**He saw it then, the glint of tears in her eyes,
the slight trembling of her lower lip.**

His fury dissolved in an instant. Reaching up, he brushed an errant curl from her face, tucking it back behind her ear tenderly. "Because you deserve better," he rasped, cupping her cheek. "You deserve happiness and security. You deserve someone who loves and cares for you." *And how I wish that person could be me.*

She drew in a trembling breath, her eyes searching his face. A tear spilled over, trailing down her cheek. He used his thumb to brush it away. And then, because he couldn't stop himself if he tried, he bent and kissed her damp cheek.

"Don't cry, Katrina," he whispered, her name escaping him of its own volition, like a benediction. He kissed her other cheek, her forehead, her nose, his lips traveling across her sweet face. And then his lips found hers, and it was as if every moment of his life had led to this.

Praise for Christina Britton and Her Novels

"For readers who like to feel all the emotions of a story."
—*Library Journal* on *Some Dukes Have All the Luck*

"Endearing, complex characters."
—*Publishers Weekly* on *Some Dukes Have All the Luck*

"Sigh-worthy fare."
—*BookPage* on *Some Dukes Have All the Luck*

"This is a knockout."
—*Publishers Weekly* on *A Duke Worth Fighting For*, starred review

"First-rate Regency fun!"
—Grace Burrowes, *New York Times* bestselling author

"Moving and heartfelt."
—*Kirkus Reviews* on *Someday My Duke Will Come*

What's a Duke
Got to Do With It

ALSO BY CHRISTINA BRITTON

What's a Duke Got to Do With It

CHRISTINA BRITTON

FOREVER

NEW YORK   BOSTON

Forever
Hachette Book Group
1290 Avenue of the Americas, New York, NY 10104
read-forever.com
twitter.com/readforeverpub

First Edition: July 2023

Forever is an imprint of Grand Central Publishing. The Forever name and logo are trademarks of Hachette Book Group, Inc.

The publisher is not responsible for websites (or their content) that are not owned by the publisher.

The Hachette Speakers Bureau provides a wide range of authors for speaking events. To find out more, go to hachettespeakersbureau.com or email HachetteSpeakers@hbgusa.com.

Forever books may be purchased in bulk for business, educational, or promotional use. For information, please contact your local bookseller or the Hachette Book Group Special Markets Department at special.markets@hbgusa.com.

ISBNs: 9781538710425 (mass market), 9781538710432 (ebook)

Printed in the United States of America

OPM

10 9 8 7 6 5 4 3 2 1

Dedicated with love to Kathryn Kramer.
You started out as the author of the first romance novel I
ever read, and are now a cherished friend.
I'm so grateful to have you in my life.

Acknowledgments

A huge thank you to my readers. Though I work in words every single day, words cannot express how much you all mean to me. I am beyond grateful for you.

Thank you to my fabulous agent, Kim Lionetti; I absolutely adore you and I'm so thankful to have you in my corner.

Thank you to my amazingly talented editor, Madeleine Colavita, and everyone at Grand Central Forever for your hard work and passion, including Grace, Dana, Luria, and so many more. I'm honored to work with all of you.

Thank you to the friends and family who have supported me. A special thanks to Jayci Lee, Hannah, Julie, and Cathy for always encouraging me and lifting my spirits when I need it most.

And, of course, last but never least, a huge thank you to my husband and children, for never faltering in your love and support of me—even if I *still* haven't put a sword with a secret compartment in the hilt in one of my stories. I love you so much.

Author's Note

WHAT'S A DUKE GOT TO DO WITH IT contains content that may distress some readers. For content warnings, please visit my website:

http://christinabritton.com/bookshelf/content-warnings/

Affectionately Yours,
Christina Britton

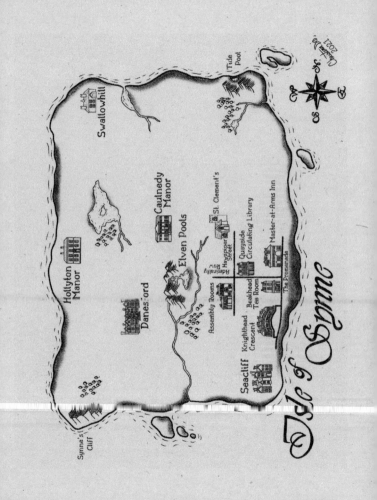

Prologue

London, 1817

"Miss Denby, how wonderful to see you here this evening."

Miss Katrina Denby's heart leapt in her chest at the sound of his voice, so close behind her his breath stirred the fine hairs at the nape of her neck. *We've been acting out a meaningless flirtation for nigh on two months now*, she told herself severely. *Tonight is certainly no different.* God knew she was fully aware he didn't mean anything by it. He was the darling of the *ton*, showering his attentions on the wallflowers and diamonds alike— and vocal about the fact that he had no plans to marry anytime soon.

Yet that did nothing to stop a kaleidoscope of butterflies from fluttering like mad in her abdomen. Nor did it stop a traitorous, hopeful voice from whispering through her mind that maybe, just maybe, he wanted something more with *her*.

That voice only grew louder as she took a step away

from her chaperone, Aunt Willa—who had not been paying any attention to her anyway—and turned to face him. Sebastian Thorne, Marquess of Marsten, smiled down at her with that endearingly crooked twist of the lips that she had come to adore over the past months of their friendship. He was one of the season's most eligible bachelors, the devilishly handsome firstborn son of the Duke of Ramsleigh, and was on every matchmaking mama's list of potentials for their daughters.

Which was exactly why he was not on her list. Not that she had a list, per se. Lists of matrimonial prospects were for those who had ambition in marriage, something she lacked completely. Of course, she did want eventually to find a man to love her and who she could love in return. But she had no lofty aspirations. Yes, it was fun to be popular and adored, to dance and flirt and receive outrageous proposals from all manner of titled, wealthy men. But affection was what she wanted more than anything, a quiet and happy home life, security and contentment and a family that loved her. All those things she had lacked throughout her life.

Useless; stupid; know your place. Her late father's cruel words were sharper for all she had not expected them. She forcefully banished them. For now, she was simply happy to no longer be rotting forgotten at her family's ancestral estate near Lincoln.

But if she did have a list, it would certainly not include Lord Marsten, who was quite openly enjoying his popularity and had been vocal in his intention to remain blissfully single. He was a rake of the first order, and as she had her own rake in the family in the form of her elder brother Francis, one of those pinks of the *ton* who flirted and charmed his way through life, she knew there was no hope in Lord

Marsten settling down until he was good and ready. Which to a rake such as him may as well be when hell froze over.

Knowing this, she had happily begun a mutual flirtation with the ever-so-charming marquess. A silent arrangement that had seemed to work perfectly for them both: he could lavish attention on her with no worry of being pursued for matrimonial purposes, and she could have something of a friend in the marquess. A novel idea for her, truly.

Yet over the past weeks, through balls and picnics and outings of all sorts, their friend groups meeting and mingling almost daily, a new awareness had cropped up where he was concerned. The playful flirtation that had bounced back and forth between them like a child's ball had transformed, the tone of the game turning more serious, more anticipatory. That same anticipation filled her now as she gazed up at him.

"Lord Marsten, I'm so happy to see you here this evening. I feared for a moment you would not arrive."

"As if I would miss an opportunity to see you," he murmured in a tone that had goose pimples dancing across her skin. "Dare I hope that you have a dance open for me? Mayhap...the supper dance?"

Katrina drew in a sharp breath. *The supper dance.* It was well known that Lord Marsten did not secure any young woman for the supper dance. He was carefully circumspect in his attentions to any one woman, and no doubt he felt the supper dance had too much expectation riding on it.

Yet here he was, asking her for that very dance, an almost vulnerable look in his eyes.

She swallowed hard, those butterflies in her stomach starting up again, their wings creating a kind of hurricane of hope within her.

"I—I do, actually," she managed, sending up a swift thanks that she had as yet not felt compelled to accept anyone for that particular set. Holding out her wrist, she offered up her dance card to him, trying and failing to stem the shaking in her limb that sent the small, intricately decorated card and pencil dancing about.

He smiled, white teeth flashing, sending her brain packing for parts unknown. Taking up the pencil and card, he quickly wrote his name in before, gently grasping her hand, he lifted it to his lips to press a kiss to her knuckles. And Katrina found herself wishing fervently that elbow-length gloves were not the fashion for balls.

"I look forward to it," he said, his voice an intimate rumble as he lowered her hand, gently squeezing her fingers before reluctantly releasing her. His smile widened. "And I do hope you will indulge me with more tales of your new puppy. Mouse, wasn't it? No doubt he is growing hale and hearty, blessed as he is with your careful ministrations."

She blinked. "You remember his name."

"Of course I do," he declared. Then, taking a step closer to her, he whispered, "I remember everything you have ever told me."

Goodness. Cheeks hot, Katrina could only gaze up at him with what she supposed was a slightly silly smile on her face. This was not their typical flirtatiousness. No, this was most definitely that something more she had felt earlier, that heightened anticipation that had her feeling as if something was about to change between them, that something momentous was about to take place. She should perhaps play coy, batting her lashes and hiding a coquettish smile behind her fan. It was quite possible that she was reading much too much into his attentions; she had a very active imagination, after all. And the last thing she wished to do was to show her hand regarding her deepening feelings when all the cards had not yet been played.

But gazing into his gray eyes, eyes that skimmed over her face with such care, as if he were memorizing her, she found herself hoping that it wasn't her imagination, that there truly was something more to this attraction between them. For she knew, with very little effort on his part, he could make her fall in love with him.

The music ended just then. And suddenly Lord Landon was there, pushing his way between them.

"Pardon me, Marsten," the baron said as he held out an arm for Katrina, "but I believe this dance is mine."

"Of course," Lord Marsten murmured, inclining his head before turning his warm gaze Katrina's way. "I shall see you later this evening, Miss Denby." And then he was gone, leaving Katrina to sigh dreamily at thoughts of being swung in his arms across the dance floor, of him escorting her into dinner and fetching her a plate, perhaps even of him taking the opportunity to sneak her away to the gardens...

"Miss Denby?" Lord Landon's voice broke into her fantasies, dragging her back to the present.

She blinked before, smiling, she placed her hand on his sleeve and allowed him to lead her onto the floor. "Forgive me, Lord Landon. My mind was wandering. But I admit to being surprised to see you here this evening. You are marrying Miss Lenora Hartley in two days' time if I am not mistaken."

"The wedding is scheduled, yes," he muttered evasively as they took their places. Frowning, she opened her mouth to question him further—she liked Miss Hartley, after all, and was happy for her to finally be marrying after her two failed attempts in recent years. Even if it was to someone as dull as Lord Landon.

But Lord Marsten appeared just then in the set across from her, and all other thoughts fled from her mind. He looked so very handsome tonight in his black coat and silver-threaded waistcoat and snowy cravat, his hair deliciously disheveled in rich dark brown waves. What, she wondered as the music started and she began to move automatically through the quadrille, would those locks feel like between her fingers? And what would it feel like to have that firm, generous mouth covering her own?

Her cheeks heated. Goodness, where had that come from? She had never thought of kissing the marquess before. At least, she amended, not while conscious. But one could not have control over one's dreams, could one? How many times *had* she dreamed of kissing Lord Marsten? She pursed her lips as she considered. Surely no more than a dozen at most. Though perhaps that was excessive. She smiled slightly as her gaze drifted to him once more. Had she been falling for the marquess all these weeks, then? It was only when his gaze met hers and softened, a tender look passing across his face, that she realized with a start that she had. The man had been working himself under her skin all this time, and she had not even realized it. Her smile widened, her cheeks warming further as she held his gaze. And the funny thing was, she could not even be slightly annoyed with herself at that fact. Especially as it appeared he might feel the same way.

"Miss Denby," Lord Landon called loudly in her ear as they joined hands.

Katrina's face heated. "Ah, forgive me, Lord Landon," she murmured, tearing her gaze from Lord Marsten. "I'm afraid my mind wandered again. I find myself easily distracted, I fear."

"It is understandable," he said with a small, knowing smile.

She blinked. Lord Landon had always seemed a staid, serious sort. Tonight, however, he appeared positively enigmatic. Though mayhap it was nerves. The man was set to be married soon, after all. Such a momentous occasion was bound to wreak havoc on even the most poised of people.

Which, of course, had her thinking of matrimony, and what her own future might hold in that regard. Her gaze drifted once more to Lord Marsten, her breath catching in her throat when she caught his eyes again on her. Throughout her London season, she had received several proposals of marriage, and even more declarations of love. She had never considered a single one of those men. But one dance request from Lord Marsten, some softly spoken words, a changed look in his warm gray eyes, and she was ready to dream of happily-ever-afters. She very nearly laughed. Was she such a hopeless romantic then?

The dance ended, and after clapping politely and bending his head to say something to his partner, Lord Marsten headed her way. The suddenly intent look in his eyes had her heart galloping in her chest, like a horse's hooves racing for the finish line.

"Miss Denby," he murmured, bending his head close to hers, "I thought perhaps we might—"

Before he could finish, however, a servant came rushing toward them, a missive held in his hand.

"My lord," the footman said, holding the letter out to the marquess, "this has just come for you. It is quite urgent; the messenger is waiting even now for your reply."

Lord Marsten tore open the letter, his face going pale as his eyes scanned the paper. "It is from my father's steward. He says I must return home at once. I am sorry, Miss Denby, but I must postpone our dance for this evening."

Before she could respond, he was rushing away, and was soon swallowed up in the crowd.

* * *

A full four and twenty hours later and Katrina found that no matter how she tried to forget Lord Marsten, she could not. Was his father well? Was the marquess even now on his way to see him? When would she see the marquess again?

"Enough," she told herself forcefully as she climbed into bed and pulled the sheets up over herself, being careful not to disturb her new pet. But the puppy was oblivious to anything just then. Belly full, Mouse snored softly on his back, his huge paws splayed at awkward angles, one large ear covering his eyes. Smiling tenderly, she gently brushed his ear back from his face.

"He asked after you, you know," she whispered. "Lord Marsten. And he remembered your name. What do you think of that?"

In answer, Mouse snorted in his sleep, his legs jerking. Laughing softly, Katrina settled back against her pillows, and in no time had drifted off in dreams of being held in Lord Marsten's arms...

Until a high-pitched barking woke her. Eyes flying open, her lovely dream gone in a puff of smoke, Katrina attempted to figure out just where she was and what that god-awful racket could be. She spied Mouse beside her in a fitful ray of moonlight, small body vibrating, ears jumping with each yip and woof, his entire focus on the window. And then she looked up and saw a dark form easing over the windowsill and into her room.

The scream that ripped from her throat was loud and long, and halted only by the hand that slapped over her mouth.

"Please, Miss Denby," a voice panted in her ear, the man's moist breath making her cringe, "don't be afraid. It is only me."

Me? Me who? But the question remained unasked—through no decision of her own, as that hand over her mouth remained firmly in place, the sweaty palm holding her lips closed.

Mouse, however, was under no such constraints. His barks went on, an endless litany of yelps. The intruder attempted to reach for the puppy while still holding on to her but was unsuccessful as Mouse tumbled back out of his reach, a black-and-white ball of fury, legs flailing as he rolled across the coverlet, his barks never ceasing.

"Damnation, he will have the entire house waking," the man holding Katrina hissed.

As if on cue, the door to her room burst open, crashing against the wall with a sickening crunch. And then light invaded the space, finally bathing the face of the intruder.

Lord Landon?

She blinked up at him. Surely not. The man was set to marry Miss Lenora Hartley in the morning. He could not be here, in her bedroom, accosting her.

But no, it was him, from his thin brown hair to his long nose, to his small, close-set eyes.

And then her brother's voice confirmed it.

"Landon!" he roared, lamp swinging wildly as he rushed into the room, sending the shadows to dancing until

Katrina thought she might be sick. "Get your fucking hands off my sister."

But Francis did not wait for Lord Landon to move. In an instant he was beside the baron, hand on his neckcloth, hauling him from the bed. Katrina, finally free, fell back against the rumpled bedsheets.

"Denby, wait!" Lord Landon cried. As Francis slammed him against the wall, the baron grunted in pain, grabbing onto Francis's wrists. "Denby, it's not what you think."

"Isn't it?" Francis growled. "Because it looked like you were attempting to force yourself upon my sister."

Lord Landon's face went white, his gaze swiveling wildly between Francis and Katrina. "Gad no. I would never. I love Katrina, with all my heart."

He looked at her fully then, his eyes pleading. "Katrina, I love you. I want you to run away with me."

"You fucking bastard," Francis snarled, pulling Lord Landon away from the wall and slamming him back against it, this time lifting him until he was nearly off his feet. "I'll kill you, I swear I will."

That, finally, propelled Katrina to break free of the shocked stupor she had been frozen in. She bolted from the bed, grabbing Francis's arm and pulling back with all her might. But she may as well have been tugging on a stone statue for all her brother was affected.

"Francis," she begged as she looked wildly at the baron's quickly purpling face, "please let him go. I'm certain Lord Landon just over imbibed. He is marrying Miss Hartley tomorrow and must be nervous."

Blessedly the hard muscles under her hands released their tension, and Lord Landon slid toward the ground.

Relief began to fill Katrina as the baron dragged in a ragged breath.

But then Lord Landon went and opened his mouth again.

"I am not drunk, but quite sober," he shouted hoarsely, throwing Francis's hands off and grabbing Katrina's hands. "In fact, I have never been more sober. And I do not give a damn what Miss Hartley's father will do to me in breaking this cursed engagement. Katrina, I love you. Marry me—"

Before the words were out of his mouth, Francis's fist connected with the baron's jaw, sending his head flying back. Blood spattered Katrina's fine lawn nightgown and across the wall.

"You shall regret this, Landon," her brother snarled. "I demand satisfaction."

"Francis, no!" Katrina cried, reaching for him. But he shook her off, his blazing eyes never leaving the baron.

"Expect my second to contact you. We meet at dawn."

A flash of fear crossed Lord Landon's pale face, mingling with the quickly deepening bruise from Francis's fist and the blood trickling down his chin, creating a horrifying mask. But he straightened and looked her brother in the eye.

"Very well," he rasped. "Dawn it is."

They both stormed out of her room, leaving the air electric with anger and fear and fury. And Katrina, holding Mouse, staring at the space where they had been, knowing nothing would ever be the same again.

Chapter 1

Miss Katrina Denby had learned years ago that as soon as life seemed to be shifting in her favor, it was invariably going to be turned on its head.

It was not as if she believed there was some force out there determined to undermine every good thing she might have. She was unimportant, after all, and therefore could never garner such fatalistic occurrences from the powers that be. No, her future was merely caught in the crosshairs of much more important and devastating events. Whether it was her parents' unexpected and tragic deaths just before her London debut, or her brother losing his arm after the duel in her honor that had sent her fleeing society in scandal, or the loss of her family's fortunes, which had prompted her to enter a life of service, she had been trapped in the undertow of the swirling maelstrom that happened around her.

She could say, with utmost confidence, that her suffering on each occasion had been mild considering what others had suffered, and so it was incredibly selfish of her to fixate on her own heartbreak. She could have been in that carriage with her parents, instead of remaining at home with a cold. And she could have been without employment prospects when she had needed to escape her increasingly dire living situation. And she could have lost her brother in that duel...

Well, she amended bleakly, she supposed she had lost him in a way. But at least he wasn't dead. And lately she had even begun to get a part of him back, her weekly letters to him, sent without fail though he had refused to acknowledge them for years, finally answered.

Now, secure in her position as companion to the irascible dowager Viscountess Tesh, the outspoken matriarch of that popular seaside resort the Isle of Synne, and in possession of the first real friends she had ever had, she felt she was finally attaining the respectability she had yearned for since that great scandal four years ago. And so she supposed she should have been prepared for yet another great upheaval. Fool that she was, however, she had instead remained blissfully unaware of the impending doom about to descend upon her.

Though how she could have ever predicted this, she thought as she looked down on a body sprawled inelegantly in the garden below her bedroom window, she didn't have a clue.

"Goodness me," she muttered, peering down into the heavily shadowed bushes. "Who in the world is that?"

The only answer she received, however, was a low *woof* from the massive canine beside her. Her sweet runt of a pup had grown considerably in the four years since she had taken over his care. Now, with paws the size of dinner plates planted on the windowsill, Mouse perked his ears and tilted his head in curiosity as he stared down at the unmoving form below them. As if he hadn't been the one to push the man out of the window.

"Oh, Mouse," she moaned. "What have you done now?"

Even if he had been able to answer, the dog would not have been given the chance. Suddenly she heard a great stomping of feet below and saw a lantern swinging wildly down the garden path, sending shadows careening through the vegetation. And then there was the butler and several footmen, faces illuminated by the glow of the lantern, all half-dressed and seemingly ready for battle if the brooms and mops they held poised like medieval swords were any indication.

"Good God, what happened?" she heard one of them ask as he knelt down to peer in the bushes. As the rest of them muttered darkly to one another, the butler came closer, the light from the lantern bathing the unknown man. Finally giving enough light for Katrina to see his identity.

Her vision went dark around the edges, and she could literally feel the blood leave her face. She did not know she had cried out, however, until the men below looked up at her in surprise.

The butler was the first to react. "Miss Denby," Jasper called out in alarm. "Perhaps it's best if you go back inside. This is no sight for a lady to witness."

But she could not. No, her horrified gaze remained glued to the supine man below. His eyes were opened wide, staring unseeing up at the inky black sky, his mouth slack, his neck bent at an unnatural angle. But it was not the realization that she was staring down at a dead man that had her frozen in shock. No, it was the man's very familiar features,

features she had seen in her nightmares more than once in the last four years.

Jasper seemed to realize something was amiss. His steely brows drawing low over his eyes, he called out, "Miss, do you know this man?"

It took her some seconds to respond. When she finally did, however, her voice sounded as if it were coming from far away.

"I do," she managed. "That is Lord Landon. The man who nearly killed my brother."

* * *

Some hours later—truly she didn't have a clue how many; all she knew was the sun had begun its ascent over the horizon- -Katrina found herself seated in Lady Tesh's private sitting room, a cup of hot tea in her hands, her employer and her dear friends surrounding her. She was certain she would eventually feel a horrible guilt for dragging them all from their beds in the middle of the night. Now, however, she was just glad they were with her.

Especially as the magistrate, Mr. Henrickson, was doing his damnedest to make Katrina feel as if she were somehow responsible for all this.

"You say you knew this Lord Landon?" He peered hard at Katrina. "And yet you do not know why he was attempting to climb into your bedroom?"

Miss Seraphina Athwart, proprietress of the Quayside Circulating Library and one of Katrina's closest friends, glared at Mr. Henrickson from her place beside Katrina on the low settee. "Just what are you implying, sir?"

she demanded, eyes narrowed dangerously behind her wire-rimmed spectacles.

He glared right back. "Miss Athwart, I don't believe this has anything at all to do with you." He smirked. "Perhaps it's best if you went back to your little bookstore and left this to me."

"It is not a *little bookstore*, but the premier circulating library on Synne," she shot back coldly. Phineas, her ever present green-and-red parrot, glared with equal chill from her shoulder.

"I think what my friend is trying to say," Miss Adelaide Peacham, owner of the Beakhead Tea Room, cut in with a complacent smile that did not reach her dark eyes, "is that Miss Denby has told you several times she has no idea why Lord Landon was attempting to gain access to her room. She has not seen the man in four years, after all."

"So she says," the magistrate drawled, disbelief ripe in his voice.

"Yes, she has said," Bronwyn, formerly Miss Pickering but recently married and now the Duchess of Buckley, bit out as she looked over her spectacles at the man. "I sincerely hope you are not doubting her word, Mr. Henrickson."

The magistrate, however, was not the least bit daunted by the possibility of insulting a duchess, if his patronizing glance Bronwyn's way was any indication.

Blessedly Lady Tesh intervened just then, preventing the situation from getting any uglier. "Mr. Henrickson," she snapped, bringing her cane down on the floor with a sharp thud lest the man dare try ignoring her, "I do believe you are through here. You can see my companion is overcome and exhausted beyond bearing. Why, she looks as if she is about to faint."

Katrina blinked. Did she? She had thought she was doing quite a good job at keeping her composure, considering the circumstances.

But a quick jab in the ribs from Seraphina had her realizing what Lady Tesh was attempting to do. Placing her teacup on the low table, she pressed a hand to her forehead and gave a low moan, swaying in her seat.

Mr. Henrickson did not look the least convinced. But what could he do? Especially when Miss Honoria Gadfeld, the vicar's eldest daughter, rose and shooed him toward the door.

"It was so very kind of you to make certain our dear Miss Denby is well," she said with a syrupy smile. "I will be certain to tell my father how wonderfully you have handled this whole horrible mess. I am sure I can speak for him when I say God will look well on you for the work you have done here this night."

"Oh!" Mr. Henrickson looked startled, then pleased as he was hustled toward the door. The man may be a blowhard, but he was a pious blowhard. Or if not pious, at least eager to earn his way into heaven by kowtowing to the local vicar. "Well, you know I do my best, Miss Gadfeld. That I do."

"Of course you do," she said complacently. "Do take care returning home; the sun is not quite up yet. And do give our best to your lovely wife."

Before the man could reply, Honoria pushed him out the door and closed it firmly in his face. She leaned back against it, her pleasant expression disappearing as she rolled her eyes heavenward.

"The blathering idiot," she mumbled.

"Kinder words than I would have used," Seraphina muttered darkly.

"Doaty lavvy heid," Phineas squawked in his strong Scottish brogue, ruffling his feathers in outrage.

"Quite right, my dear," Seraphina murmured, reaching up to give his neck a scratch. "I could not have said it better myself."

Katrina, however, was hardly aware of the exchange. The moment the man's footsteps could no longer be heard she was up and racing across the room to the door that connected into Lady Tesh's bedchamber. Yanking it open, she dropped to her knees and intercepted Mouse as he came tearing into the room, throwing her arms about him and pressing her face into his warm neck. He wiggled under her, attempting to reach her face so he might bathe it with his lolling tongue, his long tail thrashing to and fro in his joy at being invited into the group once more.

Katrina did not realize anyone had noticed her exit from the group until a soft hand landed on her shoulder and an even softer voice sounded in her ear. The scent of baked goods, Adelaide's signature perfume, surrounded Katrina like a hug.

"They aren't going to take Mouse away, Katrina," her friend said gently.

"How do you know that?" she demanded, her voice muffled by the dog's smooth fur. "What if Mr. Henrickson blames Mouse for Lord Landon's fall? What if they try him for murder? What if they sentence him to *death*?"

Which, even as she babbled question after question, she knew was ridiculous in the extreme. Yet Katrina could not stop the panic from rising in her. Mouse was all she had left, the one thing her brother had gifted her, proof that he loved her. She could not lose the dog, this one last connection to him, too.

Anyone else might have laughed at her for her idiocy. Not Adelaide, however.

"I have every faith that Mouse shall not be tried for murder," she soothed. Disentangling Katrina's arms from about the dog, she assisted her to standing. "Now," she said with a bracing smile, "why don't we get you back to bed? You must be exhausted after such a troubling night."

"Oh, yes," Honoria chimed in, rushing over to them. "That's a capital idea, my dear. Katrina, once you've gotten some rest you will be able to view the whole ordeal in a more positive light. Rather," she amended sheepishly as Adelaide shot her a disbelieving look, "not exactly positive, as a man has died—"

"What Honoria is trying so valiantly to say," Seraphina interrupted in her brisk, no-nonsense way as she approached, "is that things will not look quite so dire once you have rested. Exhaustion has a horrible effect on a person's mental capabilities. Don't you agree, Bronwyn?"

"Absolutely," the woman in question answered, joining the group that surrounded Katrina. "You are not thinking clearly, and rightly so. Rest will provide you with a clear head."

As one the four friends began to herd Katrina toward the sitting room door. She should be glad for their concern, she told herself. Yet the panic swelled up choking her, filling her with so much tension she thought she would burst.

And finally she did, breaking away from arms that should have given comfort but instead felt suffocating. It was only as she stood apart from her dear friends, the self-styled misfits called the Oddments, that she realized why she was about to jump out of her skin.

"It does not matter how much sleep I get," she managed,

hugging herself about the middle. "The fact of the matter is, this is a huge scandal, one I won't be able to escape from."

At once her friends exploded in protest. Mouse, still in the middle of them all, looked at each one in turn, huge tongue lolling from his mouth, utterly clueless as to the chaos his exuberance had caused.

Katrina, however, could not keep her gaze from Lady Tesh. Her employer had remained off to the side, silently observing, her small white dog, Freya, equally watchful on her lap. It was a disturbing break from the woman's normal brash forcefulness. Katrina knew that if anyone was going to tell her the truth of the matter, it would be her employer.

Lady Tesh did not disappoint.

"Katrina is right, of course," she said, silencing the Oddments with one stern look. "This will no doubt cause a huge scandal. If it was just some random man, we might have been able to quiet the rumors. But Lord Landon was a peer of the realm. He perished attempting to climb into Katrina's bedroom window in the dead of night. Not only that, but this was not the first time he had done so. We will not be able to sweep this under the rug."

"There, you see?" Katrina said, though she did not feel one ounce of triumph from having Lady Tesh agree with her. No, the only thing she felt just then was the overwhelming desire to curl up in a ball and cry.

"There is only one thing to be done now," she continued with much more bravado than she felt. Taking hold of Mouse's collar, she dragged him out of the group of women and, straightening her shoulders, turned to face her employer. "I'm certain my brother will welcome me back," she said bracingly—much more bravely than she felt. Francis had practically disowned her after Lord Landon's first attempt at climbing into her room, laying the fault for the whole debacle, including the duel and the loss of his arm, on her shoulders. And she could not blame him one bit for it, though she still didn't have a clue how she had encouraged the baron. But she must have done something to make the man think she would be at all receptive to such a thing.

That, however, was the past. And Francis's recent letters, after so long ignoring her attempts to contact him, had given her hope that he would accept her back. She swallowed hard. After this horrible turn of events, she feared that she may have lost whatever ground she had gained with her estranged sibling. Even so, it was painfully obvious she could not stay. "I'll pack up my things and be out of here as soon as I can manage. Will tomorrow morning suffice?"

The Oddments gasped, cries of dismay and outrage filling the room. Katrina, however, had eyes only for Lady Tesh. The woman was her employer, after all, and the entire reason she was on the Isle of Synne. The dowager had taken her in and offered her a position when Katrina had been quite without hope.

Her time on the Isle and in Lady Tesh's employ had not been without its difficulties, of course. The woman was not the easiest person to work for. She was demanding and blunt and difficult on her best days.

But she had given Katrina a home, had introduced her to the women who would become her dearest friends. And in the process had saved Katrina when she had believed everything must surely be lost.

She fully expected the woman to nod in agreement. She should have guessed, however, that Lady Tesh must have her say.

"No," the dowager viscountess murmured, "I don't think that will suffice, not at all."

Katrina's stomach dropped. "You wish me to leave earlier than that? Very well, I'm certain I can manage to depart by this afternoon." She turned to go, dragging Mouse along with her. Lady Tesh's voice, however, stopped her in her tracks.

"No, you misunderstand me. Though," the woman muttered, "that is no surprise. Everyone seems to willfully misunderstand me." She speared Katrina with a stern glare. "You above all. Why you cannot follow simple instructions is beyond me."

Katrina, as lost as ever where the woman was concerned, could only stare open-mouthed at her. Seraphina, blessedly, was not so reticent when it came to speaking up.

"What are you saying, Lady Tesh? Surely you cannot mean to let Katrina go."

"Of course I shall not let her go," Lady Tesh snapped. "Do you think me a monster? Just because some idiot man decided it would be wise to climb up the side of a building and invite himself inside a woman's room without her consent, only to conveniently fall and break his damned neck? No, I shall not punish Katrina for that."

There was a collective sigh of relief from the inhabitants of the room. None more so than from Katrina, who was so overwhelmed she became light-headed. It was only because her hand was on Mouse's collar that she was able to keep her feet under her at all. As it was, she had to stumble to the nearest seat, dropping down into it with an inelegant grunt.

Despite her relief, though, common sense would insist on shining through.

"But, Lady Tesh," she said, her head continuing to fight

against her best interest, "you cannot want a companion with such a stain on her name."

"I took you on with a stain on your name, didn't I?" the woman demanded.

"Well . . . yes, I suppose you did—"

"And did it bother me one bit that you had a scandal attached to you?"

"I suppose not—" Katrina replied. Or, rather, tried replying, as Lady Tesh continued as if she had never spoken.

"I am well aware that men can be utter idiots when their cocks are involved."

"Lady Tesh!" Adelaide gasped, her face as red as a strawberry. "There are unmarried women present."

But Lady Tesh waved one heavily beringed hand in the air impatiently. "As if Miss Athwart here wasn't providing you with the books and pamphlets to educate yourselves on the human body and all the intimate things it's capable of," she scoffed. "And I know she is doing so because I am the one who has funded such an endeavor. One of the greatest sins men have committed against females is keeping them blithely unaware of the sexual acts. No doubt," she continued in a dark tone, "because if we were aware of just how horrible the vast majority of them are in bed, no woman would wish to lie with them. Your own husband, of course, is the exception," she said to Bronwyn with a sly sideways glance. "That Ash looks as if he knows what he's about."

Katrina was vaguely aware of the strangled laughter around her. But she had no time to react herself before Lady Tesh's piercing eyes were once more settled on her.

"You are not at fault for what that man has done. And I will not allow anyone to disparage you. As my companion, you are under my protection, and I do not take that duty lightly. And so I will hear no more talk about you leaving."

Warmth filled Katrina until she thought she would weep with it. Lady Tesh was not an affectionate woman. More often than not she was rude and outspoken and gave no care to what others thought.

Such a speech coming from her, as aggressive as it had been, was as good as a shout to the heavens that she cared.

Even so, it would not be right to let the woman take on the full burden of this. It could not have been easy for her to hire such a person—Katrina recalled all too well the chilly reception she had received from much of Synne before Lady Tesh had stepped in and set everyone straight. But it would be doubly difficult now, with the old scandal resurrected in such a violent manner, and not only resurrected but also compounded upon. "If my brother insists I return home," she managed around the lump in her throat, "I will return to him, and save you from whatever repercussions might arise from this."

For the barest of moments, Katrina thought she saw pity darken the woman's heavily lined face. But in a second it was gone, replaced with a gentleness that Katrina had never seen from her employer.

"Very well, you may write to him. But if he refuses, you shall stay with me. Is that understood?"

Swallowing down tears that burned her throat, Katrina nodded. "Yes, Lady Tesh."

Though as the woman shuffled back to her bed and Katrina's friends helped her back to her own, she didn't know which she dreaded more: returning to her brother or having no recourse but to remain a burden to these people she loved.

Chapter 2

Sebastian Thorne, Duke of Ramsleigh, paused at the bottom of the steps leading up to the Grosvenor Square town house. No, he didn't pause; rather, he froze, his feet seemingly unable to move farther. He just stopped himself from letting loose the string of profanities that knocked at his lips and would have no doubt had every curious lady and gentleman—of which there were a prodigious number walking up and down the street at this time of the morning—dropping into dead faints.

What the devil was wrong with him? Once he secured Miss Bridling's hand, his family would be saved. And not just his family, but every family who relied on the Ramsleigh title for their livelihoods. He would be given the means to fix their roofs, put food on their tables, expand their flocks, and see that their fields were properly sown. Not to mention repairing Ramsleigh Castle's own leaking roof and crumbling plaster and broken windows. And he would be able to provide his sisters dowries of their own. Ones that would not be as large as they should be, of course, considering they were daughters of a duke, but enough to ensure they secured respectable husbands, as well as providing them with a safety net should they ever find themselves again in a position of looming poverty.

Yet even with all this hanging in the balance, their salvation finally within reach, he found his feet unable to propel him forward to claim it.

Expelling a harsh breath, he gritted his teeth and forced his legs to move. One step, then another, then another, until, finally, he was before the shining black door. He raised a disturbingly heavy hand, let the brass knocker fall.

Before the sound died down the door was thrown wide. Lord Cartmel's dour butler stood there, as if he had been waiting for Sebastian the whole while.

And no doubt he had been. It was no secret that Sebastian had been courting Miss Bridling nearly from the moment he had met her two months ago. And he'd made no secret that he'd intended to make her an offer this very afternoon. He cast a glance back at the people milling about in the square, which had become a veritable crowd since he'd arrived. Every eye was turned his way and remained on him, though they had been caught blatantly staring. He heaved a sigh and turned back to face the butler. No doubt they did not want to miss the commencement of the match of the season. It really was too bad the possible groom-to-be was wishing he was anywhere else but here.

The butler bowed. "Your Grace. Shall I let Miss Bridling know you are here?"

As if the man didn't know very well that Sebastian was not here to see Miss Bridling at all. Keeping his face impassive, he just stopped himself from tugging nervously at his jacket. "Actually," he said as he stepped inside the cool, cavernous front hall and the door closed behind him, blessedly leaving the gawking crowd behind, "I am here to see Lord Cartmel. If you could inform him of my presence?"

"Very good, Your Grace," the butler intoned, not a flicker of surprise in his eyes. "If you will have a seat in the rose sitting room, I shall see if the baron is home."

Before Sebastian could acquiesce, a soft voice sounded behind him.

"There is no sense in falling on ceremony, Curtis. Father is expecting you, Your Grace. I shall show you to the study."

The butler bowed and backed away. "As you wish, Miss Bridling."

Sebastian turned to face his future wife. It was not ego that made him so certain her father would accept his suit, or that the lady would accept his proposal. No, he knew what Lord Cartmel was after: a dukedom for his beloved daughter. No matter that the dukedom had been besieged with scandals and creditors in the past years, no matter that not many families would wish to take on the immense burden of bringing the dukedom back to what it had been— not to mention that of its soiled reputation—there was still much a title could buy. Including the only daughter of one of the richest men in England.

That particular woman was looking at him right now, her face as smooth and impassive as ever, her lips ever-so-slightly curved in that barely-there smile that held not a hint of warmth in it. Miss Diane Bridling was nothing if not poised and proper.

Yet every now and then, Sebastian was certain he

caught sight of something just a bit more in her gaze. Like now, as her lips hiked up ever so slightly, giving her an almost sardonic expression. "Your Grace," she said in neutral tones, dropping into a curtsy that was neither too shallow nor too deep. "If you will follow me?"

At his nod, she turned about, leading the way deeper into the bowels of the house. Sebastian had the sudden insane feeling that he was being buried alive. He fought the urge to gasp for breath, but instead straightened his shoulders and tightened his hands into fists at his side. So focused was he on remaining in control, however, that he did not immediately realize he had not said a single word to his soon-to-be fiancée.

Dear God, was this how their life together would be? Polite indifference, barely speaking, never truly knowing one another? Of course, their entire courtship had been thus, with just the exact number of dances, the proper time together with the necessary chaperones, talking of the weather and not much else. He did not know whether she preferred champagne to wine, did not know if she would rather live in London or in the country. He did not even know what her favorite color was.

And just then, facing down his future, he felt the burning urge to learn all he could. Perhaps then he might be able to reconcile himself to such a life. If he knew something, anything personal about this woman who was to take him to her bed and bear his children, mayhap there was hope they could be, if not happy, at least fairly content. Or, rather, at least not miserable.

She stopped before a closed door and raised her hand to knock. Before Sebastian could think better of it, he gently captured that hand in his own and turned her to face him.

She gasped, brown eyes widening. They were lovely eyes, fringed with a generous number of curling lashes. Truthfully, she herself was immensely lovely, with her smooth skin and dark, wavy hair and delicate features. Yet try as he might to feel more for this woman, Sebastian only felt a hollowness.

No one can compare to that other one, the one who made your heart beat in the strangest manner and had you fairly trembling with need for her.

Sebastian nearly gasped and stumbled back. He had not thought of Miss Katrina Denby in more years than he could count. Well, he amended, that wasn't necessarily true. He had thought of her, especially when he was alone at night. But those thoughts had been too painful to focus on for long, memories from the *before-times*, when life had been good and his future had seemed as bright and shiny as a new penny. When he'd not had to worry about debt and grief and helping those under his care to do something so basic as survive.

Damn it, he'd been a selfish bastard. But he'd learned soon enough that his life had been an illusion. His father had died unexpectedly, and Sebastian had been forced to leave London, to return home and begin the impossible job of digging his family and tenants free of the literal mountain of debt and scandal his father had buried them under. There had been no time to think of that girl who had captured his heart, and who could have been so much more to him had they been given more time.

Not that any promises had been made, nor any declarations spoken. No, they had never gone beyond friendship and a wonderful flirtation.

Yet he had begun to want so much more with her toward

the end, had even been ready to tell her of his feelings and begin courting her in earnest for all and sundry to see. And though he knew it was not the least bit beneficial or healthy, he could not help thinking on occasion that things might have turned out quite differently had his father not been so damned selfish, if he had not lost everything due to gambling, then concocted that false investment scheme that had left so many families on the verge of bankruptcy, ruining the Ramsleigh title in the process—and if Sebastian had not then been forced to liquidate everything not nailed down to pay for the sins of his father. If all that had not occurred, would he have declared his love for Miss Denby that very night of the ball when everything had instead fallen apart? Would she have returned his feelings and accepted his suit? And would he have spent the rest of his life with her, building a family with her, loving her...?

But no, he would not think of that any longer, he told himself brutally as he looked down into Miss Bridling's startled features. This was his life now, forced to take a woman to wife who obviously had no wish to marry him, if the slight curl of distaste to her upper lip as she took in his gloved hand on her wrist was any indication. In an instant he released her, then just as quickly dropped any thoughts of Miss Denby from his mind. She was the past, a time he had best forget if he was to move forward. This woman before him was his future. No matter how painfully obvious it was that neither of them wanted that future.

"Miss Bridling," he said, "forgive me. I acted without thinking. I merely wished for a moment with you before I go in to see your father."

At once her face smoothed, any hint of emotion leaching from it. But there was the slightest tightening at the corners of her lips, as if she were annoyed. "Very well," she replied, clasping her hands before her and looking at him in expectation. "What was it you wished to say?"

He opened his mouth to speak. But nothing emerged. What the devil did he want to say? Truly, he didn't have a clue. There wasn't much he could say. They both knew why he was here, and what would happen once he disappeared behind her father's study door. And he was immensely sad, for both of them. For all the possibilities being stolen from them today, all for money, and status, and expectations.

But he couldn't say any of that. Yet he had to say something, for she was looking at him in increasing impatience. Finally, just as she pressed her lips tight and made to turn for the study door again, he found his tongue.

"What is your favorite color?"

She gaped at him. "My what?"

"Your favorite color," he replied lamely. As she continued to look on him with disbelief ripe on her face, he added, "so I might send you flowers. When this is all done."

She blinked. "Oh. Purple. I love purple." The faintest hint of humor lit her face before it disappeared altogether, leaving almost sadness behind. "Do you know, no one has ever asked me that before."

Before he could make out what to say to that, she resolutely turned and opened the door.

"Father, His Grace is here to see you."

And then Lord Cartmel's gruff voice boomed out into the hall. "Thank you, Diane. Come in, Ramsleigh."

Miss Bridling barely looked Sebastian's way as she dipped into a graceful curtsy and hurried off. Leaving Sebastian alone with her father. Heaving a sigh, knowing he could not put it off a moment longer, Sebastian strode inside, closing the door behind him. Trying with all his might not to think of the sound as a death knell.

Cartmel sat behind his massive desk, neat piles of paper placed just so on the gleaming desktop, quills in precise lines, all showing the careful control the baron had over every aspect of his life. As Sebastian moved forward, the man stood and held out a hand.

"Ramsleigh," he said, his voice like gravel beneath a boot. "Good to see you. Though I think we both know why you're here. Shall we move to the chairs before the hearth so we might be more comfortable?"

Like father, like daughter in their no-nonsense manner. Cartmel was amazingly capable; knowing that the dukedom would have just such a capable duchess in the man's daughter should have been a relief. Yet it made Sebastian feel as if he were in a runaway carriage with no way to escape it, no way to stop it.

Nevertheless he nodded and followed Cartmel to the chairs in question, sinking down into the one indicated as the man made his way to the sideboard.

"Brandy?"

"Yes, please."

The baron turned to pour the drinks, the splash of liquor and the clink of crystal filling the air. "Though we both know why you're here," he said, making his way back to Sebastian, handing him one of the drinks and sitting across from him, "I do think we'd best do this the right way. I've been waiting a long time for this moment, you see, and wish to savor it."

If Sebastian had been a cat, he rather thought his hackles would have raised at such a remark. So the man wished him to dance like a marionette on a string, did he? Taking a deep draught of the brandy, focusing on the burn of it as it traveled down to his empty stomach, he turned his mind to Ramsleigh Castle, and the village surrounding it. Bernard Fenley's children needed the thatched roof above their heads to be repaired so they did not need to fear another winter. And Hazel Munsbridge needed to know she would not be forced to sell her body to feed her sisters. And Charles Porrid's flock needed to be expanded after the sickness that had wiped out nearly every one of his ewes the season before.

So many people counting on him. He could not allow his pride to cause them even a moment's more suffering.

Clearing his expression so only pleasantness remained, he looked Cartmel in the eyes—eyes that held too much enjoyment in their crafty depths for Sebastian's liking—and said, clearly and distinctly, "Lord Cartmel, I would be honored if you would accept my suit for your daughter's hand in marriage."

The baron did not answer right away, instead gazing at Sebastian over the rim of his glass. Finally, when Sebastian thought his lips would crack from the strain of keeping them in a pleasant line, the man spoke.

"As you know, Ramsleigh, I have made it no secret that I abhor what your father did. He lied, and cheated, and stole, ruining so many lives with his hoax of an investment scheme. And many of the men he swindled, I consider dear friends."

How Sebastian kept his composure he would never know. He was well aware that his father's sins had not been forgotten by the *ton*. There had been too many seemingly innocuous comments made in passing, too many cold glances, too many calls not returned and invitations mislaid to be mere coincidence.

Yet he had never been attacked as directly as Lord Cartmel was doing just then. His fingers tightened about the glass in his hand until he thought the crystal would shatter; his teeth pressed so hard together he was certain they would turn to dust. But manage to remain calm he did, looking Cartmel in the eye until his own burned from the effort.

"Yes," he replied softly. "I am aware of that. And you also must know that I do not, nor have I ever, condoned what my father did. Not only that, but I have done all in my power to rectify the mistakes he made."

Cartmel twirled the glass in his hand, swirling the reddish amber liquid inside until it resembled nothing so much as a hurricane in his grasp, all the while keeping his gaze unerringly on Sebastian. "Mistakes," he mused. "An interesting choice of words. A mistake, after all, implies an action is unintended. Whereas your father's actions were quite deliberately calculated."

The bastard. Forcefully tamping down the shame and fury that frothed in his gut, it took every bit of Sebastian's self-control to keep from storming from the room. He knew he could talk until he was blue in the face, explaining how he had been completely oblivious to what his father had been up to until after his untimely death, how he had tracked down every last lender and investor and paid them back with interest, how he'd been paying in unimaginable ways every day since.

But looking into Cartmel's flat, cold eyes—eyes that resembled a shark's—he knew those excuses would fall on

deaf ears. And he knew that after months of the man courting Sebastian's title as ruthlessly as Sebastian had courted
Miss Bridling and her dowry, this was the final test, the one
last hurdle to jump before Cartmel gave Sebastian the salvation he was trying so damn hard to reach.

Sebastian's stomach lurched at how cold and mercenary
the whole blasted thing was.

Still Lord Cartmel waited. With utmost will, Sebastian
inclined his head, a silent acceptance of the baron's cruel
words. He had taken on every burden and bit of blame
his father's actions had created; he would certainly not
stop now.

Cartmel's smile widened. "I'm glad we have gotten
that out of the way then. But before I give my consent—
no easy thing, you know, for Diane is my dearest and only
daughter—I have one thing I need you to do for me."

Alarm bells clanged about in Sebastian's head. What the
devil was this? Was the man not going to give his blessing
today? Was he going to continue to dangle Sebastian over
the precipice? His tension was gone in an instant, replaced
by a fury so bitter he could taste it.

"I don't understand, my lord," he gritted.

For the first time in the exchange, Cartmel's ever-present
composure cracked. Though it was no mere press of
lips. Lines of tension bracketed his mouth as he shifted
in his seat, his eyes tightening at the corners. But he did
not answer right away. No, he took a sip of his brandy,
observed the way the light caught in the liquor. Sebastian
might have thought he was simply increasing the suspense,
attempting to make Sebastian squirm. Yet he saw in the
way Cartmel's Adam's apple bobbed furiously that he was
nervous.

Again those alarm bells pealed, louder than before. Whatever it was the baron had to say, it was not good.

Just when Sebastian thought he would go mad from waiting, the other man spoke.

"I have always let my children know that I shall find a spouse for them, one that will provide a benefit to this family. Diane is proving obedient, of course. But my son has shown himself to be quite difficult in this regard. I have recently been made aware that he has become some-what...enamored of a certain woman of dubious virtue. I would have been happy to let the boy sow his oats, of course. Men of our station, as you know, keep mistresses and such. There is no shame in it. Indeed, it is expected, to help relieve our more manly urges."

No shame for the man, perhaps. Sebastian breathed slow and deep as he thought of the women involved in such situations, who were vilified while the man was applauded.

"But it seems Harlow is not content to merely pump the girl and be done with her," Cartmel continued, his compo-sure cracking as anger saturated his features, turning his complexion florid. "Nor is he happy to set her up in a house of her own and visit her on occasion, no matter I offered him the funds to do so. No, the damned boy insists he will marry her."

His brows drew low in fury. "It's his need to be a savior, no doubt. He always was enamored of the idea of playing a knight in shining armor. And when he rescued *that actress* from an overzealous admirer one evening it must have brought up those grandiose delusions that he revels in. Why else would the boy claim to have fallen in love with such a creature?" He made a rude noise. "Can you imagine? My son, the latest in a line that goes back as far as the Norse invasion, marrying that—that—*creature*? An actress! A woman who has been with half of London. My son shall be a laughingstock. And our revered lineage shall be soiled beyond redemption."

How Sebastian did not roll his eyes, he would never know. *Revered lineage, my arse.* He had heard of the connection, of course. Miss Mirabel Hutton was popular, and beautiful, and talented, her company much sought after. And she was also worth ten of Mr. Harlow Bridling, a boy not yet three and twenty who was as ridiculous as any one person could be.

But it made no sense why the baron was bringing this up to Sebastian. "I'm sorry, my lord, but I don't understand how I fit into all of this."

Cartmel sat forward, spearing Sebastian with an intense look. "I want you to take the boy away from London, distract him, make him forget this woman, show him a good time." His expression hardened—well, it became harder than it already was, a feat unto itself. "And make certain he remains with you and doesn't run off to elope with that strumpet. If you do this for our family, I shall gladly give my support to your marriage with my daughter."

Sebastian gaped at him. His future hung on the whim of a young man who believed himself in love? "You cannot be serious."

At once the fervent look faded from the man's face, replaced with his typical haughty coldness as he sat back. "I assure you, I am quite serious."

"And if he falls in love with another unsuitable young lady while we're away from the capital?" Sebastian demanded. Truly, so much could go wrong here, it was frightening.

But the baron merely waved a hand in dismissal. "That will be dealt with should the time come. The main objective now is to remove Miss Hutton from his mind."

He speared Sebastian with a hard glare. "This is my one condition to you marrying my daughter. You need to prove that you can be loyal to this family."

When Sebastian continued to gape at him, the baron narrowed his eyes. "You either do this for our family, Ramsleigh, or you can see yourself out the door. What shall it be?"

Dear God, the man was serious. Effectively backed into the proverbial corner, Sebastian saw no way out of it. He would have to see this done.

"Very well, my lord," he replied through stiff lips. "Is there any place in particular you wish for me to take your son?"

"I have already sent word to an old family friend, Lady Tesh, that you shall both be arriving posthaste, and so you may set off first thing tomorrow, the better to get the boy out of London before he does something rash. The Isle of Synne is secluded enough that Harlow shall be quite effectively stuck there, and it is not yet their summer season, so I can be assured that any fortune hunters will be few and far between. I've a mind to match the boy with an heiress while he's out of the city, to recoup the coffers I shall be depleting on you should you manage to succeed in this endeavor."

He sat forward, his expression giving no quarter. "Provide him with the time and distance necessary to break his infatuation and you shall have my Diane and her generous dowry."

Once again that nausea rose up in Sebastian, nearly choking him. But what could he do? He stood, placing his drink on a small side table, the sound of it like a shot in the tense stillness of the room. "I shall begin preparations at once," he managed, turning and striding from the room. Feeling as if he had signed a deal with the devil himself.

Chapter 3

A month. It had been a month since Lord Landon's death. Every day of that month, without fail—more often than not, several times a day, much to Lady Tesh's annoyance—Katrina had checked the post with equal parts hope and dread, certain her brother would insist she return home at once.

And every day she was met with increasing unease as the silence from Francis continued. Until today.

Katrina bit her lip as she glanced down at her brother's bold, sharp handwriting. The butler had brought the missive to her just as she was about to depart for her weekly meeting with the Oddments. It should have been the ideal time to read it; she was essentially alone in the carriage save for Mouse, with no demands from Lady Tesh to take her away from giving her full attention to her brother's words.

But once she and her pet were safely ensconced within the plush interior, and they were on their way to Seraphina's circulating library, Katrina found she couldn't bring herself to open the letter. Once she read its contents, no matter what it said, it would bring her grief. If her brother wished for her to return home, she would gain her only relation back, but she would be leaving everything she knew and loved here. And if Francis did not want her to return, she would stay with Lady Tesh and her friends and this place she had come to adore, but she would also know for certain that any hope that she and Francis could fully reconcile was over.

And, the irony was, she didn't want either of them. Or, rather, she wanted the best of both.

So overwhelmed was she, however, by what the letter might contain, she remained frozen on her seat, unable to lift so much as a finger to break the seal. Before she quite knew what was happening, the coach slowed to a stop before the Quayside Circulating Library and the door opened to reveal Lady Tesh's driver.

"Miss Denby, we've arrived," he said when Katrina just stared at him in incomprehension.

"Oh! Yes, thank you, Henry," she mumbled. Then, stuffing the missive into her reticule and grabbing Mouse's lead, she descended to the pavement with as much poise as she was able. Which, regrettably, was not much, considering the disordered state of her mind, as well as Mouse's excitement over seeing some of his very favorite people in the world. But eventually she managed to tug her dog into the Quayside, stood by while he gave enthusiastic greetings to Seraphina's two younger sisters, Elspeth and Millicent, then left the girls to their duties behind the counter while she made her way to the rich blue brocade curtain at the back of the shop and the small office that doubled as a parlor beyond.

But no matter how she attempted to school her features into pleasant unconcern—something she had never been much good at—it did not take her friends long to realize that something was wrong.

Honoria, in the process of rubbing the ears of a very grateful Mouse, froze when she spotted Katrina's face. "Who died?" she demanded.

"No one died," Katrina insisted as every eye sharpened in alarm on her. But no matter that she raised her chin and forced a smile to her lips, there was no hiding the tremble in said lips as she took a seat in one of the room's comfortably overstuffed chairs. Nor could she stop her hands from nervously clutching her reticule to her chest, as if to hide what lay within.

"Of course no one has died," Adelaide soothed, leaning across the space between their chairs and laying a hand on her arm. "But it is quite obvious something is wrong. What is it, my dear?"

But no matter that Katrina opened her mouth to answer her friend, nothing emerged. What could she say? That she had finally received a letter from her brother, something she had been openly anxious about for a month? That though she had desperately wanted to hear from him, she was now too frightened to read his missive? It sounded ridiculous even to her.

Bronwyn, as sharp as ever, adjusted her spectacles and narrowed her eyes, taking in Katrina's appearance as if she were studying her precious insects. "What is in your reticule, Katrina?" she asked quietly.

In answer, Katrina loosened her grip on the bag just enough to extract the now crumpled letter. Instant understanding saturated every face in the room.

"Your brother has written," Seraphina said. Her face was, as ever, stern. But there was something troubled in her eyes.

"Yes," Katrina rasped, looking down to the letter in her hand, then just as quickly looking away, as if she might discern what it contained simply by observing her brother's sharp scrawl.

Adelaide's hand on her arm tightened in comfort. "What does he say?" she asked quietly, her sweet voice threaded through with tension.

"I—I don't know," Katrina whispered. "I haven't read it yet."

There was a beat of silence. And then, Honoria's voice filling the small room, "What the blazes do you mean you haven't read it?"

"Honoria," Adelaide reprimanded gently.

"Oh, don't tell me you aren't just as surprised as me," Honoria shot back. She returned her attention to Katrina. "You've been waiting for that blasted letter for a month. It's all you've talked about. And you haven't read it yet?"

Miserable, Katrina could only shake her head.

"Honoria," Adelaide tried again, her voice sharper this time. "Enough."

"No, she's right," Katrina said. "I should have opened it the moment I received it. But once I read it . . ."

Her voice trailed off, unable to finish the sentence. But her friends knew her heart better than anyone.

"Once you read it, you shall have your answer," Seraphina replied quietly. "And it may not be the answer you want."

"And so you keep it shut up, much like shutting up a cat in a box," Bronwyn mused. Excitement began to light her eyes, which glittered behind the lenses of her spectacles. "While it's in the box, it can be both alive and dead."

"A paradox," Seraphina said thoughtfully, looking at Bronwyn, one auburn brow raised. "Interesting. Do you suppose—"

"I do believe," Adelaide cut in loudly, "that we should focus on the problem at hand, ladies." Returning her attention to Katrina, she gentled her tone. "Is that why you haven't opened the letter yet? You fear what his answer might be?"

"Yes."

Suddenly Honoria was before her, snatching the letter from Katrina's grasp. "Well, there is only one way to fix that particular problem," she declared. "We open and read it for you."

This time Adelaide did not resort to merely a verbal reminder that their friend had crossed a line. In an instant she was on her feet, diving for the paper.

"You most certainly shall not," she declared, straining to reach the missive.

Honoria, however, was considerably taller than Adelaide, and able to lift the letter thoroughly out of reach. "Oh, come along," she said. "Even you in all your patience and goodness must want to know what the letter contains."

"That is neither here nor there," Adelaide gritted, straining up on her toes to reach the piece of foolscap, giving a tiny hop for good measure. "We are not the ones who should be deciding when and where the letter is opened."

"Oh, for goodness' sake." Seraphina sighed, rising and plucking the letter from Honoria's hand with ease. "Katrina," she said in a carrying voice to drown out

Honoria's objections, "would you like one of us to open the letter for you?"

The room went silent, each woman turning to Katrina, seemingly with bated breath. Katrina, for her part, bit her lip in uncertainty. Then, before she could think better of it—really, it was the ideal plan, for she would have her dear friends surrounding and supporting her no matter what the letter read—she closed her eyes tight and nodded.

"Yes. Do it. Please, before I lose my nerve."

There was a general sound of scuffling, quiet quarreling as it was decided who would do the deed. And then silence descended, broken only by the sound of the seal being opened.

Then and only then did Katrina dare to open her eyes. Adelaide had the letter in her hands and was carefully unfolding it From her spot beside her, Katrina could see the letter was short, a worryingly concise message. In the next moment Adelaide, face tight with unease, began to read aloud.

"Katrina, I am—"

Adelaide paused, looking about the room in outraged disbelief before her gaze finally came to rest on Katrina. And there was so much pity in her dark eyes that Katrina felt she might cast up her accounts then and there.

But it was too late to put Bronwyn's hypothetical cat back in its box. Straightening her shoulders, she swallowed down her bile and said with as much poise as she could manage, "Please finish."

Pressing her lips tight, Adelaide nodded and turned resolutely back to the letter in her hands. Her voice shook as she continued. *"I am ashamed of you, even more so than I was four years ago. Do not contact me again, and do not return home; there is no place for you here. Francis."*

How strange, Katrina thought a moment later, for while her friends had not uttered even the faintest noise at the commencement of the letter, a peculiar rhythmic rushing filled the room now, a sound that grew louder and louder with each passing second. It took her some moments to realize the sound was her blood rushing in her ears. When spots began to swim in her vision and she swayed in her seat, she came to the troubling conclusion that she had not drawn breath for some time. It was not until Adelaide's hand took tight hold of her arm, however, that she was able to inhale at all.

She dragged in a great gulp of air, her head clearing as she fought to right herself. All the while her friends' voices surrounded her, muffled at first, then growing clearer, their outrage a palpable thing.

"How could he?"

"The bloody idiot."

"If he was here, I would call him out and shoot off his other arm."

"Ye scabby bawbag," Phineas joined in.

"You are quite right in that, darling," Seraphina growled as she patted her pet. "He truly is a filthy, horrible scrotum of a man."

Mouse, his giant head swiveling about, ears perked forward, let loose a low whine from his deep chest. When he moved to Katrina and placed his head in her lap, looking up at her with those large, soulful eyes of his, Katrina could hold her grief in no more. To her utter mortification, sobs erupted from her, shaking her body as she cradled the dog's head.

At once her friends' fury transformed to worry. They surrounded her, their arms going about her, hands stroking her back and her hair as she bent over Mouse and pressed her face into his neck.

"Oh, darling," Adelaide soothed. "I know it must pain you."

"You have still got a home on Synne," Bronwyn murmured. "We shall always be here for you."

"As selfish as it is, we are glad you're to stay," Seraphina added quietly.

Finally Katrina's sobs subsided. She raised her face and looked about her circle of friends. It was true, she had not wanted to leave this place or her friends, or even Lady Tesh.

Only she had not realized how much it would hurt to lose her brother again. And this time she feared it was for good.

Adelaide passed her a handkerchief. "I am sorry, dearest."

Katrina managed a wan smile as she dabbed at her wet cheeks. "I should have expected as much, I suppose. But now I have my answer, don't I? I can move forward."

"That's right," Seraphina said, giving her a bracing smile.

"And the first order of business in this new future of yours," Honoria declared, grabbing at one of the plates on the low table in the center of the room and holding it out to Katrina, "is to fill your belly. Adelaide has brought us some magnificent goodies from the Beakhead, and they will set you to rights in an instant."

"And I already have a bundle in my bag for Ash's sisters, so you've no need to worry about leaving some for them," Bronwyn said.

"Oh, we weren't going to worry about that," Honoria

said archly. "When Adelaide's baking is in question, it is every person for themselves."

As chatter once more filled the room—Katrina knew what they were about, trying to distract her from her brother's letter and the pain it had given her—she took a sponge cake from the platter. But she had no stomach for it. As surreptitiously as she could manage, she passed the treat to Mouse, who inhaled it without hesitation.

Yes, it was true she had her answer now. There was no more wondering, no more worrying. Her path was set before her. She was still safe, still had a home and a living. It was more than so many could claim.

But that did not stop the sorrow that burrowed deep in her heart. Though she and Francis had never been particularly close, after their parents' deaths he had become everything to her. And now even he was lost to her. And it was so much more final than the first time he had sent her away. Then, no matter the dire straits she had found herself in, she had been certain it was a temporary thing. Now, however...

The time with the Oddments, usually something that sped by, passed with aching slowness. Katrina tried with all her might to disguise her heartache—not that her friends would have blamed her a bit for it, but she did not want to cause them a moment's more distress from her reaction to Francis's letter. When it was time to leave, however, it was made painfully obvious to her that she had failed spectacularly at disguising her emotions as, upon Katrina saying her farewells and gathering Mouse, Bronwyn sidled up beside her.

"Walk me out?" she asked gently, linking an arm through hers.

Flushing, Katrina nodded and accompanied her friend through the blue curtain and into the Quayside.

"How are you feeling?" Bronwyn murmured as they nodded their farewells to the two younger Athwart girls—and pointedly ignored the matron nearby, who nodded Bronwyn's way before giving Katrina a cold glance and turning up her nose.

Katrina, cheeks burning from the cut direct—something she had seen a fair amount of in the last month, though the people who lowered themselves to such acts were careful not to do so in Lady Tesh's presence—did her best to focus on her friend's question. "As well as can be, I suppose."

Bronwyn nodded in understanding. "As you know, I've dealt with my fair share of troublesome family members, and was even set to be banished from home. And though our situations are in no way the same, know that should you ever have need of an ear to fill, I am here for you, day or night."

Tears burned Katrina's eyes. "Thank you, Bronwyn," she managed. She remembered that time too well when, not even a year ago, Bronwyn had been a victim of her parents' ambitions, when they had tightened the reins so brutally her friend had been in danger of losing everything that was precious to her.

She looked at her friend as they stepped out onto Admiralty Row. The afternoon sun glinted off Bronwyn's spectacles, shone on her relaxed, content expression. How different she was from the strained, anxious woman she had been then.

"How did you do it, Bronwyn?" she found herself asking. "How did you manage to get past that time?"

"Well, marrying Ash did help." She laughed, and her

sharp, narrow face lit up. But she quickly sobered. Pulling Katrina off to the side of the walkway, she peered closely at her.

"Although I rather think you're asking about my reconciliation with my family. My situation was nothing like what you are enduring, my dear. And I don't have any answers for you, though I wish with all my heart I did. But know that we are always here for you, no matter what path your life may take."

Katrina gave her friend a watery smile, beyond words. Though none of her friends had wished for her to leave Synne and return to her brother, they had nevertheless supported her in her decision to do what she had thought was right. And though they had mentioned how happy they were that she was remaining on Synne, it had been their expressions that had been proof of just how deep that relief and happiness had been.

And Katrina was glad to be staying, as well. She loved it here on Synne, with her friends, with Lady Tesh. She had found a home in them all.

So why was she not content? What was this uncomfortable itch under her skin?

As she said her farewells and made her way to Lady Tesh's carriage, she chewed at her lip, trying to make sense of her emotions. Yes, she missed her brother. But it was something more, wasn't it? It did not strike her just what that thing was, however, until an unfamiliar voice hissed in her ear.

"You should be ashamed of yourself, going out amongst decent folk."

Katrina, stunned, looked up into the angry face of

the same woman who had given her the cut direct in the Quayside.

"P-pardon?" she stammered.

The matron looked her up and down, her thin lip curling. "Lady Tesh may have kept you on," the woman said, her voice so sharp Katrina was shocked it did not slice her to ribbons, "and she may have prevented anyone from saying anything, but know you are not wanted here, girl, by any of us."

With that she sniffed, and turning her nose up, she marched on.

A chill came over Katrina as she watched the woman return to the Quayside, and she hugged herself about the middle. It felt, quite literally, as if a bucket of ice water had been poured over her head, then seeped straight to her bones. She had known it had not been easy for Lady Tesh to convince many of the people of Synne to accept Katrina after Lord Landon's death. From squashing rumors, to fielding questions from the local magistrate and Lord Landon's people, to exerting her impressive and formidable reputation in an attempt at seeing that Katrina was not ostracized, there had not been an idle moment spent. Even so, that had not stopped the quantity of angry, hateful looks Katrina had received.

But she had not realized the peoples' hatred ran quite so deep.

Which was ridiculous, really; why would anyone concern themselves with the likes of her? Mayhap that woman's opinion was not a commonly held one. Dragging in a shaky breath, she looked about at the busy street. And blanched when she caught more than one face peering coldly at her.

Just then a young woman passed her on the pavement, yanking her skirts to the side, as if she feared to contaminate them with Katrina's presence, her narrow features pinched with distaste as she looked Katrina up and down.

Dear God, had she been so blind this past month, so buried under her own concerns, that she had completely overlooked how the residents of Synne truly perceived her? Not that it was such a foreign experience for her, she thought loweringly as she and Mouse hurried up inside the carriage and she closed the curtains to prevent further acidic glares from reaching her. No, ever since that first scandal four years ago, she had been an outcast, shunned by the people who used to be her friends. Or, at least, those who she had believed to be her friends.

Since she had come to Synne, however, she had begun to think that was all behind her, that she could finally live a respectable life.

She recalled the matron's hateful words, the disgust of the young woman, the angry looks of the people. How wrong she had been.

But even worse than how they perceived her, Lady Tesh was receiving censure for protecting her. In one fell swoop Katrina had damaged, perhaps irreparably, the dowager viscountess's standing in the community. Tears sprang to her eyes as the realization hit her. Dear God, was she to contaminate everything she touched in her life? And would the others who cared about her be equally harmed? The crowd had seemed unseasonably small at the Quayside, hadn't it? And hadn't the patronage at the Beakhead Tea Room seemed to have grown smaller in the past weeks, something she had noticed when she and Lady Tesh had arrived for their weekly visit just days ago?

It all spread out before her now, like brilliant red strings connecting each seemingly separate event. And she was at the center of it all. But how could she gain respectability again so that those she cared for were no longer damaged by her presence?

At once Bronwyn's words drifted through her mind: *marrying Ash did help.* Marriage. She mulled it over, tried the word on. Yes, her friend had been right; their situations were quite different. Yet Katrina could not think of another way to protect herself from further talk and heal her reputation.

Not that Katrina believed anyone would want her with such a stain upon her name. She pressed her lips tight and absently rubbed Mouse's silky ear. No, she was not the popular debutante any longer, as she had been when she was young. There were not scores of men lined up to dance with her, no bouquets filling her home to bursting.

Nor was there any man who she had developed a tendre for, as there had been in the *before-times*...

At once an image of Lord Marsten swam up in her mind, tall and deliciously dark and handsome. She had purposely refused to think of him in the past four years. But as fragile as she was in that moment, there was no stopping the remembrances this time. She sucked in a sharp breath as memories crashed over her head, a veritable wave of emotions. She could still recall how she had felt that last night with him, how she had thought perhaps he might want more than a mere flirtation, the happiness and hope that had burst to life within her at the realization that she had begun to fall in love with him without even realizing it.

But then he had been forced to leave London—only later did she learn it was due to his father's death—and the scandal with Lord Landon and the duel with her brother broke soon after. And she had put that wonderful, attentive, devil-may-care man from her thoughts. It was too painful to remember him. Lord Marsten encapsulated all her previous hopes and dreams, the yearnings of a young woman's very soul. And with the devastation of the past years, and more recently the newest scandal to visit her doorstep—or, rather, bedroom window—those yearnings brought her only pain, her *what-ifs* too difficult to bear.

But she would not do this to herself, would not remember that man and the possibilities of such a bright future at his side. She would put him from her mind and not think of him again. She would focus on her future, and what she could do to alleviate the pain she was bringing to those she cared for most. And if she had to find a man to marry to do it, to gain back a bit of her old respectability so she might protect those nearest and dearest to her, she would.

She chewed on her lip. She could ask Lady Tesh for help, of course. The woman was a consummate matchmaker and had been frustrated beyond bearing at her lack of success to match Katrina in the past; she would no doubt relish the chance to try again. But she would wish to find some beau of good society, someone with a title and fortune. And Katrina, quite frankly, did not have the time to wait for something that seemed an impossibility, not with her friends' livelihoods being threatened. No, Katrina would have to look elsewhere for a husband.

Mayhap there was some hardworking man on Synne who would still take her. Hadn't Mr. Kendrick shown an interest in her recently, even with the newest scandal, though he was old enough to be her grandfather? Mayhap Mr. Finley, who always seemed a touch friendlier than was comfortable. Or Mr. Young, a widower with a dozen or so children, who had been vocal about finding a bride. Yes, that wife would merely be a kind of indentured servant to care for his brood. She sighed, blinking back tears. But at this point in her life, she could not afford to be choosy. And perhaps, if she were to enter into a respectable marriage, she would not be such a burden to those she loved.

So mired in the possible benefits such a dismal endeavor might bring, she did not immediately notice when the carriage slowed before Seacliff's massive front doors. Finally, however, she roused herself to leave the carriage and make her way inside. It would do no good to look so dismal. She would not give Lady Tesh a moment to regret all she had done for her.

Jasper approached as she entered.

"Lady Tesh is in the drawing room, miss," he intoned. "Her guests have arrived, and she has asked me to direct you to her."

Lady Tesh's guests. Of course, how could she have forgotten? Rousing a smile though it was the very last thing she felt like doing, she thanked Jasper and hurried to the drawing room, releasing Mouse from his lead as she did so. It was Lord Cartmel's son, wasn't it? What was the man's name? Mr. Bridling? Yes, she believed that was it. And a companion, though Lady Tesh had not informed her who that might be. They would have company at Seacliff, and would no doubt be out and about showing them the sights. And Katrina would not have all that much time to focus on her own sad problems. Which was a relief. Though she knew she should decide on which man to encourage in a possible suit with all haste, she certainly did not have the heart for such a depressing endeavor.

Reaching the drawing room, she took a deep breath and ducked inside, rushing across the carpet toward the group at the far side of the room. "Lady Tesh, I'm sorry I'm late," she said in a cheerful voice that was nevertheless brittle to her own ears. "I did not realize your guests would be arriving so early—"

The trio turned to face her, and Katrina lost her breath entirely as she was struck by one very familiar, once-so-dear-to-her face. "Lord Marsten," she breathed, her feet stumbling to a halt not five feet from that man. No, she reminded herself hazily, he was no longer Lord Marsten but the Duke of Ramsleigh. Dear God, it was as if her remembrance of him had acted as some kind of spell, summoning him from the ruin of her former dreams. He stood then, like her hopes rising from the dead, and she clutched a hand to her chest, as if it could hold that pounding organ back from galloping straight out of her chest. Goodness, it was him, in the flesh.

And so much flesh. Her gaze roved hungrily over him. He had always been well-formed, of course, with his broad shoulders and slim hips that the current fashions fit with impressive perfection. Now, however, there was so much more to him, his shoulders broader, his chest massive. And his thighs. Dear God in heaven, had they always filled out his trousers so well?

But it was his face that arrested her attention. There was that same dark, wavy hair, just a tad too long; those same lips, deliciously generous, ones she had dreamed of kissing on more than one occasion. And, most importantly, there were those piercing gray eyes with their fringe of impossibly long lashes. They widened as they took her in. He opened his mouth, as if about to speak.

Whatever he had been about to say, however, was lost as a sudden booming woof rent the air. It was not until she heard the scrambling of nails and the thudding of giant paws on the polished wood floor, however, that she understood just what that woof heralded. By then, Mouse had already rounded the drawing room door. She froze as he galloped into the room. His head swiveled in their direction, jowls swaying, tongue lolling, what appeared to be almost a grin on his face at the sight of them—or, rather, the newest inhabitants. Another great bark sounded, fairly shaking the cups on their saucers, and he was racing across the room. Right for the duke.

Time slowed, Katrina's eyes widening in horror, knowing what was about to come. There was nothing Mouse liked more than to greet newcomers, particularly males, by shoving his head in the most inappropriate places. Before she could open her mouth to stop the animal, however, suddenly the duke was in front of her, planting himself between her and Mouse. Like a knight of old preparing to do battle with a fire-breathing dragon.

In the next instant Mouse's great snout, given a clear shot to that body part he loved most, arrowed straight for the duke's . . . nether regions. And with a strangled "Uargh!" the duke doubled over, dropping like a felled tree.

Chapter 4

Perhaps if Sebastian had been in full possession of his faculties, perhaps if he had not still been reeling from seeing Miss Denby again—dear God, it truly was her—he might have understood sooner that it was merely a dog that was racing toward them like a demented stampeding elephant.

As the situation had stood, however, he had seen her, the one woman who had ever made him want more from life, the one who had made him dream things he had never expected to dream, and he had been shocked to his core. In a split second he had felt the worries of the past years melt away as he'd stared into her clear blue eyes. He had been overcome by the urge to rush to her, to take her hand in his and never let go now that he had found her again.

It had been in that moment, however, that the dog—if one could even call a creature of that size a dog—had torn into the drawing room. Sebastian had acted on instinct alone, positioning himself between Miss Denby—Lady Tesh and Bridling had been far from his thoughts though they were right next to him—and the huge black-and-white flailing beast that was barreling toward them at full speed.

He'd braced himself, feet planted wide, fists raised. No doubt some part of him expected to be leapt upon and torn limb from limb. What he did *not* expect, however, was for a huge yet decidedly canine snout to run straight into his...ahem.

He must have yelled out. At least he thought he had. There was the echo of something tortured and quite loud that bounced about in his brain. All he was aware of, however, was pain exploding in that most sensitive place. He doubled over, his face planting in the wriggling black-and-white back of what he now knew to be a dog but was much more the size of a pony. Or a small horse.

"Oh!" Miss Denby cried, her voice sounding as if from a distance for all his ears were ringing. "I am so very sorry Mouse! Stop this at once, you are being very naughty."

And then the beast was dragged from his person. And Sebastian, lacking that canine body to keep him upright, and much to his chagrin—if he had been at all capable of feeling chagrin just then—dropped like a stone.

For the next several seconds, he felt caught in some limbo, his ears filling with cotton, his vision going dark about the edges. Until, that was, he finally managed to drag a shuddering breath back into his empty lungs. It was then he heard Lady Tesh's voice ringing through the air.

"Katrina, I told you to keep that blasted beast contained."

"I'm sorry, my lady. I did not even think of locking him up before coming here."

"A dire mistake, one the poor duke is now paying for."

There was a groan then, rising over their voices. It took him some seconds to realize that the sound was coming from him. And only because Miss Denby dropped to her knees beside him and took his face in her hands. He knew *that* because his eyes snapped open at the sensation of her cool fingers on his skin—something that should not feel as wonderful as it did. Especially considering what condition the other aspects of his person were in.

"I am so sorry, does it hurt much?"

But, though he could now breathe and though he knew he must be capable of speech, he could not find the voice to answer her, for the sight that met his eyes hit him like a punch to the gut.

Miss Denby's face was sweetly flushed, and so close to his own that, had he been at all capable of it, he could have easily risen up mere inches to take her lips in a kiss. It was something he had ached to do four years ago, and apparently that urge had not quieted in him—no matter what his present physical state was. How was it she was even more lovely than before? Her face was heart-shaped, her cheeks like apples, her eyes tilted up ever so slightly at the corners and with a thick fringe of lashes that practically reached to her delicately arched brow. Her hair was like spun gold, curling at her temples and caressing the side of her long neck. And her lips...ah, God, those lips, bow-shaped, with the most delectably full bottom lip, so plump it creased in the center. A lip made for kissing.

"He's not answering me," Miss Denby gasped, blessedly unaware of his inappropriate thoughts, looking up at Lady Tesh even as she reached out to push the massive canine away. "Not *now* Mouse," she cried before turning back to

Sebastian, her voice more desperate than before. "Your Grace, please answer me."

Finally, he found his voice. But only because her use of such a form of address directed to him—something he had never heard from her sweet lips before—had been like a bucket of ice water poured over his head. He was not the same ignorant, conceited young man he had been so long ago, after all. No, his days of dreaming of anything with this woman were well and truly over.

"I'm fine," he croaked, attempting to sit up and distance himself from her. "Truly."

She let loose a relieved breath. It fanned his face, smelling of whatever sweet thing she had partaken of last and something else, something utterly feminine and delicious.

"Thank goodness," she breathed. "Oh! But let me help you up."

Before he knew what she was about, she leveraged herself to her feet, bent over him, and jammed her hands under his arms. Which only managed to thrust her bosom into his face. That, accompanied by the sounds of effort she was making from that delectable mouth as she attempted to lift him by sheer will, were doing the most unfortunate things to his body.

When one particularly vigorous attempt nearly caused her breasts to spill free of their delicate muslin prison, however, he finally regained the sense he needed to put a stop to her efforts.

"I can manage," he croaked, waving his hands in the air in a bid for her to stop.

She did, immediately, stepping back and dragging the still wriggling dog with her, looking as miserable as any one person could.

Somehow—he would never know how, for he was bound and determined to erase this moment from his mind the instant he escaped from her presence—he managed to get to his feet. And he was left staring down at the beast that had caused the chaos.

It did not look nearly as menacing as it had when it had been running full tilt toward them, though it was still impressively huge, even from Sebastian's taller-than-average height. Mayhap that was because it was next to Miss Denby, who was incredibly petite. He had a feeling that, if she had been at all inclined to, she could have ridden the beast like a horse.

But there really was no denying it was larger than any dog he had ever seen. Paws like dinner plates, a madly wagging tail that could no doubt do considerable damage, a deep chest. All topped by a comically large head, made even more laughable by the fact that everything drooped on it, from ears to eyes to jowls. As he stared, its tongue lolled out of its mouth, uncurling like a great pink banner, making it appear for all the world as if the dog were grinning at him.

And then a memory surfaced, one that hit him with all the force of a kick to the chest.

"This is Mouse? But I thought he was the runt of his litter."

Something akin to pain muddied her gaze. "You remember," she whispered.

I remember everything you have ever told me. The words were as clear as the day he first said them to her at that fateful ball in London

But he was drifting into forbidden waters. He could not go back to that time. Not ever.

Clearing his throat, he took a surreptitious step back

and said, "He is an impressive dog. Much larger than I expected, that is certain."

"He was supposed to have been locked up upon Miss Denby's return," Lady Tesh said from her seat, which she had not budged from. She laid her hand on her own calmly seated pet, as if to say, *This is what a proper dog is supposed to be.*

Suddenly she frowned. "But I do think introducing your pet before proper *human* introductions have been made is quite beyond the pale. Though," she drawled, looking back and forth between Sebastian and Miss Denby, "it seems, Your Grace, you are acquainted with my companion already."

"Your companion," Sebastian repeated, looking sharply at Miss Denby once more. After his retreat from London following his father's death, he had been too immersed in his own troubles, too preoccupied with his own cares and grief, to have heard any of society's gossip. He may as well have been on another planet for how completely he had separated himself from everything. A part of him had assumed that Miss Denby had found a husband, that she would have a home of her own and blond children frolicking at her feet and all the happiness she deserved. It had been that assumption—and the pain it brought him—that had prevented him from asking after her upon his return to London.

But in all that time, he had never once thought that Miss Denby might have been reduced to a *companion*, a position that only those of greatly reduced circumstances and with no family to care for them took on.

He looked her up and down, seeing her with new eyes. If there was anything he had learned in the past years himself, it was how to hide the visible proofs of a sudden reversal of fortune. And he saw that proof in Miss Denby, most obviously in her muslin gown which, while lovely, was years out of fashion and showed signs of being mended more than once. Her jewelry, too, was simple, a small gold heart, secured not with a chain but rather with an inexpensive ribbon. What had happened to put her in such a position?

But she must have seen his too-obvious perusal of her person, for she flushed mightily, her apple cheeks going bright pink. He hurriedly rearranged his features, looking away—and immediately caught sight of Bridling gaping at her. Ah, yes, Bridling. The reason he was here on this godforsaken Isle when he should be planning a wedding to Miss Bridling and her fifty thousand pounds and getting ready to save his family and tenants from something so much worse than mere ruination.

Miss Bridling. Damnation, in the past minutes, transfixed as he had been by Miss Denby and how she made him feel, so achingly similar to what he had felt as a carefree young man, he had completely forgotten her. He set his shoulders and drew in a steadying breath. He would not do so again.

"But forgive me," he murmured. "You are so right, Lady Tesh; I am being incredibly rude. Miss Denby, please allow me to introduce you to Mr. Harlow Bridling. Bridling, this is Miss Katrina Denby, an old acquaintance of mine."

Miss Denby smiled at Bridling and dipped into a pretty curtsy. "Sir, it is a pleasure."

Sebastian expected Bridling to mutter a greeting and fall back into the sullen mood he had been in since leaving London. The boy had not been at all happy to be forced away from his lady love, declaring loudly to anyone who would listen that this time away from her would make no difference in his feelings, and that he would marry her with or without his father's blessing.

Now, however, he looked like a changed man. His face was alight with interest, a smile softening his formerly pinched features. He stepped up before Miss Denby, taking her hand in his, bowing low over it, and pressing his lips to her knuckles.

"The pleasure, I assure you, is all mine, Miss Denby," he said in a low, intimate tone.

Sebastian blinked. What the devil?

Miss Denby looked equally taken aback. "Er, thank you, Mr. Bridling," she replied in that clear, sweet voice of hers.

A jolt of something bitter chased away the remnants of shock that were still present in Sebastian's body. Bridling looked utterly taken with Miss Denby, as if he had been struck by Cupid's bow. Not that Sebastian could blame the man. She had always been a stunning woman, almost too beautiful to be real. That, along with her sweet nature, had made her one of the most popular ladies in London during her time there, a diamond of the first water.

And her looks had not altered in the intervening years of what must have no doubt been stressful circumstances. If anything, she was even more lovely, an ethereal fairy, almost otherworldly. No, he could not blame Bridling for his instant attraction.

That, however, did not mean he understood this acidic gall that soured his stomach. What the devil was it? Certainly not jealousy. He was angling to marry Bridling's sister, after all. It was his whole reason for dragging the boy here, to distract him from thoughts of his actress and

thereby win Lord Cartmel's approval of Sebastian's suit.
And if these first minutes in Miss Denby's presence were
any indication, it would not take much at all to dissuade
Bridling from wanting to marry a woman who his father
had decreed was an improper match.

Yet no matter how firmly he told himself that Miss
Denby was not for him and therefore he should not care
who Bridling's affections might stray to, the sour feeling in
his gut persisted, even growing as he watched the boy gift
Miss Denby with what he no doubt thought of as a melting
smile. The blasted little rake.

But Bridling was not through surprising him. Nor, it
seemed, was he about to make things easy for Sebastian.

"You know, Miss Denby," he said, "you remind me so
very much of my darling Mirabel."

Miss Denby gave him a confused little smile. "Mirabel?"

"Yes!" Bridling's eyes shone with excitement, his chest
fairly puffing up with pride. "Miss Mirabel Hutton, London's premier actress. No!" He corrected himself, his gaze
going slightly dreamy. "*England's* premier actress, for she
outshines any other."

"She is your fiancée, sir?" Miss Denby queried politely.

"Not yet," Bridling said, shooting an almost defiant look
at Sebastian before returning his gaze to Miss Denby. "But
she soon shall be. Once I return to London, I intend to ask
her to be my wife."

"My early felicitations, Mr. Bridling," Miss Denby said
with a smile.

Blessedly, Lady Tesh was through being ignored and put
an end to Bridling's effusions.

"Sit, all of you," she snapped. "My neck aches from
looking up at you."

They did as they were bid, though Miss Denby sank into her own chair near the dowager viscountess with seeming reluctance. "Shouldn't I bring Mouse to my room, my lady?"

"What is the point? He will no doubt find a way to escape. No, the damage is done. He shall remain, and when we are done with our tea we shall all take a walk out of doors so the beast might have his exercise. I would show His Grace and Mr. Bridling Seacliff's gardens, and we may discuss our plans for the next weeks. If, that is," she drawled, sending Bridling a droll look, "you are more amenable to this trip, my boy."

"Why would I not be amenable?" he asked, giving Lady Tesh a wide smile before returning his attention to Miss Denby. "I am quite anxious to begin planning my time here. The Isle is a lovely place. And its inhabitants equally so, it seems. It shall be a wonderful little holiday before I return to my Mirabel and begin life as an adoring husband."

It was blatant flirting, not at all subtly done, and punctuated in the most baffling way with that pointed mention of Miss Hutton. Truly, Sebastian could not make heads or tails of Bridling. No matter how confounding he was acting, however, Sebastian had no choice but to watch the boy carefully and pray that Cartmel knew his son enough that this mad scheme would work.

Just then the dog—which Miss Denby had been doing her best to control with a firm hand on the creature's collar while simultaneously attempting to balance a delicate teacup in the other hand—suddenly broke free of her grasp.

"Mouse," Miss Denby cried out, even as Lady Tesh heaved a loud, beleaguered sigh.

"That is a fine pet you have," Bridling said, scooting

forward in his seat and patting his knee. "Come here, dog. I say, come here."

But the animal ignored Bridling completely. Instead, and with a bright look of determination it its eyes, it worked its way around the low tea table, large tail coming dangerously close to swiping the whole tea set to the ground, and made a beeline to Sebastian.

"You naughty thing," Miss Denby said, rising to her feet, no doubt intending to go after her pet. "Come back here at once."

But though Sebastian knew it would be best to let her fetch the creature, he instead found himself holding up a hand to stop her.

"It's quite all right, Miss Denby." He looked down at the dog—well, not so far down, for it was nearly on eye level with him now that he was sitting.

Miss Denby, however, did not look any easier. "If you are certain," she said as she gingerly resumed her seat.

"I am," he stated with firmness before turning to the dog. "Now, my good man, can you behave yourself?"

Seeming to sense he would not be turned away, the dog heaved a happy sigh and rested his quite heavy, quite solid head in Sebastian's lap, looking up at him as if there was no place he would rather be in the world.

To Sebastian's credit, he did not flinch when the dog's head came in such close contact with his private area again. He did, however, allow himself a silent mourning for his trousers, which would no doubt need to be disposed of once the dog's drool was done with them. It was an expense he could ill afford.

"That is most kind of you," Miss Denby said with a beatific smile. "He truly does like you, Your Grace."

Which should not have affected Sebastian as deeply as it did. But with her looking at him as if he were a saint among men, he suddenly felt one hundred feet tall.

"He likes everyone," Lady Tesh muttered.

Bridling, of course, spoiled man-child that he was, could not be left out of the conversation. "I have a great many hounds back at our country seat. Cartmel Manor boasts extensive grounds, you know, and has some of the finest hunting in Somerset. Have you ever been to Somerset, Miss Denby?"

"Er, no," she answered with an uncertain smile, seeming to drag her attention away from Sebastian and her dog with difficulty. "No, I have not had the pleasure."

Bridling smiled wide. "I hope I may one day have the pleasure of your visit there. I say," he continued, fairly bouncing in his seat as he turned to Sebastian, "as you and Miss Denby are old friends, mayhap you can invite her for the wedding festivities when you tie the knot with Diane."

Sebastian flinched. It was well known that he was pursuing Miss Bridling, but his suit had not exactly been accepted yet. He glared at Bridling. All of it, of course, hinging on this boy with his seemingly mercurial affections.

And, apparently, the news had not traveled so far as Synne if Miss Denby's reaction was any indication. "You are set to be married, Your Grace?" she asked quietly.

Why, he thought as he looked at her pale face, did the thought of succeeding in his desperate suit of Miss Bridling suddenly sit so very wrong with him? Or, at least, more wrong than before. And why did he feel as if he had betrayed this woman? Yes, he had at one time wished to make a future with her. And yes, he had begun to make advances toward her to show where his affection had lain.

And yes, she had seemed to welcome those advances quite enthusiastically.

But there had never been an understanding between them. No, things had been quite thoroughly derailed before they'd even had a chance to see where their futures might lead—and if those futures might have joined together down the same path in life.

That did nothing, however, to ease the sudden and inexplicable ache in his chest. He just stopped himself from rubbing a fist into said chest, instead focusing on the silky-smooth ears of Mouse, whose head was still firmly planted in his lap. "It is not finalized," he said lamely, shooting Bridling a dark look.

Bridling, of course, was oblivious to the chaos he had just unleashed. He blithely bit into a biscuit, glancing about the room with a wide smile. "Ramsleigh is, of course, being modest," he said around the biscuit. "He has been pursuing my sister for months now, you know. It's only a matter of time before my father accepts." He gave a loud laugh, punching Sebastian in the shoulder. "You're a blasted duke, after all, no matter your unfortunate history. I'm looking forward to having a duke for a brother."

Which should have given Sebastian peace of mind as to his plans for the future and all he had to accomplish to save his tenants. Yet as he glanced at Miss Denby, noting the sudden loss of color in her cheeks and the way her smile trembled on her lips before falling altogether, he found himself wishing for a different future entirely.

Chapter 5

*H*e was getting married.

Those four words clattered noisily about in Katrina's head, as they had since she'd learned of his future matrimonial prospects just hours before. And they still had the power to take her breath away. It should not come as such a blow, of course. Not only was he highly eligible, as well as expected to marry and produce an heir, but she had never had anything serious with him. Yes, they had indulged in a mild flirtation. And yes, she had thought perhaps he might want more with him. And she had wanted that *more* with him. So much more.

But that had been years ago, and she had not seen or heard from him since. It was expected that he would have found someone by now. Which he had. And if Lady Tesh's comments in the intervening hours since learning of the duke's upcoming nuptials were to be believed, the woman was a respectable, smart, and immensely wealthy heiress. The duke, by all accounts, could not do better.

All that reasoning, however, didn't do a thing to sooth the ache in her chest for the path her life could have taken except for her going off on a few horrible detours—or, rather, her being forcefully shoved in different directions. A path that would have been so much more lovely than the one she was planning now, trying to decide which of the awful men on Synne who might consider taking her on as a wife would be the most palatable.

She sighed, taking the stick from Mouse's mouth and lobbing it across the side lawn. Though summer was fast approaching and the weather had begun to reflect that, having been beautifully warm and clear earlier that afternoon, it seemed the wind had decided to stir itself up and commiserate with her lowered spirits now. It had brought in an abundance of gray clouds, set the trees to swaying, had her skirts snapping about her ankles, and dried the tears in her eyes before they could spill over.

Hugging her arms about her middle, she listlessly watched as her pet galloped across the grass. Tea was over with, the tour of the gardens that had followed done, and Katrina had been given a short respite to exercise an increasingly restless Mouse. A fact she could only be grateful for, this small break giving her a chance to breathe for the first time since she had laid eyes on the duke.

Mouse came tearing toward her, stick held aloft in his teeth with pride. She held out her hand for it absently, then threw it as hard as she could manage. But instead of chasing after it, as he had been doing for the past quarter hour, Mouse suddenly appeared intensely interested in something behind her. Then, letting loose a joyful, boom-ing woof, he loped past her toward the house.

It did not take Katrina more than a second to realize who was there. Mouse had become incredibly attached to the duke from the moment he had met the man, sticking close to his side throughout the afternoon, hardly giving Mr. Bridling a glance. And wasn't it just her luck that the man who was causing her such troubled thoughts would have found her in her one moment of peace? Nevertheless, she plastered a smile to her face and turned.

The duke stood not twenty paces away, looking even more delicious than he had just hours before. His dark, wavy hair was tossed here and there by the breeze, and Katrina found herself ridiculously jealous of that wind.

"Hello," he said, looking up from Mouse, who was wrig-gling happily between the man's legs. "I was just getting some fresh air and did not intend to disturb you. Forgive me, I'll leave you to your solitude."

Which was what she wanted. Wasn't it?

But looking at the serious, stark expression on his face, she recalled not for the first time since his arrival the young man he had been, so sweet despite his rakish reputation. She had thought his altered attitude this afternoon had been due to being in a new place, with new people. She had always been a bit anxious in new settings, after all, and it took her some time to relax enough to smile and talk with any ease.

But he had never been like that, she reminded herself. He had always seemed to thrive in such settings. It was part of what had made him so in demand, that natural liveliness. He had always been at the center of any gathering, the first to join an outing, the one with the loudest laugh and brightest smile.

Now, however, with the mischievous gleam gone from his eyes and his face settled into serious lines, he seemed as far removed from that devil-may-care rogue as any one person could possibly be. What had happened to turn him into a shadow of the person he had been? And why did she so badly wish to find out what it was?

In her typical fashion, her mouth was quicker than her mind. And even as she was coming to the realization that it was best if they kept their distance from one another and she should let him return to the house, she found herself saying, "No, stay, please. We have not had time to catch up after so long."

She wished she could recall the words the moment they left her lips. The last thing she should want was time alone with this man. But it was too late. Giving a jerky nod, he gave Mouse a final pat and made his way to where Katrina stood.

"You have got quite a strong throwing arm," he said as Mouse, having gotten his greeting out of the way, happily ambled off after his stick.

Katrina, eyes forcefully glued to her pet, shrugged. "It comes from years of practice. Mouse needs an immense amount of exercise and loves this particular game more than any other."

"I recall how you worried about him when he was a puppy," the duke said, his voice quiet. "I am glad to see he has grown up hale and healthy."

She looked up at him, oddly touched that he would remember such a detail. Which was an immense mistake. The moment she met his gray eyes—almost the same hue as the darkened sky above their heads—she felt it straight to her toes.

"T-thank you," she managed, tearing her gaze away. She gave a nervous laugh. "Though it really is too bad you had to leave London before I could tell you how healthy he was quickly becoming even back then. Oh! Forgive me," she said, cheeks hot, cursing herself ten times a bumbling fool for her unthinking words. "But you left because of your father's death. Which you know, of course. Seeing as he was your father. Please accept my belated condolences. As well as my heartfelt apologies."

She felt rather than saw him turn toward her. "Thank you for your condolences. But why are you apologizing? It certainly is not your fault he died so suddenly."

If possible, her cheeks burned hotter. She bit her lip, accepting the stick back from Mouse before throwing it with such force it bounced several times along the ground in a wild pattern, much to Mouse's delight. "No, what I meant was, I am sorry if my presence here has caused you any discomfort. It cannot be easy to see someone you were once acquainted with in such reduced circumstances. Not that I am ungrateful for my position. I shall be eternally grateful to Lady Tesh for taking me on when I had no other recourse." She shrugged awkwardly. "Even so."

For a long moment he remained silent, though whether from pity or disgust or discomfort she didn't have a clue. She kept her gaze on Mouse's distant rollicking form, having no wish to learn what the reason was for the duke's silence. It would not be the first time that she had run into someone from the *before-times*, after all, and she had seen her fair share of all three of those unfortunate emotions directed at her.

But it would be a much harder pill to swallow from *him*.

Finally he spoke, his voice a gentle rumble, much gentler than she expected. "The only distress I might feel is thinking of what you must have gone through over the past years. It is my fault entirely, however, for being surprised at all. I admit, I purposely didn't ask after you upon my return to society several months ago."

His tone changed then, became lighter, almost rueful, and she had the feeling he was smiling. "I suppose I never wished to learn that you could be happily married to some lucky fellow somewhere."

She could not have stopped herself from looking up at him if she tried. "You did not want to know if I had married?" she whispered.

"Ridiculous, isn't it?" His gray eyes scoured her face, and though he still smiled, there was something sad in it. "I never had any claim on you, after all."

Hadn't he, though? It had been affection for him that had her keeping every other suitor at bay . . . as well as what made figuring out which man to encourage now so much harder. Though she knew that even if she had a dozen polite, handsome young men to choose from, it would have still been difficult. No, nigh on impossible. No one had ever made her feel even a portion of what he used to make her feel. And still made her feel, apparently, if the return of those long-dormant butterflies in her stomach was any indication.

But no, she reminded herself brutally, he was not for her. "You are getting married," she said, a kind of reminder to herself and him both, her voice overloud in the late afternoon air.

Her words seemed to unlock something in him. Or, rather, to lock something up, the ease he had begun to have with her gone in an instant. He immediately straightened, a flash of what appeared to be regret or pain in his eyes before they went completely flat. "Yes. That is, I am hoping Miss Bridling accepts my hand. Which I plan to secure once I return to London with her brother."

Katrina swallowed down the bitterness that filled her mouth, managing to dredge up what she hoped was a bright smile. "I am happy for you," she murmured. It was a blatant lie, of course. She was the farthest thing from happy there was. Especially as his engagement—or near-engagement—made him so much farther from her; as it stood, he may as well have been on the moon.

Not that he had not already been far from her in terms of status. The ruined sister of a baronet, and a duke? It would have caused talk even when she had been respectable. But the fact that he was planning to marry another made him untouchable. She had destroyed one possible marriage, after all, and would do everything in her power to keep from doing such a thing again.

Granted, she had not encouraged Lord Landon on that first occasion. And the man's previous fiancée, Lenora—whom he would have married the day after that first climb through Katrina's bedroom window four years ago—had gone on to marry Lady Tesh's nephew, the Duke of Dane, and now lived in marital bliss right here on Synne. It was Lenora who had secured Katrina the position of companion to Lady Tesh when she had learned of the reduced circumstances Katrina was in. The whole horrible scandal had come full circle.

But no matter the positive outcome—for Lenora, at least—the debacle with Lord Landon and Lenora had cemented in Katrina the determination to be especially careful where other women's fiancés or husbands were concerned. Which the duke was. Or, at least, nearly, which was as good as. No, even if she wished it, there could be nothing between her and the duke.

Which she did *not* wish. Not in the least.

But the silence had gone on much too long. And if there was anything Katrina did not deal well with, it was silence. And especially a tense silence, of which this certainly was one.

She watched as Mouse returned, this time galloping toward the duke instead of her, patiently waiting for the man to take his stick. The duke took it, throwing it even farther than Katrina could ever manage, sending Mouse into raptures as he bounded after it. And still the silence stretched. Her muscles tightened, her mind a blank slate, unable to come up with a single thing to say to this man she had wanted so much once upon a time.

She had to get away from him. That was all there was to it. She would gather Mouse and hurry to Lady Tesh, and use that woman as a kind of buffer for the next weeks so she would not have to find herself in another uncomfortable situation with the duke. And so, drawing a deep breath, she prepared to call Mouse back and excuse herself.

The duke spoke, however, his voice so quiet she almost didn't hear it for the blood rushing in her ears.

"Why did you never marry?"

If he had reached out and slapped her, she would not have been so shocked. Or hurt. Granted, he had admitted to purposely not asking after her upon his return to society, not wanting to know if she had married. But there could be no possible way he did not know of the scandal of four years ago. The news had been spread far and wide, printed in every newspaper in the country, spewed from every person's lips. And anyone who knew that history would know why she had never married. It was almost cruel for him to ask such a thing.

"I rather think," she said through numb lips, "that there are plenty of reasons why I would have never married. Or, rather," she continued when he merely stared in incomprehension at her, "one very specific reason."

Dawning understanding lit his face. "Ah, you mean your reversal in fortune."

Despite herself, Katrina let loose an unamused bark of laughter. She had certainly never heard it referred to in such terms before. "If you call becoming embroiled in a scandal not of my own making, my reputation ruined beyond repair, and nearly losing my brother in a duel a reversal of fortune," she muttered more to herself.

Which, she supposed, she should not have said aloud. He certainly didn't need the whole blasted thing repeated to him. It was a well-known story, after all. She expected him to nod in commiseration or appear uncomfortably abashed. What she did not expect, however, was the look of confusion on his face.

Her heart stuttered in her chest as a horrible idea took root. Dear God, was it possible that he didn't know about the scandal? No, surely not. It was a preposterous idea. Practically all of England knew.

In the next moment, however, her fears were confirmed.

"What are you talking about?"

She blinked myopically at him. "Y-you don't know?"

"Know what?"

More blinking. Truly, he would think she had something in her eye at this rate.

Which really was the least of her concerns. Especially if he truly didn't know a blasted thing about the scandal, or the duel, or all the messiness surrounding those horrible events.

But just to be certain—and because she was apparently a bit masochistic—she said, "About Lord Landon climbing in my bedroom window all those years ago? And my brother challenging him to a duel? And Francis losing his arm and sending me away and turning to gambling and losing everything?"

With each question put to him, the duke's expression grew more horrified until, by the end, his jaw had dropped open a considerable degree. She swallowed hard. Well, she certainly had her answer, didn't she? But now she felt vaguely ill. Here was quite possibly the only man in England who did not know about her scandalous past, and she had gone and told him the whole of it.

Well, not the whole. Nausea made her stomach pitch and roll like the deck of a ship. There was still the whole debacle with Lord Landon returning and then proceeding to try *again* to climb into her window, but instead falling to his death. But that was neither here nor there.

The duke, however, seemed no better off than she was. He blinked several times—it must be catching, this eye malady that made one flutter one's lashes like a debutante— before clearing his throat and shifting from foot to foot. "Ah. Er, yes. That is, no, I had no idea. After my father's death, I'm afraid I was quite consumed with everything that needed to be done. Between that and Ramsleigh Castle's isolation, I did not learn any of the goings-on in society until my return just months ago."

"And you did not ask after me on purpose," she finished lamely.

He managed a smile, but it was a sickly thing. "Quite."

But, much to her shock, he was not through, not by far.

"As you have told me your scandal, it's only fair that I tell you mine. If you are as unaware of it as I was of yours, of course."

"Your scandal," she repeated blankly. "You were involved in a scandal?"

"Yes." He cleared his throat. "Or, rather, my father was. Which, of course, means I am as well. As you were not apprised of it, it would appear as if you are every bit as isolated from news here as I was at Ramsleigh Castle. I assure you, it was the talk of the town for some time, and I am still recovering. You see, after losing the majority of his fortune to creditors, my father tried to recoup his losses by creating a false investment scheme. He bilked numerous people out of their money, then promptly lost everything. I have spent a good portion of the past four years making reparations, paying it all back, with interest."

He smiled again, though this time there was a spark of humor in his eyes. Well, perhaps not humor, but there was something there, a recognition of just how ridiculous this whole thing was.

"And so," he continued, "we are two peas in a pod, us scandalous creatures."

Katrina did not think it possible she could laugh just then. But she found her lips quirking in humor, then a chuckle escaping, which she hastily held back with tightly pressed lips.

He cocked one eyebrow, his eyes shining with reluctant mirth. "Don't stop yourself on my account," he murmured.

Which succeeded in loosening the last bit of control she had on her inappropriate bout of humor. A laugh broke free that she could not contain no matter how hard she tried. In the next instant she found herself doubled over, giggles pouring from her.

She feared the duke might find offense in her reaction. He certainly never meant for her to be so overtaken with amusement as this. But his deep chuckles joined her own, rough and tumbling from his lips in a jumble, like a bunch of rocks in the neck of a river that was finally worked free. Soon they were both roaring with laughter, the freeing sound of it joining with the distant sound of the waves crashing against the cliffs and the lowing of the wind through the trees.

Their laughter trailed off, reduced to the occasional chuckle. But their smiles remained. They gazed at each other, and for the first time since his arrival, Katrina felt she saw something of that man he had once been. For perhaps the first time in four years, the band about her chest loosened, a band she had not even realized was there.

In the next moment, however, it was back in place, tighter than ever.

"I say," Mr. Bridling said as he emerged from the house and made his way toward them, "you two are awfully jolly. Mind letting me in on the joke?"

Those words, as innocuous as they were, had all the power of a wall going up between her and the duke. A quick glance at that man as she surreptitiously stepped back—she had not even realized she had stepped closer to him—and she saw the serious, austere duke had returned. His eyes, cool once more, passed over her before coming to rest on Mr. Bridling.

"I thought you would be resting in your room, preparing for dinner," he remarked to the younger man.

"No doubt," Mr. Bridling murmured, looking back and forth between Katrina and the duke with narrowed eyes.

Katrina involuntarily flinched. She had erred, and greatly. She had a very specific place in this world now, one that did not include falling back into the old friendliness she used to share with the duke. She was not a diamond of the first water any longer, was not society's darling. No, she was a companion, who desperately needed her position. At least until she saw her plan through and found some poor man willing to take her on as a wife.

The duke had a need to marry, as well. But whereas Katrina would be content to find anyone respectable, the duke was set to marry Miss Bridling, Mr. Bridling's sister. She saw it clearly now that he had given her the full story: his father's scandal; how he'd needed to make reparations to those his father had wronged; his isolation from society followed by his sudden reappearance just months ago; his swift near-engagement to Miss Bridling, a wealthy heiress. He *needed* this marriage to save the dukedom.

Yes, she had erred in falling into such friendliness with the duke. But it was not only for her. She watched with increasing unease while Mr. Bridling continued to eye them both with suspicion. She would not ruin the duke's chances with Miss Bridling. But what could she say to diffuse this increasingly tense situation?

Blessedly, Mouse appeared just then, bounding up to them. Managing a bright smile even as she drew upon her old talents for conversing—something she had not had to use since her time in London—she took hold of the dog's collar, preventing him from going to his new favorite person, and turned to the young man.

"Oh, we were just laughing at this silly beast. But it is

getting late, and Lady Tesh must be expecting me. Mr. Bridling, perhaps you might accompany me inside, for I wish to hear more of your Miss Hutton. It has been years since I was in London and I do not recall hearing her name. Would I have seen her in anything, I wonder? I do hope you shall tell me everything."

As she'd hoped, the man's suspicious look melted away, to be replaced by bright-eyed pleasure. "I would like nothing better, Miss Denby," he said, holding out an arm to her.

Placing her fingers on his sleeve, she let him lead her inside, nodding briefly the duke's way—making certain not to look at him, for if she did, she feared she might cry.

Chapter 6

"Miss Denby," Lady Tesh said later that evening as they lounged in the drawing room after dinner, "I find myself needing entertainment. Play us something."

Miss Denby, who had been in the process of securing a shawl around her employer's shoulders, hastily rose. "Is there anything you wish to hear?"

"Something jolly," Lady Tesh said with a stern look. "None of those sad ballads you've been playing of late. And Mr. Bridling," she continued as Miss Denby hurried to the pianoforte, Mouse close to her side, "you shall turn the pages for her."

"It would be my pleasure," Bridling said gallantly, following Miss Denby with alacrity.

Sebastian, for his part, couldn't seem to take his gaze from Miss Denby. It had been the same since his arrival, of course, his eyes drawn to the busy, graceful way she moved, some part of her always in motion. Like now, as she adjusted her skirts over the bench and riffled through the music sheets before her. She blushed prettily as Bridling approached, her hand smoothing over her pet's head, as if to seek comfort there, her soft laugh as Bridling spoke to her causing Sebastian's stomach to clench in the most disconcerting way.

Focus on Bridling, he told himself brutally. Sebastian was to marry the man's sister, after all. The whole point of this trip was to make certain that event, required to protect his family and those who relied on him, took place.

But no matter how forcefully he tried to set his traitorous mind on the path it was supposed to travel, his attention would invariably drift to Miss Denby, his eyes tracing the curve of her cheek, noting with a pang the deep dimple when she smiled, caressing the graceful arch of her neck as she bent her head to focus on the keys. How many times had he sat just like this, watching her hungrily from afar? And then, later, when he had gotten bolder and approached her, offering to turn the pages just as Bridling was doing for her now? She had gazed up at him with her sweet smile, and he'd felt on top of the world.

And then it had all come crashing down on his head.

"Your Grace," Lady Tesh said, blessedly drawing his attention from the delectable sight of Miss Denby, "I thought it might be nice to have a private moment to get to know one another better."

Sebastian inclined his head. "I would like that," he replied by rote, though he felt anything but. The dowager was an incredibly shrewd woman, and the crafty look in her sharp eyes made him feel he would not like the conversation to come, not one bit. Would she remark on his former relationship with her companion? She had seemed to be watching them closely throughout the afternoon and evening, after all. If even Bridling had noticed the friendliness between them, there was no doubt in his mind that the dowager must have noticed as well. For a moment he cursed himself ten times a fool for putting Miss Denby's position in dire straits.

But that was not what the woman wished to discuss, it seemed. Though the relief he should have felt was lacking, considering the true reason she wished to speak with him.

The woman pursed her lips, looking closely at him. "You may not be aware," she began thoughtfully, "but I knew your father many years ago, when he was a young man."

Shoulders tense, he fought for a bland expression, though inside he was a riot of emotion. Most people who wished to talk of his father did so out of a morbid curiosity to see how he would react. He had learned that particular lesson during his months in London, and had taught himself to remain virtually emotionless when the subject was brought up. Externally, at least. Internally, he was not so lucky, his gut invariably clenching with equal parts grief and anger for all his father had done, and all Sebastian was now forced to deal with in the aftermath.

"Is that so?" he queried lightly now.

"Indeed. I did not know him well, of course. He was a young buck around the same time that my son was searching for a bride, and so the present Lord Tesh knows him much better than I ever did."

She narrowed her eyes, as if taking measure of Sebastian. Then, without warning, her expression softened. "I have heard about what transpired some years ago, of course. But I have also heard of your actions to repair the mess you were handed. That was quite honorable of you."

Sebastian had not thought anything she could have said could have shocked him. But he had been wrong. A thickness filled his throat, and he forcefully attempted to swallow it down. "That is kind of you to say," he managed. "But it is not any more than anyone else would have done."

"Now, that is not remotely true," she replied, much more gently than he thought her capable of. "It takes incredible fortitude to make such things right. Though, I daresay, you are not used to kindness when it comes to such things."

What could he say to that? No, kindness had been the furthest thing from anyone's thoughts when his father or the scandal was brought up. More often than not, the emotion that seemed to be present was a cruel glee.

Lady Tesh seemed to sense he needed a moment, for she pointedly turned her attention to the pianoforte. Sebastian glanced that way as well, thankful for the reprieve—and immediately felt the full weight of his mistake. Miss Denby had been all he'd wanted before his father's death. And while he had been able to work toward recouping much of what had been lost, she was the one thing he could never claim again—and the one aspect of the whole mess he regretted most.

"They make a fine pair, do they not?"

Sebastian felt as if he'd been punched. He gaped at the dowager. "I'm sorry?"

But the woman was looking at Miss Denby and Bridling with close interest. "Mr. Bridling and my companion," she explained, nodding their way. "They are both so attractive, it is like looking at a painting, don't you agree?" She looked at him then, obviously waiting for a reply.

But what the devil could he say to that? Not what he truly wished to say, of course, which was that if she thought to match Miss Denby with that popinjay Bridling, it would be over his dead body.

"I suppose," was what he finally came up with. A pathetic response, of course. Why it made the dowager smile so widely, however, he didn't have a clue.

"Not that anything can come of it, of course," Lady Tesh mused, turning to look back at the couple again. "Not with Mr. Bridling's affections being secured quite thoroughly elsewhere. Though I admit to being surprised that his father would allow it. Lord Cartmel will have a very specific idea of exactly whom his children will marry, after all. But I suppose you know that better than anyone."

What could he say to that? Blessedly, he didn't have to say a damn thing, for she continued.

"I, of course, received a letter from Mr. Bridling's father regarding his son's sudden visit before your arrival. However, he did not inform me why a lively young man in good health would wish to visit a decrepit old woman in this sleepy place."

"I would hardly call you decrepit, Lady Tesh," he said.

The woman pursed her lips and lifted one steely gray brow. "And you are not answering the question, Your Grace," she drawled. "While flattery will typically get you everywhere—and I am vain enough that I shall happily tuck that compliment away for later use—in this moment it shall not distract me in the least. So tell me, why is Mr. Bridling truly here? It is all too obvious he did not come willingly, and that he would be only too happy to have remained in London with his actress."

The woman was entirely too quick. But after a hasty rumination, Sebastian could not come up with a good reason why he should not tell Lady Tesh the whole truth of it, especially as she had seemingly figured out a decent portion of it already, and in less than a day. It would only help to have her as an ally, after all.

Leaning forward, planting his elbows on his knees, he said, "Very well, I shall tell you. But I'm certain Lord Cartmel would wish me to impart this to you in the strictest confidence."

"Of course. I am the soul of discretion." He must have looked dubious, however, for she laughed. "I know well and good when to keep my mouth shut. Which, I assume, has been a main component in my longevity. If I spoke of the majority of the things I have heard in confidence, I would not now be of this earth." Again a chuckle.

Despite himself, Sebastian found himself smiling. The dowager viscountess was one of a kind, that was a certainty.

Before he could think better of it, he lowered his voice and said, "As you have noted, Mr. Brídling has gone and fallen in love with the actress Miss Mirabel Hutton. And you are right in that Lord Cartmel does not approve of her. The baron was of the opinion that some time away from the woman would do the boy some good."

The dowager rolled her eyes, waving a hand dismissively in the air. "Cartmel is a stick in the mud. To go to such lengths due to the woman's profession?" She made a rude sound.

Sebastian choked on a laugh. "You do not see anything wrong with the match then?"

"Of course not," she returned. "Why, I have known my fair share of actresses in my day and they were a jolly bunch to a one. But there is no accounting for taste, especially from someone as stodgy as Cartmel. But I assume your presence here has a purpose, and you are to *assist* the boy into forgetting his actress?" At his reluctant nod she continued. "As I suspected. And, knowing Lord Cartmel as long as I have, no doubt he is also holding something over your head to ensure your help. Considering I am all too aware of what your father did to the dukedom before his untimely passing, and considering it has been mentioned that you are expected to make a match of it with Lord Cartmel's daughter, I am going to guess that the girl's dowry is a large one...and you have desperate need of it. Do I have the right of it?"

Truly, the woman was the most frightening person he had ever known. "Are you a mind reader, then?" he muttered with reluctant admiration.

"I shall take that as a yes," she remarked dryly. "Well, if that is the case, what are your plans for the boy?"

Which was a question he had not been prepared for. He shrugged. "I did not have any specific plans, to be honest," he replied. "As Lord Cartmel was of the mind that Bridling would quickly tire of his actress with time and distance, I did not think it necessary to plan anything."

"Then you are as big a fool as he is," she scoffed. "And, of course, this means I shall have to get involved."

She heaved a heavy sigh, as if she could not think of anything she wished to do less. But Sebastian saw the glint of excitement in her eyes as she pursed her lips in thought.

Without warning she thumped her cane on the ground, as if punctuating what she had said.

"But I do think we are done here, at least for the time being. Why don't you take over for Bridling, Your Grace, and send the boy here so I may get a sense of what might work best to turn his head."

Bemused, confused, and all manner of *-useds*, Sebastian

did as he was bid, standing and making his way toward the pianoforte. It was only when Bridling was on his way to Lady Tesh's side, however, and Sebastian looked down on Miss Denby's sweet face that he realized what a fatal mistake this had been. For he suddenly felt himself transported to those long-ago days when his future had been bright and his dreams centered around a smile from those large blue eyes.

* * *

Katrina's fingers slipped on the keys as she gazed up at the duke. No surprise, as her heart was frolicking about in her chest like a gamboling puppy at his closeness. The discordant sound clanged through the room, making her wince. Mouse, whose head had been pressed against the instrument as he liked to do when she played, pulled away and whined.

"Miss Denby," Lady Tesh called out, "is there a problem?"

Heat suffused her cheeks as she patted Mouse's head in reassurance and looked back to the music sheet. "Not at all, my lady."

With incredible willpower—truly, it took no less than her entire focus, considering the very warm, very male figure now stationed at her side—Katrina once more found her place in the song and began to play. The cheerful tune filled the air, mingling with the low murmur of voices coming from Lady Tesh and Mr. Bridling's direction. She could do this, she told herself bracingly as her fingers moved over the keys. The duke was just an old friend. There was no reason to be nervous around him.

Just then he reached past her, turning the page—and

nearly turning her head as well as those strong fingers came into view. The smell of pine reached her, so reminiscent of those times he used to station himself at her side for just this reason that she nearly melted right into the bench.

Perhaps, she thought with no little panic, if they were to fall into conversation, she wouldn't be quite so physically aware of his presence. His personality was so altered, after all, that conversing with him should remind her that she was not the popular debutante flirting with London's premiere rake any longer. Clearing her throat, she said, "You appeared a bit distressed, Your Grace, while talking to Lady Tesh. I do hope the dowager wasn't too forward in her words to you. She can be . . . blunt at times."

"At times, eh?"

Despite herself, she laughed, though it was a nervous thing, considering the effect he was having on her. "She does take some getting used to. But she is kind, in her own way. I daresay I could not have survived the past years in her employ if she were not. She tends to terrify those of a weaker constitution, of which I am regrettably one. Of course, not everyone can be so strong-willed. And I am glad Lady Tesh is so fierce. At least, when it is not being directed toward me."

"And you are happy here?"

The question, so quietly said, so gentle, took her completely off guard. Blessedly the song ended just then, and though the notes fell away a bit too abruptly, it was not so jarring that anyone would notice. She looked up into the duke's face, trying to understand where such a question had come from. The worry there, buried deep in his eyes but there regardless, made her heart lurch in her chest.

"I am," she rasped. Then, unable to help herself, she added, "As happy as I can be."

Which did nothing to alleviate his worry if the deepening divot between his brows was any indication. She should not have been so honest. He had enough to worry about, after all. He did not need to concern himself with her as well.

But they had remained silently staring at one another too long. Though it was not Lady Tesh's strident voice shattering the tension between them; rather it was Mouse, who was apparently not quite through with listening to music. He was suddenly there beside her, rearing up, huge paws coming down on the keys, creating a discordant explosion of sound that had Katrina wincing.

"Miss Denby," Lady Tesh called out, "do play something else so that beast of yours behaves."

"Yes, Lady Tesh," Katrina replied, even as she pushed her pet away from the instrument. "Very well, you naughty thing," she hissed before blindly grabbing the next music sheet in the pile beside her and beginning to play. Anything to settle her pet and the dowager. Too late, however, she realized the song was all too familiar, a sweet love ballad she had played once before with the duke—then Lord Marsten—standing at her elbow. He had flirted with her, distracting her mind from her nerves at playing before a crowd. Did he recall that night? Surely not, she comforted herself. The man had much more important things to concern himself with.

But one surreptitious look at his face made her realize he did indeed remember. Very well.

His lips quirked without a trace of humor as he reached

forward to turn the page for her. "That night seems so long ago, does it not?"

His voice was quiet, threaded through with something achingly familiar, a regret she knew all too well. "Yes," she managed. In truth, it seemed like a lifetime.

But they were growing maudlin, his expression taking on undertones of sadness. To lighten the mood, she nodded her head toward Lady Tesh and Mr. Bridling, who were quite thoroughly engrossed in whatever it was they were discussing. "Though I cannot recall a more rapt audience," she said wryly.

His expression shifted, the curve of his lips transforming to a true smile, his eyes joining in as they danced with mirth. Her breath caught in her throat as the memories that had overtaken her before bombarded her with more force.

But things were different now, weren't they? Not only because her circumstances were pathetically reduced. No, *he* was different, too. Yes, he was a duke now, about to marry, with troubles and responsibilities on his head. But those were only surface differences. Even when laughing, she saw something had altered deep in him, a seriousness that had not been present before having taken root.

Though he was not the only one who had altered in the four years since they had known one another, she reminded herself severely. She could not expect them to be the same people they had been, could she? *Foolish girl.* "A positive change, surely," she continued a bit breathlessly, trying to redirect her attentions back to the music she was playing, "for I can botch the notes to my heart's content."

"Oh, but you never botched the notes," he returned gallantly, with that altered echo of the rake he had been. "And besides, look at your pet. I daresay you could simply wiggle your fingers over the keys in a cacophonous mess and he would be more than content."

She cast a quick look at Mouse and, despite herself, laughed softly. As was his usual pose when she was playing, he leaned against the smooth wood of the instrument, one of the few times he was truly calm and quiet, his eyes closed in bliss.

"I admit it has been wonderful that my music, as uninspiring as it is, can touch a creature in such a visceral way. My brother was forever telling me to quiet my playing. He was prone to over imbibing, and claimed the sound of the pianoforte wreaked havoc on his head..."

Her voice trailed off at that, her mood shifting fully to melancholy in an instant. She had kept herself from recalling such things; it was painful to remember that brother whom she had never been close to yet had wanted to have a relationship with more than just about anything.

She had not realized she had stopped playing until Mouse once more made himself known. Though it was not to insist she play more. No, as ever he was sensitive to her moods, ready and willing to offer comfort when she needed it. His wet nose nudged under her arm, his large, solid head pushing into her side. She started, automatically wrapping her arms about his neck, glancing up at the duke. There was that worried frown marring his brow again. Though this time confusion and curiosity were also there in his eyes. He opened his mouth, and she knew he intended to ask her about Francis. They had run with the same crowd in London, and while they had not been close, they had been friends of sorts. The duke would no doubt wonder how her brother was doing, why he had allowed their fortunes to reverse so completely, and why he had let his sister take on the position of a companion.

The thought of fielding such questions made her so exhausted she wanted to weep.

In an instant she was on her feet. "Forgive me," she murmured. "My fingers have cramped. Please make my excuses to Lady Tesh." She hurried from the room, Mouse close to her side. Wondering how the devil she was supposed to get through these next weeks when the duke, no matter how altered he may be—or perhaps because of it—made her equal parts grieve and yearn for what might have been.

Chapter 7

I vow," Bridling said as he strode into Sebastian's room the following evening, "I have never seen such a collection of lovely girls in all my life as I did when we visited the town center this afternoon. I admit I was furious with you and Father when you cooked up this plan to spirit me away for God knows how long, and in such a far-off, sleepy little place." Here he made a face, his thoughts on Synne's attributes clear. Not that Sebastian didn't know well and good what Bridling thought of the place; he had been the recipient of the boy's ire for the entire four-day journey here.

"But now I do believe it is genius," Bridling continued. He strode to the cheval glass in the corner, licking his finger and smoothing down his brows, looking at his face this way and that. "Though, of course, I miss my darling Mirabel dreadfully, I can see now that this whole endeavor will be good fun. A kind of last holiday as a bachelor, if you will."

Sebastian breathed deep and slow, focusing on the

carefully metered action to keep himself from saying something he would certainly regret. They had been on the Isle a mere day, he told himself; of course the boy had not had time to forget his actress. Now that Lady Tesh was working in concert with him to distract Bridling from his infatuation, it should not take long to complete the job he had been sent here to do. Especially if the way the boy continued to eye Miss Denby whenever she was in the same room was any indication.

At the memory of how Bridling had leaned in close to Miss Denby when they had visited Seacliff's library after their return from town, his chest brushing her arm under pretense of reaching for a book on a high shelf for her, the muscles in Sebastian's shoulders seized. It had taken every bit of willpower he possessed to keep from grasping the boy by his collar and dragging him from Miss Denby's person. Such were the actions of a jealous lover. Of which he most certainly was *not*.

That fact, however, did not diminish the memories such a scene had reawakened, of the times he had ached to brush up against Miss Denby, just for the chance to touch her. Despite the flirtation they had indulged in when they had been in London, there had been some unspoken agreement between them that nothing would come of it. She out of everyone in London had seemed to understand that he had not been remotely interested in marriage, and he had been able to relax around her in ways he hadn't been able to with anyone else.

Well, he rectified wryly, he had not been remotely interested until those final days, when he had realized his feelings for her had shifted to something more. But even so, he had never followed through on the urge to touch her.

All but for that one time...

In a flash he recalled that halcyon spring day, the birds chirping so merrily in Hyde Park, the group of gentlemen he had been out riding with coming upon Miss Denby and her group of friends. How he and his friends had dismounted to walk with the ladies, and he had found himself beside Miss Denby. And how his hand had reached out seemingly of its own accord in her direction—only to find her fingers extended in just such a way...

He hastily shook his head to dispel the memory, forcing his attention back to the preening peacock before him. He had a job to do here, and he'd be damned if he'd let anything distract him from it, be it a lovely miss who dredged up things best left in the past, or the spoiled heir of a powerful baron. The stakes were too high.

"And it shall be a holiday you won't soon forget, I daresay." Sebastian lifted his chin as his valet secured a sapphire stickpin in the folds of his cravat—glass, of course, the actual jewel having been sold off long ago to pay for repairs to the tenants' cottages. "Lady Tesh has quite the schedule of events for us. Starting with this evening."

"Ah, yes, dinner at the Duke of Dane's." Bridling gave a humorless chuckle. "I daresay even my esteemed father cannot complain about that."

No, the man certainly would not. Especially as Sebastian and the Duke of Dane would not be the only dukes present. He had been informed, along with other prestigious personages from Synne society, the Duke of Buckley and his bride, one of Miss Denby's closest friends, would be in attendance as well. It would be a veritable buffet of dukes.

For a moment he amused himself with wondering just

what a group of dukes was called. An *audacity* of dukes, perhaps? Or an *effrontery*?

His lips twisted. Perhaps it was a *futility* of dukes. For he could not see a purpose to the blasted title, no matter that everyone else seemed to hold it in such high regard.

For a moment he thought of his father, a man he had revered, and all the people he had hurt. All the tenants and farmers he had ignored and overlooked and, in the process, caused to suffer so damn much.

His gaze drifted to Bridling, who was still looking closely at himself in the glass. Which, of course, caused his thoughts to drift to that man's sister. Miss Bridling was Sebastian's salvation. Yet he was not ignorant of the fact that she had never asked to be sacrificed on the altar of both of their fathers' greed, his for money and hers for power. He would do everything he could to make certain she was not unhappy, that she did not regret her life.

Though as they left his room and made their way below stairs, and he was met with the sight of Miss Denby in her outdated pink gown and simply pinned hair that somehow made her even lovelier than the high society miss she'd been before, he knew that he would not be so lucky.

* * *

Perhaps it had been seeing the duke again that had made Katrina completely forget the confrontation with the woman outside the Quayside Circulating Library just two days ago. And perhaps it had been her constant determination to not notice his presence at Seacliff, all while being pathetically aware of him, that had caused her to forget that the dinner tonight at Danesford was the first true event she was to attend since Lord Landon's death, a fairly sizable gathering of some of the more notable members of Synne society. Maybe if she had remembered, she might have been prepared for what happened upon her arrival. Even so, she wasn't certain it would have hurt any less.

Extricating herself from Lady Tesh's side as that woman made the necessary introductions of the duke and Mr. Bridling to the milling guests, she hurried to Honoria. Her friend embraced her, kissing her on the cheek. Which should not have been all that unusual. They were uncommonly close, after all. But Honoria's hug was a touch longer and tighter than usual. It only took Katrina a moment to find out what was different about tonight.

"Now, don't panic," Honoria murmured with a stiff smile. She took hold of Katrina's suddenly cold hands, pulling her to a settee off to the side of the massive drawing room.

"Oh, God," Katrina moaned as dread coursed through her. Though her friend's expression was pleasant if strained, the look in her eyes could only be described as a healthy mix of fury and regret. "What now?"

Honoria took a deep, steadying breath before saying, her voice trembling, "My father has refused to come."

Katrina blinked. Whatever she had expected her friend to say, it certainly wasn't that. "I see."

Which she didn't, not in the least. Blessedly her friend understood that and set about explaining, though with the furthest thing from pleasure imaginable.

"It seems he thought it a prudent message to send to his congregation that he would not socialize with...such a scandalous female."

A ringing started up in Katrina's ears. She had always

liked Honoria's father. The vicar had seemed a good man, who had not only taken on the complete care of his own two daughters after his wife's untimely death, but also his two nieces as well when his brother and that man's wife had died. And he had always treated Katrina with, if not friendliness, then at least respect.

Now, however…

"I am so sorry, Katrina," her friend whispered, tightening her grip on Katrina's fingers. "I told him he was being an old fool, that I could not believe he could go so completely against the teachings of that book he reveres so much. But he would not listen to me."

"It's all right," Katrina responded. But it was a mechanical response, sounding as if it was said by someone else, and from a great distance. Dear God, the vicar was willing to anger not only Lady Tesh, but also the Dukes of Dane and Buckley and their wives as well with such a snub? That it was aimed at her notwithstanding, Katrina was well versed in society, and knew that such an action would be seen as an insult to every titled person present. He must hate her very much to invite their wrath.

Bronwyn approached just then, the worry and anger on her face a mirror to Honoria's. "Have you told her?" she asked as she sat on Katrina's other side.

"Yes," Honoria answered, frowning at Katrina. "Though she does appear awfully pale, doesn't she?"

"It's to be expected," Bronwyn murmured, placing an arm about Katrina's shoulders, which Katrina suspected was as much to keep her from falling to the floor as it was to show solidarity with her. "Katrina, dear, are you well? Should I tell Lady Tesh you wish to return home?"

Before Katrina could answer, however, Honoria spoke

up, her voice sharp. "She most certainly shall not retreat. She will stay right where she is and hold her head high. And we shall be right there beside her."

"I rather think that decision should be up to Katrina," Bronwyn gritted.

"And her decision shall be to stay."

"You are still speaking for her."

"If you think I am going to allow her to turn tail and flee," Honoria snapped, "you have got another think coming."

"Please," Katrina managed, her voice reed thin but strong enough to silence both women, "don't fight. It's all right, Bronwyn. I shall stay." She gave them a sickly smile. "I would rather be here with the both of you than alone in my room thinking anyway."

Bronwyn, however, did not look the least convinced. "If you're certain."

"I am," Katrina replied, with much more conviction than she felt. "Now, let us join the others so we don't cause any talk."

Or any more talk than was already being had. As they rose and crossed the room, Katrina was painfully aware of more than one eye following her, as well as the hiss of whispered conversation. And it was not due to her outdated gown, either, though she had just added some embroidered roses at the hem to camouflage a small tear. No, these gazes and whispers were decidedly nonfriendly in nature, fairly burning her back as she passed.

Finally they reached the small party at the far end of the room. Lenora, Duchess of Dane, smiled reassuringly at Katrina as she sidled up to Lady Tesh's side. Which, of course, meant that the young duchess was aware of the vicar's stance. Katrina's cheeks burned.

"Katrina, dear," she said, "I was just telling Lady Tesh that you must bring Mouse for a visit. Our Charlotte adores him, you know."

"That is because she is two, and more than happy to terrorize anything larger than her," her husband, Peter, said with a sly smile for Lady Tesh. "I rather think she gets that from my dear aunt."

"She is lucky to get such a trait from me," Lady Tesh replied archly to her nephew. "You don't want anyone walking over her."

"They would not dare," Peter replied with a chuckle.

"I am sure you have realized, Ramsleigh," Ash, Duke of Buckley, said to the other man, "that Lady Tesh is quite the formidable woman. As a matter of fact, it seems most of the women on Synne have that particular trait in some degree or another, my own dear bride included." He tucked an arm about Bronwyn's waist and smiled down at her.

"Perhaps it is something in the water," Peter mumbled, smirking as his wife playfully elbowed him in the side.

"I have the utmost respect for Lady Tesh, I assure you," the duke—the Duke of Ramsleigh, that is; goodness, there were so many dukes—said, bowing in that woman's direction. "I daresay if the world was run by strong, formidable women instead of men, we would be in a sight better shape than we are."

"Oh, you'll do just fine here," Ash murmured approvingly.

All the while, as they talked and laughed, Katrina busied herself with adjusting Lady Tesh's shawl and seeing to Freya. As she smoothed the wisp of unruly fur atop the dog's head, however, she noticed her fingers were trembling. And not just a small bit, but quite violently. It would be easy enough, of course, to attribute her spate of nerves to Honoria's revelation of the vicar and his cruel message. Such a thing was powerful enough to affect her for some time.

But Katrina knew there was more to it. And as she glanced up and caught Lenora gazing at her in worry, she knew what it was. Having been with Lady Tesh for more than two years now, she had learned how to blend into the background easily enough. While everyone was typically kind to her, she was never at the center of the discourse. It was not her place, after all.

But tonight she felt inexplicably as if she were standing center stage at Drury Lane, with the lights bright and burning on her. And she hated it, so much she thought she would be ill.

Maybe she should have listened to Bronwyn and returned to Seacliff. There was still time to depart, wasn't there? She could leave, and have the carriage sent back for the rest of the party, and spend the rest of the evening curled in bed with Mouse. Or she could sit at her small desk and write out that list of men she might be able to marry, thereby setting in motion the events needed to finally claim some respectability.

Before she could inform Lady Tesh of her wishes, however, the butler arrived and announced dinner. And then there was no time to slink away like a dog with its tail between its legs. Lady Tesh needed her assistance, and Freya required attention, and she did not want to cause a fuss. Or, at least, no more a fuss than she already had.

Dinner was a torturous affair. Lenora had, of course, made certain to have the seat and place setting the vicar would have used removed before the guests arrived in the dining room, so there was no empty seat screaming at Katrina that she was a scandalous female. But it did not go without her noticing that the young man on her other side pointedly ignored her. Nor did she fail to notice the Duke of Ramsleigh looking at her with a troubled frown throughout the evening. Was even he aware of the slight that had been made against her? Dear God, how he must pity her. Which was somehow worse than the vicar's cruel opinion.

By the time the meal was over, Katrina's nerves were about to shatter. She assisted Lady Tesh back to the drawing room and saw she was settled comfortably. But when she would have sat beside that woman, she froze, her stomach lurching. She couldn't do it. She could not sit and smile and pretend everything was well when her life was in shambles. If she did not get some air this very moment, she knew without a doubt she would scream. Or cast up her accounts. And truly, in that moment she didn't know which would be worse.

Turning to Bronwyn, who sat near Lady Tesh, she passed Freya to her. "I think I need to use the retiring room," she said.

Bronwyn, of course, saw through her brittle unconcern. "Take all the time you need," she whispered. "I'll distract Lady Tesh."

Katrina wanted to throw her arms about her friend's neck in thanks. Instead she gave her a trembling smile and bolted from the room. But she did not go to the retiring room. Instead she made for the closest outside door, rushing through it into the cool evening air. Only then, with the clear inky sky and multitude of stars above her head, could she breathe. But it was not a normal, calming inhale. Rather, it was a shuddering gulp of breath, the air hitting her lungs seeming to awaken all her frustration and fear and anguish. Soon sobs were ripping from her chest. *This is ridiculous*, her mind scolded as she hugged her arms about her middle, as if to hold herself together. *You are weak. You are pathetic. It's only what you deserve.*

But the more her mind scolded her—the echo of what she had heard throughout her childhood, a cruel drum in her head—the harder she cried. She was barely aware of the door opening behind her, or the voice calling her name. It was only when a hand gently gripped her arm that she realized she was no longer alone. Before she could think to react, however, she was pulled into a strong embrace, and a familiar scent of pine assailed her senses. *The duke.*

She should pull away. He was not for her, after all. And if they were ever found here, it would ruin his chances with Miss Bridling. She could not allow that. But when his strong hands rubbed over her back, soothing her in ways she had not thought possible, she could no more pull away than she could fly to the moon above their heads. Letting loose a weary sigh, she melted into him, her arms stealing about his waist. And one small corner of her brain thought that she would be quite content to never let him go.

Chapter 8

Sebastian had sensed something was wrong with Miss Denby the moment they arrived at Danesford. Her friend had whisked her away and whispered something to her, and the blood had quite literally drained from her face. He had ached to go to her and ask her what had happened.

But no, it was not his place. She had her friends surrounding her, and he had his duty to Lady Tesh and their hosts. There were people to meet—or, on occasion, reacquaint himself with, as he had known the Duchess of Dane, then Miss Lenora Hartley, and the Duke of Buckley, then the co-owner of London's premier gaming hell, during his time in London before his father's death. And Miss Denby was in a safe, familiar place. Nothing untoward could happen to her here.

Or so he had thought. It was not until they were seated at the long mahogany table for dinner that he realized maybe Miss Denby was not in a safe place after all.

The woman seated beside him, Mrs. Pickering, mother to the Duchess of Buckley he had been informed—on multiple occasions—leaned in close as they began their soup. "It is shameful Lady Tesh has kept *her* on after such a sordid scandal," she murmured in outraged tones, motioning with her spoon toward Miss Denby.

He stared at her, certain he had not heard her right. He should ignore her, of course. If there was anything he had learned over the past years, it was that giving such gossips the attention they craved, even if that was to squash rumors, only succeeded in adding kindling to the fire.

Yet he found that though he knew better, he could not help responding.

"That was four years ago," he gritted. "One would think that people would have moved on from it by now."

As expected, the woman's eyes fairly glowed with her success at capturing his attention. She tittered. "Ah, my dear duke, but this latest scandal was a mere month ago. Though I suppose you wouldn't have heard just yet, being so new to Synne, as well as residing under Lady Tesh's roof. The dowager viscountess has been working quite hard at keeping the whole thing bottled up tight."

A month? What the devil was she talking about? But though he schooled his features into disinterest, it was much too late. Mrs. Pickering had already got a whiff of his blood and was not about to release her jaws from about his neck.

"That poor Lord Landon fellow must have been utterly bewitched by her to have attempted to climb into her bedroom window again upon his return to England. Though this time he fell to his death, didn't he? How Lady Tesh can hope to keep this from getting out, I'll never know." She smiled, an almost feral thing. "But now that the vicar himself has refused to be in the same room as her, there will be no stopping the good people of Synne from shunning Miss Denby as they ought. I only wish my darling daughter would follow suit. I have told her on more than one occasion that it does not look well for a duchess to befriend such a person. But she will not listen to me, no matter that I am her mother." She sniffed in offense.

Fury had boiled up in Sebastian at the woman's ramblings. But putting her in her place would do no one any good, most of all Miss Denby. And so he had pointedly turned his back on Mrs. Pickering and her cruelties, letting his silence do what his words could not in such a setting— all the while doing his best to ignore the effect the woman's words had on his curiosity.

Lord Landon had returned, and tried once more to climb into Miss Denby's window a mere month ago? And he had *died*? What the devil? He had known Landon during his time in London, of course, though not well. The man had been boring, and serious, not at all the kind of person Sebastian had been in the habit of running wild with. He could not imagine him becoming so passionate about anything that he would have not only got himself embroiled in a duel and sent into exile, but also lost him his life.

His gaze had once more drifted to Miss Denby. Though perhaps in this particular case he could understand only too well. There had been a time he would have done just about anything for a single smile from her...

He shook his head to clear his mind. Not only was he very nearly engaged to Miss Bridling, therefore making any such thoughts about another woman highly inappropriate, but he was letting Mrs. Pickering and her cruel gossiping get to him. It was just such speculation that had no doubt made Miss Denby's life a living hell. As it was even now. The man on her left, a young and fashionable pink, pointedly turned his nose up when she ventured to draw him into conversation. Miss Denby, of course, had noticed, and her skin, which had become uncommonly pale upon their appearance at Danesford, became even more wan, more strained. When the women left the men to their port at the conclusion of the meal, it did not take those men long to begin gossiping. And talk immediately went to Miss Denby.

"Still cannot believe Lady Tesh has kept that girl on," one man huffed, twirling his glass between his fingers. "Dane, perhaps you can talk to your aunt, let her know that she should let Miss Denby go. It isn't reflecting well on her to have such a person in her employ."

Fury roared to life in Sebastian, a consuming fire, so hot he feared he would scorch the table where he gripped it to keep from lunging for the man's throat. Blessedly the Duke of Dane's cold voice stopped him.

"Mr. Pickering," he bit out, "though you are Bronwyn's father and Buckley's father-in-law"—here he nodded to Buckley, who sat at his side—"if you speak of Miss Denby or my aunt in such a manner again, you and your wife will no longer be welcome at my table. And that goes for any of you," he continued, eyeing each man in turn, his unusually pale blue eyes like chips of glacial ice, freezing each man in their place. "Both women are very dear to myself and my wife, and I will not hear them insulted. Isn't that right, Buckley?"

The Duke of Buckley, who up until then had been watching the proceedings with his dark eyes narrowed dangerously, uncurled from his unassuming relaxed pose, his lean form threaded through with power, like a great cat sighting down its prey. "You have the right of it. Any person who talks ill of them shall have the both of us to answer to."

The Duke of Dane was, of course, a huge behemoth of a man, more like a Viking than a duke, and frightening enough to behold angry. But with Buckley beside him, a man Sebastian knew to possess a well-deserved reputation for ruthlessness, it was enough to make every man at that table look decidedly ill.

Catching Dane's and Buckley's eyes as the other inhabitants of the room fell into quiet conversation, he nodded his thanks before, murmuring to Bridling that he needed air, he rose and made his way from the room. It was not a lie, of course. He did need air, and desperately. After the events of the past hours, he had the horrible feeling that if he did not begin moving, he would shatter from the force he was using to hold himself together.

But all thoughts for himself fled the moment he stepped into the hallway. At the far end was a familiar blond figure in pale pink, racing down the corridor as if her life depended on it.

He did not hesitate to follow her. Whatever had happened in the time since she'd left the dining room, it must be horrible indeed. In a moment his long legs brought him to the side door she had slipped through.

Her sob was the first thing he heard upon stepping out into the garden. That sound, so forlorn, so full of hopelessness, had his heart seizing in his chest. He called her name, looking wildly about the dark landscape for her, quickly finding her just off the side of the path. At the sight of her, head bent, arms hugging her middle, he wasted no time hurrying to her and pulling her into his arms.

He had wanted this for years, he realized as she fit against his body. How many times had he dreamed of holding her? And it felt just as heavenly as he had imagined it would.

But now was not the time, he quickly berated himself. In truth, it would never be the time for such musings. That fact hit him with all the finality of a door slammed in his face. And with it came anger, at himself, at his father. Why had he held back four years ago? Why had he been so determined to hold on to his bachelorhood? And why the hell had his father been so damn selfish that he had brought ruination to the family and destroyed forever his children's chances for love and happiness?

Useless recriminations. All he could do now was quiet his regrets and focus his attentions on soothing Miss Denby as best he could.

He rubbed his hands up and down her back, helplessness coursing through him as she shook against him. Finally, after what seemed an eternity, her sobs quieted and she relaxed into him. He should pull back then. They could not stay out here forever, after all. Eventually someone would come looking for one of them, and they certainly could not be found alone together in such a compromising position. Not only would it destroy any chance he had with Miss Bridling, but it would also endanger whatever tenuous position Miss Denby had left in Synne society after Landon's latest—and fatal—actions.

But try as he might, he could not put her away from him. Instead, he found himself holding her closer, leaning his cheek against the crown of her head, breathing in the scent of her. It was intoxicating, her own sweet floral scent mixed with the cool, fresh night air.

Finally, however, Miss Denby seemed to at last regain her senses. Her body, so soft and slight against his, tensed. And then, wedging her hands between their bodies, she gently pushed.

He stepped back immediately, letting his arms fall. The loss of her against him was acute, but he brutally squashed the traitorous feeling.

"I'm sorry," he murmured, looking down at her. The moon was waning, and the shadows long. Yet he could still see the details of her face, though they were bathed in silvery light and leeched of all color. Her eyes were wide in her pale face, teeth worrying at her full lower lip. He forcibly looked away from the tantalizing sight.

"I'm sorry," he repeated. "I shouldn't have been so forward."

She hastily wiped at her damp cheeks. "You were not forward at all. You were merely comforting me. I should be the one to apologize for making such a spectacle of myself."

"You did not make a spectacle of yourself," he murmured. "In fact, I don't think I have ever seen such bravery in the face of such cruelty."

Once more her eyes found his, though this time filled with shame. "You saw his cut direct then?" she whispered, her voice cracking. Before he could answer, her face twisted and she turned away. She looked up at the cloudless sky, the hundreds of pinpricks of light like diamonds above her head. "But of course you saw. How could anyone have missed it? And no doubt you heard why he acted in such a way as well. After the vicar's pointed absence, everyone in the dining room must have been talking about it one way or another. And you were sitting next to Mrs. Pickering, the biggest gossip of them all. Though I shouldn't talk of her in such a way, seeing as she's my dear friend Bronwyn's mother."

His heart ached at the pain lacing her words. "I would say to pay them no heed, but I know firsthand how such things can affect a person."

The look she gave him could only be described as suspicious. "That is all you have to say on the matter?"

He shrugged. "What would you have me say? I'm the last person who should be judging anyone for being embroiled in such a mess."

"But my scandal from four years ago has revisited me," she insisted. "Worse, this time the man died when he attempted to climb in my bedroom window."

"I think," he said gently, "that is Lord Landon's fault and not yours."

He rather thought if he had stood on his hands and danced a jig with his fingertips he would not have shocked her more. Her jaw dropped nearly to her chest. And then her eyes welled, shimmering in the moonlight with unshed tears.

Before he could think to pass her a handkerchief, however, she quickly rallied. "It is kind of you to say, of course," she said, quickly pressing the heels of her hands to her cheeks, no doubt to stem the tide rising there. "But most of Synne society does not agree. Lord Landon's actions and subsequent death, no matter that I had no control or knowledge of them, has painted me with a broad brush. He may as well have branded my forehead, for all people can't seem to see to the me beyond the scandal. And worse, it is spreading to those I love best. My friends, Lady Tesh; all are being polluted as well. And there is not a thing I can do about it. Except—"

Her speech stalled out, as if she had lost her burst of bravado mid-sentence. He held his breath. And for some unknown reason he felt unaccountably tense for what she might have been about to say. And then she spoke again, and he knew why.

"Except to marry."

"Marry?" The word came out on a hot breath, his shock obvious in it. Was she set to marry someone then? And why did the idea pain him so, especially as he was set to marry someone himself?

She nodded. "Yes. I have come to the conclusion that, should I marry, I can, if not silence, at least quiet these damaging rumors. I can start anew, put my past behind me. And hopefully gain some portion of respectability back."

"Who?" he found himself asking, the word bursting from his chest for all he had no desire to know the answer.

To his surprise, she shrugged. "I've no clue, to be honest." And then she laughed, a bitter thing, such a foreign sound coming from her lips. "Despite my unfortunate reputation, I assume there are still a handful of men on Synne who would not be opposed to take me as wife."

Her words carried a sting to them, and he could not fail to acknowledge they were at least partially aimed toward him. And well deserved, too, for how unfeeling he was in his one-word questions.

"I'm sorry. I never meant to make you feel as if it was an impossibility."

Her face crumpled, her brief bout of bravado gone. "Once more, you have no need to apologize. I daresay if I were the one looking in from the outside, I would react in much the same manner."

But when she made to head back into the house, he couldn't help but stop her.

"Don't do that," he said softly.

She turned back to him with wide eyes that reflected the stars above their heads. "Don't return to the party?" She gave a sad laugh. "As much as I would wish it, I don't think that's possible."

"No," he replied. "Don't shrug off my apology."

She continued to stare at him, as if what he said was utter nonsense and she could not comprehend he was even saying it. And his heart broke a little. It was all too obvious she believed she did not deserve his apology. Unable to help himself, he stepped closer and took her hand in his. She inhaled, a soft sound he felt down to his toes.

"No matter that I did not mean to insult you, I did. You should not have to accept that behavior. You deserve to be respected." His grip tightened on her fingers, anger burning under his skin as he thought of what she had been subjected to that evening. "And if I could force those people that insulted you tonight to apologize, I would."

For the first time in their exchange, she smiled a true smile. Her eyes still held hints of wryness, however, proof that she did not believe him one bit.

"You are kind, Your Grace," she said, squeezing his fingers before releasing them with seeming reluctance. "Not that I am surprised, as you have always been kind. But we had best return."

She was right. They had spent far too long out here as it was, each second courting disaster. He wished he could continue to convince her that she was worthy of respect. More than that, however, he was loath to leave her.

But it was necessary. "You go on inside first," he managed, stepping aside so she could pass him on the path. "It wouldn't do to be seen returning together."

Was that regret that flashed across her face? But mayhap it was just the shifting moonlight making it appear so, for the next moment she nodded and hurried forward. Before she opened the side door, however, she turned back to face him.

"Thank you," she whispered, "for not judging me, for being a friend."

And then she was gone. He stared at the place she had been for a long time, trying to ignore the quiet part of him that wished he could be much more.

Chapter 9

*A*fter the debacle at Danesford the evening before, the very last thing Katrina wanted to do was to attend the weekly subscription ball at the Assembly Rooms. But Lady Tesh refused to hear a single one of her pleas.

"I blame myself, of course," the dowager viscountess said, looking up from cooing over Freya, who was lounging in as unconcerned a manner as a dog was capable of on Lady Tesh's massive four-poster bed. "I allowed you to absent yourself from most of our outings and hide away here at Seacliff. Perhaps if I had been firmer with you from the start, we could have squashed this talk right away. Instead it festered into something ugly, and now the blasted vicar has gone and run with it. But if you think I'm going to allow you to skulk at home any longer, beaten down by these horrible people, you are quite wrong. As a matter of fact, I am going to make a declaration for this evening that you shall not sit beside me all night long as you typically do, but shall dance every dance."

Katrina gaped at her. "You cannot mean it."

"Oh, I do mean it," her employer stated, eyeing her severely before passing a small, gilded brush to her maid. "Be certain to brush my darling Freya well before putting her to bed, do you hear? Otherwise her sweet fur gets horribly matted." As the maid, accepting the brush with a stoicism that only years of such orders could have achieved, turned to fuss over the dog, Lady Tesh returned her attention to Katrina.

"You shall not allow them to cow you," she ordered. "You shall hold your head high and ignore their pathetic chattering, and soon it will be behind you. Just as it was the first time."

Which sounded entirely too much like Honoria, so much so that Katrina felt the insane urge to laugh bubble up in her. Blessedly she managed to swallow it back. It would not have been a laugh of amusement; rather, it would have been a wild thing, that no doubt would have preceded tears. And she was done crying. Especially after the mess that had been last night.

As she followed Lady Tesh from the room, however, and they made their way below stairs in preparation to leave for the evening, she found herself remembering how the duke had held her in his arms during her bout of tears, and she was forced to come to the conclusion that mayhap last night had not been all bad. And when he had looked at her not with condemnation or pity but a gentle worry, when he had insisted she deserved respect, she had not felt like a scandalous young woman whose life had been ruined beyond redemption. No, she had felt like a woman who was cherished deeply.

But that had not lasted long. In truth, that feeling, as freeing as it had been, had disappeared the moment she had returned to the drawing room. Letting her guard down had been a dangerous thing; it made the cold shoulders and snubbing that much more painful. She could not forget what society saw her as. After all, they certainly would not. Now, as she was about to embark on an outing so much more public than last night, she held on with both hands to the reminder of who she was.

Something that was, unfortunately, necessary when she saw His Grace waiting with Mr. Bridling by the front door. The way he looked at her, with a kindness that bordered on affection and tenderness, made her ache to throw off the opinions of others until it was just the two of them. It was tempting, yes. But what would happen when he left in just a couple of weeks? He would go off, marry his Miss Bridling. And nothing would be different for Katrina. She would still have this scandal hanging over her head, would still have to worry how it was affecting those she cared for most. Worse, if she did not rein in these quickly growing feelings for him, she would wind up mourning the loss of him, someone she could never claim for her own.

And as she turned away from his greeting with barely a smile, she determined to remember that.

* * *

Which was no easier to remember an hour later as she stood at the side of the long ball room, the crown jewel of the Assembly Rooms, and her traitorous eyes searched out and found the duke for what must have been the hundredth time that night.

No hard thing. The man was one of the tallest in attendance. And to Katrina's eyes, he was the handsomest by far. But after all the scolding she had given herself regarding the man, you would think she would know better.

She was saved from further silent berating by a cane smacking her shin. Yelping, she jumped back, looking down at Lady Tesh, who brandished said cane at her threateningly.

"I told you to dance, girl," the woman said, glaring at her.

Katrina blinked. "But…no one has asked me." Which the woman must surely know, seated as she had been the whole while beside Katrina.

Lady Tesh rolled her eyes. "That is because you are stuck to my side like a limpet. And if there is anything a potential dance partner does not want, that's me as an audience." Here she smirked, no doubt fully aware of how terrifying she was to most of Synne. The woman wore her irascibleness like a badge of honor.

But her self-satisfied expression was quickly replaced with her customary sternness. "Now off you go," she said, flapping her cane in Katrina's direction, causing Katrina to stumble back lest she be the recipient of yet another attack by that frighteningly active piece of wood. "If I don't see you dancing tonight, I shall let you go on the spot."

With that, she turned away to talk to the woman on her other side. Katrina, with no other recourse, bit her lip and edged away from the long line of seats reserved especially for the more elderly of Synne's population. Lady Tesh could order her to dance all she wanted. But if no one asked her, there was not much she could do about it.

And it did not appear as if anyone was inclined to ask her any time soon. Especially as every time she came near a group, the members of that group invariably eyed her with distaste and turned their backs on her. After the third such reaction, Katrina, feeling suddenly exhausted, quickly scurried to an empty corner at the far side of the long room.

How different this experience was from when she was young. Then, she had been highly in demand, so much so that she had not been able to sit once during a ball. Each evening she had returned to their London town home after hours and hours of dancing, her feet and head aching horribly.

And yet she had been so very happy. Or, at least, she had believed she was. She had not thought anything could ruin the veritable charm that her life had become after being so thoroughly ignored throughout her childhood. After feeling lonely for so long, she had found herself popular, and courted, and had reveled in the attention.

But it had all been so fleeting. And when scandal had come calling at her door—or, rather, her bedroom window—not a one of those fine people who had claimed to be her friends had stood by her side. Every one of them had turned their backs on her, spewing gossip and cruelties with glee. And she had been made painfully aware that her life had been a mirage.

Now, at least, she had friends aplenty. Though, as luck would have it, none of them were here tonight. But perhaps that was a blessing. She did not want to consider what the Oddments might have to say to her if they knew what her plans for her future were. Her eyes scanned the crowd, seeking out the few men she had managed to single out as possible husbands. Mr. Young was, of course, not here tonight, as he was no doubt home with his brood. And Mr. Kendrick had proclaimed more than once that he was too old for such events, as it made his gout flare up horribly.

But there was one man she could count on to be here. Her gaze found Mr. Finley, then a short distance away. He stood at the edge of a group of young women, talking and laughing with a petite brunette in bright yellow. The girl blushed at the attention, smiling shyly. As Mr. Finley moved closer to her, however, the girl's friends closed ranks and separated them, bobbing curtseys as they all shuffled away.

It was not the first time Katrina had witnessed a scene of that sort with the man. Mr. Finley, while friendly and attentive, always at the center of whatever event was happening on Synne, had a way of looking at a woman that somehow did not feel...quite right. She would not say her skin crawled whenever he settled his interested gaze on her. But some muted alarm went off in her head that she could not begin to understand.

Just then he turned and spied Katrina. A wide smile spread over his face as he nodded her way.

Despite herself, Katrina shivered. If she had choices aplenty, she would have hurried away, as she usually did when he was near. But Synne was not exactly thick with suitors, especially not for someone of her reputation. And so, taking a steadying breath, she offered a smile in return. It was no doubt a tense, pathetic thing. She was not an actress, after all, and had never been particularly adept at feigning emotions she did not feel.

But she must have done a good enough job at it, for Mr. Finley's eyes flared with surprise before narrowing in obvious interest. Smoothing his hand over his slick hair, he strode toward her.

"Miss Denby," he murmured in an amiable tone that nevertheless had her muscles tensing as if prepared to take flight, "how lovely to see you. But I cannot believe my good fortune in finding you without your employer nearby. Has she given you the evening off then?"

It was with utmost will that Katrina kept her pathetic excuse for a smile intact. "Indeed she has, Mr. Finley. She has bid me to dance the evening away."

"Which you are not doing," he said, making a show of looking about for her nonexistent partners. "Though I suppose that has more to do with the events of a month ago. Otherwise your loveliness would have them lining up in droves."

Katrina just kept herself from blanching at the mention of the scandal. At least the man was showing interest in her. Sadly enough, she could not ask for better than that.

Swallowing hard, she said in as flirtatious a manner as she was able, "That is because no one has asked me yet."

"Is that so?" the man murmured. "Well, then, allow me to be the first. Miss Denby, will you do me the honor of the next dance?"

It was what she had wanted, of course. But that didn't make in any easier to say, "I would be delighted."

Nor did it make it any easier to take his hand. Thank goodness they were wearing gloves, she thought a bit wildly as he guided her toward the floor. She did not think she could hide her unease were he to touch her with his perpetually sweaty palms.

Which, of course, made her think of what happened between two people who were married, in the privacy of their bedroom. Something she was all too familiar with, considering the abundance of material Lady Tesh had sponsored and that Seraphina supplied to the unmarried young women of Synne through the Quayside Circulating Library. If she married this man, he would touch her in those intimate ways. And there was nothing she could do to stop it.

For a wild moment, as he pulled her into his arms for the waltz—of course it was a blasted waltz—she was overtaken by the urge to run. It was with incredible willpower that she allowed his arms to come about her. This one dance was not a promise of more to come, after all. Despite her very limited choices, she did not have to take the first man who came along promising respectability.

But as the first strains of the song started and Mr. Finley swung her in a turn, Katrina had the impression that she had erred horribly, and respectability was the last thing on the man's mind.

That feeling was not lessened—rather, it worsened considerably—as Mr. Finley brought her a touch closer than proper and leaned in to speak in her ear. "I admit, Miss Denby, I did not think I would ever be able to entice you to a dance. I don't suppose my sudden luck has anything to do with the death of a particular gentleman some weeks past as he fell from your bedroom window?" When she merely gaped at him, feeling as if she had been slapped, he chuckled. "Have no fear, my dear. I am not so picky as all that. I don't mind a woman with a bit of history to her. Especially one with such...endowments as yourself."

With that, he tugged her even closer, so suddenly Katrina gasped, and leered down her bodice.

Before she could think how to react—she knew now without a doubt that Mr. Finley did not have matrimony on his mind at all but something far less permanent—a sudden masculine hand on the man's shoulder had them stopping dead in the middle of the dance floor. Stunned, she looked up to see the duke's furious face glaring down at Mr. Finley.

"Forgive me, but it seems, sir, that you have taken my set with the young lady."

* * *

Sebastian had known that the last thing Katrina needed was for him to make a scene on her behalf. She was suffering enough from the latest scandal. And he had managed to heed that voice of reason in his head as she walked out into the set with her dance partner. For all of ten seconds.

But when that disgusting man had blatantly pulled her closer and leered at her in such a way, there was nothing on heaven or earth that could have stopped him from racing to her side and extracting her from the arms of that libertine.

The libertine in question, some oily-haired coxcomb whom Sebastian had blessedly not had the displeasure of meeting, gaped up at him. "I say," he sputtered, "what is the meaning of this?"

Sebastian, heedless of the dancing couples that twirled around them, smiled. But it was not one of friendliness. No, this was a mere baring of teeth, something that made the man before him flinch. "I said, this set with Miss Denby was promised to me."

Mr. Oily's meager chest puffed up like an enraged rooster. "Look here, I don't know who you are, but Miss Denby promised this set to me. Isn't that right, Miss Denby?"

And then he did something incredibly stupid. Or, at least stupider than what he had already done in ogling Miss

Denby. He snaked an arm about her waist and yanked her closer to his side.

Even then Sebastian might have been able to step back and assess the situation—had Miss Denby not winced.

In an instant he planted a hand once more on Mr. Leering's shoulder. Though this time it was not just a firm means to stop the man in his tracks. No, this time he squeezed, pressing his thumb into the sensitive hollow between his collarbone and the curve of his neck.

Mr. Disgusting gasped, his arm dropping from Miss Denby as if she were a hot coal as he broke free of Sebastian's hold. Sebastian, not quite done with the man, leaned close to his ear.

"If I see you treating the lady in such a way again, I will do much worse to you. Now off with you."

The man did not need further encouragement. Giving Sebastian a furious glance, and Miss Denby no glance at all, he bolted from the floor. Leaving the two of them blessedly alone. Or as alone as two people could be in the middle of a crowded dance floor full of gawking people.

Which, of course, made him realize that he had been an utter fool in drawing so much unwanted attention to Miss Denby. No, more than a fool; he had been an unmitigated arse, not much better than the other man in his treatment of her in this public setting. Clearing his throat, he looked apologetically her way, certain she would give him a well-earned tongue-lashing for his boorish behavior.

But no, she appeared wan, her eyes glazed. Concern flooded him and he took hold of her hand. Even through her glove he could tell it was ice cold.

"I'm sorry," he murmured. "So very sorry, Miss Denby." Then, knowing they could not just stand there in the middle of the floor, and needing to detract attention from Miss Denby, he gently tugged her toward him. "I cannot apologize enough for my actions. But let us dance so we don't draw any more attention our way."

She did so mechanically, placing her hand on his shoulder, allowing him to lead her in the steps. Her gaze remained fixed unseeing on his cravat, and he thought perhaps she would remain silent for the remainder of the dance—however much was left after that little scuffle. But suddenly her voice, a brittle thing, reached him.

"Thank you for that," she said.

Stunned, he could not think how to formulate a response.

But it seemed Katrina was not quite through. She looked up at him with eyes that were brimming with frustration. "Nevertheless, I am more than capable of handling men like Mr. Finley on my own. I cannot have you stepping in every time I am dealing with a prospective husband."

"You are so very right. It was not my place to—" Suddenly he stopped, the meaning of her words finally sinking in. He gaped at her. "Prospective husband? That horrible man? You must be joking."

"I assure you, I'm not." Her lips twisted, pain flashing in the clear blue of her eyes. "There are not many men who would willingly take on a wife with such a reputation. I need to look at all my options."

His hand tightened on hers. "But surely you don't mean to consider someone like *him*? Dear God, he was ogling your...endowments," he finished lamely.

She shrugged. "I admit, I made an error in Mr. Finley. But I was fully aware of that fact and was prepared to retreat before you stepped in and made me once more a subject of gossip."

Here she looked nervously about them. When Sebastian followed her gaze, he saw that, sure enough, they were still garnering more than their fair share of stares. Damnation. He had been trying to help, and he had only made things more awful for her.

That glaring truth was only made worse when, with the end of the waltz, Bridling suddenly came bounding up to them.

"I say, Ramsleigh, that was a sight to behold. And a damn good idea—oh, pardon me, Miss Denby—for these country bumpkins cannot fail to silence their gossiping if you and I take Miss Denby to the floor. A blasted duke, and an heir to an extremely powerful baron? They shall be no match for our combined support. But are you well?" he asked, looking on Miss Denby with concern. "Do you need air?"

"N-no. I'm well, thank you," she managed. Her cheeks, which until then had been unnaturally pale, burst forth in a riot of color.

Bridling smiled wide. "Then will you honor me with a dance?" he asked, holding out his hand.

She nodded tightly, placing her trembling fingers in his. "If you wish it, sir."

Sebastian watched them take their places before, frowning, he strode to the side of the room. But he did not stop there. No, he kept going, to the side door, flinging it open and stepping out into the cool night air. The long colonnade was empty, the only souls about being the quietly talking coachmen and sleepy horses that lined the street, waiting for their passengers. And Sebastian was fervently grateful for the respite from humanity.

Miss Denby was a danger to all his carefully laid plans. Not that she had done anything to deserve such condemnation, of course. She was only ever her sweet, unassuming, kind self. But he had always been deeply affected by her, whether he wished it or not. And now, seeing her in such dire straits, knowing she felt compelled to marry whatever man might come along and give her respectability, no matter how miserable she might be, he felt a helplessness and anger coursing through him that he could not seem to contain.

He clenched his teeth tight, looking out over the dark landscape, breathing in deep of the briny ocean air. But contain it he must. Not only was it no business of his, but his own future security, and those who relied on him, depended on him distancing himself from Miss Denby's troubles and letting her do what she must.

If only I could marry her myself.

The thought, a mere whisper of an idea through the halls of his mind, nevertheless shook him down to the foundation of his soul. He quickly shut it up, turning the lock on it for good measure. No, he would not even contemplate that *what if.* Whatever chance they'd had for a future was well and truly gone. He had his life to live and she had hers—including doing what she felt she had to regarding finding a husband.

His lips twisted as he looked over his shoulder toward the sound of music and laughter coming from the Assembly Rooms. He just prayed that whoever else she had singled out as a future life partner, they were a sight better than tonight's dubious choice.

Chapter 10

*Y*our Grace."

Sebastian, in the process of passing the drawing room as he headed out for a brisk ride the following morning—preferably one that would not take him anywhere near where Miss Denby might be—stopped and peered inside. "Lady Tesh," he said, striding within the room and bowing. "I did not expect to see you up so early. I hope you slept well after the revelries of last night?"

"Oh, I never have trouble sleeping, I assure you," she replied. Then, waving a gnarled hand toward the high-backed chair to her right, she said, "I would be most appreciative if you would join me. I believe you and I are due for another talk."

Unease latched on to the base of his skull. Just like the last time she had cornered him to talk privately on the night of his arrival at Seacliff, there was something premeditated in this whole thing. Though this time there was something more in her gaze, a craftiness and suspicion. But how could he refuse? And so, bowing once more, he sank into the chair she indicated.

For a moment she watched him closely, her sharp brown eyes, without a hint of milkiness as so many of her age had, seeming to take in everything. Freya, seated in the woman's lap, gazed at him with equal narrow-eyed interest. Sebastian, feeling as if he were being called to the carpet for some ungodly reason, could only sit and wait while the woman gathered her thoughts. Was she going to comment on his behavior the night before in causing further talk about her companion? God knew he had been kicking himself in the arse about it ever since; he could not blame the elderly woman a bit should she wish to rake him over the coals.

Finally, after what seemed an eternity, she spoke. But it was not about Katrina at all.

"How do you think Mr. Bridling has responded to our schedule thus far?"

His relief was so acute, he nearly sagged in his seat. Blasted idiot, he berated himself, to suspect that she had wanted to ambush him in regard to Miss Denby. How the devil had he forgotten about his understanding with the dowager viscountess to distract Bridling from thoughts of his paramour?

"Ah, Bridling." He cleared his throat and shifted in his chair. "I do believe he has thoroughly enjoyed the events you have planned."

She cocked one sharp eyebrow high on her forehead, the lines about her mouth deepening as she pursed her lips, a decidedly arch look. "However," she prompted.

She was too quick, this woman. "However," he continued obediently, almost sheepishly, "Bridling is used to a fast set in London. And while dinner parties and balls are wonderful diversions, I do believe the boy needs something a bit...more. If that is not too presumptuous of me, of course," he hurried to say, for Lady Tesh had gone uncommonly still and narrowed her eyes in such a way that he was certain she was preparing to give him a sharp tongue-lashing for daring to insult her schedule.

Much to his surprise, however, the dowager did not do anything of the sort.

"Of course," she said, dipping her head in acknowledgment. "That was quite a misstep on my part, wasn't it? But you will forgive me. I am an old woman, and my mind is not what it used to be."

It was on the tip of his tongue to denounce such a statement—Lady Tesh was sharper of mind than most of his contemporaries—but she waved a hand in the air and continued blithely on.

"Let us say that the past two days were a dress rehearsal, and we may now move on to the performance at hand. It is time to dazzle the boy. Which means, of course, that we cannot rely on Synne's typical population. No, we must surround him with all manner of pretty women and lively young men."

He looked at her with a new appreciation. "I assume you have a group of young people in mind?"

Her smile was pure cat-that-licked-the-cream. "I certainly do. Though," she continued, her mood turning in an instant, a frown pulling down on her face, "it may not be as easy as it should be, not with the vicar spreading his tales of Miss Denby and her unfortunate history. After the events of the last two nights, I fear it shall only grow worse before it gets better."

Sebastian, who had begun to relax some, tensed at that. The anger that had been simmering in him over the past two evenings boiled up. Would that he could denounce those who would malign her—especially the vicar, from whom most of the vitriol seemed to originate.

Lady Tesh, blessedly, was not as blinded as he by anger—a good thing, for if he continued to insert himself into situations as clumsily as he had last night, there was no telling what more damage he might do to Miss Denby's reputation. The dowager straightened, looking as certain and capable as anyone he had ever known. "But that only means I shall have to be more creative in my invitations. The three grown children of the Marquess of Ilford are all godchildren of mine and not a half day's journey from Synne. And my landscape designer, Mr. Mishra, is just outside Whitby with his own children. I shall write to them all immediately. Do let Jasper know that I require a quantity of paper and ink."

Impressed and, if truth be told, almost frightened by her quick competence, Sebastian made to rise and do as he had been bid. Before he could, however, the dowager viscountess's voice halted him.

"One more thing before you go, Your Grace."

Pausing, Sebastian glanced at the dowager. But she did not smile or look crafty now. No, her expression was almost solemn in nature. The anxiety he'd felt upon entering the room returned then tenfold.

His fingers tightened on the arms of his chair as he settled back into the plush cushions. "Yes, my lady?"

"Are you infatuated with my companion?"

If she had swung her cane at him and punched a hole in his chest, he would not have been more stunned. He fought to draw breath. "Pardon?"

If anything, the dowager's expression became more serious. "You have both been open with the fact, of course, that you were friends back in London. But after watching you the last few days, I get the feeling there may have been something more between you. And after last night..." Here her voice trailed off, and she shrugged.

Of course I'm not infatuated with her. The words were simple enough, shouting through his mind. He willed them to cross the barrier of his lips. But no matter how he tried, they would not come. Swallowing hard, he finally managed, "Miss Denby is my friend and nothing more."

It would have satisfied most people. Not Lady Tesh. Her gaze became almost sad. "And what of your upcoming engagement with Mr. Bridling's sister?"

It did not escape his notice that Lady Tesh did not ask him what his feelings were for Miss Bridling. Swallowing down the lump of sadness that had settled in his throat, he said, "It will happen. So long as we are successful with her brother, that is."

"I see," she said. And he saw from the mournful way she considered him that she did indeed understand, only too well.

But Sebastian could not take a moment more of this interrogation. Rising abruptly, he bowed and strode from the room. But he could not leave behind the empty sense of loss Lady Tesh's questions had created.

* * *

Katrina had not been prepared for anything out of the ordinary when the Seacliff party made a sojourn to the beach that abutted the busy Promenade two days following the disaster of an evening at the Assembly Rooms. Granted, she had not expected such a trip at all. Lady Tesh was not keen to traverse over sand, considering her need for a cane. But Mr. Bridling was youthful and exuberant, and so she supposed her employer wished to show him all the places where the younger people tended to congregate to make his time on Synne more to his liking.

But this, she thought as she looked out over the group of busily chattering young people all bunched within what was obviously an elegant, boisterous picnic of sorts, was shocking to say the least.

Lady Tesh must have seen the stunned look on her face. As the phaeton slowed she leaned in and said, "I thought Mr. Bridling could do with a bit of lighthearted fun."

Katrina blinked as she looked at her employer. Lady Tesh had been the one to put this all together? Which should not have surprised her, she supposed. Lady Tesh was brilliant at knowing just what was needed for her guests.

Yet looking on the motley group of young people spread out over luxurious blankets and rugs, under large white tents that resembled billowing triangular clouds, all of them talking and laughing, she couldn't help but be highly impressed. Mr. Bridling was a spirited man straight from London, and this was just the kind of outing to appeal to someone of his personality.

But along with that awe was a healthy dose of fear. Since the ball, she had felt decidedly bruised and battered. True, the fact that the duke and Mr. Bridling had danced with her had helped some with how others had treated her. Even so, she had been sadly devoid of dance partners the rest of the evening.

She scanned the crowd anxiously as she descended from

the phaeton and accepted Freya from Lady Tesh. Blessedly it seemed all of the people present today had not been at that cursed ball. In fact, it appeared as if a good portion of today's guests did not live on Synne at all; rather they lived nearby on the mainland and visited Lady Tesh on occasion, and so perhaps they might not know about her unfortunate reputation. They had always been kind to her in the past. She bit her lip, sending up a prayer that they would continue to be kind to her today as well.

The duke, who had arrived on horseback alongside Mr. Bridling, approached then and held out his arm to Lady Tesh. "Do you require assistance, my lady?"

In answer, the dowager viscountess batted her lashes coquettishly at him and placed her hand on his sleeve. Katrina, bemused, could only stare after them.

Suddenly Mr. Bridling was at her side. "Miss Denby," he said with a wide smile, holding out his arm, "it would be my honor."

"Oh! Er, thank you," she said, shifting Freya's slight weight and taking the man's proffered arm. They made their way down the path that had been cut into the stone, soon reaching the sandy expanse of beach and the group of revelers.

Honoria, who had been lounging on a blanket with her sister, Miss Emmeline Gadfeld, and her two cousins, the Misses Felicity and Coralie Gadfeld, rose to her feet and hurried to Katrina's side. "Well, isn't this jolly?" she said, taking Katrina's arm once Freya was placed in Lady Tesh's lap. "Lady Tesh, I cannot thank you enough for your kind invitation. This is the perfect occasion to prepare us for the upcoming summer season."

Lady Tesh, seated now in a massive plush chair beneath the shade of one of the tents, tilted her head as she observed

Honoria. "And did you have any trouble with your esteemed father?" she asked quietly.

The smile that had been spread across Honoria's full cheeks faltered. "I daresay we would have had trouble— if I had told him where we were heading off to. Not that I lied outright to him. Even I with my outrageous ways would not do something so sinful as to lie to a vicar." Here she laughed, though it held a strained quality to it. "But I thought it would be better for everyone if I simply left our destination unsaid."

"You are a smart woman, Miss Gadfeld," Lady Tesh said, lifting one silver eyebrow, her eyes twinkling. "I always knew I liked you."

"The feeling is mutual, my lady," Honoria replied, this time with a full grin before she returned her attention to Katrina. "Well then, come along. There's fun to be had."

Katrina blinked. "I cannot leave Lady Tesh, Honoria."

"Nonsense," Lady Tesh barked from her seat. "I have given Miss Gadfeld here orders that she is to keep you away from me. You are a young person as well, after all, and should enjoy the day as much as anyone else. And besides, I have brought Violet for any need I may have."

Sure enough, the lady's maid appeared just then, ducking under the tent and making her way to the dowager's side.

Katrina, stunned, stared dumbly at them both. "If you're certain, my lady."

"Of course I am. Now off with you," she said, swinging her cane in Katrina's direction.

Which, of course, left Katrina with no recourse. Numb, she allowed Honoria to pull her along to the group that lounged nearby.

"I don't understand," she whispered to her friend, even as she wrung her hands together in anxiety. "First the ball two nights ago, now this? One would think Lady Tesh wishes to be rid of me."

"Oh, my dear," Honoria said, rolling her eyes in Katrina's direction. "I should have known you would fret over something of this manner. You always were one to overthink things. If Lady Tesh was done with you, don't you think she would simply let you go?"

"Well, I suppose," Katrina admitted reluctantly.

"Lady Tesh does not suffer those she does not like," Honoria continued. "She knows you have been through so much in the last weeks, not least of which is due to my own father's actions." Here her stern, certain expression faltered, a look of sadness passing through her eyes. But it was quickly gone, and she gave Katrina a bracing smile. "But let us forget all that and enjoy this lovely day."

She was right. Of course she was right. Even so, Katrina could not relax. After weeks of coldness from so many members of Synne society, she was not ready for further cut directs.

Surprisingly, however, those cut directs did not come. As she and Honoria inserted themselves into the jolly group spread out across the blankets, more than one person sent her smiles of welcome.

"Miss Denby," Miss Regina Hargrove, Ash's half-sister, called out with a wide smile, "Coralie and I were planning on combing the beach for shells later. Do say you'll join us. You always have such a sharp eye and see things we do not."

"Oh, yes, do join us," Miss Coralie Gadfeld, Honoria's youngest cousin, joined in as she removed her bonnet from her tight black curls and dabbed at her forehead with a handkerchief. "We are planning on making a game of who finds the most. You shall be on my team." Here she gave Regina a mischievous smile.

Regina gasped. "You cretin!" she exclaimed before, with a laugh, she grabbed the bonnet from her friend's hands and jumped to her feet, racing across the sand. Cora-lie, squealing, ran after her, lifting her skirts high above her ankles to make up for Regina's own trouser-clad legs.

"And so you see," Honoria murmured in Katrina's ear, "you have nothing to fear from anyone here. Now enjoy yourself, will you?"

Easier said than done, of course, even with the unexpected friendliness of this particular group. No small part due to the duke, who had lowered himself to the blanket across from her. Why, oh why, did he draw her eye so completely?

Well, she rectified, she supposed it wasn't hard to figure out. Clad in buff breeches and a light green jacket, his dark hair with hints of copper throughout ruffled by the ocean breeze, his features relaxed as he took in the happy group around them, he looked so much like that man she had begun to fall in love with four years ago that she could not breathe for a moment.

Blessedly Lady Paulette, the Marquess of Ilford's only daughter and one of Lady Tesh's numerous godchildren, spoke up then. "I have not been to Synne in too long." She gave a happy sigh as she looked out across the sand, straw-berry blond curls caressing her flushed cheeks. "I was so happy my brothers and I received Lady Tesh's invitation. What do you think the dowager has planned?"

"The question should be, what don't I have planned?" Lady Tesh called from her place beneath the tent.

As if on cue, a group of footmen approached, holding aloft the items needed for pall-mall and battledore and shuttlecock, as well as an assortment of balls and kites and other equipment. At the same time, a wiry, grizzled fellow made his way over the sand toward them, a line of donkeys following like obedient schoolchildren behind him.

"I've got the asses you requested, Lady Tesh," he said with a gap-toothed grin. "All sweet-natured, perfect for a bit of a ride over the sand."

"By God, this is a splendid surprise," Mr. Bridling exclaimed, taking it all in. He rose to his feet, eyes alight with excitement, looking much like a young boy preparing for a grand holiday as he turned to the nearest lady and held out a hand. "Miss Mishra, what should we do first?"

Miss Laila Mishra, daughter of Mr. Mishra, who was not only Lady Tesh's landscape architect for the folly she recently had built but also her good friend, smiled and took Mr. Bridling's proffered hand, allowing him to assist her to her feet. "I hardly know," she replied, shaking out her skirts and tucking a jet-black lock of hair behind her ear. "What think you, brother?"

Mr. Emir Mishra grinned. "As my strength is battledore and shuttlecock, and you are abysmal at it, I shall have to suggest that."

"Oh, you beast. Mr. Bridling," she continued, turning toward that man, "shall we join forces to take my brother down?"

Mr. Bridling grinned. "It would be my honor."

Soon they were off, the other partygoers following, even Honoria as she accompanied her younger sister, her eagle eyes on Lord Wesley Beckett, one of the Marquess of Ilfold's younger sons, who was sticking close to Emmeline's heels. Leaving Katrina alone with the duke.

Clearing her throat, she looked his way—her cheeks heating when she saw his gaze quite firmly on her. "You don't wish to join in with the game, Your Grace?" she managed.

His lips quirked up on one side, more of a wry gesture than anything. "Ah, no. Such things aren't for me any longer, I'm afraid."

That brought her up short. Gone again was that hint of the carefree man he had been, and back in his place was the serious, dour man he had become. "You don't mean that," she blurted.

"I assure you, I do."

Katrina frowned. "But that is ridiculous. It is not so long ago that you used to be at the center of such revelries."

His eyes, so solemn they made her heart crack, found hers. "Much has changed since then, I fear," he replied softly, then blanched. "And once again I have inadvertently insulted you. My apologies. You know as well as I, even more so, how much has changed since those days."

Katrina felt the blood drain from her face. Indeed she did.

But she would not focus on that. Nor did she want him to focus on all they had lost. Shifting forward on the blanket, she smiled. "That may be," she said, "but I do hate to see your talents for such games go to waste. I recall, after all, just how many of the young gentlemen you bested. You were quite the dashing athlete, and I cannot imagine you have lost those abilities."

He laughed that rough, unused laugh of his, his features

softening with relief that the uncomfortable moment had passed. "And how many did you best? I vow, Miss Denby, you seem to have forgotten your own talents."

"Nonsense," she declared a bit self-consciously. "I'm certain you all let me win. I was never able to practice such games in my childhood, and so cannot have been as accomplished as you seem to imply."

That laugh again, though this time perhaps less rusty. "You may rest assured, I was too prideful to have done anything but try my hardest to win. No, your victories were entirely your own. It seems you have a natural talent."

Unused to being praised in such a way, Katrina's cheeks heated. "Are you saying," she said in an attempt at deflection from such a kindness given to her, "that you are not so prideful now?"

His eyes shone with humor. "Miss Denby, are you attempting to verify if I would allow you to win now, just because I am not that conceited young man I used to be?"

In answer she rose, dusting off her skirts and holding out a hand to him. "There is only one way to answer that, isn't there?"

He considered her for a time, a small half smile on his face that could be either humor or exasperation. "That invitation is too tempting to pass up," he finally said, the words a low rumble.

Why did it feel as though that innocent statement held a deeper meaning? She did not have long to dissect it, for he reached up, clasping her hand, and she quite forgot what they had been discussing as awareness centered on where their palms met.

It was pure instinct that had her planting her feet wide

and tugging as he maneuvered his feet beneath him and rose to standing. What she had not counted on, however, was how little help he actually needed from her—nor had she counted on her own strength. Much like Mouse when he had a rope between his teeth and her on the other end of it, she tugged much harder than was warranted. He gave a surprised grunt, nearly flying forward, just catching himself before he crashed into her and brought them both back down to the sand.

It was a simple mistake, one that should have been laughed off as they parted and went about their day. Except Katrina committed a fatal error: she glanced up. That was all it took, apparently, one quick look at his face, and she was lost. Her breath, which had grown shallow upon that first touch, was sucked right out of her chest at the sight of his gray eyes peering into hers, at those full lips parted ever so slightly, at the small divot between his brows as he gazed down at her. She ached to smooth that line, to press her finger to the indentation in his chin, to trail the pads of her fingers over his hard jaw and dive into the thick waves of hair at the nape of his neck...

"I say, Ramsleigh, you're taking your sweet time," Mr. Bridling called out. "Come and join in our game, and Miss Denby with you. Unless, of course, you fear me getting the better of you." He laughed uproariously, the sound dancing along the breeze.

The duke looked down at Katrina, his lips kicking up in a rueful smile. "What say you, Miss Denby? Shall we?"

Katrina smiled and nodded, allowing him to lead her over the sand. All the while thinking she would follow him to the ends of the earth if he asked her.

* * *

The very last thing Katrina expected when following Sebastian out onto the flat expanse of sand toward the others was to enjoy herself. Yes, she had suggested they join the others, but to bring a smile to the duke's face more than anything. She had quickly come to the conclusion, however, that perhaps she had needed this bit of lighthearted fun as much as he had.

She swung at the cork bird, feeling the vibration of it hitting the strings of her racquet with a satisfying thwack. A cheer went up from the group around her, and she grinned. No, she had not expected to enjoy herself. Yet here she was.

"Miss Denby, that was a brilliant hit," Miss Mishra called out, bouncing on the balls of her feet in her excitement.

"Even more so for the fact that your brother missed it?" Mr. Mishra said with a wink for his sister.

"Well, that certainly didn't hurt my enthusiasm," Miss Mishra quipped.

"I suppose I should have warned you," the duke called out as the shuttlecock went airborne again, hit up into the air by Mr. Bridling's enthusiastic swing, "Miss Denby is brilliant at this game. I saw her once put a dozen London gentlemen to shame in the middle of Hyde Park." The cork bird flew his way just then, and he drew his baddledore back, hitting the shuttlecock with terrifying precision toward Katrina.

"You shall not distract me, Your Grace, by bringing up my past triumphs," she called out, hitting the shuttlecock back toward him, her heart flying right along with it. It had been so many years since she had experienced this joy. She felt, quite literally, as if she had found a part of herself that had been missing.

That fact was compounded upon a moment later as the bit of cork dropped to the sand at the duke's feet. Grinning in a carefree way she had not seen since his arrival on Synne, he performed a gallant bow her way.

"Well done, Miss Denby," he murmured. "You have not lost your touch, I see."

Why did it feel as if he meant more than her talent for the game? But Katrina was too happy to look at it too closely.

Lord Martin Beckett, Lord Wesley Beckett's younger brother and still at university if the ginger fuzz sprinkled across his upper lip was any indication, looked at her with bright eyes. "I vow, Miss Denby, I don't believe I have ever seen any female play such a fine game before."

"Female?" Regina queried archly, pushing a lock of sable hair out of her face. "I daresay that was a fine game regardless of gender."

But Lord Martin was not the least offended that his prejudice had been called out. He laughed, the sound as carefree as the gentleman himself. "You are correct in that, Miss Hargrove. But surely there is something Miss Denby is not good at. Say, footraces?" He looked to the duke. "What say you, Your Grace? Do we have a chance at that, do you think?"

The duke pretended to consider Katrina, his lips pursed in thought. Katrina, for her part, felt that look straight down to her soul. Especially when his gaze transformed into something more, something decidedly admiring. Her insides turned to mush, her legs to jelly. Truthfully, her entire body went a bit soft and warm all at once.

"I daresay," he murmured, the intimate sound of it

making the liquification of her body complete, "that Miss Denby can do anything she puts her mind to."

The moment stretched out, the warm glow in Katrina's stomach expanding through her limbs, to the tips of her fingers and toes. It was a foreign feeling, one she had only known during her brief time in London, when she had been able to forget the harsh lessons of a lifetime that had taught her she was unimportant, that she did not matter. She had seemed to matter then. More important, she had seemed to matter to *him*.

The shrill call of a seabird rent the air just then. Blinking his eyes, he rearranged his face back into the easy lines it had been in as he looked to the others.

"But the only way to find out is to try," he said with some of that old cheerfulness and natural magnetism he'd had and that had been buried in the intervening years of hardship. "Shall we attempt to redeem ourselves, gentlemen?"

As one the group agreed heartily, moving to a flat length of sand down the beach, laughing and talking the whole while. Katrina followed behind, making her slow way across the sand, watching the others with a small smile on her face. She had not realized until now how much she had lost with Lord Landon climbing into her bedroom window back in London. For so many years she had tried not to think about how her life had changed. She had instead focused solely on moving forward, on survival.

But with Lady Tesh's proclamation that she join in on the fun, she had begun to remember. She wondered if, later, in the privacy of her bedroom with this afternoon well behind her, she would feel grief for the direction her life had taken. Would she mourn all she used to have? Especially as this moment in time could only be just that: a moment, a brief and wonderful interlude.

But she would not think on it now. Her gaze snagged on the duke laughing with Mr. Mishra as they decided on where to draw the line in the sand, drawing her further into the memories of how life had been before the scandal that had upended her life. No, she thought with a smile, she would hold on to this moment with both hands for as long as she could.

Chapter 11

Sebastian had not thought Lady Tesh could outdo the picnic at the beach. While Bridling had been jolly enough attending the dinner party and ball, there was a new light to his eyes today, a joy and excitement Sebastian had not seen in the boy since leaving London. And not once in that long afternoon of excess and sport had Bridling mentioned his actress, the biggest proof of the victory that the day had wrought.

As the day progressed to evening, however, he found himself impressed despite himself. If any setting could tempt Bridling from settling down too early, it would be this.

The wide path sandwiched between the street and the beach with the ocean beyond was a busy, cheerful thoroughfare, no doubt a popular attraction in the summer months. Colorful lanterns were strung over the pedestrians' heads, and as night fell they lit in glorious washes of brilliantly tinted light, bathing mirth-filled faces in all the hues of the rainbow. Groups of musicians were interspersed along the pavement, the cheerful melodies from their instruments mingling with the conversation and laughter, completing the festive air of it all. Here and there small stalls were set up, with wares ranging from meat pies to bundles of sweet nuts to painted fans to posies.

Bridling was like a puppy bouncing among the myriad members of their party, his face alight with a smile so wide his cheeks must ache. As Sebastian watched, bemused, Bridling said something to Lord Wesley, throwing his arm about the man's shoulders and laughing uproariously, as if they had known one another all their lives. The boy had made fast friends with all the gentlemen that day, and had already made plans to meet up with them the following afternoon.

He had also begun showing a more than passing interest in the young women, his eyes going decidedly moony in appearance as he gazed at the tight group of them a short way down the path. There did not seem to be one particular woman to garner his attentions. Well, Sebastian amended with a frown, that statement was not entirely true. There had been times during that jolly afternoon when Bridling had looked at Katrina slightly longer than necessary, had laughed in a jarringly intimate way with her, had touched her arm with an air bordering on familiar.

But perhaps it had been his imagination. He was not showing any particular interest in her now; rather, he appeared to be taken with all of them as a whole. Something that brought an incredible amount of relief to Sebastian. Not because Bridling no longer seemed interested solely in Miss Denby, he told himself fiercely. He was most certainly not jealous of any attention the boy might give her. But the more the boy was dazzled by the idea of other women, the less he would think of his actress, and the more secure Sebastian's claim on Miss Bridling would be.

Which, of course, had him thinking of Miss Denby again. Which was horribly inconvenient; there was no reason at all that thoughts of his future intended should lead him into thinking of another. God knew Miss Bridling did not deserve it. No, she deserved nothing but the utmost loyalty from him.

Yet no matter how he berated himself, he could not seem to stop his gaze from drifting to Miss Denby. She stood near the collection of young women and beside Lady Tesh, beneath a pink lantern that made it appear as if she was blushing from head to foot. Her hair, which had come undone during their long day of sports—of which she had won a fair amount, much to his delight—had been plaited and pinned at the nape of her neck in a loose chignon. Stray tendrils of pale hair curled against her cheek and along the long column of her neck, caressing those places he itched to touch.

But more powerful than all that was the brightness of her eyes, the softness of her smile. The day in the sun, laughing and running about with the others, had done wonders for her, bringing a light to her eyes that reminded him so much of the girl he had begun to fall for that his chest ached with it. But she was made all the more beautiful for the new maturity in her gaze. That maturity had not been there in their youth. Then she had been all stardust, glittering and joyful.

Now, there was a depth to her that called to him. With

a gentleness and kindness that only a transcendence over heartache and pain could bring about, she had somehow drawn him from the windowless room he had locked himself in since his father's death and into the light. He was not a fool, of course. He knew this was temporary, a mere interlude from the seriousness and worry that his life had become.

But her ability to remind him that there was still some joy left in him had been a precious gift.

"Your Grace," Lady Tesh barked, impatience threaded through her sharp voice. "Are you ignoring me on purpose?"

Sebastian blinked, his face heating as he tore his gaze from Miss Denby and approached them. "My apologies, my lady," he murmured.

But the diminutive dowager did not appear the least mollified, her effrontery obvious.

"You should be sorry," she grumbled, "for I now shall have to repeat myself. I will be taking a sedan chair to visit with a dear friend, and I would have you and Miss Denby act as chaperones of sorts for this motley group. I shall meet you there when you are through. And have no fear; Miss Denby knows the house. I certainly cannot count on you to pay attention enough to remember."

With that parting shot she made her hobbling way to the waiting sedan chair, settling within, accepting Freya from Miss Denby before starting off down the street.

Bemused, Sebastian looked Miss Denby's way. Her eyes were dancing with laughter in the colorful glow of the lanterns.

"You must have been quite thoroughly distracted to receive such a reprimand from Lady Tesh," she murmured.

What would she say if she knew the reason for my

distraction? Giving her a wry smile, he held out his arm. "We are to act as chaperones, are we?" he murmured, attempting to ignore the jolt of electricity from the touch of her fingers on his sleeve.

She looked over at the rest of their party, who had moved to listen to a young girl singing an operetta, her voice clear and haunting. A small smile lifted her lips. "Apparently so. Though she might rethink matters if she knew that you used to be a consummate rake."

"Oh, now, I don't think I would have described myself as a *consummate* rake. I was merely an *adequate* rake, I assure you."

She laughed, the sound mingling with the music, filling him up with a kind of joy. It was the first true laugh he had heard from her since his arrival; he had forgotten what the sound of it could do to him.

Suddenly she sighed, a wistful sound. "Do you recall that night at Vauxhall? It was truly beautiful there. This reminds me of that, you know."

The memory of that night took shape in his mind, how he had seen her in her dinner box with a group of her friends, the small smile she had given him when he'd approached, how he had promenaded with her around the Grove before asking her to dance. How he'd longed to take her on the Dark Walk and kiss her senseless.

"All it needs is ham thin enough to see through," he said now.

She laughed again, but it was a quiet, subdued sound. Guiding her around a group of boisterously talking elderly men, he found an unpopulated area of the path with a clear view of the rest of their party before, stopping, he turned to her.

"Do you miss it?"

Of course she would know immediately he was not referring to Vauxhall, but the life they'd had. "Sometimes." She gave him a sad smile. "I think it would be strange if I did not. Especially considering what has become of me since."

At once he felt as if he had kicked a kitten. "Damnation, Miss Denby," he said gruffly, "I'm so sorry—"

But she held up a hand to stop him. "I know you told me the night of the dinner party that I should accept apologies given. But truly, your apology now is uncalled for. After all, I could certainly ask the same of you. And I shall. Do *you* miss it?"

Only the times that you were part of. The words very nearly escaped his lips, and he was shocked at how utterly true they were. Thinking back, he had not truly enjoyed all the constant movement and stimulation and entertainment. It had merely been a way to alleviate the boredom of having no direction or purpose. Only he had not realized that until Miss Denby had arrived in London, dazzling him with her sweetness and innocence and the utterly artless way she viewed everything around her.

Blessedly he was able to hold the words back, however, instead parroting what she had said. "Sometimes."

Again that sad smile. "We are a melancholy duo, are we not? But you have gained a bit of your old life back again. You shall marry, and take your rightful place, and all shall be right in your world."

Nothing shall be right ever again. Once more unbidden words whispered through his mind. This time, however, instead of mulling them over he forcefully pushed them away.

"As will you," he responded quietly. "Once you find that husband and marry as you wish to do."

"Yes."

They fell quiet, each mired in their own thoughts. A bubble of sadness in the midst of happy revelry. Just then Bridling and his new friends broke away, heading for the posey stall. They bought armfuls of the small bundles of flowers, then proceeded to hand them out to every female in their purview. Suddenly Bridling approached.

"For you, Miss Denby," he said with a gallant bow before, with a broad wink, he made his way back to his friends. Talking animatedly, they started off down The Promenade, following the young women.

Miss Denby brought the small bundle to her nose, sniffing appreciatively before tucking it in her bodice. "Mr. Bridling is such a lively gentleman," she observed as, her arm tucked once more in Sebastian's, they followed behind the rest of the party. "Is his sister much the same?"

For a moment frustration reared. He did not wish to talk of Miss Bridling. But he knew Miss Denby had the right of it. It was a lovely thing to talk of the past. But they must realize it was well and truly behind them. They could only look toward the future. And his future was Miss Bridling.

"Actually, no," he replied. "She is much like her father. Do you recall Lord Cartmel?"

"Not well, no. He was a serious man, if I remember correctly."

Which was putting it mildly. "Yes, he is serious, as well as a brilliant businessman. His daughter has inherited his talents and is wonderfully competent."

Which was not the language of a lover by any means. Blessedly Miss Denby did not seem to notice.

"She sounds wonderful." She gave a little sigh. "What I wouldn't do to be considered wonderfully competent. But I fear I shall always be seen as slightly silly."

Offended despite himself, he stopped and stared in outrage down at her. "Who has said that about you?"

She shrugged, seemingly unbothered. Except for the slight tightening at the corners of her mouth, which betrayed her hurt over the moniker. "My brother Francis used to say it often enough."

Sir Francis Denby. Sebastian had been friends of a sort with the man at one point. Well, no more than an acquaintance, really. Yet he had known him enough to feel concern over the fact that he had fought in a duel and lost an arm—as well as to wonder what the blazes had possessed the man to drag his family fortunes so low that his sister had been forced to work as a companion. He ached to ask Miss Denby about her brother now, just as he had when she had mentioned him that night she had played the pianoforte for them. But she had so quickly changed the subject, her discomfort with it plain as day.

The last thing he wished to do was to cause her further discomfort or dismay. And so instead he replied quietly while starting off after the others, "Well, your brother was wrong."

She did not respond. But he saw the deepening of the dimple at her cheek, proof that what he had said pleased her.

Suddenly there was a shriek and a shout from the crowd up ahead. And then Bridling's voice rose above it all.

"Ramsleigh, stop that man!"

In an instant Sebastian saw who he was referring to: a figure in dark clothes, running his way. And in his hand was what appeared to be a reticule.

He wasted no time, stepping away from Miss Denby and into the path of the person who was no doubt a thief. The man's eyes widened when he saw Sebastian, but though he tried to redirect his steps, he was too late. Sebastian leapt at the man, tackling him to the ground.

"Geroff me!" the thief cried, panic flaring in his eyes as he struggled beneath Sebastian's weight.

Sebastian did, but only so he could haul the man to his feet. He plucked the reticule from his fingers, handing it off to Miss Denby before taking the man by the collar and bringing his face close to his. He was grubby, his hair unkempt, dirt smudging his cheeks. But beneath all that it was too obvious how young he was, no more than fifteen or sixteen at most.

Reaching into his pocket with one hand, he extracted a handful of banknotes and pushed them into the boy's hand. The thief's eyes widened in confusion.

"Wot th' blazes?"

"I know times must be difficult for you," he said low. "But there are other ways to obtain what you need. Do not steal from the young ladies again. Do you understand?"

He expected any number of reactions from the boy, from censure to anger to humor that Sebastian could be so stupid as to hand over money like some reward for such a crime. Instead, however, the boy's eyes welled with tears. Sebastian released him then. The boy looked at him for a long moment before, giving Sebastian a quick nod, he disappeared into the crowd.

Miss Denby sidled up to him, the pilfered reticule pressed to her chest as she grasped at his sleeve with her free hand. "Are you well? You are not hurt, are you?"

"No, I am not hurt," he murmured. And the smile she

gifted him with, full of both admiration and a pride he could not recall ever seeing, made him feel as if he were on top of the world.

* * *

Nothing had prepared Katrina for how affected she would become when Sebastian let the thief go, even giving him money from his own pocket—money he could ill afford, if his desperate need for funds was any indication. He could have easily seen that the man was punished for his thievery, and indeed most would have agreed with the need for such a thing. He must learn his lesson, they would say. Not knowing—or caring—that the lesson would have destroyed the boy's life.

But no, he had been kind, and generous. And Katrina knew if she wasn't careful, she would be in danger of falling in love with him just as much as, if not more than, she had four years ago.

The rest of their party approached then, pushing through the crowd that had gathered at first sign of the scuffle but were dispersing now that the excitement was done with. Mr. Bridling was at the front of the group, and on his arm was Lady Paulette, her hair askew, her face pale with shock.

Katrina hurried forward and put an arm around the girl. "Goodness, are you all right?"

"I'm fine, Miss Denby," she replied with a wan smile. "Thank you ever so much."

"Did you catch the thief, Ramsleigh?" Mr. Bridling demanded, looking about for the man.

"Yes," the duke replied. He motioned toward Katrina,

who still held the reticule in her grip. "Long enough to get that."

Lady Paulette exclaimed in relief, accepting the reticule from Katrina. "Oh goodness, you retrieved it. Thank you ever so much."

But there was no relief on Mr. Bridling's face. Instead his irritation seemed to only grow. "You mean you let that criminal get away?"

"It is no matter," Lady Paulette said. "I am just happy to have my bag back." She turned glowing eyes up to Mr. Bridling. "You were so very heroic, sir. Without you catching me, I should have fallen into the road and under the wheels of that carriage for certain."

Lady Paulette's effusions did much to erase whatever ire Mr. Bridling still held on to. He smiled down at her, his chest puffing up with pride. "It was nothing, nothing at all. I'm quite used to London, you know, and a quick mind is necessary in such a busy place. It seems, however, that even on this idyllic Isle there are thieves aplenty. But you've no need to fear, my lady, when you are in my company."

Katrina must have looked confused at the exchange, for Miss Mishra approached. "Mr. Bridling was quite heroic," she explained. "The thief jarred Lady Paulette, and she nearly fell into the path of a hackney. But Mr. Bridling pulled her to safety."

"He was indeed heroic, Honoria chimed in, taking a break from her constant bustle around her sister and cousins. "But I do think that is the perfect ending to our evening, for nothing so exciting can top that. We had all best be getting home; it has been a long day, and Father will be wondering where we are. And anyway, Lady Paulette will need rest after her ordeal."

"Oh, but you must allow us to call Lady Tesh's carriage for you," Katrina said.

It was not anything out of the ordinary. Lady Tesh had done as much herself for not only the Gadfeld girls, but also for any number of young ladies to prevent them from walking alone.

The look Honoria gave her, however, was full of regret. "Thank you, dear," she said quietly, "but I do think it's best if we don't."

In a moment Katrina was reminded of her true standing in Synne society. Honoria had not told her father they had meant to spend the day with Lady Tesh. Which meant, of course, her friend had purposely kept the vicar in the dark because of Katrina's presence. She felt the blood leave her face as, attempting an unconcerned smile, she nodded. "Of course."

Honoria, however, saw through her ruse. She grasped her hand, pulling her off to the side of the path. "I'm so sorry, Katrina. It's just that Father doesn't know we were with you, you see."

Katrina held up a hand, fighting to keep her smile intact though she wanted to cry. "Please, don't feel you need to explain. It's quite all right, Honoria. Only do let us secure a hackney at least."

"A hackney?" Miss Mishra exclaimed with a warm smile. "Nonsense. My brother is going carousing with the other gentlemen, and so I would be most obliged for the company in my carriage if you're amenable."

Honoria accepted with thanks, quickly gathering the younger Gadfeld girls before returning to Katrina.

"I'm so sorry again, my dear," she whispered in her ear as she embraced her. Then, with a parting kiss on the cheek, she was off, looking for all the world like a mother hen as she herded her charges back along the path.

Katrina watched them go, suddenly exhausted beyond bearing. The day had been perfect, these people Lady Tesh had amassed together for the purpose of entertaining Mr. Bridling also treating Katrina with kindness and acceptance. But nothing had changed, she realized as she glanced about at the people walking to and fro on the path and saw more than one cold glare directed her way. In truth things had grown worse, one of her dearest friends feeling as though she had to sneak behind her own father's back to spend a day with Katrina. She had best recall she was still a social pariah.

She looked at the duke, who was in quiet conversation with Mr. Bridling, his soon-to-be brother-in-law. And she had better remember that she was not who she used to be. And never would be again.

Chapter 12

*M*iss Denby," Lady Tesh barked, "what have you done to your pet? Or, rather, not done, for I vow he is more out of control than usual. Did you take him on his morning exercise?"

Katrina, in the process of retrieving her cup from the carpet while simultaneously blotting up the tea that had been spilt and dodging Mouse's madly wagging tail—which had been the reason the teacup was on the floor in the first place—felt her cheeks burn hot. "I'm so sorry, my lady," she mumbled. "I did take him. But it appears it may not have been enough. Perhaps it was due to us being gone so long yesterday for the picnic and the evening entertainment after."

Which, of course, only increased Lady Tesh's ire. "Are you blaming *this*"—here she waved an outraged hand at Mouse—"on *me*?"

Katrina blanched. "Of course not, my lady," she hastened

to reply, resuming her seat and attempting to push Mouse's bottom to sitting. She may as well have been pushing at a brick wall, for all the attention the dog paid her. No, he was quite firmly focused on the duke.

Blessedly that man hastened to assist her. "Sit, Mouse," he said in a firm tone.

The dog, of course, listened, his behind falling heavily to the floor. Right on Katrina's foot. Wincing, she pulled her bruised toes out from under her pet. "Thank you for your assistance, Your Grace," she said, avoiding his gaze. Just as she had been avoiding it since the breaking up of their party following the robbery the evening before. Though it was not without difficulty, his mere presence drawing her like a moth to a flame.

"Your Grace," Lady Tesh said, obviously done with the slight detour of a debacle with Mouse, "as we are without Mr. Bridling today"—here she sent a pointed look to the ceiling above their heads in the direction of where Mr. Bridling was no doubt sleeping off a great quantity of drink— "perhaps you might like to explore the area below the cliffs. There is a fine beach down there, and a fairly private place to swim if you're so inclined."

Out of the corner of her eye, Katrina saw the duke tilt his head. "That sounds most welcome."

"Splendid," Lady Tesh said, clapping her hands together. "It is not an easy place to find, however, the path down hidden behind some rocks. Miss Denby will show you the way."

Katrina, in the process of taking a sip of her replenished tea, promptly choked. Gasping for breath, eyes watering, she looked at her employer in disbelief. "Pardon?"

Lady Tesh scowled. "I vow, Miss Denby, you really must

take care. But are you asking my pardon for choking, or because you did not understand what I had said?"

"Er...both?" Katrina managed, wiping at her streaming eyes.

The dowager sighed dramatically. "I do not know what is so difficult to understand about it all. Your pet requires a great deal of exercise today. A trip to the beach should more than do that. And the duke requires a guide. It is the perfect scenario."

Dear God, the woman actually wanted her to walk off alone with the duke? She cast him a mortified look, which of course made her even more painfully aware of why time alone with the man was not a good idea. Her body hummed in the strangest way—it actually hummed, every nerve vibrating in awareness—just at the sight of him. She swallowed hard.

And the duke, it seemed, was of much the same mind, his gray eyes wide when they met hers. "I'm certain if you give me the directions, I can find my way," he said to the dowager.

"Nonsense," she dismissed, feeding Freya a small bit of biscuit. "You would never find it. No, Miss Denby must show you."

But Katrina was not about to give in to such a scheme so easily. "Perhaps one of the footmen would be best suited," she tried.

"What, and pull them from their duties?" Lady Tesh barked, glaring at her. "I vow, that is most selfish of you. As if they, and indeed all, of my servants, don't have enough to do without taking over duties given to you."

Once more Katrina blanched. "I'm sorry, my lady."

Lady Tesh pursed her lips. "You can apologize by

readying yourself and your pet for your outing. And you as well, Your Grace," the dowager said. "I've a mind to nap, and you are both delaying my much-needed rest. Off with you now."

With that she turned her attention from them and began cooing at Freya, who sat at her side on a gilt brocade cushion. Leaving Katrina and the duke with no option but to rise and leave.

Katrina hurried out ahead of the duke, pulling Mouse along with her, sending up a quick prayer that she would be able to survive the afternoon with her sanity intact.

* * *

Not for the first time since heading out for the much-lauded beach did Sebastian curse Bridling and his weak ability to hold his liquor. That was, of course, in between bouts of condemnation at himself for how utterly transfixed he was by Miss Denby. Good God, how was it possible she became more lovely each and every day? One would think he would have grown used to her looks by now, being in her presence nearly every waking moment since his arrival on Synne. But no, each time he looked at her it was as if he were seeing her for the first time. He was enchanted, dazzled. And hard-pressed to look away again.

Like now, as he held out a hand to steady her on a particularly steep area of the path and chanced to look at her face when she made a small, agitated noise. Her lips, those perfectly plump lips, were parted, and as he watched, her tongue darted out to moisten them. Fire shot through him, from the top of his head to the tips of his toes. Swallowing hard, he forced his attention back to the path.

"Are you well?" he asked. Mayhap this trip had been too much for her. Her color seemed quite high, after all. And her breath, wasn't it coming a touch faster than it should?

"I'm fine," she replied, yanking her hand from his. Which, of course, made him realize he had retained it much longer than he should have. Which, naturally, caused his own face to heat.

Blessedly they reached the bottom of the path then. Mouse, with a booming bark, bounded across the beach toward some seabirds, sending sand flying up from his massive paws. The creatures squawked in outrage, taking to the sky. Mouse, of course, took no offense, merrily chasing another group.

Despite himself, Sebastian smiled. "I daresay your Mouse is the most cheerful fellow I have ever met," he remarked as he and Katrina made their way across the sand.

She laughed lightly. "He does bring me joy. I'm ever so grateful Lady Tesh allowed me to bring him when she took me on as her companion. I truly don't know what I would do without him, not only because he is my dearest and most loyal companion, but that he also was a gift from my brother."

He gave her a curious sideways look. Once again she'd mentioned Sir Francis. Though this time he did not sense the same agitation as before. Was she ready to talk about him then?

"I recall you telling me all those years ago that your brother's dog had a litter and Mouse was the runt," he said carefully. "You seemed happy when he gave you the puppy to care for."

She nodded, a small smile on her lips that was neverthe-less more sad than happy. "Perhaps Francis did it to keep me quiet over the matter, as I was quite vocal in my anxiety over the puppy's health. Or perhaps it was easier than disposing of it." She shrugged. "Nevertheless, I still cannot help but cherish the fact that he listened to me and lessened my anxiety. Which, of course, makes Mouse doubly precious to me."

Sebastian's chest ached for her. Having known Sir Francis, even though he had not known him well, he could say with certainty that the man had not given the puppy to his sister to benefit her, but rather himself, something she must subconsciously be aware of, though she would insist on looking at it in a more positive light.

Which, of course, made him wonder what had led the man to pawn his sister off as a companion. Yes, he'd lost an arm, and his fortune as well. Yet Sebastian could not understand how the man could have left Miss Denby out to dry. No matter the scandal that had befallen her and the repercussions it had wrought, she was still his sister. He should have taken care of her and protected her regardless of the circumstances.

For a moment he thought of his own sisters, Rachel and Gracie, safe at Ramsleigh Castle. Despite their dire straits, he had never once considered abandoning them. Everything he did, every decision he made, was for the people who counted on him for their livelihoods. But first and foremost were his sisters. Their happiness and future security were everything to him. No matter what they might become embroiled in, no matter what they might do, he would never forsake them.

"And where is your brother now?" The question came without him meaning for it to, peppered with his growing anger at the man.

Thank goodness Miss Denby did not hear the emotions behind the question. She gave a small sigh, looking out over the ocean. "Back at our country estate, Denby Hall, near Lincoln. It was the only property he managed to retain after... well, after. He retreated there upon the loss of his limb and has been there ever since from my understanding."

"From your understanding? But you did not come here for several years after that. Where were you in all that time?"

She looked down, kicking at a small stone, and so he could not see how his question affected her. But he could hear it in her voice, the slight tightness, the sadness. "A small cottage, in Suffolk. It was our mother's property and came to the family upon her marriage to our father. Francis thought it was best, you see, that I should be removed from society completely."

He clenched his hands tight at his sides, the small voice that told him to leave it alone disintegrating in his growing anger for what she had been through. "He packed you off to live alone in some cottage?"

She blushed, her mouth pinching at the corners. "Well, I was not completely alone. I did have my aunt with me."

"The aunt who acted as your chaperone throughout your time in London?" He recalled the woman well, a Miss Willa Horace. She had been no proper chaperone, forever gossiping and indulging in outrageous outfits and over imbibing on expensive liquor. Was it any wonder Landon had thought he could get away with accosting Miss Denby in her own bedroom, with such people looking out for her? No doubt Sir Francis's banishment of his sister had been as much to punish the aunt as it had been to punish Miss Denby.

"Yes," Miss Denby replied, her tone subdued. "But Aunt Willa was not happy there. I daresay we were not a good fit, our personalities too much like oil and water." She gave a nervous laugh before quickly sobering. "It was during my time there that I received a letter from Lenora, the Duchess of Dane. She had heard of my...situation and wished to know if she could assist me in any way. And then she offered me the position of companion to Lady Tesh. By that time money was quite tight; my brother was not answering my letters or supplying us with the much-needed funds to survive. I suppose there was much on his mind, so I cannot blame him for letting us slip through the cracks. But I saw no other alternative, so I agreed to Lenora's proposal, with the understanding that I would take on my duties by the end of that year. I had hoped, you see, that things might turn around and I would have no reason to take the position after all. But then Francis lost that property as well, and I was forced to come here as Lady Tesh's companion much sooner than had been planned. Blessedly Aunt Willa found a home with some old friends of hers. I sent her money whenever I could, until her death just over a year ago."

"And your brother let you take such a position instead of bringing you to live with him at your family home?"

Finally she seemed to hear the fury in his voice. She glanced at him, eyes opened wide in surprise. "You are angry."

"Of course I am angry," he bit out. He ran a hand through his hair, taking a deep breath of calming ocean air. Yet it only made him more agitated, reminding him why Miss Denby was in this location in the first place. Yes, it was beautiful here. And yes, she had a good position and friends who cared for her.

But the truth of the matter was, her brother should have taken care of her. He should not have abandoned her to cruel gossip and the vagaries of an uncertain fate.

"If your brother were here right now," he said in a voice so low it was nearly stolen by the breeze, "I would not be responsible for what I did to him."

"He did everything he could for me," she replied, her voice trembling.

"Did he?" he demanded. He looked at her then. She stood several feet away, her arms wrapped about her middle, looking as outraged as he had ever seen her. "Can you truly agree that he did everything he could have, everything he *should* have, where you are concerned?"

If anything, she appeared more mulish, her chin jutting out and her brows drawing together. "You don't know what you're talking about," she replied tremulously. "He treated me much better than I deserved."

"Than you *deserved*?" He could not have heard that right. He took a step toward her, ignoring the faint floral scent of her soap, his focus on her stubborn features. "You deserved to be protected and cared for, not left for the wolves."

"He did not leave me to the wolves," she insisted. "I am blessed in so many ways. I have a roof over my head, food in my belly, people who care for me."

"Through no help from him."

She glared up at him, stepping forward so they were toe to toe, her small form vibrating with her anger. "He is my brother. I won't have you speaking of him in such a way."

"Someone has to," he gritted. "Someone has to stop your defense of him."

"Why?" she demanded. "Why must my defense of my brother, my only living relative, stop?"

He saw it then, the glint of tears in her eyes, the slight trembling of her lower lip. His fury dissolved in an instant. Reaching up, he brushed an errant curl from her face, tucking it back behind her ear tenderly. "Because you deserve better," he rasped, cupping her cheek. "You deserve happiness and security. You deserve someone who loves and cares for you." *And how I wish that person could be me.*

She drew in a trembling breath, her eyes searching his face. A tear spilled over, trailing down her cheek. He used his thumb to brush it away. And then, because he couldn't stop himself if he tried, he bent and kissed her damp cheek.

"Don't cry, Katrina," he whispered, her name escaping him of its own volition, like a benediction. He kissed her other cheek, her forehead, her nose, his lips traveling across her sweet face. And then his lips found hers, and it was as if every moment of his life had led to this.

* * *

She should have been shocked at his kiss. He was not for her, after all; he was nearly engaged to another. The last thing he should be doing was kissing *her*.

Yet she wasn't shocked. Nothing had ever felt more right.

Her hands came up, twining about his neck, her fingers diving into the thick, wavy locks of hair at the nape of his neck. The strands were silk under her touch, curling around and through her fingers like a caress, and she flexed those fingers, drawing him closer. He groaned into her mouth, his arms coming around her waist, drawing her up and against the hard length of his body. She gasped as her breasts pressed against the broad expanse of his chest, as her belly met his, and he immediately tilted his head, plunging his tongue into her mouth. Her senses were overwhelmed, the taste of his tongue against hers, sweet and heady and utterly delicious, sending her mind spinning.

His hands, those strong, capable hands, trailed up her spine, bunched in her gown, massaged into her muscles. She sighed into his mouth, even as his name echoed through her mind: *Sebastian*. He was no longer the Duke of Ramsleigh, no longer His Grace. No, from this moment forward he was *Sebastian* to her, the dearest part of her heart.

Mouse's warm body pressing into her side and his faint whine had her reluctantly pulling back. Her eyes fluttered open, and she looked up into Sebastian's face. He was closer than he had ever been, so close she could see the faint ring of brown around his iris.

"Goodness," she whispered.

His gaze caressed her face, as if he were memorizing her. "I have wanted to do that for four years," he murmured.

"As have I," she managed. And it was true. She recalled that last night in London before everything fell apart, how she had hoped beyond hope that he would begin courting her, how she had imagined him walking with her into the garden and kissing her. And before that, before she had even begun to realize her feelings for him had gone beyond mere friendship, how night after night she had dreamed of him taking her in his arms.

But never in her wildest imaginings, even after all the pamphlets and books Lady Tesh had supplied, had she imagined something so incredible, something that not only brought her body to life, but her heart as well. Something she felt down to the very bottom of her soul.

The moment of awe did not last long, however. In the

blink of an eye she recalled just what had happened in those four years…as well as what was to come. Namely, Sebastian's near engagement to Miss Bridling.

Hastily stepping back, she smoothed the front of her dress down with shaking hands and then caressed the top of Mouse's head. Fool, fool woman. How could she have forgotten herself so completely? Perhaps she truly was as hopeless as her parents used to say she was, really was as horrible as everyone on Synne seemed to think. For no matter her determination to never again interfere with a relationship, she had done just that in kissing Sebastian.

And then, to make her mortification complete, Sebastian spoke the two words that destroyed her more than any others could. "I'm sorry."

"Don't apologize," she choked out. "I cannot accept your apology for this." *It means you regret it. And I can stand anything but that.*

She drew in a deep breath, raising her gaze to his. And the self-condemnation in his eyes was like a punch to the chest. He hated himself for his part in it. And she could not accept that. Not when she had been only too happy to fall into his arms.

"And please don't regret it. I am glad it happened. The once. But I think we can both agree it cannot happen again."

"No." His voice broke on the word and he cleared his throat, trying again. "No, it shall not happen again."

It was what she had wanted, a verbal agreement between them that this would remain a solitary event. They would get through the remainder of his trip on Synne and would put this moment behind them. He would marry his Miss Bridling and save his dukedom. She would search out and marry whichever gentleman on Synne was willing to take her on, thereby saving her reputation, as well as that of her friends and employer. And she and Sebastian need never see one another again.

But as she gathered up Mouse and headed for the path that led back to Seacliff, she knew she would regret the possible life she had lost with Sebastian until the end of time.

* * *

Sebastian watched her go, hands clenched into fists at his sides, fighting that part of himself that shouted inside his head, urging him to go after her. What he had done in kissing Katrina had been abhorrent. Not only was it a complete betrayal of Miss Bridling and the vow she expected him to make to her, not only was it a betrayal of his family and the families counting on him to make that all-important match, but it also had been a betrayal of Katrina as well. She was going through so much after the devastation of Landon's asinine climb into her bedroom window. She certainly did not need him pawing at her, threatening whatever tenuous hold she still retained in Synne society.

He watched her until she and Mouse were out of sight. Only then was he able to breathe. He dragged in great gulps of the cool sea breeze, letting the brine and life of it fill him up, praying it could cleanse his mind of all thought of Katrina. Yet she remained firmly planted, the roots of memory deep, clinging to the rocks of his heart. And there, he feared, she would stay.

Picking up a pebble from the sand, he lobbed it across the churning waves. What the blazes had he been thinking? But that was no difficult answer to come to. He hadn't been thinking. He had looked down into her pain-filled eyes, and his need to comfort her had drowned out all else, even common sense. And then that need to comfort had transformed into something else, something deep and impossible for him to ignore. Something he had attempted to keep buried for four long years and that had clawed to the surface in one shining moment of weakness.

And apparently he was still weak. He could not stop the remembrance of her in his arms, the feel of her body pressed to his and her mouth under his own. It had been everything he had ever dreamed and more, like a piece of a puzzle falling into place. His body stirred to life again as the memory of her tongue sliding against his overwhelmed him in sensation, and he closed his eyes, as if he could blot it out. But, fool that he was, it only made the memory that much more acute, his need for her climbing to a painful degree.

His eyes flew open, his hands clawing at his cravat. He would purge her from his thoughts in any way he knew how. And right now that meant shocking some sense back into his errant body. Ripping his clothes off, tossing them to the sand in his haste, he did not stop until every inch of fabric had been torn from his body. Then, without hesitation, he strode into the unforgiving sea. The cold was like needles on his skin as he dove into the waves. He welcomed it, forcing himself through the rolling waves, until his feet could no longer reach the shifting, sandy bottom. His arms worked then, cutting through the water as he swam out. Praying with each stroke that he could leave Katrina far behind.

Chapter 13

No matter that Sebastian pushed himself until his muscles screamed and his extremities turned blue with the cold, no matter that the waves beat at him as if Nature herself was punishing him for his actions, there was no getting away from thoughts of Katrina. No, she clung to him, refusing to let go. Or, rather, he clung to *her*, for he could not lay the fault of this at her feet. She had not asked for any of this, had not invited his attentions, had not flirted or seduced him. She had merely been *Katrina*, the object of his affections, and he had been powerless against the pull of her, like the tide and the moon.

But while he could not control his thoughts of her, he had to at least make it appear as if he could. No one's eyes were sharper than those of the formidable Lady Tesh.

"Did you have a pleasant time at the beach this afternoon, Your Grace?" she asked after dinner that evening.

Her gaze flitted back and forth between Sebastian and Katrina, as if she were watching a tennis match.

And no wonder, for Katrina was looking decidedly pale. She had hardly said a word during dinner, her gaze fixed to her plate. Even now, she kept her eyes averted, fairly glued to the embroidery in her hands. Mouse, in a break from his typical exuberance, remained quietly stuck to her side like a burr.

Summoning up a smile, he replied, "Indeed. It was most invigorating."

The dowager nodded in satisfaction. "My dear husband, God rest his soul, used to love swimming there. He did so nearly every day, in fact, even in the dead of winter, up until his last days. It is wonderful for the constitution."

"I should love to try my hand at it," Bridling said, looking up from the deck of cards in his hands, which he was shuffling over and over again in a maddening *shush* of sound. He gave Katrina a melting smile. "Mayhap you might show me the way there as well, Miss Denby, if you plan on bringing Mouse down for his exercise again."

Over my dead body. A thought that disturbed Sebastian to his core. No doubt the boy's attentions to Katrina were nothing but a mild flirtation. But even if Bridling did have a particular interest in her, Sebastian certainly had no claim on her.

Even so, he found himself saying, "I would be happy to show you the way myself, Bridling. I've a mind to visit the spot often during our time here." His gaze drifted to Katrina, caressing the curve of her cheek and the rise and fall of her bosom beneath the modest neckline of her gown before he hastily yanked it away at his body's reaction to the sight of her. Oh yes, he would be visiting the beach quite often, indeed.

"Splendid," Lady Tesh said. "The path is not an easy one, but you both are hale and hearty gentlemen. And," she added, giving Bridling a sly look, "I do believe a plunge in the water is good for the effects of over-imbibing as well. Perhaps you should have joined them this morning, Mr. Bridling. It could have been of benefit to you."

"No doubt." Bridling laughed. "Though I will be certain to keep it in mind for the next time I'm in such a state."

"The next time? Then I assume you are planning on more nights like last night." The dowager nodded in satisfaction. "I am glad for it. They are a good bunch of young men. And no one of your years and spirit can want to spend all their time with an old woman like me."

"Nonsense," Bridling replied gallantly. "It brings me great joy to spend time with you."

Lady Tesh considered him. "You are quite the charmer, young man, when you put your mind to it. Though I don't know why I'm at all surprised, considering your rescue of Lady Paulette from that thief. It is all anyone can seem to talk about, as is proof by the multitude of female callers I received this afternoon while you were sleeping off the effects of your drinking."

Which was news to Sebastian. And Katrina, as well, if the way her brow furrowed in confusion was any indication.

"We had callers, my lady?"

"Yes," that woman drawled. "And you may have been aware of it had you not taken to your room after your return from the beach. Of course you would become light-headed after such an excursion. You are forever forgetting your bonnet, and the sun does play havoc with one."

Katrina had retreated to her room? Had it been due to their kiss? Had she truly been so affected? Despite himself, Sebastian cast her a glance. Her color was bright from the reprimand, but she held her head high as she asked, a determined gleam in her eye, "Who came to call, my lady?"

"Who? Let me see if I can recall." The older woman took a sip of her wine, pursing her lips in thought. "Ah, yes. Miss Mishra, of course, along with Lady Paulette. As well as Miss Pulman, and Miss Newton. Oh, and Miss Verity."

Was it Sebastian, or did Katrina suddenly appear incredibly focused? She sat forward, her body tense. "Miss Pulman, you say? Mr. Kendrick's granddaughter?"

Lady Tesh scowled. "You know very well who I am referring to, young lady. There is only one Miss Pulman on Synne."

But for the first time, Katrina did not cower beneath Lady Tesh's harsh words. "I, er, have some ribbon I promised to her, is all. But we shall see them tomorrow during our trip to the Beakhead Tea Room, as that is their usual time to visit as well. I shall bring the ribbon then."

She was lying. He knew it as certainly as he knew his own name. Katrina was one of the most honest, most kind people he knew, and there was something off about the way she was speaking, some nervousness and harshness to her tone that belied her words. Before he could make sense of it, however, Bridling spoke up.

"What a pity I was not well for their visits," he said with a small frown of regret. "I should have so loved to have met with such splendid company. Especially that of Lady Paulette; I wish to see for myself that she is well, you see."

All too soon it was time to retire. Sebastian stood slowly, reluctant to face the restless night that was sure to come. As they were leaving the drawing room, however, Lady Tesh stopped him.

"Your Grace, there were some letters that arrived for you this afternoon. As I was not certain when you would return from the beach I had one of the maids leave them on the desk in your room. I apologize for not recalling earlier; it must have slipped my mind."

Giving the dowager his thanks and wishing her and the rest of the party good night—all while doing his best to keep from staring with hungry eyes at Katrina—Sebastian hurried to his room and the promised letters. There were very few people who would be writing to him during his stay on Synne, and even fewer he wished to hear from. In truth, the only ones in that latter group were his sisters. He had not seen them in too long, not since leaving home for London, and he missed them dreadfully. It was the longest they had been without each other since their father's death, and over the past four years they had leaned on one another for support. Though they had written often during his absence, helping him to feel connected to them, it had been difficult being without them by his side.

Blessedly, one of the letters was indeed from them. His eldest sister Rachel's flowery scrawl stared up at him from the gleaming top of the oak desk, and the sight of it eased the band about his chest. He quickly broke the seal, his eyes tripping over words that fairly bounced across the page, each girl taking turns writing about the goings-on at Ramsleigh Castle and peppering him with questions about how he was getting on.

But there was something hidden in their missive, a darker undertone he had not read before, though they would camouflage it with their typical cheerfulness.

*Mrs. Greaves has been fixing the most interest-
ing meals, and I vow they are barely palatable.
How you would laugh to see the faces we make
in trying to swallow her food down. Gracie has
declared she will learn to cook and has raided the
kitchens for all manner of books to teach herself
such a talent. I daresay by the time you return
with your bride, our sister shall be able to create
a feast to rival any you've had while in London.*

His heart wrenched in his chest. If Mrs. Greaves, the
housekeeper, was lowering herself to cook the meals for his
sisters, that could mean only one thing: they'd had to let
the cook go. He ran a hand over his face. Dear God, he had
nearly ruined everything this afternoon in kissing Katrina.
What the devil was he doing? His sisters were counting on
him. Everyone at Ramsleigh Castle was counting on him.

But no, he was lusting after Katrina. He was a damn
selfish bastard.

Placing the letter down on the desk with care, he set
his jaw and purposely reached for the next. If there was
anything that could cement his determination to keep his
course, it was a letter from Lord Cartmel, as the sharp,
angular scrawl across the front declared.

The baron's letter was short and to the point.

Ramsleigh.

*As you receive this you will have been on Synne for
nearly a sennight, and I pray you have not forgotten your reason for being there. I have begun talks
with our solicitors to expedite matters—should*

you succeed in what you were sent to accomplish in distracting my son from thoughts of that woman. My daughter and I await your return to London with the news we hope to hear.

Yrs,
Cartmel

Sebastian's fist closed around the expensive paper, crushing it in his grip. He wanted to cast it into the fire, to see the man's words consumed by flame and turned to ash.

Instead he forced his fingers open and smoothed it on the desk, tucking it into a drawer along with the letter from his sisters. Better to have these physical reminders of why he was here. And as he readied himself for bed, and his thoughts turned once again to the feel of Katrina in his arms and her mouth under his, he knew he would need them.

* * *

The moment they entered the Beakhead Tea Room the following afternoon, Katrina was busy searching for Mr. Kendrick. Lady Tesh's casual mention of the visit of that man's granddaughter had reminded her that he was on her list of hopefuls. And after her misstep at the beach with Sebastian, something Katrina's threadbare reputation could ill afford, she had come to the sobering conclusion that she did not have time to lose if she was to find a husband and claim a semblance of respectability again. Especially as their arrival at the Beakhead seemed to herald the hasty exit of several patrons, each one casting a dark look Katrina's way as they did so.

But the elderly gentleman was not to be seen. Had she missed him? Or was he among the seemingly growing multitude who were now trying to avoid her at all cost? Panic reared in her breast. She did not have many chances to socialize, especially now that half of Synne was shunning her. The last thing she wanted to do was to wait a week to see Mr. Kendrick and ascertain his interest in her—much less if he was even willing to be in the same room with her.

They were shown to their seats then. As Adelaide, having taken their order, was making to walk back to the kitchens, Katrina reached out for her. Adelaide, giving her a quizzical look, leaned in close.

"Has Mr. Kendrick and his granddaughter arrived today?"

The curious look on Adelaide's face increased. And no wonder, for Katrina had never been close with either of those people. As a matter of fact, she had been more than happy to join in with her friends when they had discussed their distaste for the man's all-too-obvious attempts to find a very young wife—which would be wife number four, if memory served—to sire his still-needed male heir.

"No, dear," Adelaide answered, lowering her tone to match Katrina's. "I haven't seen them yet."

"Miss Denby," Lady Tesh said, her voice ringing through the room, "you shall see Miss Peacham tomorrow for your Oddments meeting; please let the woman see to her business."

"I'm sorry, Lady Tesh," Katrina mumbled as, face flaming, she turned back to their party and Adelaide, bobbing a quick curtsy, hurried off.

"Oddments, eh?" Mr. Bridling asked with interest. "And what, pray tell, is an Oddment, Miss Denby?"

"I am. That is," Katrina stuttered as she busied herself settling Freya on the chair between her and Lady Tesh, "my friends are. Or, rather, that's what we call ourselves. Because we are . . . well, odd."

"I would never in my life give you such a moniker, Miss Denby," Mr. Bridling said gallantly.

She managed a smile at the man. He was young, yes, and spirited. But he was nice and had never been anything but kind to her. "That is sweet of you to say."

Adelaide returned then, busying herself in setting a teapot and cups down before them, drawing Lady Tesh's and Mr. Bridling's attentions as she told them of the newest pastries she had concocted. As they talked, Sebastian leaned toward her. Though she didn't so much see it as feel it, in every nerve in her body, the magnetic pull of him calling to her.

"For once I have to agree with Bridling," he said, his voice low. "You are not odd, in any sense of the word."

"I daresay most of society would beg to differ with you on that, Your Grace," she mumbled.

The noise he made could only be construed as rude. "I think both you and I can agree that society can go hang."

Despite herself she sputtered on a laugh. When her eyes met his, she saw the wry humor in their gray depths.

"Come along, Miss Denby," he drawled. "You have to admit that society has not done either of us much good in the past."

"No," she agreed, "you're right in that. It has given both of us nothing but headaches." She sighed, picking at the tablecloth with her nails. "It really is too bad that one cannot live on scandal, or we would both be quite well-off."

"Rich as Croesus." He smiled, a weak thing, before it

fell away completely. "Have you not kept in contact with any of your old friends?"

She thought of the group she had been part of in London, that collection of beautiful, fashionable young women that had invited her into their midst once she had begun to show the smallest bit of popularity. How she had loved to be part of something so glamorous and admired.

Yet how quickly they had abandoned her when the scandal broke. "Oh, they were not friends," she said now, trying and failing to ignore the twinge of pain in her chest at the remembrance of all the letters she had written to them that had been returned unopened. "Not really. I never knew any of them outside those few months in London."

He gazed at her soberly for a time. "And you had no friends before that trip?"

She shook her head, recalling those lonely days of her childhood. "No. Papa was of the mind that children, especially girl children, were no more important than a vase on the mantel, used for decoration and nothing more. He saw no need to court the friendship of what he saw as inferior neighbors for my benefit, and kept us quite sequestered in his supposed importance."

He shook his head solemnly. "That is horrible."

She shrugged. "Such was my life, I'm afraid. But I take it your sisters were not treated in such a way?"

"God no." A small smile lifted his lips, his eyes turning inward. "Not that Rachel or Gracie would have allowed it. They have always been frighteningly outgoing and seemed to need socialization like they needed air to breathe. If the neighborhood children did not come to visit them, my sisters invariably were searching them out."

"Oh, that sounds lovely." She sighed. "I should have loved to have met them."

"I wish you could meet them," he murmured low. "I think they would adore you."

"Would they?" she asked, much more earnestly than she had intended to.

But he did not seem to hear anything untoward. He smiled again. And then his hand found hers beneath the table, strong and comforting. "Absolutely."

His eyes were full of some nameless emotion as he gazed at her, the warmth from his fingers on her own stealing through to her bones. A question formed in her mind then: *And would you adore me as well?* But she could not give voice to that, especially as the meaning of adoration from him was so different. Instead, unable to help herself, her thumb came up to caress the backs of his fingers.

The expression in his eyes changed in an instant, the nameless emotion that had been hovering in the misty gray depths dissipating to reveal a kind of light shining through the darkness. His breath hitched and his gaze caressed her face before dropping down to focus on her lips. Dear God, she wanted him to kiss her. No matter they were in public, she wanted nothing more than to have him close the distance between them and take her lips with his. She wanted to melt into his embrace and never, ever, emerge from it. Without meaning to, she began to sway toward him.

Adelaide's overly bright voice rose up close to Katrina's ear as a plate of biscuits was thrust between her and Sebastian.

"I do think you will like these, Your Grace," her friend

was saying. "Lemon poppy seed, a favorite of many of my customers."

Katrina, startled, looked up into her friend's brittle smile. But Adelaide wasn't looking at her. No, she was looking down at Katrina's hand—which was still entwined with Sebastian's.

Blanching, Katrina hastily yanked her hand away. She had no idea what Sebastian's reaction might be, however, for her entire focus was on Adelaide, who was looking back and forth between her and the duke with mounting concern.

"Adelaide—" Katrina began.

Her friend leaned forward, under pretense of pushing the plate of biscuits farther toward the center of the table, and brought her mouth close to Katrina's ear. "We will talk about it later, when we have a moment in private."

Nodding miserably, Katrina looked down to her lap. She knew her friend would not spread tales of her improper actions with Sebastian. Adelaide was loyal, and Katrina trusted her with her life.

But that did not mean she would not have words to say about this. Or that she would not get the other Oddments involved if she deemed it necessary. Katrina swallowed hard. And she did not want to think what her other friends might say about this, after all she had put them through in the last weeks.

Just then the bell above the door jingled, and Miss Pulman and her grandfather stepped into the Beakhead, like a sign from the heavens.

"Oh, Grandpapa," Miss Pulman said brightly, "look who is here. Lady Tesh, so lovely to see you again. Your Grace, Mr. Bridling." She nodded to each in turn before giving Katrina a stiff smile. "Miss Denby," she muttered.

Her expression shifted back to her typical pleasant demeanor. "But I wanted to speak with you, Mr. Bridling, about your gallant saving of Lady Paulette just the other evening, and I was so very disappointed to miss you during my visit to Seacliff. Let me see that my grandfather is settled and I shall be right with you, for I *must* hear the details from your very own lips."

Which was an opportunity Katrina could not pass up. She stood, her chair scraping against the wooden floor. "Oh, but allow me to see to your grandfather's comfort, Miss Pulman," she said, "and you can take my seat for the time being."

Miss Pulman blinked at her. "Oh, er, thank you, Miss Denby. That is most kind."

In a moment Katrina was across the room, sidling up to the elderly Mr. Kendrick as his granddaughter slid into the empty seat beside Sebastian.

"Mr. Kendrick," Katrina said with a wide smile as Miss Pulman exploded into raptures over a beaming Mr. Bridling at the other table, "how lovely to see you here this afternoon. I pray you're doing well?"

"As well as can be," the man bit out, grunting as he eased into a chair. He raised one wiry brow, his milky blue eyes glittering as he peered at her. "Though I daresay a sight better now that I have such lovely company. Especially as you would hardly give me the time of day before."

Katrina, in the process of sitting across from the man and smoothing out her skirts, promptly choked on air. She rallied quickly, however, forcing a wide smile. "Now, that cannot possibly be true," she prevaricated.

"It is, and you know it." He narrowed his eyes and leaned forward. "I don't suppose this has anything to do with the latest scandal to visit you. I vow, Miss Denby, you are certainly a magnet for those types of things, aren't you?"

Katrina, of course, didn't have the foggiest idea how to respond to that except to blush violently. Mr. Kendrick heaved a great sigh before, nodding, he reached out and took Katrina by the chin.

Muscles seizing in shock, Katrina could only stare at the man as he brought his face closer to hers. Good God, was he going to *kiss* her? Her stomach roiled at the very idea, and for a moment she feared she would cast up her accounts then and there all over the man.

Blessedly, however, he had no intention of doing something so outrageous—and unwelcome. Instead he studied Katrina's face, turning it this way and that.

"Your skin is not spotty, I'll give you that," he muttered. "And you've got good features, if a bit too fine. Do your eyes trouble you?"

"N-no," Katrina managed.

The man nodded. "Good. I won't have any heir of mine inheriting bad eyes. After all, look at me. Four and sixty, and never needed spectacles a day in my life. Though I will insist on waiting until you've had your courses before bedding you. I don't give a damn if you were with that other fellow, the one who broke his neck trying to get to you, but I won't have any cuckoos in the nest, if you know what I mean. Now," he continued, leaning in closer, "open your mouth for me, gel, so I might see your teeth."

Before Katrina could even think to do as he asked, however, a strong hand on Mr. Kendrick's wrist had him releasing her. Dazed, Katrina looked up to see Sebastian glaring down at the older man.

"I would appreciate," he said, his voice even and

measured and yet containing a dangerous tension that had the hairs on the back of her neck standing on end, "that you not maul the young lady and study her like a horse for sale."

"I say," Mr. Kendrick sputtered as he glared up at Sebastian, "I don't know who you think you are, but you cannot handle me in such a way, sir."

"Oh, but forgive me for not introducing myself," Sebastian drawled, bowing his head. "I am Sebastian Thorne, Duke of Ramsleigh."

The blood drained from the older man's face, giving his pasty skin a gray cast. "Ah, er, pleased to make your acquaintance, Your Grace."

"I cannot say I feel the same," Sebastian answered coldly before, turning to Katrina, he gently placed a hand under her arm. "Miss Denby, your tea grows cold."

But Katrina, who was now coming to the realization that Sebastian's interference had once more knocked another prospective husband off her pathetically small list, snapped. Yanking away from his touch, she stood and, not caring that she was making an absolute spectacle of herself, stormed for the door. The bell above her head swung wildly as she threw the panel wide, the clang of it jarring her eardrums, but she hardly heard it for the blood rushing in her ears. Even as she raced across The Promenade to the path beyond, however, even as she dragged huge gulps of ocean air into her lungs to calm herself, there was no taking away the maelstrom of emotions that sat like an agitated ball in the pit of her stomach. Though whether it was due to losing another prospect, or relief that she had lost him, she could not tell.

She had never felt more humiliated, more like an object, than she had in the moment Mr. Kendrick had taken her chin in his hands. Sebastian had been right, of course, in that the man had been studying her like a horse for sale.

Yet what had she expected? She, with a reputation shredded not once, but twice? She, with no prospects other than the worst of the worst Synne had to offer? And all while pining for the one man she could never, ever have.

"Katrina."

She groaned, wiping at her wet cheeks before turning to face him. Of course he had followed her out here.

"What do you want, Sebastian?"

The agony on his face nearly had the tears returning.

"You cannot tell me you mean to take that man as a husband," he rasped.

Exhaustion pulled down on her, and she would have given just about anything to return to Seacliff and her bed and put this whole mess behind her. Unable to look him in the eyes a moment longer—eyes that contained much more pain than she was worth—she looked out to the water line. The churning waves rushed in with a rumble, frothy surf tumbling across the sand before retreating in a hush, like a spurned lover, only to return. A never-ending cycle.

"My choices are limited, as you well know," she managed, wrapping her arms about her middle. "Mr. Kendrick would have provided me with the respectability I need." A respectability that was now even more out of reach than before. Hopelessness fell over her again, but this time it was threaded through with anger: anger at him for interfering; anger at herself for her relief that he had; anger at the world for vilifying women while men were not held to the same standards.

She turned her face to his, her voice hard. "Though Mr.

Kendrick will certainly not consider me now, not after your treatment of him."

His expression only became bleaker. "I am more sorry than I can say. I should not have interfered."

Her chest ached at the self-recrimination in his voice. But she would not soften. "No, you should not have. You have made my position even more untenable. Mr. Kendrick was one of the few men who would consider marrying a woman with such a history."

Which finally dragged a response from him that was not self-condemnation. No, this one was decidedly angry. "Those who would pass up a chance to have you by their side are fools."

She sucked in a sharp breath. His eyes seemed to burn as he gazed down at her, his voice harsh and working its way through her, wrapping about her heart. Would that he was free...

She shook her head sharply, dispelling the aching thought. There was no sense going down that path; it would only bring pain and regret.

He seemed to sense that what he had said was inappropriate. Clearing his throat, he blinked several times in rapid succession, as if expelling something uncomfortable from his eye. "What I meant to say was, there must be more men than you have considered that would be happy to take you for a wife."

Of course she had misread what he had said. *Foolish thing.*

"I assure you," she said, "I have given it plenty of thought."

He frowned, his frustration palpable. "But to settle for a perverted reprobate or a man old enough to be your grandfather who looks at you as if you're an object he's considering buying?" He closed his eyes, blowing out a sharp breath, and seemingly his agitation with it. His eyes were back to bleak when he opened them again. "I am sorry. That was not well done of me. You do not deserve this. You do not deserve any of this. But there has to be someone else for you."

Her frustration, however, was more expansive, more consuming than his could ever be. "Do you think I have not considered someone else? Do you think I want to marry those men? Of course I have considered everyone else. I've lain awake for hours wracking my brain for any other option that would grant me the respectability I need to protect those I care for. But you saw the way those people left the Beakhead when we arrived. This whole mess is affecting Adelaide's very livelihood. In addition, you must be more than aware of the fact that my dear friend Honoria Gadfeld is now forced to conceal from her father when she wishes to spend time with me and Lady Tesh. She is lying to a vicar to keep her continuing relationship with me under wraps. And only God knows what is befalling my other friends. Not only that, but the respect Lady Tesh has garnered over the decades is now tarnished. People talk about her behind her back, they malign her. And I cannot stand that it is because of me—"

Her voice cracked, her words eaten up by the breeze blowing in off the sea. She turned away from him, looking to the horizon. Just two nights ago she had walked this same stretch of pavement on Sebastian's arm, beneath colorful lanterns and serenaded by musicians, surrounded by the laughter of her friends, and she had been able to forget, for a short time at least, all the troubles that plagued her.

But here in the bright light of day she could not ignore it.

Sebastian remained behind her, silent, and she could feel the tension rolling off him in waves, like fog rolling in from the ocean. She drew in a deep breath and hugged her arms about her middle, keeping her gaze far, far away from him. If she saw pity in his gaze she would break.

"And so, to answer your question," she continued low, "I have considered every avenue possible to me, every other man who might be willing or able to take me on. Most see me as a social pariah that would be fine to bed, but certainly not fine to wed. The few that are left are part of a very small list, and it grows smaller each time you step in with the determination to save me from a horrible fate. But I assure you, I would much rather be unhappy in a respectable marriage than to give my loved ones a moment more grief from just trying to be my friend."

She turned then, but it was not to face him. No, she looked back at the Beakhead. Adelaide was standing in the open door, worry plain on her face. Just further proof that she was no good to her friends as she was.

"Let me help you."

Those four quiet words, said in his wonderfully deep voice, were like a slap to the face. "How can you possibly help me?" she demanded.

"I won't interfere any longer for one." He tried for a smile, an attempt no doubt at lightheartedness. But it quickly fell away, leaving nothing but strain in its wake. "Mayhap I can help you find someone more suitable. Someone who can treat you with the respect you deserve, who can make you happy—"

A harsh laugh escaped her lips, so rough he flinched. Ah, God, was this what she had sunk to? That the man she had been well on the way to falling in love with would have to help her find someone willing to marry her?

"There is no need for that, I assure you," she managed. "I'll be heading back to Seacliff now. Please tell Lady Tesh I am ill and will send the carriage back for you all."

With that she strode off, praying with all her might that she could make it to the carriage before she broke down.

Chapter 14

*O*nce again I am forced to corner you, Your Grace, to get to the bottom of things."

Sebastian, who had rushed to open his bedroom door with the wild hope that Katrina was the one knocking after they had all retired for the night, stared down at Lady Tesh's stooped form in sober realization. What had he thought would happen if it had been Katrina at the door? Did he think she would have come with the express intent of having him kiss her again, even though they had both agreed such a thing was to never be repeated, and it was the last thing he should want with both their futures on the line? Or, worse, did he think she had decided to take him up on his asinine offer to help her find a man to marry?

What the hell had he been thinking? Even now, hours later, that question battered his brain like a pugilist's fists. Just the thought of her marrying another made him slightly ill; did he think he would be able to traipse about Synne looking for a fiancé for her? That he could assist her in flirting with another and gaining their admiration?

Not that it should be something that troubled him. He was set to marry another, after all—if things went well with Bridling, that was. And Katrina deserved happiness. He should want her to find someone who could give her everything she required.

Yet the very idea of her being held by another man, of making a life with him and having his children and growing old with him, had bile rising up until his chest and throat burned with it.

But Lady Tesh was waiting. And woe to the man who made the dowager wait on anything.

Straightening his shirt—and insanely grateful that he was still wearing said shirt, as well as his trousers—he stepped aside and motioned her within. "Would you like to come in, my lady?"

"Indeed." So saying, she swept past him, her gauzy bright pink robe trailing behind her, Freya trotting along at her heels. She made her way to the half-circle of seats before the fire, sinking down into one of the overstuffed chairs with a sigh. Freya jumped up into her lap, curling into a ball and closing her eyes.

"It has been some time since I was alone in another man's bedchamber, you know," she mused as Sebastian settled himself in the chair across from her. "Regrettably I am past the time when such a thing is considered scandalous. Though in my day I daresay you would have been more than happy to have me at your door in a nightrobe." She smiled, looking for all the world like a cat that licked the cream, eyes narrowed in thought. "You're just my type, after all."

Sebastian gaped at her. Surely the woman wasn't flirting with him. In the next moment, however, her expression sobered, the lightheartedness gone in the blink of an eye.

"Miss Denby will reveal nothing of what went on at the Beakhead this afternoon. Or, at least, not the truth of the matter. She would insist she was feeling ill and you saw her in distress, thus the reason for your interference in her conversation with Mr. Kendrick. She also insists you went after her to make certain she got home safely."

Lady Tesh speared him with a stern look. "Miss Denby, however, has always been an appalling liar, and this time is no exception. But she looked as though she might shatter when I questioned her on it, and I did not want to add to her distress. And so I come to you, Your Grace, to hear the true story of what happened this afternoon."

He could easily dismiss the dowager and send her back to her bed. It would be no hard thing to corroborate Katrina's story.

But Lady Tesh blinked quickly then, as if she were holding back tears, and he saw the worry for Katrina in the sheen of moisture in her sharp brown eyes and the lines of tension bracketing her mouth. The whiteness of her knuckles where they held her cane, the strain in her knotted fingers, was proof of her attempt to retain control over her emotions. The woman was worried for her companion, and deeply so.

Sighing wearily, he ran a hand over his face. That made two of them.

"I cannot divulge what Miss Denby does not wish to have revealed," he replied gently. "And I wish there was something I could say to ease your mind. But there is not."

Lady Tesh's shoulders, which until then had been held in

a rigid line, drooped. She closed her eyes, as if in pain. "I was worried you would say something like that."

"I am sorry," he replied softly.

She pursed her lips. "You know, I could attempt to force it out of you."

His lips twitched at her attempt at humor. "You could certainly try, my lady."

"Hmm. It might be fun, at that." But the lightheartedness of the moment was short-lived. Looking suddenly a decade older, she sighed heavily, as if the weight of the world were on her shoulders.

"I have done all I can for her these last weeks. But with the vicar grabbing hold of the scandal like a dog with a bone and spreading his vitriol, I fear I will fail in protecting her. But this is not your concern. I will leave you to your rest. Come along, Freya."

The dog jumped down and headed for the door as Lady Tesh made to rise. Sebastian, still reeling from such a defeated speech from the dowager, hurriedly rose and assisted her to standing. He had thought surely Katrina must be exaggerating when she spoke of needing to protect her employer. But here was proof that she had a right to worry about the older woman. Though he had not known Lady Tesh long, he was still shocked at the change in her as she admitted to what she perceived as her failure in protecting her companion.

"Why has Miss Denby never married?"

The words tumbled from his lips, unbidden, and he wanted to kick himself the moment they emerged. Especially when Lady Tesh turned and speared him with those sharp eyes of hers that saw much, much more than they should. But there was nothing to be done now; the words

were out, and there was no taking them back. He raised his
head and continued as if he had meant to question her on it.

"I am fully aware that the scandal four years ago has
harmed her in ways I cannot begin to imagine." Here fury
sizzled under his skin for all Landon had put her through.
He quickly brought it under control lest Lady Tesh see more
than he wished for her to.

"But she is young and beautiful." *And sweet, and kind,
and incredible...* "And she has regained some respectability while she has been in your employ." Which Landon
once again destroyed. Again that fury, though this time it
took some effort to control. "Surely there has been someone who has shown interest in her."

Blessedly Lady Tesh did not seem to see anything suspicious in his line of questioning. Lacing her fingers over
the head of her cane, she sighed. "Much to my frustration,
there has not. Or, rather," she amended with a wry smile,
"there has been no one to capture Miss Denby's interest.
Oh, I have tried to find someone for her, you may believe
that." She laughed quietly. "I fancy myself as something of
a matchmaker, you see, and had hoped to add Miss Denby
to my list of successes. And there have been many successes, you may be assured."

Her expression altered then, the lines of her face deepening. "It is yet one more thing I failed at with her. And
now I fear it will be even more difficult than before."

Which Katrina had proved to him. He recalled her frustration with him that afternoon, the sheen of tears in her
eyes, and the acidic guilt that had begun to corrode his gut
returned even stronger. Pressing a fist to his stomach in a
fruitless attempt to relieve it, he said, "But surely there are
men who are receptive to her, despite the recent tragedy.

The young men who joined our excursion to the beach, for instance, did not seem to look at her with anything but kindness."

But he had finally gone too far in his concern. The dowager narrowed her eyes, a preternatural stillness coming over her features. "You have an uncommon interest in Miss Denby's future."

His face heated, but he maintained eye contact with Lady Tesh. God knew it would not do to show he had been cowed; she would scent the blood and go in for the kill if he did. "She is merely my friend," he replied quietly, sending up a prayer that she believed him—as well as a prayer that he believed it himself, for anything more was an impossibility. "It grieves me to see her so maligned. I daresay I would feel the same for any young woman put in such a position."

"Hmm," was her thoughtful reply, a sound that made the hairs stand up on the back of his neck. If there was anything that could make the dowager dangerous, that was piquing her curiosity.

But it seemed luck was on his side tonight. She appeared to shrug off whatever suspicions she had and continued. "While I would love nothing better than for Miss Denby to find happiness with one of those young men, they are either still in university or already promised to another, and so it is an impossibility. But I have taken up enough of your time. I shall see you tomorrow morning."

She made to leave. As she reached the door, however, she turned back to him, eyes full of a desperate pleading.

"I'm glad to know she has at least you to confide in. Please continue to watch out for her, Your Grace."

With that she was gone, the door closing softly behind

her. Leaving Sebastian to stare in dismay after her. For
watching after Katrina was the very last thing he could do.

* * *

For the first time since arriving on Synne and befriend-
ing the Oddments, Katrina dreaded going to their weekly
meeting.

She stepped down from Lady Tesh's carriage with
Mouse in tow, dragging in a deep breath as she prepared to
hurry through the Quayside to the blue velvet curtain at the
back of the shop. Would there be more cold stares and cruelties from the patrons as she passed through the circulating library? And if she were to make it through unscathed,
what would be waiting for her behind that blue curtain and
in Seraphina's small office? Had Adelaide told them all
what happened yesterday at the Beakhead?

Just as she gathered her courage and took the first step
toward the entrance to the Quayside, however, a figure
materialized from the shadows near the door and rushed
toward her. But it was not a ruffian intent on her purse. Nor
was it that horrible woman from last week or anyone like
her, determined to let Katrina know what a scandalous person she was. No, it was Adelaide, looking as somber and
determined as Katrina had ever seen her. Before Katrina
could call out a greeting, Adelaide grabbed her arm, dragging her and Mouse down the street to a private alcove near
a small silhouette shop. And Katrina quickly learned the
answer to those questions that had been preying on her
since the day before. Or, at least, one of them.

"I have not told the others what happened yesterday," she
whispered, eyeing the passersby cautiously to make certain

they were not being overheard. "I wanted you to know that before we joined them."

Relief coursed through Katrina, so potent she could taste it. But it was short-lived.

"That is not to say you and I will not have a conversation about it," she continued. She bit her lip, her large brown eyes brimming with worry.

"I was simply ill," Katrina mumbled, directing her attention to Mouse as he attempted to greet every person who passed by their small alcove. Though controlling him was only part of the reason she became so focused on her pet; the rest was to prevent Adelaide from becoming aware that she was lying through her teeth. Just as she had lied to Lady Tesh all day yesterday when asked about the commotion at the Beakhead.

"That is not what I wish to discuss at all, and you know it," her friend said quietly. She laid a gentle hand on Katrina's arm. "Is something going on between you and the duke?"

Ah, God, she had forgotten that Adelaide had witnessed her holding hands with Sebastian. It would not be as easy to deflect this particular issue, of course. But deflect she must try.

"He was merely concerned for me is all. He saw I was not feeling well, and was attempting to comfort me."

But Adelaide did not look the least bit convinced. "That is not what it looked like, Katrina. It appeared as if there might be something…more going on between the two of you."

"His Grace is engaged," Katrina replied tightly. "Or very nearly, which to me, as you well know, is as good as being engaged. Especially since he and the young woman and her family all seem to have an understanding. Nothing can happen between the duke and I."

But Katrina's attempt to distract her friend failed, miserably. "Which is a very convenient way of skirting the question," Adelaide murmured.

Katrina pulled Mouse close to her side and nervously rubbed at his silky ears. "The duke and I have determined that nothing shall happen between us."

Adelaide raised one black eyebrow. "You are getting closer. Try again."

Sighing, Katrina let out a small growl of frustration. "Very well. We kissed. Are you happy now?"

But Adelaide did not look the least bit happy. In fact, the expression in her eyes could only be described as mournful. "No, actually, I'm not. What happened, Katrina?"

The memory of his arms about her, of his mouth on hers, nearly overwhelmed her then. Dragging in a deep breath, she managed, "It does not matter what happened. But it did not go past a kiss, and we both agreed it would not happen again."

Adelaide was quiet for a moment, though to Katrina her silence was louder than the clamor of carriages and conversation surrounding them. Finally she spoke.

"Mayhap it would be best if you stay with one of us for the time being."

Despite herself, Katrina could not tamp down the hurt that surged in her like a tidal wave. "You don't trust me to even be in the same house as the duke?"

"It is not that, dearest," Adelaide hurried to say. "Of course I trust you. It is the duke I don't trust. He is virile, and powerful, and though I know Lady Tesh will do all in her power to protect you, when a man of his station takes it in his mind to do something there is not much that can stop him."

The one small, reasonable part of Katrina's brain knew that her friend was only worried for her and was trying to help. But it was overshadowed by outrage, and a powerful urge to protect Sebastian. "The duke has never been anything but proper to me," she said heatedly. "He would never take advantage of me. He is the kindest, the gentlest, the most considerate man I have ever known, and I won't have you thinking such horrid things about him."

Which, she realized after the words had left her mouth, had probably not been the wisest thing to say, for Adelaide was gaping at her like a fish on market day.

"Oh my goodness, Katrina," she whispered. "You are falling in love with the duke."

Katrina blanched. *Of course she wasn't.* The words should be easy enough to say. They were already there, tripping up her throat.

Yet she couldn't seem to force them past her lips. Why? Yes, she had already been well on her way to loving him four years ago. And yes, it was true she desired him now. Their kiss had been proof of that—as well as the sleepless nights she spent thinking of him, and the way her body fairly hummed when he entered a room.

But she was also painfully aware that allowing herself to continue that falling in love with him would be a horrible mistake. Why, then, did the words denouncing any such feelings lodge in her throat like a cherry pit?

In the end she finally managed, through numb lips, "He has only been here a week," hoping it would suffice to squash any such thoughts of her being in love with Sebastian.

Once again, her friend did not look the least convinced.

"Yet another non-answer. I am well aware that you knew the duke four years ago during your time in London."

Knowing she had effectively trapped herself in a corner, Katrina closed her eyes and rubbed at the back of her aching skull, hoping to relieve some of the headache that had come upon her so suddenly. "It doesn't matter what I may or may not feel for the duke," she rasped. "He is preparing to marry Mr. Bridling's sister. There is no use in us talking about it further. And please don't mention any of this to the others. I wouldn't wish for them to worry. Now, shouldn't we be heading inside? They will be wondering where we are."

So saying, she tightened her hands on Mouse's lead and headed back to the Quayside. Adelaide, after only a moment's hesitation, followed. But as Katrina made her way back to the blue curtain, all the while trying not to notice just how few patrons were within the circulating library—or that Honoria was conspicuously absent from Seraphina's office when she opened that door—she knew she would have to work doubly hard at hiding her affections for Sebastian to keep her friends from suspecting he was more to her than he should be.

Chapter 15

*I*f there was one thing Sebastian didn't expect when he entered Bridling's room the following afternoon, it was to see him furiously scribbling away at his desk.

It's not that he had never seen the boy write...or had he? Truthfully he couldn't recall ever seeing Bridling with a quill in his hands. Or in possession of a book. Not that they had spent an inordinate amount of time together; before this trip, they had never been what one would call close, or even true acquaintances. In fact, Sebastian had barely seen the boy during the few events they had managed to attend together during the London season.

Even so, after having spent four days confined in a carriage for the drive here, as well as being in his company for more than a week since their arrival on Synne, he could not recall a single time he had witnessed Bridling doing anything remotely intellectual.

Bridling glanced up then, and a faint flush stained his

cheeks. In the next moment he was hurriedly stuffing the paper he had been working on in the desk drawer.

"Ah, you're here," he mumbled, in a tone that was not at all like his typical cheerful voice. "I had forgotten about our ride."

Which was truly peculiar, as he had appeared excited for the prospect of exploring the Isle when Sebastian had brought it up earlier—an outing Sebastian had suggested for the sole purpose of feeling Bridling out regarding Miss Hutton. The boy had not so much as mentioned his paramour over the past couple days, a strange turn of events. And one that left Sebastian equally hopeful for and dreading what was to come. If the combined efforts of Sebastian and Lady Tesh and the Isle of Synne had finally worked and turned the boy from thoughts of his actress, it meant their time here would soon come to a close. Sebastian could finally return to London and secure Miss Bridling's hand—and her fortune—having done what Lord Cartmel had required him to do.

Which also meant, of course, that he would be leaving Katrina behind, most likely never to see her again.

Unless you abandon this whole blasted plan and marry her yourself.

If Sebastian had been drinking something he would have certainly choked. No, he would not allow his mind to go down that path. It would only torture him, knowing that a future with her, something he had wanted so desperately all those years ago, would never be within his grasp. Yet now that it had been allowed to slink into his brain, he could not easily dispel it. Though dispel it he must. This was how it had to be, after all, the path he had been forced to take the moment his father took advantage of all those people. Too many were counting on this marriage with Miss Bridling, his sisters and the tenants and all those who worked at Ramsleigh Castle included; he could not destroy their futures due to any selfishness on his part. No matter how much he might want a future with Katrina.

Propping his shoulder against the doorjamb, he watched Bridling closely as he tidied up the desk, dropping the silver stopper of his ink pot in his haste. It was time to put his sole focus on the boy. And that boy, much to Sebastian's bafflement, appeared nervous, evasive, as if he would jump out of his skin if Sebastian so much as moved wrong. What the blazes was going on?

"Forgive me," the boy said. "I completely lost track of time."

"If you'd rather remain inside and complete your correspondence, we can postpone our ride for another day," Sebastian replied neutrally.

"Correspondence?" Bridling frowned, looking to the desk, as if he could not contemplate what Sebastian was talking about. "No, it wasn't correspondence. Who would I correspond with?"

"Forgive me," Sebastian murmured. "I assumed you would be writing to Miss Hutton."

"Mirabel?" Once more Bridling appeared confused. Though this time there was something more to his frown, as if he could not understand why Sebastian had brought the woman up at all. "Goodness, I have not thought of her in several days." A short bark of laughter escaped him. "Funny that, isn't it. Though with what has occurred since, can you blame me? It is not every day a man can play knight in shining armor."

For a strange moment he fell silent, his eyes going

distant and soft until, with a shake of his head, he looked back to Sebastian.

"But my apologies, I have not yet readied myself. I'll meet you downstairs in about fifteen minutes' time, shall I?"

Without waiting for an answer, he made his way to his dressing room. But not before locking up the desk tight.

Sebastian strode from the room, his heart thrumming in his chest, feeling much like a bloodhound with its first scent of fox. No, not just a scent of fox; the whole bloody fox had laid down in front of him. He could not have asked for a more viable piece of proof that Bridling's interest in his actress was waning, his dismissal of his paramour as loud as a shout that the tide was turning.

But that had not been the only thing to capture Sebastian's attention. Bridling's dismissal of Miss Hutton had appeared intermingled with something tangible, namely his reference to playing knight in shining armor. A memory surfaced then, of Cartmel's frustration that day when he'd spoken of his son's infatuation with Miss Hutton: *It's his need to be a savior, no doubt. He always was enamored of the idea of playing a knight in shining armor. And when he rescued that actress from an overzealous admirer one evening it must have brought up those grandiose delusions that he revels in.*

It was quite possible that very same thing had happened again, only this time with Lady Paulette. Was it possible he had formed a tendre for the young woman?

His steps faltered on the stairs as he considered that. Lady Paulette was from a good family. Her father, the Marquess of Ilford, possessed a lineage that even Lord Cartmel in his arrogance could not fail to be impressed by. If by some chance the young lady was beginning to replace Miss Hutton in Bridling's affections, if Bridling should fall in love with Lady Paulette, surely Cartmel would support such a match. And the price Sebastian had been expected to pay would be paid in full, no doubt with interest. The only question now was: How did he see to it that Bridling and Lady Paulette were brought into one another's orbits so Bridling's burgeoning feelings might become more fully formed and thus cement the outcome needed to end this damnable trip—and finally get Sebastian far from the temptation that was Katrina?

Katrina. But no, he would not think of her. He would focus on finishing this thing with Bridling. And there was only one person who had the necessary talent to assist him: Lady Tesh.

The woman would no doubt be in the drawing room at this time of day. So focused was he on reaching that room before his planned departure with Bridling, however, he did not immediately hear the masculine voice from within until he had already rounded the door.

At the sight of the fair, bespectacled fellow seated close to Katrina on the settee he stopped cold.

He had never seen the man before, that was certain. Who was he? And why was he sitting so bloody close to Katrina?

He did not realize just how tightly he was holding his hands into fists until the brim of his beaver hat gave a rather sickening crunch. Looking down at the article, he let loose a soft curse as he attempted to smooth the blasted brim out, all the while taking deep, fortifying breaths to calm his sudden agitation that was certainly *not* jealousy. No doubt this man was the latest in Katrina's attempts to marry and make herself respectable. He cast a furtive glance their way, taking stock of the man—as any good friend would do, surely, and not at all out of the ordinary. At least the man appeared to be a gentleman, perhaps even a quiet bookish type, not a letch or near death's door as the other two had been. While he was not in the first blush of youth, he could not be above forty, a slight bit of graying at his temples and faint lines at the corners of his eyes giving him a distinguished appearance. Add to that his neat clothing and commanding posture, and Sebastian could almost see the appeal of the man.

Almost.

When Katrina gave the other man what could be construed as a flirtatious smile, however, he knew it would take an incredible amount of effort to keep his promise to her that he would not interfere.

Blessedly he was saved from doing further damage to his much-maligned hat when Mouse spotted him. Woofing softly, the beast rose and trotted over to him, tail swinging in a happy arc. Unfortunately, the dog's attention also drew the eyes of the others his way. As Katrina's gaze met his and her smile faltered, he thought surely the whole room must have heard his heart cracking.

"Pardon me for interrupting," he managed, patting Mouse's smooth head distractedly, more to keep the beast's snout from his private area than anything else. "I was looking for Lady Tesh."

That woman—who he had completely overlooked, as focused as he had been on Katrina and her caller—spoke up from the depths of her wingback chair near the others, beckoning him closer. "Well, I am here, m'boy. But why don't you come and meet our guest. Mr. Young, I would like to introduce you to the Duke of Ramsleigh, who has accompanied my friend's son Mr. Bridling for a short holiday on Synne. Ramsleigh, this here is Mr. Young. Mr. Young owns a small farm on the far side of the Isle, a pretty little piece of property."

"Pleased to make your acquaintance, Your Grace," the man said in a solemn, monotone voice as he rose and bowed.

"We do not often get to see Mr. Young," Lady Tesh continued. "He is a widower, you know, with several children, and rarely comes into town." She eyed Katrina thoughtfully. "Imagine my surprise when he deigned to show up on my doorstep with the express purpose of calling on Miss Denby."

"I would not have thought of it had I not met Miss Denby at the Quayside just yesterday," the man said in what Sebastian was coming to think was his normal lack of any discernible inflection. "How fortuitous that my daughters asked me to fetch them sheet music during my weekly stop into town for supplies, or I would have never run into Miss Denby and received an invitation to visit."

Sebastian, who had taken the seat across from Katrina— with Mouse planting his posterior upon his foot, something the dog had taken to doing recently—watched the other man with narrowed eyes. There was no affection for her in his words, the flat, automatic quality of them making them seem completely disingenuous. Nor was there warmth in his gaze. Rather, he seemed to be sizing her up, as if he were considering hiring her on for a position in his household and was trying to determine if she would be a good fit.

Enough, you blasted idiot, he scolded himself, attempting to focus on patting Mouse's great head. Let Katrina do what she felt she needed to do. *Stay out of it.*

"I am only pleased you took me up on my invitation," Katrina said with a smile that did not reach her eyes. "It must be so very difficult for you to get away from home with all your responsibilities. I am honored you took time away to visit with us."

"I would not have missed it for the world," the farmer stated. Why was it, Sebastian thought, that the man could say something that seemed so pleasant, and yet make it sound dry and as hard to swallow as unbuttered toast?

"That being said," Mr. Young continued, rising, "I really must be getting back home. I have ten children, you see, Your Grace," he explained to Sebastian, "and since my late wife's passing it is difficult for me to get away for any length of time."

"Oh, but allow me to see you to the door," Katrina said, springing to her feet. "If, Lady Tesh, that is all right with you?"

"Certainly," the dowager murmured, waving a hand in the air.

The farmer made his farewells and departed, Katrina at his side. Sebastian watched them go, fighting the urge to bolt after them. A widower with ten children? If Katrina married him she would be nothing more than a glorified nanny. Sebastian had never met anyone so dour in his life, no matter the man's pleasant appearance. Katrina's spirit would be crushed if she were to shackle herself to such a person, he was certain of it.

No! He physically shook his head, attempting to dislodge the critical thoughts. This was Katrina's decision and he had to respect it. He *would* respect it. Even so, it took an incredible amount of effort to tear his gaze from the empty doorway—only to find Lady Tesh looking at him with a healthy dose of speculation. His face heated. Surely she would say something about his fascination with Katrina and Mr. Young—especially after his misstep last night when he had questioned why Katrina had not married. Or, barring that, she would quiz him on Mr. Young's appearance and Katrina's seemingly welcome attitude toward the man's attentions—as insipid and businesslike as they had been. And he did not know if he could trust himself to hide his feelings on that particular subject, as volatile as they were.

Blessedly, however, she didn't speak of either of those things. "You wished to see me about something, Your Grace?" she asked, patting Freya, who was currently snoozing in her lap.

Damnation, he had completely forgotten his reason for seeking her out in the first place. Forcefully putting Katrina and her questionable beau from his mind, he focused on the issue most important to him: namely, how to ensure that Bridling had completely forgotten his actress, thus sealing a stable future for all those people counting on Sebastian not to muck this up.

"I have reason to believe," he began quietly, "that Bridling may have formed a tendre for Lady Paulette."

"Lady Paulette, eh?" Lady Tesh mused. "Even Cartmel would not dare to complain of such a match."

"I am of the same mind."

She pursed her lips, idly stroking Freya's fur. "The young lady was set to return home tomorrow. But mayhap I can convince her to stay on Synne for a bit longer." Suddenly her gaze turned troubled as it drifted to the doorway. "There is the ball at the Assembly Rooms tomorrow, of course. But after our last visit there, I don't think that would be something we should attempt. At least not for the time being."

She was thinking of Katrina. Which, of course, made *him* think of Katrina, and why she was doing what she was doing in welcoming the advances of such men. She truly loved Lady Tesh and her friends, and she would relegate herself to a lifetime of unhappiness to protect them.

Did he think it was utter madness? Absolutely. There must be some other path she could take to reclaim her respectability. But for the life of him he could not think what that might be; with even the vicar villainizing her, he could not see a way out of this for her anytime soon.

Marry her yourself, you coward.

There was that voice again, louder this time. And much harder to ignore.

"What we need is something more private, like our beach excursion, to encourage intimacy between the two," Lady Tesh continued, providing him with the means to quiet those secret, troublesome desires. Suddenly she looked at Sebastian with a gleam in her eye. "Mayhap a bit of rowing on Lake Tyesmere."

A genius plan if there ever was one. Rowing in small skiffs would be the ideal way to get two people off alone. "Lady Tesh," he said with a small smile, "I do think that is a positively inspired plan."

"Well, of course it is," she replied archly. "*I* came up with it, after all."

"What did you come up with, Lady Tesh?" Katrina asked as she re-entered the room.

But Sebastian didn't hear the dowager's reply. The sight of Katrina walking toward them, her golden hair illuminated like a halo about her head as she passed through a beam of afternoon sunlight, addled his senses completely. But why? He had literally just seen her mere minutes ago; why would she have such an effect on him just by walking into the room? Especially after he had just been telling himself that he would not interfere in her life and would stand back to allow her to do what she felt needed to be done?

But she was speaking, no doubt replying to whatever it was that Lady Tesh had said. "A rowing party?" she said, eyes lighting up as she resumed her seat beside the dowager. "Oh, I do adore rowing. All that bobbing and floating in the water, like being in a dream. Why, I can still recall the last time I was out rowing. It was at a house party during my last season in London. The water was clear as glass." She turned to Sebastian, a smile lighting her face, making him feel warm from the top of his head to the tips of his toes. "Don't you remember, Seb—?"

She cut herself off, her blue eyes going wide with dismay before they dropped to her lap. But her attempt to rein herself in was too late for Sebastian. Her words brought to mind that halcyon day mere weeks before his father's death. They had been among those who had been invited to Lady Fulton's annual house party just outside of London. How often had they walked together, or sat together of an evening talking and laughing? And then there had been that one shining afternoon, where he had taken her out rowing with the rest of the party. How he had ached to row them beneath the shade of one of the many willow trees that dotted the bank, to shield them behind the dragging branches, to take her in his arms and kiss her senseless. To claim her for his own right then and there.

But he had not. No, instead he had fed the rebellion in his breast that had loudly declared he was too young to be tied down to one woman. And so instead of holding her and kissing her, as he'd ached to do with every fiber of his being, he had turned the boat about and brought her back to shore.

He had never regretted such a cowardly decision so much in his life. If he had quieted that part of himself that insisted on remaining free, if he had instead listened to his heart, he would even now be married to the most incredible woman he had ever known.

And you would have no way of pulling yourself out of the sucking pit of financial ruin you're currently in.

It was the intelligent voice in all this, the voice of reason. And he tried to step back and give it its head, to let it take over and crush the other voice that would have him aching to make a life with Katrina.

But looking at her, recalling their kiss from just days ago, and knowing how desperately he wished he could do that and more with her, he was having a devilishly hard time remembering why he had to keep his head down and forge on in the opposite direction.

Blessedly Katrina was much more reasonable than he was just then. Unfortunately, she brought up the one person Sebastian did not want to hear about.

"I don't suppose I could invite Mr. Young to our rowing party? He had such an enjoyable time here this afternoon, after all."

The muscles in Sebastian's back seized. Which was ridiculous; Katrina was no doubt hoping to secure a marriage proposal from the man, and would want to make certain they were together as much as possible, something that did not seem easy to do, considering the man's many—many—responsibilities.

Ten children? Really?

But with such a blatant request, especially after Sebastian's idiotic questions regarding Katrina's marital prospects, Lady Tesh could not fail to put two and two together. It was obvious she cared for Katrina; how would she feel about such a match?

But when he glanced at that woman, she wasn't looking at Katrina at all. In fact, she was peering at him again with a gaze so piercing he thought she must surely see to the very heart of him.

"I think that would be a lovely idea," Lady Tesh said, narrowing her eyes on him for a moment before returning her attention to her employee. "Please send off an invitation to Mr. Young, with my blessing."

As Katrina, not looking his way, ran to the desk in the corner to write off her invitation to her suitor, Sebastian took his leave. No doubt Bridling would be ready for their ride, he told himself. But deep inside he knew his quick departure had nothing at all to do with Bridling, and everything to do with needing air to clear his head of thoughts of Katrina and Mr. Young together.

Chapter 16

"Am I to assume, Miss Denby, that your recent attentions to me have something to do with the pernicious gossip of the vicar?" Mr. Young asked two days later as he pulled the oars through the water.

Katrina, in the process of settling her skirts about her in the small skiff, froze. What was it with the men she had singled out as possible husbands and their propensity to baldly state their suspicions regarding her attentions?

"Er...these last weeks have been difficult, as I'm sure you can surmise," she hedged, unable to look him in the eyes. And not only for the fact that his eyes were as cold and murky as the waters of Lake Tyesmere that they were currently gliding through. After all, she did not want this last chance at finding a husband on Synne to go as wrong as the other two had.

"No doubt," he murmured dryly. "But I will tell you here and now, Miss Denby, that I happen to despise the vicar—and indeed all men of his ilk. I am of the mind that they are hypocritical blowhards, and so his words against you only endear you to me more."

Katrina blinked. "Ah, that is... good?"

"Indeed." He squinted, looking out over the water toward the others. Katrina followed his gaze to see Mr. Bridling in one of the other skiffs, Lady Paulette opposite him with a lacy parasol held aloft above her burnished head. Their light laughter reached them, blending with the call of birds and the low murmur of conversation from several other members of their party where they lounged on the bank beneath the shade of a tree.

But it was Sebastian, with Mouse at his feet, that snagged her attention. He stood ramrod straight as he looked out over the lake, his hand on Mouse's head, his gaze piercing even from this distance. She felt, quite foolishly no doubt, that he was looking her way. Her heart constricted in her chest.

Suddenly Mr. Young stopped rowing and began to speak in his dull monotone. "That, of course, does not negate the fact that you were embroiled in a scandal of incredible magnitude. I have impressionable young daughters at home, and I would not wish to have them influenced by someone in possession of loose ways."

Beneath the wide brim of her bonnet, Katrina's face burned hot as she looked back to the man. "I assure you, Mr. Young, that my reputation is entirely unfounded."

"Hmm," was all he said before, looking her up and down as if taking stock of her, he began to pull the oars through the water again.

"I, of course, have come to the conclusion that you require a husband to repair your reputation. And that you have decided I fit the bill. Is that a fair assumption, Miss Denby?"

He looked to her for confirmation. Pressing her lips tight, she nodded stiffly.

"And it is not due to you being in the...family way?"

Her jaw dropped so quickly, she was surprised she did not have to pick it up from her lap. "O-of course not, Mr. Young," she stammered.

"Not that I can afford to be picky," he said, his voice dripping boredom despite the volatile and potentially life-altering subject of their conversation. "Everyone on the Isle knows that I am in desperate need of a wife. Especially as my sister, who as you know has been with me for some months now to help with the children, is due to marry and set up a house of her own. No, I cannot afford to be picky at all. But I would prefer not to add another man's by-blow to my already large brood."

Katrina, who felt as if she had been slapped, gazed numbly at Mr. Young. "I swear you do not have to worry on that score."

He nodded. "Good. Well then, if you can vow that your unfortunate proclivities are well and truly behind you, I would consider marrying you."

It was what she had wanted. By marrying Mr. Young, not only could she remain on Synne with her friends, but she would also gain respectability, would have a home of her own and a family to care for, would be able to protect her friends and Lady Tesh. It was ideal. And she could not deny that, though he had faults, Mr. Young was a sight better than either Mr. Finley or Mr. Kendrick.

Why, then, did she feel like crying? Why did she have

the insane urge to jump into the lake and swim for all she was worth to escape such a future?

Instead she managed a trembling smile, though in truth she felt she might be ill. "Thank you, Mr. Young," she said.

He nodded, in such a way that made it seem as if he were bestowing a great favor upon her. Which, she supposed, he was. A lowering thought, indeed.

"I will have you visit the farm for a day," he said. "That way I may see how you get on with the children. After that, I will decide if you could be a proper mother for them."

So saying, Mr. Young turned the boat back for shore. Katrina, feeling as if she had been invited to apply for a position in the man's household as a servant and not as his wife, slumped in her seat, her gaze once more drifting listlessly to where Sebastian stood. Though she was being rowed closer and closer to him, she felt as if the distance between them had never been so great.

* * *

Bridling had been successfully paired with Lady Paulette for not only some rowing, but also for the picnic that followed, and so Sebastian should feel nothing but triumph. Things were going beautifully, the boy's actress seemingly all but forgotten as he laughed and talked with the latest object of his affections. The end of their time on Synne had to be close now.

Yet instead of Sebastian relaxing with the group and reveling in his looming triumph, here he was, sitting off to the side with Mouse, trying and failing not to glare daggers at Mr. Young as he passed a plate of fruit to Katrina.

"What the blazes is wrong with me?" he mumbled.

Mouse, who had been stuck to his side like a burr all day long, turned his head and gazed at Sebastian with large, soulful eyes.

"I should be happy for her," he went on, this time directing it to the dog, who continued to look at him in solemn silence. "Mr. Young doesn't seem a bad sort. He's a boring stick in the mud, yes. And he has far too many children."

He looked back to Katrina, who was conversing with her suitor, a small, tremulous smile on her face. "But I cannot be happy. She deserves so much more. She deserves a man who loves her, who will give her the entire world."

A low whine issued from Mouse's chest, one huge paw coming up to rest on Sebastian's knee.

"Well, of course, I care for her," Sebastian said, plucking a leaf from a nearby bush and tearing it into small pieces before tossing it aside. "But I cannot be the one to marry her. As much as I may want to."

That last bit slipped out quite without him meaning to. He had been fighting it for days, that voice in his head that had been urging him to turn his back on his responsibilities and make a life with Katrina.

But hearing it aloud from his own lips made it so much more heartbreaking, an undeniable fact that threatened to shatter him.

The whine from Mouse was louder this time, more persistent. Sebastian looked down at him, and his heart twisted at the sadness in those big eyes, reflecting what was in his own heart.

"I can't marry her," he rasped. "The whole reason I'm planning on marrying Miss Bridling is to save the dukedom and all the people who rely on it. I can't sacrifice their safety and livelihoods for my own selfish reasons. I just can't. No matter how much I—"

He stopped the words before they could emerge, those damning words that there was no coming back from. But Mouse was either much smarter than Sebastian gave him credit for, or a demon sent from hell to torment him, for he let out a low woof, pushing his nose into Sebastian's chest, as if to dislodge the truth that was stuck there like a cherry pit.

"No, Mouse," he said, his voice hoarse.

But the dog was not about to give up. He pushed harder, letting loose an insistent whine for good measure.

"Fine," Sebastian managed. "Do you want me to tell you I love her? Of course I love her. How could I not? I have never known another who would so selflessly give of themselves to help others, who would give up their own chance for happiness to protect those she loves. Not only that, but she has even made certain to assist me in reclaiming some of the joy I used to have in life. And God knows I have not deserved it, not after all I have done to get in her way. She is the kindest, the sweetest, the most amazing woman I have ever known."

A humorless bark of laughter broke free from his lips. "And the cruelest part is," he continued, unable to stop himself from pouring his heart out to her dog, "I *have* considered ways I might be with her. I have spent the last two nights wracking my brain, trying to come up with a solution. Is there an old friend, perhaps, who might assist me until the dukedom finally becomes solvent? Is there a bank that might extend to me yet another loan? Is there anything else I might sell to provide the necessary money? But each possible path I see myself taking comes to a dead end. It is hopeless."

Mouse heaved a mournful sigh and laid his massive head in Sebastian's lap.

"I know, old man," he muttered, patting the dog's head. "It's highly depressing."

They remained that way for a time, each mired in his own thoughts. If dogs could be mired in thoughts, of course. Just as he was about to rise and rejoin the others, however, a sudden voice made him tense.

"The dog seems to like you, Your Grace."

Sebastian glanced up sharply to see Mr. Young peering down at him.

"Have you decided to leave Miss Denby's side then?" The question burst from his lips without him meaning for it to, burning his throat with bitter gall. *Shut up, Sebastian.*

Mr. Young frowned slightly before, holding up the pale blue piece of fabric in his grip, he said, "She was growing chilled and asked me to fetch her shawl."

More sharp retorts rose up and Sebastian forcefully swallowed them down. Truly, what the hell was wrong with him? He had vowed to Katrina he would no longer interfere in her life. And even if he hadn't, he had no right to verbally attack the man. This was Katrina's choice and hers alone. If she wanted to marry this potato with hair, that was her business.

"That's most kind of you," he managed, returning his attention to Mouse.

Mr. Young stood there for a moment, no doubt confused by Sebastian's strange pendulum of emotions. Finally he made to move off.

But Sebastian, glutton for pain as he was, spoke once more, stalling the farmer's departure.

"You will make her happy, won't you?"

The look Mr. Young sent his way could only be

described as stunned. Ah, finally some emotion, Sebastian thought bitterly.

"Miss Denby?" the man queried.

Sebastian cleared his throat. "Yes, Miss Denby. You will make certain she is happy?"

Mr. Young blinked several times before, pressing his lips tight, he said in his strange monotone, "I will endeavor to see she wants for nothing."

Which was not the same, not at all. Yet what could he do? Nodding, he turned away this time, praying the other man would leave. But he did not. The bastard.

And he was even more of a bastard for what he said next.

"As the beast likes you so much, mayhap you could take on its care after Miss Denby and I marry."

This time it was Sebastian's turn to peer in confusion at the other man. "The beast? You mean Mouse?"

"Yes." He motioned to the dog, who had raised his massive head and was looking at Mr. Young with ears pinned back. "She will need to find a home for the creature, and it seems to like you. An ideal situation to me."

Sebastian frowned. "Why would she need to find a home for Mouse?"

The laugh that broke free from Mr. Young was as dry and unemotional as his voice. "Well, she cannot bring it with her when she moves into my home. She will be much too busy to care for it."

Gaping at the other man, Sebastian slowly rose to his feet. Mouse, no doubt sensing something ugly was happening, rose as well and pressed into his side, powerful body trembling.

"You cannot force her to give up her pet," he said. "She loves Mouse more than just about anything."

But Mr. Young waved a hand in dismissal. "It is a dog, a mere animal."

"Not to Miss Denby," Sebastian replied, tension threading through him at the man's callousness. Dear God, was he truly going to force Katrina to give up her pet? "She has dealt with too much heartbreak and has lost too much already."

"Her disappointment will pass, I assure you," the man replied. Suddenly his eyes narrowed. "And as she shall be my wife, and therefore my responsibility, I shall be the one to decide what is best for her."

It was a warning, plain and simple. He may as well have declared that Katrina would be his property. Which, by law, was unfortunately all too true. Sebastian's vision went red, his body trembling as violently as Mouse at his side.

But as much as he would love to take Mr. Young by his cravat and plant him a facer, as much as he ached to team up with Mouse and frighten the man into decamping, he knew he could not. He had promised Katrina he would not interfere. And he would keep that promise—no matter how much it destroyed him to do so.

He stepped back, pulling an agitated Mouse with him, nodding his head in a sharp, jerky motion.

Mr. Young smiled, a cold thing. "Do consider taking on the animal," he said, smoothing Katrina's shawl over his arm as if he already owned her. "I would so hate to destroy it. Now if you will excuse me."

Mr. Young turned to go, but did not move a step farther. Thinking the man must wish to prolong their conversation—if one could even call such an exchange that—Sebastian prayed for strength that he could continue to rein himself in. He was damn near close to breaking his promise to Katrina as it was; he did not know how much more of the man he could take before he snapped.

Katrina's voice, however, told him it was not a wish to continue inserting his dominance over Sebastian that had made Mr. Young pause.

"Destroy what animal, Mr. Young?"

Her voice was tremulous, a kind of horrified disbelief coloring the quavering words.

The man, coward that he was, did not answer. Instead he held out her shawl.

"Forgive me for taking so long to return to you, Miss Denby," he said. "I stopped to talk to the duke and completely lost track of time. Here is your garment."

But Katrina did not take it. She clenched her hands tight before her and kept her eyes steady on her suitor.

"Mr. Young, you have not answered my question. What animal are you planning to destroy?"

Sebastian expected discomfort or guilt from the farmer. But no, the man was not done shocking him that day.

He raised one pale brow and gave Katrina a patronizing look down his nose. "You must see the wisdom of disposing of your pet. I have young children at home. I would not have them put in danger."

"Mouse is not a danger to anyone," she said through her teeth. Suddenly she paled, and shivered, her gaze going hazy—was she thinking of the accident with Lord Landon? But the alteration in her composure was brief as, rearranging her features to a calm he knew she did not feel if the slight shaking in her hands was any indication, she raised her chin and looked the farmer in the eye.

"I know we have come to something of an understanding regarding our futures," she continued. "But the one thing I shall insist on is keeping Mouse. I will not budge on that, sir."

The perpetually frigid temperature that seemed to envelop Mr. Young dropped like a stone, making his gaze positively icy as he stared down at Katrina. Every protective bone in Sebastian's body was electrified, and it took never-before tapped willpower to keep himself from stepping between the two. *You promised, you arse.*

"I see, Miss Denby," Mr. Young said, each word like icy needles, "that you are not the right fit for my family. It is bad enough you are a scandalous female. But your stubbornness on this matter proves that you are not the right caretaker for my children. Good day."

But Sebastian had heard enough. Surely, now that things had ended between the two, he could step in. As the man made to move past them toward the horses, he reached out and gripped hard to his shoulder.

"I say!" the man sputtered, attempting to pull out from Sebastian's grasp. "Release me at once."

"I shall," Sebastian drawled, "once I tell you that if you ever malign the lady again, you shall have me to answer to. Is that clear?"

Mouse chose that moment to move closer to Sebastian's side. A low rumble vibrated from his deep chest, a sound that had the farmer's eyes going from outraged to fearful in an instant.

Sebastian moved his face closer to the other man's. "I said, is that clear?"

Mr. Young, gasping, nodded jerkily, stumbling out from under Sebastian's grip and racing for the line of horses, Katrina's shawl still gripped in his hands.

For a long moment neither Sebastian nor Katrina moved.

The sounds of distant conversation and laughter were muffled by the bubble of tension they were mired in. Sebastian's fury had dissipated immediately upon Young's departure, leaving only guilt and regret in its wake for his part in the whole debacle. Finally, when Sebastian could stand the silence no longer, he attempted to speak.

"Katrina—"

"No," she cut in, the quiet word as good as a shout. She closed her eyes, breathing in deeply, her shoulders stiff and unyielding. Sebastian ached to step toward her and take her in his arms, to rub his hands over her back and shoulders and ease the strain from them.

But no, that was the very last thing he should do. Especially as, no matter that he had attempted to keep his promise to Katrina, he had still indirectly interfered, and was responsible for yet another suitor abandoning her. If he had not confronted the man about Mouse, no matter how briefly, no matter that he had retreated with the intention of letting Katrina handle it as she saw fit, she would not have overheard and would not now be in the position she was in.

When he thought he would surely snap in two from the strain, she suddenly drew in a deep, shuddering breath and turned to face him. Her eyes, those beautiful, clear blue eyes, were frighteningly flat and devoid of any emotion. It was worse than if she had been full of hate for him, and he wanted to weep

"Katrina," he rasped, "I am sorry—"

She held up a hand. "I have duties I must get back to," she said, her voice a mere whisper. "We will talk later."

With that she grabbed Mouse's heavy leather collar, pulling the dog away as she headed back to the party. And Sebastian knew he had never hated himself more.

Chapter 17

The pendulum of emotions that Katrina experienced that long—oh so very long—day was exhausting. From anxiety to relief to anger to grief and back to relief again, she was left feeling the simultaneous urge to cry and curse and laugh until her sides ached. What horrible Shakespearean comedy of errors was she in, that something so ridiculous could happen to her in the space of hours? Was she the punch line in some horrible, cruel joke?

As the evening had progressed and she had begun to gain some distance from the mess of an afternoon, however, she had been able to look at it with a semblance of reason and clarity. Was she still angry at Sebastian for inserting himself again into her plans for her future? Absolutely. But she knew now he had been attempting to keep his promise to her, and had been in the process of stepping back when she had come upon him and Mr. Young.

Which, of course, only made her feel more conflicted.

It was one thing to remain furious with Sebastian, focusing on her anger with him and nothing else. At least in that way she could keep her armor up, a hard shell shielding her from heartbreak.

But it was quite another to know he had been keeping his promise to her—no matter how bad he had been at it. That realization had her feeling raw, unable to ward off the inevitable pain.

But she could show none of her volatile emotions. Indeed, now more than ever she needed to keep a calm facade and pretend that nothing at all was wrong. Especially as her employer, the one person who stood between Katrina and complete ruination, seemed all too aware that something was horribly amiss.

Granted, Katrina would have been shocked if Lady Tesh had not noticed something momentous had occurred. The dowager was frighteningly observant, after all. And Katrina had not exactly been circumspect in her pitifully failed attempts to find a husband.

But now that Lady Tesh's lady's maid had finished readying her for bed and retired, and she had Katrina completely alone, there was nothing to stop her from quizzing Katrina to her heart's content. Which she did, with frightening focus.

"I thought nothing of it when Mr. Finley asked you to dance and was quickly sent packing at the Assembly Rooms," she began, spreading her coverlet over her lap. "I was mildly curious when the episode with Mr. Kendrick at the Beakhead occurred. But the situation revolving around Mr. Young over the past couple days has me wondering just what it is you're up to, Miss Denby."

Katrina, in the process of adjusting the pillows behind

Lady Tesh's back, flinched. And not because of any venom in her employer's voice. No, there was a decided lack of anger or frustration—an unusual occurrence, to be sure.

The gentleness in her voice, however, was more potent and devastating than any aggravation could be.

"I assure you, it was nothing at all," she replied, trying for a cheerful tone and instead fearful that she only managed to make herself sound a bit manic. "I was merely trying to be kind."

"Is that so?" Lady Tesh murmured, sounding like she did not believe Katrina one bit.

"Mmm hmm." Katrina stepped back, quickly folding her hands in front of her to prevent the dowager from seeing just how badly they were shaking. "If you don't need me for anything further, I'll retire now."

Lady Tesh pursed her lips, peering closely at Katrina, who was overcome with the sudden urge to run screaming from the room to prevent her employer from ascertaining anything in her expression. Instead she forced herself to remain utterly still, hardly breathing for all she feared she would give away.

Finally after what seemed ages Lady Tesh sighed, her gaze dropping to Freya, who was already snoring softly at her side.

"If that is the way you wish to have things, then I must respect your wishes. You may go."

Exhaling shakily, Katrina bobbed into a quick curtsy and hurried for the door. But Lady Tesh was not quite through.

"Just know, my dear," she said to Katrina's retreating back, "that you don't have to settle for a loveless union. You deserve all the happiness in the world."

But did she really? After all the trouble she had caused, after all the heartache that came part and parcel with her, did she deserve to have a happily-ever-after?

And truly, she could never claim that for herself even if she wanted to, considering the one man she had ever loved, the one man she *could* ever love, was set to marry another.

Love. That word should surprise her, yet it didn't. She had been well on the way to that emotion where Sebastian was concerned four years ago. He was so altered, no longer the man from her memories, one would think that any romantic inclinations she'd had for him would have died out.

But they hadn't. No, the more she had seen of the man he had become, the more she had come to care for him. He was no longer merely a bright and shining personality without a care in the world but a person of true depth, who had been through the fire of grief and hardship and come out the other side a better man for it. He had paid for his father's sins with interest, was doing everything he could to save his family and the people who relied upon him, had attempted to make her believe that she was worthy of respect.

And she could never be with him.

A grief overwhelming and absolute crashed over her head, a massive wave that stole her very breath and threatened to drown her. Needing to escape, Katrina mumbled something unintelligible and fled Lady Tesh's room. But once she was out in the dim, quiet hallway, the feeling did not diminish. No, it only grew, as undeniable as the tide. She wrapped her arms about her middle, as if to hold the fractured pieces of herself together in the turbulent storm of her emotions. She had to get to her room. Mouse was there, waiting for her. She would climb beneath the covers with her faithful pet and hug him tight and cry into his fur. And by morning things would not look so dire. Surely in the bright light of day she would be able to swim up toward the surface of despair she was drowning in and find a solution to her current problems. There was hope somewhere. There had to be.

But as she made for the small room that abutted Lady Tesh's, her slippers silent on the plush runner, she knew she was fooling herself. Mr. Young had been her last hope. There was no one else on Synne who would even consider taking her on as a wife, no one who could repair her shredded reputation and ensure that those she cared for were no longer harmed by their association with her.

A door down the hall suddenly opened, the sound of low male conversation reaching her. And then Sebastian's valet emerged, closing the door behind him. She watched him, numb, as he made his way down the hall and disappeared from view. And then...silence. And still she stood there, staring at Sebastian's door.

Sebastian. Anger trailed under her skin, at all she had lost, at all she would never have, made all the more potent for her newly realized feelings for him. It was a cleansing emotion, banishing the hopeless grief, and she relentlessly fed it.

Before she knew what she was doing, she was stalking down the hall, making her unerring way for Sebastian's room. Without pausing, she grasped the latch and threw the door wide.

Sebastian, standing at the dark window in his trousers and nothing else, did not even turn, "I told you, Harris, I don't require you any more tonight," he said, his voice weary.

"It is not Harris," Katrina said, closing the door behind her.

He spun about, his mouth dropping as he took her in. "Katrina, what in the blazes—?"

But Katrina hardly heard a word he said. Her entire focus snagged on the broad width of his bare chest, and there it stayed. She had imagined him undressed, of course—how could she not, as finely formed and impressive a man as he was?

But in all her daydreams—and nighttime dreams—she had never once guessed that his clothes were hiding something so beautiful. And arousing, if she was being completely honest. Even in her agitated state, she could not deny that the sight of his chest, powerfully corded with muscle, with its fine dusting of dark hair that trailed down to his flat abdomen and into the band of his trousers, all illuminated in the golden glow of the low fire, had her body reacting in the most base and primal way.

But she had not come here to ogle his attributes. She paused. Though, now that she thought of it, she truly didn't know why she had come here in the first place. All she had known at the time was she had needed to be with him.

While she stared silently at Sebastian, trying to understand what exactly it was she wanted, however, the shock on his face melted away, to be replaced by a regret so potent she was surprised she could not taste it in the air.

"Ah, God, Katrina," he said, running a hand through his hair. "I am so sorry about what happened this afternoon. I will not make excuses for my part in it. But know I never meant for you to be hurt."

"I know," she replied quietly. And she did know. Looking back on that moment, recalling the way Sebastian had stepped back from Mr. Young and lowered his head in a kind of defeat, it was all too obvious he had been attempting to make good on his promise to her. And he had not inserted himself into her conversation with the other man, remaining in the background, trusting her to do what she felt she needed to. Not until Mr. Young had insulted her beyond reason and declared there would never be anything between them did Sebastian come forward to defend her. And a glorious defense it had been.

Sebastian, however, did not seem to hear her.

"I should not have engaged in conversation with him at all," he continued. "I was ready to walk away. But then he brought up Mouse, and separating you from him—" His voice cracked, taking the words with it, and he closed his eyes, the muscles of his jaw working.

Mouse. She thought of her pet, safe in her room, and Mr. Young's cruelty came rushing back to her. She had been prepared to give up a good many things by marrying: her autonomy; her independence; her spirit.

But never had she thought any man would force her to give up her pet, the one creature who had been there for her when she feared her brother would die, who had followed her from her exile in London to that horrible cottage with her aunt, who had comforted her when her heart had nearly broken from Francis refusing to acknowledge her, who had remained by her side when she had been forced to come to the Isle to work to save herself from complete destitution.

Worse than that, however, had been Mr. Young's readiness to not only separate Katrina from Mouse, but to dispose of him. He would have readily killed her pet. And she might not have known until it was too late.

It was the first time she truly acknowledged just how close she had been to losing Mouse. Though reason told her she did not have to worry about losing him any longer, that did not stop panic from saturating every muscle in her body. She had not realized she had swayed on her feet until Sebastian was at her side. His hands gripped tight to her arms, drawing her flush against him.

"Katrina, are you well?"

His scent enveloped her, that wonderful smell of pine and soap and memories. Even more potent, the heat of him seeped into her, right down to the bone, making her realize just how chilled she had become. His skin was smooth under her palms where they rested on his sides, and she ached to trace the lines of muscles, to use the sensitive pads of her fingers to discover every inch of him until he was as familiar to her as her own body was.

It was in that moment, with their bodies pressed together, that she knew why she'd come to him tonight. And what she needed from him.

"You've no need to apologize, Sebastian," she whispered, lowering her head and rubbing her cheek to his chest.

He shuddered, his skin jumping under her touch, even as he pulled her closer. "What have I told you about respecting yourself when people apologize," he rasped, an attempt at humor, before he exhaled heavily. "I deserve your censure, not your kindness. I should have ignored Young."

"Yes, you should have," she said. "And you will be happy to know I am angry at you for the small part you played in all of it."

She raised her head and looked up into his tortured eyes. "But I also know you kept your promise to me." Her lips quirked. "However fumbling it was."

But there was no answering humor in his gaze. If anything, he appeared more miserable. "I ruined your last chance at respectability."

"No," she replied with firmness and certainty, "I ruined it myself. And I would do it again if it meant protecting Mouse."

His eyes told her he didn't believe her, that he still felt as if he were the one to blame. But Katrina felt a certain peace in her decision to stand up to Mr. Young that afternoon. Yes, her life was in shambles with no discernible way to dig herself free of the rubble. Yes, she had lost so much, a chance for a future with this man included. And she was in danger of losing even more.

But here, in this moment, in Sebastian's arms, she could forget for a time all that loss and grief. She could pretend, just for one night, that she had everything she had ever wanted.

She pressed closer to him until they were flush from breast to knee. His eyes flared wide.

"Kiss me, Sebastian," she whispered.

His sucked in a sharp breath, the dim firelight catching in the gray depths of his eyes, transforming them from regretful to shocked to hot with desire in the space of a single heartbeat. But though his arms tightened about her, he shook his head in a desperate denial.

"I can't, Katrina."

A devil perched on her shoulder then, brought on by a sudden recklessness, and she found herself asking, "Don't you wish to?"

"What?" He gaped at her. "You cannot possibly ask that."

But her moment of devilish teasing passed as swiftly as it had come. She reached up with gentle fingers to trace the tortured lines that scored his face. He drew in a shuddering breath, his eyes burning into hers.

"I know there is not a chance of a future for us, Sebastian," she said, trying and failing to ignore the slash of pain in her chest at the thought.

But she would not focus on that now. No, right now was for them, no matter what the future held.

"That does not mean we cannot embrace the small amount of time we have together." She cupped his cheek, reveling in the slight roughness beneath her palm, at the way he trembled beneath her touch, proof he was as affected as she. "Please, Sebastian. Kiss me—"

Before the words were out of her mouth he groaned, his mouth coming down on hers. She opened her mouth eagerly, meeting his tongue with hers, tightening her arms about him until not even a breath of space separated them. This was what she needed, what she had dreamed of, this falling into sensation, giving herself up to a joy so potent it sang from her every nerve. A glorious moment that would warm her for years to come.

His hands, those wonderfully strong, capable hands, kneaded into the muscles of her back, bunched into the fabric of her gown. She arched her back, a silent plea for more, even as her hands roamed up his sides and over his bare chest to twine about his neck. She could not get close enough to him. No matter how she pressed into him, no matter how tightly he held her, it was not enough. She needed more.

"Sebastian," she gasped as she tore her mouth free. She

pressed her lips to his chest, trailing a path with her tongue over his skin. He trembled under her touch, a rough sound escaping his lips. "Sebastian, I need you."

"You have me," he replied hoarsely, his hands tangling in her hair, sending locks tumbling about her shoulders. "You have all of me."

For tonight only, a cruel part of her mind whispered. She hastily shut it up tight. She would not allow reason to diminish this time with him. Tonight he was hers. And she was his.

Though her heart would remain with him for so much longer than this one stolen night.

His skin was slightly salty, and so very warm, and she reveled in the feel of him beneath her mouth. His muscles bunched and twitched beneath her greedy fingers as she skimmed over his abdomen, memorizing each delicious inch of him. When she reached the fall of his trousers, however, suddenly his hands were on hers, stopping them.

"Katrina," he rasped, his voice agonized in the quiet of the room.

She raised her head, gazing up at him, knowing her love for him shone from her eyes and not caring. "I want you to love me, Sebastian," she whispered.

But he was shaking his head. "You don't know what you're asking."

"I do." She smiled, for she had never been so sure of anything in her life. There was no feeling of wrongness in what she wished to do with Sebastian. In fact, nothing in her life had ever felt so right. She loved him. And however dire or heartbreaking her future may be, she knew she would never regret claiming a night with him.

"I do know what I'm asking," she repeated. She cupped

his cheek with her palm, feeling his jaw clench beneath her touch, proof of his tightly held control. "I want you, Sebastian. I want to have one beautiful night with you, to forget everything and everyone else. I want to pretend, just for a few hours, that all is right with the world, that I belong to you and you alone."

He closed his eyes and groaned, a tortured sound, turning his head and pressing a desperate kiss to her palm. When he looked back at her, there were tears glistening in his eyes, shining like precious diamonds in the low firelight.

"Yes," he breathed, his gaze trailing over her face, the most precious caress. "For just tonight, you are mine. And I am yours."

And then his mouth was back on hers, more desperate this time. How was it, she wondered blearily as their lips and tongues clashed and their hands roamed over one another's bodies, that a person could feel equal parts joy and heartbreak? That one could simultaneously get everything one had ever wanted while knowing everything one ever dreaded was soon to come?

But she would not focus on the heartbreak of their inevitable parting. No, tonight was for joy, and coming together. And love. For she would never love another as much as she did this man, the other half of her.

Their desperate fingers made quick work of their clothes as they blindly stumbled toward the bed, leaving a trail in their wake: first her gown, then her corset, then his trousers. Before they tumbled to the mattress, however, Sebastian stopped and pulled back. For a moment she feared he had come to his senses and would put a stop to this once and for all.

But no, there was only gentleness and desire in his eyes as he drank her in. Then he reached down, grasping the hem of her chemise, and pulled it up and over her head.

She should perhaps feel shy, or ashamed, or scandalous as his eyes roved over her naked body. But as his gaze turned hot and his breath quickened, she felt only pride that he desired her.

"You are beautiful," he whispered, stepping closer, his hands skimming up her torso, light as a butterfly wing, trailing over her rib cage, along the side of her breast. She held her breath, her eyes growing heavy and her legs going weak until, finally, he cupped her breast in his palm. A low moan escaped her lips as his thumb grazed her nipple and a shaft of pure fire blossomed between her legs.

"No, you are more than beautiful," he rasped, his other arm coming around her to bring her close. "You are exquisite." And then he dipped his head, taking her nipple in his mouth.

Katrina arched her back over his supporting arm, the only thing keeping her upright even as her fingers dove into the soft, dark waves of his hair, holding his head prisoner against her breast. She bit her lip to hold back the cry that rose up in her. Dear God, she had never expected something like this. She had read of the sensations that the human body could feel in the throes of passion, of course, the pamphlets and books that Lady Tesh had supplied to the Quayside having given her a fairly comprehensive idea of what could occur between two people in bed. And Bronwyn's recounting of her intimate moments with her husband, Ash, as minimal and evasive as those were, had made her aware that the sexual act between two people who truly loved one another could be indescribably beautiful.

But she had never in her life imagined this was possible, this ecstasy that was quickly stealing through her body, filling her with both a heady languidness and a frantic need. And then he lifted her in his arms and lowered her to the bed, quickly divesting himself of his smalls before coming down over her, and she knew this was only the beginning.

* * *

At the feel of her bare skin against his, so damn silky and smooth, Sebastian shuddered. Dear God, she was heaven in his arms. He had never in his life experienced something so exquisitely beautiful. Was this what love did then? Did it bring a closeness previously unimaginable, making it seem as if his heart beating against her own was somehow in synch, that they were of one mind, one heart?

When her legs parted to accommodate his hips, however, he lost all ability to think coherently. Ah, yes, this was heaven, right here on earth.

"Katrina," he managed, his lips brushing hers, taking her rapid breath into his lungs before trailing his mouth over her cheek to the long, arching column of her throat. "Katrina, what you do to me."

But as her sweet voice breathed his name, filling his heart, he also knew he had to hold onto a semblance of reason. She was upset and hurting. He could not take advantage of her.

And she was not his to claim.

Pulling back, he gazed down into her flushed face. Which may have been a monumental mistake. With her kiss-bruised lips and pale hair in a tumbled halo about her head, she was so beautiful his chest ached.

And then she opened those glorious eyes of hers, the clear blue of them filled with so much love and trust he nearly fell back into the spell of her without a second thought.

But her future happiness was too important to him. He cared too much for her to see her have even a moment's regret from this.

No, he more than cared for her. He loved her, with his entire body and soul.

"Katrina," he murmured, smoothing a lock of hair back from her cheek, "we have to stop. We cannot do this. For once it is done, there is no coming back from it."

Which should have been like ice water to their passions. Surely now she would see the folly of their actions and put a stop to it once and for all. Which made him want to simultaneously weep and curse.

But she did not appear the least bit confused or horrified by what they were about to do. No, her eyes were clear and certain as they gazed into his.

"I know there is no future for us, Sebastian," she murmured sadly, cupping his cheek. "But I also know that, no matter where our futures lead us, I want this memory with you to carry with me always. I want these few hours of happiness with you to take with me. Because I love you, so very much."

His breath caught in his throat, his eyes burning, joy and grief swirling like a maelstrom in his chest. "Don't say that," he pleaded. "You cannot love me."

"Of course I can," she declared, with a simplicity that almost made him believe he was worthy of her love, "You are a good man, Sebastian, much more than you may believe."

The sadness in her eyes deepened, making them well

with tears until they spilled over, down her temples into her hair. "Both of us have been dealt a cruel fate through no fault of our own," she whispered. "Don't we deserve to claim a small bit of joy? Even if it's just for one night?"

And in her arms, it made perfect sense. Why couldn't they be selfish for one night, to take instead of give? To claim happiness, however fleeting?

"Yes," he managed through a throat thick with unshed tears. "One night, together."

She smiled, and it was as if the sun emerged from behind a dark gray cloud. "Together," she whispered before dragging his head down to hers.

It was a promise, as surely as any vows that could be spoken. But instead of vows for a future together, it was a vow to claim the here and now. To revel in what little time they could have together with no regrets. It was like a key, unlocking them from any inhibitions, any doubt. His hands roamed the silky curves of her body, reveling in the exquisite softness of her skin, even as his lips tangled with hers. But he needed to taste more of her. He needed to explore every inch of her until he had her memorized, so he could remember this achingly beautiful moment in the long, lonely years to come.

He trailed his mouth over her cheek to her neck, bathing her with hungry kisses. Soft, eager sounds escaped from her full lips, making his body hard with need. He wanted her, so badly it was nearly all consuming. But he refused to let her leave his bed without giving her every bit of himself and more. And so he trailed his mouth lower, to the sweet mounds of her breasts, down the slight roundness of her stomach, until he was settled between her trembling thighs.

"Sebastian."

He looked up the glorious expanse of her body to find her gazing down at him. But there was no fear or surprise or embarrassment in her eyes. Only heat, and desire, and a trust that he felt down to his soul.

"Will you let me taste you, Katrina?" he whispered, his breath fanning the thatch of soft, pale curls at the juncture of her thighs.

She gasped, her mouth falling open. But her eyes never left his as she nodded.

He did not need further invitation. He was hungry for her, his heart thumping as he breathed in the scent of her. And then his mouth was on her, taking her in, dragging his tongue over her, drinking in the sweetness of her essence. She writhed under his touch, gasps and moans and small cries escaping her lips. He was about to raise his head to make certain she was well, but suddenly her hands were on his head, holding him in place. Chuckling, letting the vibration of the sound caress her, he gladly renewed his efforts and more. With infinite care he eased one finger into her tight depths. Her heat surrounded him, her inner muscles gripping him greedily, and he nearly spent himself right there on the sheets like a green boy.

But he would let nothing distract him from giving her everything he could. Moving his finger in and out of her, his tongue and lips loving the small bud of her pleasure, he focused entirely on the response of her body. Each whimper and moan, each twitch of muscle, each clench of her fingers in his hair was as potent as any aphrodisiac. And when she began to rock against his mouth, when her thighs began to tremble on each side of his head, when her soft cries became a low keening, he knew she was close. Moving faster, faster, he brought her to the pinnacle and over, until she shattered under his mouth.

Before the tremors of pleasure had passed through her body he was beside her, pulling her into his arms, dragging her close. She burrowed into his embrace, her arms coming about his waist.

"Sebastian," she gasped, her labored breath fanning across his chest. "My God, I never imagined..."

"I know," he murmured into the crown of her hair. "I never imagined, either." Which was all too true. How was it possible he felt this utter contentment and closeness? Was he hard as a rod of steel? Hell yes. Did he ache to sink into her and lose himself in her? Also, yes.

But her climaxing under his mouth had been the single most amazing thing he had ever experienced.

* * *

That was the single most amazing thing she had ever experienced. And as Katrina lay in Sebastian's arms, their hearts pounding in time to one another's, their ragged breaths mingling in the dark quiet of the room, she knew she wanted more. So much more.

Rising up on one elbow, she gazed down at him, her hand cupping his cheek. "I want to feel you inside me, Sebastian," she murmured.

His manhood, which had been hard before, twitched against her leg. He grasped her hand to his face, the fire in his eyes flaring, becoming an inferno. And then his hand moved to the back of her head, pulling her down for a searing kiss that had desire pooling once more in her belly, made all the more potent as she tasted herself on his tongue. In a moment she was beneath him, and he was settling between her legs, and the dull tip of him was pressing to her core.

"Katrina," he murmured thickly.

She smiled up at him. "I love you, Sebastian."

He exhaled, his eyes searching hers, his heart in his eyes. She did not expect him to say it back. In fact, she did not want him to, knowing how it must destroy him, considering what his future responsibilities had to be.

But she saw the love in his eyes, felt it straight down to her heart.

He took her lips again, a kiss full of so much tenderness it brought tears to her eyes. And then he pushed inside her.

Inch by slow inch he filled her, infinitely careful as her body adjusted to him. Finally he was buried to the hilt. Pulling back, he looked down at her. "Are you well, Katrina?"

But Katrina, who had quickly become consumed once more at the feel of him inside her, was beyond words. In answer she wrapped her legs about his hips, drawing him in even deeper.

"Please, Sebastian," she begged.

It was as if her words had snapped some invisible chain within him that had been holding him back. He groaned, his mouth crashing down on hers, even as his hips began to move, drawing him out of her, then within, his pace increasing, the tension building. Her body responded, electricity sizzling along her skin and focusing on that place where their bodies met, a current of energy snapping and sizzling, growing in brilliance until, in a burst of light, she came apart in his arms.

With a growl he pulled out of her before, with a shout muffled in her shoulder, he spent himself in the sheets. Then she was back in his arms, his grip so tight on her it felt as if he would never let her go.

And for one shining moment, Katrina let herself believe that was true.

Chapter 18

Katrina didn't know what had made her think that one night with Sebastian would ever be enough. Especially as every time she looked at him in the day following, she was reminded of the things he had done to her, how he'd made her body sing...and how very right it had felt to give herself to the man she loved.

And if the heated glances and small smiles he kept sending her way were any indication, he was thinking of last night as well. Though, of course, not the love part. Her buoyant mood stumbled a bit at that. Yes, it was true she had been unable to hold her own emotions back. It had seemed imperative last night that she let him know that her decision to be with him was no idle thing. But though she had seen his affection for her in his eyes, though she suspected he might love her in return, she did not want him to declare himself to her and have that burden on his soul. If he was to save the dukedom, he could not marry her, someone who had nothing to her name but an overlarge dog and a soiled reputation.

The reminder of that last item threatened to make her mood crumble to dust completely. Her life was being held together by nothing but spiderwebs and wishes as it was; any misstep on her part would destroy her and everyone who loved her.

But as her heart twisted in her chest at the thought of never again experiencing the joy of being with him, she found herself wondering a bit desperately what one more day of bliss could hurt in the grand scheme of things. Could she be selfish for one more day? To claim a sliver more of happiness? If the way he was looking at her was any indication, over the rim of his teacup and with the most meltingly delicious heat in his gray eyes, he was wondering the exact same thing.

But Lady Tesh was speaking. And if Katrina did not want her employer to suspect anything between her and Sebastian, she had best pay attention.

"I do hope you do not grow tired of so much nature, Mr. Bridling," Lady Tesh said, referring to their planned excursion to the Elven Pools for the following day. She fed a small piece of biscuit to Freya. "I know it is not like the pursuits you have become used to in London. But as you know, Synne is a much quieter place, and so what we can offer is limited in that regard."

"Not at all," Mr. Bridling said with a wide smile. "It is refreshing. I vow, I would be more than happy to remain here on the Isle all my days. Especially as it has provided me the chance to get to become acquainted with such lovely people." Here he turned and gazed at Katrina, his expression warm.

She blushed, inclining her head. But her attention was not snagged for long, quickly drifting, her gaze finding Sebastian. He looked so utterly delicious this afternoon, the claret color of his jacket bringing out faint auburn highlights in his hair—hair she had gripped tight last night as he loved between her legs with his mouth. Which, of course, made her attention shift to said mouth. He took a bite from a small sandwich just then, his tongue sweeping out to catch a crumb from his lips in an erotic swipe. A small, needy sound rose up in her chest before she could call it back.

Lady Tesh looked at her in alarm. "Miss Denby, are you quite well?"

Face hot, Katrina could not bring herself to meet her employer's eyes. Surely that woman would see the truth branded across her face, proof of just where her mind had gone. Instead she nodded jerkily and, bringing her hand to her mouth, coughed.

"Forgive me," she croaked. "I choked on a bit of biscuit."

Which really was the most ridiculous excuse she could have come up with, considering Katrina had not even partaken of the biscuits. But Lady Tesh, blessedly, seemed to take her at her word. Or, at least, she did not verbally accuse her of lying.

"Hmm, is that so?" Lady Tesh murmured. "Well, refresh your tea then, girl. I can't stand to hear you coughing. It grates on my nerves."

Inclining her head, Katrina did as she was told, praying no one saw how her hands shook as she lifted the silver teapot. A prayer that was quickly proven ineffective as she raised her eyes to Sebastian and saw the small, crooked smile on his lips.

But she could not feel embarrassment. No, her chest was too warm for that unwelcome emotion, her heart pounding too wildly, the hummingbirds that had apparently taken perch in her stomach fluttering too madly. Which was only exacerbated as he scratched Mouse behind the ear and the dog gazed up at him in adoration. If she had not already been in love, that sight right there, of him showing her beloved pet such affection, would have done it for her. She heaved a small, happy sigh.

"Truly, Miss Denby," Lady Tesh barked, shattering the moment, "one would think you are coming down with something. I do hope you are not growing ill."

Clearing her throat and tearing her gaze from the heart-warming sight of Sebastian and Mouse leaning against one another, Katrina hastily responded, "Of course not, my lady. I have never been better."

"Perhaps you simply need some air," the woman muttered.

As if on cue, Freya rose and stretched before hopping down from her place beside Lady Tesh and trotting to the doors that led to the garden. There she paused, looking back imperiously at the gathered humans.

"Yes, Freya, that is a splendid idea," Lady Tesh said before turning back to Katrina. "Miss Denby, why don't you take the dogs out for some exercise. And Your Grace can accompany you, seeing as Mouse has taken such a liking to him."

Which was just too wonderful an offer for Katrina to refuse. She rose, Sebastian along with her, and together they walked out the garden door and into the warm early summer air. Freya trotted imperiously ahead down the path that abutted the house and toward the side lawn, glancing with disdain at Mouse as he galloped past her with glorious abandon. Not a word was said between Katrina and Sebastian as they sedately followed the canines; indeed, not even a look passed between them. Yet Katrina could not have been more aware of Sebastian if she had tried. His presence seemed to reach across the short, charged space between them, touching her physically, making her shiver with a heady anticipation.

And then she did not have to anticipate any longer. The moment they passed beneath a trellis of climbing roses and were concealed from the house Sebastian's hand was on her arm, pulling her into his embrace. She went eagerly, her arms going around his neck, her mouth opening under his. Their tongues twined, the taste of him making her eyes roll back in her head, and she moaned into his mouth even as she arched against him, a silent plea for more.

"My God, I've missed you," he rasped as he pulled back and began raining kisses down the side of her throat. "Tell me you have missed me, too."

"More than I can ever say," she whispered, her fingers diving into the soft waves of his hair. Their mingled breathing was ragged in her ear, the perfect accompaniment to the distant crash of the waves at the bottom of the cliff that ran alongside Seacliff, making her feel as if even the sea itself were in league with them.

His hands gripped her bottom, pressing her into him. "Do you feel what you do to me? I want you, so badly I can hardly breathe."

"One night was not enough," she replied. She dipped her head, kissed his ear, ran her tongue around the whorl there. He shivered under her touch, making her smile at the joy it gave her. That such a magnificent, powerful man could be affected by her was heady indeed.

"Surely one more night could not hurt," she continued, the words breathless. She ran her hands over the breadth of his shoulders, reveling at the power under the layers of his clothes even as she wished fervently that she could do away with those clothes and explore his delicious skin and corded muscles once more.

He raised his head, and the yearning in his eyes made her lose her breath entirely.

"No, one more night could not hurt," he murmured, cupping her cheek. He looked down to her lips, a ragged breath escaping his own. "Though I don't know if I can wait for tonight."

"So don't wait." She took his hand, placing it on her breast, curling his fingers over the softness there, and was rewarded with a low groan that rumbled up from his chest.

Just as he was about to speak, however, Mouse's booming woof sounded, reminding them that they were not in a private place. With one final, gentle kiss, he pulled back, that lopsided smile back in place as he gazed down at her.

"Though obviously we cannot indulge in such things here," she murmured with a smile of her own. Tugging her clothes to rights and running her fingers over her hair to check for any stray locks that might have escaped, she took the arm he offered and they started off again after the dogs.

But he was not through with her. Not by far.

"When?" he demanded hotly as they walked down the gravel path, his large hand covering her own, his thumb doing wicked things to the inside of her wrist.

A thrill went through her, and it took everything in her not to grab him by the lapels, drag him behind the hedges, and have her way with him.

"While Lady Tesh takes her nap before dinner," she whispered. "Meet me in the library."

"I'll be there," he replied, and she heard more than saw the smile in his voice, a reflection of what was in her own heart.

* * *

The planned rendezvous with Katrina was all Sebastian could think about in the hours that followed their walk in the garden. Dear God, she consumed him. *This is just temporary*, he tried telling himself, not for the first time that day.

Yet every time he thought of her, how she had responded to his touch, how she had fallen apart in his arms the night before—and how hungrily she had kissed him in the garden—he had an increasingly difficult time remembering that fact. Because he wanted more with her, so much more. In fact, he never wanted to let her go.

Marry her. God, he wanted to, so badly he ached with it. Her sweet declaration of love, so pure and certain, had unlocked something in him he had thought forever shut up, a hope for the future he had hardly dared to acknowledge. Once more he scoured his brain for a solution so he might be with her. And once more he came up empty-handed. His lines of credit with the banks were already well past their breaking point, his friendships with anyone who might be able to assist him dissolved, every property and jewel and valuable gone to creditors. Hell, he wasn't even so good at cards that he could attempt to recoup his lost fortune through gambling. Not that he would ever attempt that. Not after what his father's losses at the tables had wrought.

But there had to be something he was missing, some solution that would allow him to find happiness and love with the woman who meant everything to him without hurting everyone else he cared for in the process.

"Can you believe something so ridiculous, Ramsleigh?" Bridling said.

Sebastian, starting guiltily, looked over at the other man. They were just returning from a quick ride, and to Sebastian's dismay, he realized he had been quite thoroughly ignoring his companion. He had intended on using this time with Bridling to further his interest in Lady Paulette and distract him from his actress—but that had been before last night, and Katrina.

Katrina. He sighed dreamily, then just as quickly yanked himself back from drowning once more in thoughts of her.

"Ah, sorry about that," he replied, shifting in his saddle. "What was it you were saying?"

Luckily, Bridling did not appear as if he suspected anything was amiss. Good-natured fellow that he was, he merely smiled and rolled his eyes playfully at Sebastian's inattentiveness before explaining, "Only that Lady Tesh has got it in everyone's heads that I've made a match of it with Lady Paulette. I swear, I don't know how the dowager came up with something of that sort. Even Lady Paulette's brothers are teasing me over it."

A preternatural stillness came over Sebastian. "You don't care for Lady Paulette?" he found himself asking.

The snort that emerged from Bridling's lips only increased the unease in Sebastian's gut. "Good God, not you, too. Of course I don't care for Lady Paulette. At least, not in any way that is not pure friendship. She's a nice enough girl. But certainly not for me." He smiled, his eyes going distant. "I like a different type of woman entirely."

Sebastian stared at him, a rhythmic sound rushing in his ears. It took him some seconds to realize it was the heavy beating of his heart. "But what was all that about playing knight in shining armor?"

Bridling stared at him before exploding in laughter. "And you thought I meant Lady Paulette? Oh, you cannot be serious."

"But you rescued her," Sebastian insisted. "That night on The Promenade, from the thief."

"It was an entirely different rescue I was referring to," he said with a knowing wink.

In a moment Sebastian knew he had erred, and horribly. It had seemed obvious to him at the time, of course, that Bridling had been referring to Lady Paulette. His rescue of her from the thief had been all anyone was able to talk about, and the boy's pleasure in his newfound fame had been quite obvious.

But who could it be that had captured his interest? Who else had the boy rescued, if not Lady Paulette? Before he could quiz the boy on just who had captured his affections, however, they reached the stable yard and two grooms rushed out to take their horses from them followed quickly by a footman.

"Your Grace, Mr. Bridling," the footman said, "these letters have just arrived for you, and the messenger instructed they were to be given to you immediately."

Alarmed, Sebastian accepted his missive, quickly glancing at the return address. Cartmel? What the devil?

Bridling, however, was not so concerned at what could be the cause of such haste. Scoffing, he glared at the letter. "Typical. Father is always aiming for the dramatic to manipulate people." Nevertheless, he broke the seal and scanned the missive. The bored look on his face was quickly replaced by outrage as his eyes traveled across the paper.

"The old bastard," he spat. "He thinks he can plan out my life like he is doing to my sister's?" He crumpled the paper in his fist before, without a word, he stormed off toward the house.

Sebastian, mumbling his thanks to the footman and grooms, followed Bridling at a slower pace even as he opened his own letter. No doubt it would inform him what had upset the other man to such a degree.

To his surprise, a soiled piece of paper fell out, landing in the dirt at his feet. Frowning, he paused to pick it up—but Cartmel's sharp words on the original missive caught his eye and stopped him cold.

> *Ramsleigh,*
>
> *I have decided on a wife for the boy and shall be arriving within two days of you receiving this to see the match occurs posthaste. Make certain he is ready to take his proper place in this family, or you shall not.*
>
> *Cartmel*

Anger seethed in Sebastian. The old bastard. No wonder Bridling had been so furious. He was passionate, and a dreamer, a good-natured fellow not out to harm anyone. Why could the old man not let his son live his life? It would serve the baron right if his son cut ties with him.

Sebastian sucked in a sharp breath, stunned at not only the ferocity of his own thoughts, but also the path they had taken. He was wishing for Bridling to take a stand and live his life? What the devil was wrong with him? His whole purpose for coming to Synne with the boy was to make certain he did as his father required him to do, to forget his actress and marry a woman of the old man's choosing, to do what was expected of him.

Yet in the past fortnight he had begun to see that the boy was not just a spoiled, silly person on the cusp of manhood, not just an extension of his father, but a person in his own right with hopes and dreams. And so much like his old self that it made his chest ache.

Ah, yes, he saw it now, the ghost of who Sebastian used to be in the bit of sunshine that was Bridling. He mourned for his old self then, who had been destroyed in his father's greed. And the same thing would happen to Bridling, with Cartmel reining him in and breaking his spirit.

It was nothing out of the ordinary, of course. It happened to children every day, the forceful molding of the soul for duty and honor. Now, however, it seemed the worst kind of crime. Why the change of heart? Why had his views of familial duty changed so drastically in two short weeks?

It did not take him long, however, to know just what it had been. Or, rather, who: Katrina. These past weeks she had reminded him of who he had been before his father had died and left their family in such dire straits. He had spent the past four years trying to do what was right, what was expected. And for what? To be at the mercy of some power-hungry baron who would force his children to marry people they did not love, all for his own selfish gains? If Cartmel was in front of him right now, he would gladly punch him in the nose.

But what did he expect? It was the way things were done, wasn't it? Children sacrificing their futures for the good of their family. It was what he was doing, in setting out to marry Miss Bridling, as well as what Miss Bridling was doing in marrying him. And it was what Katrina was determined to do, though hers was not for the sake of family, but of those she loved just the same.

So much misery and heartache. And for what? So honor and reputation and fortunes were protected? What good were those things, what good was any of it, if one did not have love?

He cursed low, remembering Katrina's declarations of love the night before. And he had never told her how he felt. He had ached to. Oh, how he had ached to. But something had held him back. He'd thought it was to protect her, to keep her heart from breaking even more when they inevitably parted. And to lessen the guilt he would feel in betraying Miss Bridling by marrying her when his heart openly belonged to another.

But that had only been a portion of it. In truth, he had been protecting himself as well. Somewhere inside of himself he had believed that if he never told her how he felt, he could shield himself from pain and guilt down the road. But there would be no avoiding the guilt of marrying a woman when his heart could never be hers. Nor could he ever escape the pain of being forever separated from that one person who had come to mean everything to him.

And in a moment he knew: he had to tell Katrina how he felt, before it was too late.

Fire sparked in his gut. What he would do after that, he didn't have a damn clue. But he had to tell her, had to let her know that her love was not one-sided, that he felt just the same. And then maybe they could find a solution to their futures, together.

As he made to stride off for the house and Katrina, however, his boot kicked up something pale in the gravel path. He stared down at it blankly. Ah, yes, the piece of paper from Cartmel's missive. No doubt it was simply more instructions, more threats, a way to make certain Sebastian did his bidding. He glared down at it, tempted to crush it under his heel. But at the last second he bent and picked it up, opening it.

His stomach dropped. There, in his father's familiar shaky scrawl, was a promise of payment of the exorbitant sum of one thousand pounds. And in the corner, in sharp contrast, fresh ink.

Paid in full by Conrad Bridling, Lord Cartmel.

Nausea roiled in his stomach as he stared down at that small notation. He had thought he had managed to track down each and every one of his father's creditors. Yet there were still some out there, no doubt waiting in the wings like the vultures they were. There truly was no end in sight.

Exhaustion saturated every inch of him, and he ran a hand over his face as the fire that had begun to burn so bright in his belly sputtered and went out. For a moment, a single shining moment, he had thought he might be able to have everything he had ever dreamed of. He had thought he might find a way to overcome all the strife that had been piled at his feet and claim happiness and love for himself with Katrina.

He saw now that had been a mere fevered dream. He looked at Seacliff, imagining Katrina within those stone walls, about to leave Lady Tesh to her nap as she must be right now, descending the main stairs to the library to wait for him, and his heart fractured. As much as he wanted to spend one more afternoon and evening in her arms, as much as he wanted to lose himself in her for just a short while, to forget all that was expected of him, he knew he could not. It was not fair to him, or to Miss Bridling, who was expecting his suit any day now. And it was most certainly not fair to Katrina, who had declared herself to him so sweetly the night before, who looked at him with such trust in her eyes. Who was suffering so deeply from a reputation not of her own making and was trying everything in her power to repair it and protect those she loved.

No, he had to end things with her now. Setting his jaw, he started off for Seacliff. The only question now was, How irreparable would the damage be to both their hearts?

Chapter 19

*T*he time Katrina spent waiting in the library for Sebastian to arrive seemed to tick by as if the clock on the mantel had been submerged in treacle. And how should she spend that time? Not in reading, that was certain. Though she was in a library, the thought of trying to focus on written words made her want to pull her hair out. No, Katrina was mentally incapable of doing anything of the sort. Instead she nervously moved about the room, trying to find the perfect position to be in when Sebastian finally arrived. Should she be by the window, looking out at the garden, letting the late afternoon sun caress her features? Should she perch on a chair and pretend to read? Should she recline on the settee, aiming for a seductive pose?

In the end it was all for nothing. As the door opened she was nervously pacing the carpet before the hearth, no doubt looking as manic as any one person could be.

But that all faded away when she turned to look at Sebastian. He was still wearing his riding clothes, the pale breeches and green-tailed frock coat and riding boots making him look incredibly dashing. Her breath stalled in her chest as she took him in. "Sebastian," she breathed.

Before she could move forward and into his arms, however, the solemn expression in his eyes made her feet freeze to the floor. Alarm bells pealed in her head, discordant and jarring. Something was wrong.

And then he spoke her name, and his mournful tone was like a nail in a coffin.

"Katrina."

She stared at him across the expanse of carpet, afraid to ask what had occurred, knowing it would be the end of whatever they had briefly shared. But nothing was going to stop the wheels of time from turning, no matter how she might wish it otherwise.

"I've heard from Miss Bridling's father. He'll be arriving on Synne in the next couple days."

Miss Bridling. Of course. She swallowed hard, hugging her arms about her middle. How had she forgotten about Miss Bridling, and what she was to Sebastian?

But that did not take her long to figure out: she was in love with Sebastian, had given herself to him. Who in their right mind would wish to think of the man's future wife at a time like that?

"I . . . see," she managed.

"I did not expect it," he continued, his voice sounding muffled, as if there were cotton in her ears. "I believed Bridling and I were to remain on Synne for perhaps a week or two more and then return to London. But it seems the baron has other plans."

"You truly don't need to explain it to me, Your Grace," she mumbled. Legs shaking so violently she feared she would crumple on the spot, she sank down into the closest chair, fingers gripping tight to the arms. Nonetheless she tried for an uncaring smile as she looked his way. Or, rather, looked at his left ear, because there was no way she was going to be able to look him in the eye, not if she wanted to retain even an ounce of her fragile composure.

"This is for the best," she continued, her voice reed thin. "We both have so much at stake, after all, and each moment spent in...intimacy threatens everything we are working for. In fact," she continued a bit louder, seemingly unable to stop the word vomit escaping from her lips, "I was coming here to tell you it would be best if we were to stop all further private meetings. I need to repair my reputation, not shatter it into a million pieces. I am so very happy we're of the same mind. It makes it so much easier for all involved don't you agree—?"

He was kneeling before her in a moment. "I am sorry, Katrina," he murmured in that same tender voice she had come to love, taking her hand in his. Her fingers must be incredibly chilled, for his fingers were like fire wrapped about her own.

She swallowed hard, looking down at their joined fingers, trying not to cry. "You've nothing to be sorry for, truly."

"But I do," he murmured. "You deserve so much better than this."

"No, I don't," Katrina whispered bitterly without meaning to.

He sucked in a sharp breath. Then his finger hooked under her chin, raising her gaze to his. And the pain in his eyes nearly broke her.

"You do, Katrina," he murmured hoarsely. "You deserve everything that is fine and good in life."

But she only shook her head. He could repeat those same words over and over until his face turned blue, and she would never believe them.

"Katrina," he breathed, the sound the same low, mournful lowing as the wind, his thumb rubbing against her jaw. The ache in her chest spread, until it nearly engulfed her. How she longed to lean into his touch, to close her eyes, to raise her lips to his.

But no, they could never indulge in something of that sort, ever again.

Jerking back from his touch, she dropped her gaze again. But not before she saw the flash of grief in his eyes. And she very nearly broke.

Now, however, was not the time to lose her composure. No, she could not do that, not until she was alone, where she might indulge her volatile emotions to her heart's content.

"If you don't mind, I actually need to return to my duties," she said in as neutral a tone as she could manage, pushing to standing so quickly that Sebastian nearly lost his balance attempting to get out of her way. She moved to the desk in the corner, riffling through the papers there, hoping she looked like she actually knew what she was doing, and not what she was actually doing, which was trying her hardest not to burst into tears.

"Lady Tesh has asked that I find something new to read to her," she continued. "I fear she grows bored of the latest Sarah Burney and is looking for something new and exciting. I promised her I would locate her copies of the *Gaia Review and Repository* so we might catch up on S. L. Keys's serial. It's all the rage, you know. It fairly oozes intrigue and excitement. Forbidden romance; betrayal; mystery and adventure. But I am rambling, aren't I? And I don't have time to ramble. Truly, I don't have time for any further conversation, as you can imagine. Lady Tesh can be demanding. Not that I mind in the least. It is a joy to work for her. But I really must ask that you leave so I might do my job. You understand."

"Of course," Sebastian murmured. Out of the corner of her eye she saw him pause before finally heading for the door. She held her breath, trying to ignore the sharp pain in her chest as he reached for the latch.

Instead of heading out into the hall and leaving her in peace, however, he turned back to her.

"I just want you to be happy, Katrina. No matter what path your life takes, I just want you to be happy."

And then he was out the door, closing it softly behind him.

Katrina stood behind the desk, staring at that door, numb inside and out. The sound of his boots on the hall floor faded, silence descending around her like a wet cloak, the only sound the incessant ticking of the mantel clock, and still she did not move. She had been a fool, a damn fool. Not for giving so much of herself to Sebastian. No, she could never regret being with him, loving him, so completely.

But she had been a fool to think she could get past it so easily, that she would be able to put it behind her and forget.

Drawing in a shaky breath, she made her own way toward the door. She would retire to her room for the next hour and allow herself to fall apart and soak in her grief. And when that hour was through, she would do what she always did: she would pick herself up and put herself back together and move forward.

* * *

By the following afternoon, however, Katrina was coming to the sobering realization that moving forward would be much more difficult than she had hoped.

Not that she had thought it would be a simple walk in the park. None of the upheavals in her life had been easy to move on from, after all. But living, for however short a time, under the same roof as Sebastian was taking its toll on her. Especially when he stood in a beam of sunshine as he was just across the drive with Mouse and Mr. Bridling, the afternoon light making the faint auburn highlights in his hair glow and showcasing the impressive breadth of his shoulders. Despite herself, she let out a forlorn little exhale.

"Sighing again, eh, Miss Denby?" Lady Tesh murmured.

"My apologies, my lady," Katrina replied, jerking her gaze from Sebastian as she secured Freya more comfortably in her arms—arms that were beginning to ache for how long she had been holding the dog. They had been standing in the drive for an inordinately long time, waiting for their guests so they could depart for the Elven Pools. While Lady Tesh could not accompany them—the path to reach the pools was too difficult for the dowager to access—she had insisted on being present to see them off. Even Katrina was to join in on the outing, at the dowager's insistence. No matter how desperately she had tried to get out of it after her break with Sebastian the day before.

But the time to depart had come and gone some half hour past, and still there was no sign of the Mishras, Lady Paulette and her brothers, or Honoria and her relations. "I was simply wondering where the others were," Katrina finished.

From the deep divot between the dowager's brows as she turned to scan the empty drive, it was obvious she was wondering that very same thing. But besides the faint jangle of tackle from Lady Tesh's waiting carriages, the low rumble of male voices as Sebastian and Mr. Bridling spoke, and the distant roar of waves crashing against the cliffs below the house, there was not a sound.

"Mayhap the invitations did not have the correct time?" Katrina ventured. Though even she was not consoled by such a thought. Lady Tesh was frighteningly competent and thorough; she would not have made a mistake of that magnitude.

"Perhaps," the dowager replied unconvincingly. "Mr. Bridling," she called. "Did your friends say anything when you saw them last night, some indication that they would not join us today?"

That man, who had been talking in a low voice to Sebastian, tension bracketing his mouth, appeared not to hear the dowager at first. His mood had seemed to change since yesterday afternoon, his typical bright cheerfulness having turned to melancholy. At Katrina's side, Lady Tesh called out again, repeating her question. Mr. Bridling started, looking the dowager's way before striding across the drive toward them. "My apologies, my lady. I did not hear you at first. No, they did not say a word. They seemed quite eager for the excursion, in fact."

"Hmm, peculiar," the dowager murmured.

Sebastian approached, and it took every bit of Katrina's willpower not to look his way. "If you would like, I can ride into town. Lord Wesley and Lord Martin and Lady Paulette are staying at a house in Knighthead Crescent; I can visit there first."

Before Lady Tesh could answer, however, a sudden rhythmic thundering sounded from the road leading to Seacliff. Had their guests arrived then? But it did not take long to recognize that this was not some cart and pony, or a carriage, or even a group of riders. No, this was one single rider approaching.

And then the visitor cleared the tree line, and Katrina's stomach dropped.

"Mr. Gadfeld," Katrina breathed through a throat gone tight with anxiety. She had not seen Honoria's father since before the scandal, when he had begun to openly smear her reputation to all and sundry. Hands suddenly shaking, she quickly deposited Freya on the ground before reaching for Mouse as, no doubt sensing her anxiety, he moved close to her and pressed into her side.

"What in God's name is the vicar doing here?" Lady Tesh asked.

It seemed, however, that Mr. Gadfeld was not going to make them wonder for long. "Lady Tesh," he called out as he pulled his horse to a stop and swung down from the saddle. "you may cease your waiting, for no one is coming. I have made certain to warn the guardians of each of the young people you have been coercing to join you just what a damaging influence you are having on them."

"Mr. Gadfeld," Lady Tesh said, her voice shaking in her outrage, "you had no right. No right at all."

"I had every right," the man shot back as he approached

the dowager, his steps angry on the gravel drive. "Just what do you think you are about encouraging my girls to lie to me?"

Before the man could reach Lady Tesh, however, Sebastian was there, stepping between them. "Forgive me, sir," he said, his calm tone doing nothing to hide the danger roiling beneath the surface, "but I don't believe we have been introduced. I am Sebastian Thorne, Duke of Ramsleigh, and this gentleman here is Mr. Harlow Bridling." Here he motioned to Mr. Bridling, who, after his initial moment of alarm, stepped up beside Sebastian to form a sort of wall before the vicar.

"We are guests of Lady Tesh," Sebastian continued, crossing his arms over his chest. "And as such, we demand you treat the dowager viscountess with all the respect she is warranted."

But Mr. Gadfeld, it seemed, was too outraged to take heed of the warning in Sebastian's voice. "I shall give her respect when she earns it. And coercing my daughters and nieces into lying to me to go on outings with *that creature*"—here he pointed Katrina's way, making her gasp and stumble back—"is beyond the pale."

So stunned was Katrina by Mr. Gadfeld's words, she was at first insensible to everything else. It was not until Mouse's body vibrated against her side with a low, guttural growl that Katrina was able to tear her eyes away from the vicar to look at her pet. His hackles were raised, his ears flat against his head. But it was his eyes that had the breath leaving her body. They appeared as if they were on fire, and focused unerringly on Mr. Gadfeld as that man glared up at Sebastian. She had never seen her pet in such a state. He had never possessed a violent bone in his body, and she had feared more than once that if she was ever set upon by foot-pads, he would be more than happy to shower them with kisses rather than go in for a proper attack.

Yet here he was, looking as if he were about to leap upon the vicar and tear him limb from limb. Curling her fingers tight around his thick leather collar, she held on for all she was worth as she looked wildly at Sebastian's back. His shoulders were tense under the fine deep blue wool of his coat, his hands clenching into fists at his sides. But it was his voice that had her instinctively shrinking back; it was filled with even more danger than Mouse's low growl.

"If I ever hear you speaking of the young lady in such a way," he said, the rumble of his voice vibrating the very air with raw, dark electricity, "you shall pay for the insult."

Mr. Gadfeld's eyes, which had been narrowed in fury, widened with outrage. "You would not threaten a man of the cloth."

"Oh, I most certainly would," Sebastian said. "And it appears Miss Denby's pet is ready and willing as well."

Lady Tesh, apparently having had enough, stepped between Sebastian and Mr. Bridling, cane swinging as she motioned them to the sides. "Mr. Gadfeld," she snapped, "as a man of the cloth, you should be the first to show grace in any situation. Your treatment of my companion has been grossly unfair."

Though he looked askance at Sebastian and Mouse, no doubt to make certain they were remaining in their places, the vicar did not look the least bit cowed. "I cannot con-done such a person flaunting her scandals in my parish," he said to Lady Tesh, looking down his hooked nose at her. "And I refuse to allow this Jezebel around young, impressionable girls like my daughters and nieces. You would do well to fire her immediately before she completely destroys your standing in this community."

He turned to Katrina then, and his eyes blazed with a righteous fire. "If you had any self-respect, Miss Denby, you would not subject the good people of Synne to further damage from your presence. Can't you see what you are doing? Do you have no sense of decency?"

Once more Sebastian was before the vicar, though this time there was no barely leashed control. He grabbed the white cloth at Mr. Gadfeld's throat, nearly lifting him off his feet. Katrina cried out, tightening her grip on Mouse's collar.

"Please, Your Grace," she begged, "don't. It is not worth it." Though what she truly wanted to say was *she* was not worth it. Not one bit. The vicar's attack of Lady Tesh and herself was only what she had expected. She had hoped, had *prayed*, that she was blowing the damage she was causing out of proportion.

Here, however, was proof she had not been. And it was not going to get better, was not going to go away.

Sebastian gazed back at her, equal parts fury and agony in his eyes before, closing them tight and expelling a harsh breath, he released Mr. Gadfeld.

The vicar stumbled back, face red as he adjusted his cloth and ran a hand over his balding crown. "You shall regret this," he said, glaring at them all in turn. Then, striding to his horse and swinging himself up in the saddle, he thundered back down the drive.

They were all silent in shock for a long moment, the sounds of the horse's retreating steps and the pounding in Katrina's ears blending together until they seemed one and the same.

"Well, I never," Lady Tesh said, frowning. "That self-righteous prig. He must have been quite busy this morning, convincing everyone to stay away."

She looked at Katrina then, her expression showing merely annoyance. But Katrina had been with her long enough that she saw the unnaturally pale cast to her skin and the wild worry in her eyes beneath the mild expression.

"Miss Denby," she said, "I do believe your pet is in an agitated state. Mayhap it would be best if you returned him to your room. And while you are there, you may as well take the rest of the afternoon off. I shall not have need of you, for I plan to nap until evening at the least."

Tears sprang to Katrina's eyes, but she purposely blinked them back. She knew just what the woman was trying to do. Lady Tesh was attempting to give her time alone to recover from the scene the vicar had made. She could not have loved the dowager more.

Nor could she have despised herself more. She ached to do as Lady Tesh suggested, to hide in her room and pretend everything was well and allow her employer to handle all the ugliness that would surely follow this horrible afternoon.

But she could not allow Lady Tesh, or anyone else, to take that burden on any longer.

"Thank you, my lady," she murmured before, dipping into a curtsy, she started off for the house. She would use these next hours to take the proverbial bull by the horns and find a solution to this increasingly untenable situation. They could not go on any longer as they were.

Sebastian's voice, however, stopped her cold.

"Mayhap I should accompany Miss Denby back to her rooms."

No! The single word froze in her throat. She could not be alone with Sebastian right now. Her composure was hanging on by a frayed thread as it was.

Blessedly she did not have to give voice to her refusal, for Mr. Bridling stepped in and saved her.

"I have need to return to my room anyway, Ramsleigh. I'll accompany Miss Denby."

Before Sebastian could respond, Mr. Bridling was at her side, offering his arm. "Shall we, Miss Denby?"

She took it with gratitude, allowing him to lead her into the house. It was only when they were well out of sight of Sebastian and Lady Tesh that she felt she could finally exhale.

But this was still no time to let down her guard, she reminded herself brutally as she and Mr. Bridling and Mouse made their way up the stairs. Nor would there be time to fall apart. No, now was the time to take action. She had thought she could find a man to marry to salvage her standing in the Synne community. But each of those men had either been the wrong fit or had been chased off by Sebastian—or both. And now she was out of time. With the vicar fairly frothing at the mouth in his fury and outrage, Katrina's time to act was well and truly past. Mr. Gadfeld was now openly in opposition to Lady Tesh, and her dear Honoria was no doubt suffering horribly from the fight and breach of trust with her father. Katrina had no other option. She had to remove herself from Synne and the lives of the people she cared for immediately.

But where could she go? The answer was clear, of course: Francis. But would he turn her away the moment she showed up on his doorstep? Would he make good on his threat to cut her off completely? Or would he finally, for the first time in his life, act like a true and proper brother?

Well, she thought bleakly as her grip tightened on Mouse's collar, there really was only one way to find out, wasn't there? She didn't have any alternative, none at all. Unless some poor soul came forward and declared himself and begged to take her as his wife, she was out of options.

Just then she and Mr. Bridling reached her bedroom door. But instead of bidding her farewell and leaving her to her own devices, the man turned to face her.

"Miss Denby," he began gently.

She blinked at the tender, earnest look in his eyes. If she didn't know better, she would think Mr. Bridling had developed feelings for her.

But no, she told herself brutally, he was very much in love with his Miss Hutton. No doubt he was simply worried for her after the scene in the front drive. He was a sweet, kind man, after all, and though he had not been as vocal as Sebastian in defending her, he had stepped between her and Mr. Gadfeld. And he must see the physical proof of just how much that confrontation had taken out of her.

But no matter how she tried to excuse the way he gazed at her, there was no excusing the words that came out of his mouth as he moved a step closer.

"Miss Denby, surely you must have seen how deep my regard for you has become in these two weeks since my arrival on Synne. Your opinion is important to me. And now that the future my father is planning for me is at hand, there is only one question I have to ask you."

Before Katrina could squeak out even a sound, Mr. Bridling took her hand in both of his. As she gazed into his fervent eyes in a kind of fatalistic horror, she couldn't help but think that she certainly never expected her prayers to be answered so quickly.

Chapter 20

$\mathcal{H}$ours later and Sebastian was still cursing himself for his ham-handed way of dealing with the vicar. Had the man been a rude, cruel prig who had deserved to have his insulting words shoved down his holy throat? Absolutely. But Sebastian also knew that his own reaction to the man verbally attacking Katrina had been beyond the pale. While he could not regret putting himself between the vicar and Katrina, he knew he had been wrong to lay hands on the man. And now Lady Tesh's own standing in the community had become a fragile thing. Or, rather, more fragile than it had already been.

But the dowager had not said a thing regarding his actions once Katrina and Bridling had disappeared back into the house—no matter how much he had deserved a good tongue-lashing. Instead she had quietly suggested he do as he liked for the rest of the afternoon, then had busily gone about her duties in seeing that the planned picnic was

canceled. Now, hours later, having joined her in the drawing room in preparation for dinner, he knew he could not
leave things unsaid.

"I am sorry, Lady Tesh," he said, running a hand through
his hair as he took the seat across from her, "more sorry
than you can know that I embarrassed you in such a way. If
I could go back in time and stop myself from grabbing the
vicar I would."

To his surprise, however, Lady Tesh let out a rude noise.
"I'm not sorry," she said, waving her hand in dismissal. "I
only wish I could have done it myself. Mr. Gadfeld, for all
his talk of doing good and right, is a pompous arse who
needs to be brought down a peg or two and learn some
humility."

She set her gaze on him, eyeing him closely. "Though I
admit I was surprised at the violence of your feelings. You
must care for my companion very much to have been so
affected."

If she only knew how deeply he cared. Even thinking
of it now, of the vicar's burning, angry eyes on her and his
hateful words rending the air, all directed to that person
Sebastian loved the most in this world, he felt the same fury
consume him all over again. Fighting it back, he cleared
his throat and replied in as neutral a tone as he could manage, "Miss Denby is a dear friend. I could not allow her to
be insulted in such a way. I daresay I would have done the
same for anyone."

Besides a thoughtful "Hmm," Lady Tesh was silent for
some minutes. Sebastian, however, didn't dare look her
way. She was terrifyingly smart, after all, and he did not
want to give any of his emotions away to her. Katrina would

have a hard enough time after he left, what with the scandal and dealing with the vicar, without her employer guessing that he was in love with her.

As if she had seen into his heart, however, Lady Tesh murmured thoughtfully, "Perhaps it is for the best that you will be leaving Synne soon."

Sucking in a sharp breath, thinking she might have read his feelings on his face, he said, "My lady?"

The dowager sighed, her gnarled fingers listlessly dragging through the unruly mop atop her pet's head. "Cartmel will not be happy that I subjected his son to such a scandal. He is all about appearances, after all. As you must be fully aware, seeing what he was forcing you to do to gain his approval of your marriage to his daughter."

She looked at him fully then. "How happy you must be to leave this place behind, to get on with your marriage and move on with your life."

I'm not happy, not at all. The words very nearly escaped his lips, the deepest truth of his soul. More than anything, he wanted to make a life with Katrina, to have children with her, to grow old with her. An image came unbidden to his mind, of him sitting with her late at night after their children had gone to bed, of her smiling with eyes gently lined from too many smiles, of him taking up her hand in his and placing a gentle, loving kiss on her knuckles...

Pain ripped through his chest, and he rubbed absently at the spot. But he could never have those things. They were impossible dreams, the taunting of his heart. So cruel they took his breath away. Pressing his lips tight to stave off the grief for what could never be, he looked down to his lap and fought back the tears that threatened.

Suddenly a heavy pounding started up on the front door. Sebastian was out of his seat in an instant, hands in fists at his side. Had Gadfeld returned to finish what he had started? Did he intend to renew his attacks on Lady Tesh and Katrina? He set his jaw, widening his stance as the sounds of the butler heading for the door reached them. If the vicar dared to attack either woman again, Sebastian was going to make certain the man met his maker much sooner than he no doubt intended to. Maybe then he would finally see the error of his ways.

But it was not Gadfeld at the door. No, a literal herd of feet sounded in the hall, heading their way, several voices mingled together in an anxious melee. And then Miss Honoria Gadfeld, the vicar's eldest, entered the room, followed closely by Miss Peacham, Miss Athwart and her parrot, and the Duchess of Buckley.

"Dear God, it's the Oddments," Lady Tesh muttered as the newcomers all piled into the drawing room. "What in the world?"

"Lady Tesh," Miss Gadfeld said, dropping into the seat beside the dowager, her face wan and eyes red-rimmed but otherwise looking as ferocious as a mother bear about to defend her cubs, "I cannot apologize enough for what my father said to you and Katrina. It is unforgivable, and I want you to know I will not stand for it. I have already moved out of his home and in with Adelaide at the Beakhead, and will not talk to him again until he apologizes to you both and makes amends for his horrible actions."

"My dear girl," Lady Tesh said, in a kinder voice than Sebastian could recall ever hearing from her, "you've no reason to apologize."

"But I do," the young woman insisted. "If I had stood up

to my father from the start and let him know how foolish he was in waging this battle against Katrina and yourself, if I had not lied to him and snuck around behind his back, he would have never had cause to attack you all like that. And so you see, it is as much my fault as it is his—"

Her voice broke and she looked down to her lap, appearing as miserable as any one person could.

"It is *not* your fault," Miss Peacham declared fiercely, standing close to her friend and laying a comforting hand on her shoulder. "You know as well as any of us that there was nothing you could have done to change your father's mind. He is incredibly bullheaded once he sets his mind on something."

"Adelaide is right," the duchess said, pushing her spectacles up her nose, looking as fierce as someone of her small stature and fay-like appearance could. "And we do not believe for one moment that you did not attempt to sway his mind on the matter. We know you better than anyone, and are fully aware that the battles you must have waged were brutal."

"But we are women, after all," Miss Athwart said, her tone bitter as she sent a hot glare Sebastian's way, "and men are wont to look down on us and ignore us, though we know better most of the time."

"I'll gie ye a skelpit lug!" Phineas squawked from her shoulder.

"Oh, don't attack His Grace, Miss Athwart," Lady Tesh said with a small smile his way. "And you either, Phineas, for the duke was quite ferocious in his protection of us. Especially when Miss Denby's honor was questioned."

"Was he now?" Miss Peacham murmured thoughtfully, looking at Sebastian.

"Interesting," the duchess said, her tone contemplative as she peered at Sebastian over the tops of her spectacles.

Even Miss Gadfeld seemed to have forgotten her self-imposed misery enough to perk up, raising her head to look at Sebastian. "That is quite heroic of you, Your Grace."

Sebastian, for his part, did not think his face could attain a higher degree of heat, so inflamed did it feel with so many women looking at him in loaded curiosity. "I assure you," he muttered, "and I told Lady Tesh as much before you arrived, I would have done the same for anyone who was being attacked in such a way."

"Hmm," was Lady Tesh's answer once again. Though this time it seemed as if there were an echo, for that very same thoughtful sound was mimicked by the young women surrounding her.

Blessedly their attention was soon diverted, for Miss Athwart, after looking about, frowned and asked, "Just where *is* Katrina?"

Why that simple question had him feeling suddenly chilled he didn't know. Until Lady Tesh spoke, with a frown that mirrored Miss Athwart's.

"I'm not certain. Though Mr. Bridling is tardy as well. I wonder what is keeping them?"

She looked at the clock above the mantel, and it was only in that moment that Sebastian remembered the hour, and that they were supposed to have gone into dinner—here he followed the dowager's gaze and started—some quarter hour past. Had Katrina stayed away because she was still recovering from Mr. Gadfeld's visit? He frowned. No matter the upset of the afternoon, it was not like Katrina to not send word to her employer that she was unwell. And even if that were the case, that was no reason for Bridling to have stayed away.

The chill that had settled over him soaked through his skin to his bones. Without thinking, he stood. "I'll go check on them, shall I?" Before any of them could reply he was out the door, striding up the stairs.

He didn't even pause at Bridling's closed door, instead rushing straight on to Katrina's. Behind him he vaguely heard the muffled thumping of multiple feet on the plush hallway runner, knew Katrina's friends were following him, and that it might cause suspicion that he was so familiar with her that he would go to her room himself instead of sending one of the others. But he didn't care. His sole emotion was fear. Was she crying even now? Had she made herself ill? But when he opened her door, his anxiety not allowing him to wait for her answer to his knock, he felt the utter void of the space and knew it was so much worse than that. For he knew in an instant she was gone.

He stood frozen in the doorway, his gaze wildly scanning the small space, grasping at any bit of proof that she might return: there was a book she had left on her bedside table, Mouse's bed in the corner, her shawl draped across a chair.

But despite these very physical things that proved she had lived here, her presence had been stripped from the sparse space.

But surely he was being paranoid. Fighting to control his breathing, he looked over his shoulder to her friends. They would not be so panicked. They would say she had gone out to walk Mouse or would recall that she had an appointment somewhere.

But they looked just as fearful as he felt. Miss Athwart was the first to move, pushing past him into the room, heading straight for the bed. It was only as she bent to retrieve something from the coverlet that he saw the letter there, with Lady Tesh's name carefully penned on the front. The look on Miss Athwart's face could only be described as agonized as she held it aloft with shaking fingers. On her shoulder, her parrot swayed back and forth in an obvious sign of stress.

Sebastian, however, did not wait for them to open the letter and read its contents. He spun about, hurrying through the tight knot of women and down the hall. And then he was pushing into Bridling's room—a room that was equally as empty of a presence as Katrina's—and rushing to the desk in the corner. In his mind he recalled that not-so-long-ago day when he had entered this space and found Bridling hurriedly hiding something he had been penning. He recalled the dreamy look in his eyes, his talk of playing knight in shining armor, his dismissal of his actress though just days before he had been loudly proclaiming to all and sundry how in love he was with her. He had been so certain Bridling had begun to fall for Lady Paulette after his rescue of that woman from the thief on The Promenade. Until the boy had summarily dismissed such an idea as ridiculous.

He had not begun to guess who might have captured the boy's attentions. Now a horrible idea had come to him. It wasn't until he pried open the locked drawer in the desk with a penknife and pulled out the sheaf of papers there, all covered in Bridling's flowery, messy writing, that he knew his fears were not unfounded.

...Tonight I took part in saving Miss Denby from a fate worse than death when Ramsleigh

*and I came to her rescue in the Assembly
Rooms... would have certainly suffered from
the embarrassment of such a scene had we not
stepped in... Miss Denby is the kindest person I
have ever had the good fortune to meet... cannot
begin to describe the high regard I hold for her...*

Nausea roiled in Sebastian's stomach as he crumpled the
paper in his fist. Damnation, how had he missed this? How
had he been so blind? And now Bridling had run off with
Katrina.

He had to go after them.

He was out the door before the thought was even done,
running to his room, quickly changing out of his evening attire and tossing on whatever was comfortable and
could take hard riding. After hastily packing a small bag
of essentials he rushed back down to the drawing room.
He would take his leave of Lady Tesh and hurry to the
stables to saddle a horse, and could overtake them before
long. They did not have that much of a head start on him;
a matter of hours at the most. With them in a carriage and
he on horseback, he would be able to cover much more
ground than they could. They would not come close to the
Scottish border before he found them, he was certain of it.

That, however, did not stop the desperate beating of his
heart as he thought of Katrina, who must have felt she had no
other choice after all the matches he had ruined for her, after
Gadfeld's cruel words, which had been a vicious reminder of
what she felt she had to do to protect those she cared about.
And after their night together, and then his break from her
after. His thoughts so overwhelmed him that he did not
immediately realize that Lady Tesh and the Oddments had

been joined by another in the drawing room. At the sight of the familiar man standing just off to the side of their tight group, however, his blood turned to ice, his boots freezing to the carpet.

"Cartmel," he hissed.

The baron pursed his lips and raised an eyebrow as he took Sebastian in. "Not sure why you look as if you've seen a ghost, Ramsleigh," he said. "You knew very well I was coming. Or, rather," he continued, narrowing his eyes and tilting his head as he considered Sebastian, "you look as if you've seen a demon."

If the horns fit. But Sebastian did not have time for the man's sarcasm. "Forgive me," he murmured, turning to Lady Tesh, who appeared as wan as he had ever seen her, what appeared to be Katrina's note in her hand as the Oddments surrounded her like ladies in waiting at court with their queen. "Did she give you any particulars as to where they are going?"

"No," the dowager said faintly. "Only that she is safe and not to worry."

Sebastian nodded grimly. It was a safe bet they were headed to Scotland. "I will go and fetch her back," he swore. "They can't have gotten far. I will have her back here safe with you before morning."

As Lady Tesh gazed up at him with full eyes, Cartmel stepped into the fray. "You shall have who back, Ramsleigh?"

Grinding his back teeth together to prevent the escape of the words he wished to say to this man—that it was none of his bloody business and he could go fuck himself—he turned to the baron and said curtly, "Your son has run off with Lady

Tesh's companion, Miss Denby. I am going to locate them and return them to Seacliff. Now, if you will excuse me?"

He turned to go, not waiting for the man to respond. Before he could take two steps, however, Cartmel's furious voice rang through the room.

"Miss Denby? Miss Katrina Denby? *She* is your companion?" He swore, long and loud, a string of profanity that scorched the air.

"Cartmel," Sebastian growled. "Mind your tongue; there are ladies present."

"Oh, we don't mind such language, I assure you," Miss Athwart drawled, the first she had spoken since learning of her friend's disappearance.

"I don't give a damn if the queen consort herself is here," Cartmel snapped, ignoring Miss Athwart and, indeed, all of the women, his furious glare centered on Sebastian. "Do you mean to tell me you knew that scandalous creature was here, and you did not inform me? And now my son has run off with her? Dear God, that Harlow should tie himself to her. I would have rather he married that actress than a *whore*."

How Sebastian did not hit the baron he would never know. His body literally vibrated with fury as he faced the man. "Never speak of the lady in such a manner again."

Cartmel's eyes widened in outrage. "You dare to speak to me like that? I hold your future in my hands, Ramsleigh. You had best step down, lest you see the dukedom remain in the muck where your father sank it."

Damn it, the man was right. But Sebastian was finding it hard to care about anything but Katrina. Katrina, who had been fighting for so long to protect the people who loved her, who had only wanted respectability, at the sake of her own happiness.

And he had destroyed each and every chance she had taken. And here he was, planning to do it again.

He nearly blanched. Dear God, he truly was about to do it all over again. He had been prepared to run off after her and stop her from marrying Bridling. Just the idea of the two of them together made Sebastian physically ill. But if this was what Katrina wanted, who was he to destroy her chance at making a proper life for herself?

As if Cartmel had heard his tortured thoughts, the baron stepped up before him until they were nearly toe to toe. "But what the devil are you waiting for? Go after them."

"No," Sebastian said slowly, though the words burned his throat. "No, I won't."

"What?" Cartmel demanded, his face going red.

Sebastian looked him in the eye. "I'm not going after them," he repeated.

Cartmel's florid complexion went positively purple. "You shall, Ramsleigh, or you can consider yourself barred from marrying my daughter."

Sebastian tightened his hands into fists at those acidic yet expected words. The one goal he'd had these past months had been to marry Miss Bridling and her fortune, his one chance to save the dukedom and all who counted on it.

But looking into Cartmel's flat, cruel eyes, he knew that if he followed the baron's orders, he would not only be this man's puppet for the remainder of his life, not only commit the innocent Miss Bridling to a lifetime of marriage with a man who could never love her, but he would also destroy Katrina in the bargain.

And that last he could not accept.

"Actually," he said quietly, "I find I must respectfully remove myself from consideration for your daughter's hand. It would not be fair to her to be married to a man who can never give her all that she deserves."

He drew himself up so Cartmel, growing increasingly furious with each word that dropped from Sebastian's lips, had to crane his neck to keep eye contact with him. "I will not go after Bridling and Miss Denby. And neither will you. You will allow this marriage to take place, and welcome Miss Denby into your family. Furthermore, you will squash any rumors about her, and publicly proclaim your happiness that she is marrying your son."

Cartmel gaped like a fish. "You cannot be serious."

"I assure you, I am very serious."

If anything, the baron appeared more furious. "You're a fucking idiot," he snarled. "You have nothing to your name except a moldering pile of stones with some dubious claim to historical importance. You thought the dukedom was in ruins before? Just wait until I am done with you."

But Sebastian hardly heard him past mention of Ramsleigh Castle. An idea was beginning to form that was so outrageous he could not quite comprehend the full scope of what it might mean. Though he could never sell the place, entailed as it was, that did not mean it did not hold value.

Before he could fully comprehend that he might have a way out of this mess—and a way to marry Katrina and claim all the happiness in the world if he could get to her before she reached Scotland with Bridling—an unexpected voice rang out through the room, releasing the tension like a sword slicing through bindings.

"You won't do a damn thing to His Grace," Bridling said, striding into the room, his expression as furious as Sebastian had ever seen it. And, next to him, a person he never expected to see: the man's sister.

"Diane," Cartmel barked, "I told you to remain in the carriage."

But Sebastian did not wait for her to answer, for his entire attention had diverted to Bridling. "Where is she?" he demanded, striding forward. "Where is Miss Denby? If you have abandoned her, I swear—"

But Bridling did not look the least bit perturbed. Instead he grinned widely, looking at his sister. "See, didn't I tell you he was in love with her?"

Before Sebastian could understand what the devil the boy was talking about, Miss Bridling returned her brother's smile before turning it on Sebastian. "I am glad. It makes this all so much easier."

Sebastian, however, wasn't about to waste even a second trying to unravel the mysterious back and forth between the siblings. "Where is Katrina?" he demanded. "You eloped with her; why are you not on your way together to Gretna Green as we speak?"

Whatever response he might have expected, it certainly wasn't the delighted laughter that spilled from the boy's lips. "Eloped? With Miss Denby? Whatever put that idea in your head?" He laughed again. "Ah, I suppose my little bit of acting to throw you off the scent did the trick. Forgive me, Ramsleigh. I had to protect my interests, you see. But no, I never lost my love for my darling Mirabel. And I certainly never replaced her in my affections with Miss Denby. No, I respect her opinion, and asked her to assist me in deciding what to do about Miss Hutton, now that my father has set my life in stone for me. With her help I have decided I shall return to London and ask Mirabel to marry me." His expression softened. "Miss Denby was of the opinion that if one were to find love, one should hold on to it with both hands and never let it go."

As Sebastian's heart lurched in his chest at that, Cartmel approached, his florid face back to purple rage.

"Miss Hutton?" he roared. "No, I forbid it. You shall not marry that creature."

Bridling turned to his father, the same fury from before back on his face. "I can, and I shall. I should have stood up to you long ago where Mirabel was concerned, instead of wasting time trying to make you understand that my heart shall never belong to another." His lip curled. "But you never cared about that, did you? Just as you never cared what Diane might want for her own life, instead foisting her off on the largest title you could find." He turned to Sebastian with a sheepish look. "My apologies, Ramsleigh. Nothing personal, you understand."

"No offense taken," Sebastian muttered, even as his mind spun like a child's top trying to make sense of it all.

But one thing he did not have to make sense of was his feelings for Katrina. And that a future with her was finally possible.

Before he could claim that future, however, there was one person embroiled in this whole mess he had to confront. He turned to her now, dreading what was to come for all he respected her. "Miss Bridling—" he began.

But that woman was faster than him by far. "No, please, Your Grace. Let me speak. There is something I have been aching to say to you since you left London all those weeks ago. While my father was under the impression that I accompanied him to make certain your proposal was completed, in actuality I came to break things off with you. The last time we saw one another and you asked me my favorite color, it may have been a simple question, yet after much rumination it made me realize that perhaps I deserve so much more."

"You do," her brother said fervently. "You absolutely do."

"Rubbish!" their father spat. "A child's place is to obey their parents and do as they're told."

"No," Bridling said, with a maturity and confidence that Sebastian had never witnessed in him before, "it is not. Our place is to live happy and fulfilling lives."

"Happy and fulfilling, eh?" Cartmel demanded. "We'll see how happy and fulfilled you are when you are cut off without a penny to your name."

That, it seemed, was Lady Tesh's cue to intervene. "I have given safe haven to more than one young person in need of support and a place to stay," she declared, giving Cartmel a disgusted look before smiling in encouragement at the Bridling siblings. "I daresay I can do it again. Especially as," she continued, arching one brow at Sebastian, "I may be losing my companion?"

Katrina. Dear God, where the devil was she? Before he could so much as breathe a word in question, Bridling spoke up.

"I dropped her off at the vicarage, at her request," he said softly. "You can find her there. Use my carriage; it is already in the front drive."

"Good luck, Your Grace," Miss Bridling said, with a smile warmer than any he had ever seen from her.

Sebastian did not need further encouragement. Taking Miss Bridling's hand in his, pressing it in thanks, he was soon out the door, racing for the stables. Had everything that he had been working toward unraveled? Yes. Would there be hardships in this unfinished plan he had mapped out in his head? Also yes.

But with Katrina by his side, he felt he could do anything. As long as they were together.

Chapter 21

Just knock, Katrina. You can do it.

Katrina took a deep breath, peeking out from the shrubbery she was hiding behind for what must have been the hundredth time. The vicarage was just across the road, the two-story stone house a perfect match to the ancient stone church close by, candles glowing through the rippled glass of the windows as evening took hold of the land. There was the front door she had walked through more times than she could count, the fenced garden where Honoria had spent so many hours tending to her late mother's roses, the small wooden structure where Emmeline's chickens clucked sleepily.

And, somewhere inside, Mr. Gadfeld no doubt busy scribbling away this Sunday's sermon about how loose women who allowed men into their bedroom windows were destined to burn in hellfire for all eternity.

She was tempted to turn tail and flee. Not that it was

any different from the last thirty minutes as she attempted to build up the courage to knock on that familiar door and confront the man who had worked so hard at making her life hell. But the longer she waited the harder it would be to move her leaden feet forward.

Mouse, it seemed, was of the same mind, and as exasperated with her as she was with herself. Giving a huff, he shoved his nose into her hip.

"I know, darling," she murmured. "I know." Looking down into his large brown eyes, so solemn as he gazed up at her, she attempted a smile. But it was a weak thing, and died before finding purchase. So many emotions had torn through her throughout this long, horrible day. From heartbreak at being in Sebastian's company, to devastation when Mr. Gadfeld verbally attacked her; then in quick succession, shock when she believed Mr. Bridling to be proposing, relief when she learned he was merely being dramatic in his wish for her counsel regarding Miss Hutton, and determination when she decided to accompany him on his travels. Her plan had been simple: have him take a small detour to her brother's home near Lincoln on his way back to London, where she would finally take the proverbial bull by the horns and force Francis to acknowledge her existence.

But when they were finally on their way, and Katrina had a moment to think as the carriage had trundled toward the ferry that would take them to the mainland, she had realized that she did not want to go where she was not wanted, was tired of trying to insert herself in the life of a person who had cut her out of his life as completely and irrevocably as the doctor who had cut off Francis's arm. No, she wanted to fight, to stay where she was loved. Lady Tesh loved her. And the Oddments loved her.

And Sebastian loved her.

She shook her head fiercely to dislodge the painful thought. Yes, though he had not said the words she was certain he loved her. But he had other people to consider, people whose entire lives were riding on his marriage to Miss Bridling. She could not be the source of heartache and ruin for him.

But she could fight for this life she had built on Synne. And that began with confronting the one person who had attempted to destroy that life.

Setting her jaw, she reached for the bag at her feet and hefted it up, taking Mouse's lead in her other hand. "Come along, Mouse," she said as, with a focused glare on the vicarage through the growing gloom, she stalked across the road and through the gate, up to the heavy oak door.

Katrina expected the pinch-faced housekeeper to answer her knock. What she did not expect, however, was the vicar himself to throw open the door almost immediately. Nor did she expect the look of wild hope in his eyes—followed by a despair quickly banked as he saw who was at his door.

"Miss Denby," he muttered. "What are you doing here?"

Keep calm. The man would not react well if she attacked him on the spot. And besides, she realized belatedly as she took in his unkempt appearance, he looked strangely frazzled, his typical cool composure cracked beyond recognition. His thinning hair had a flyaway look to it, his clerical collar was crooked. But more disturbing was the look of brokenness in his eyes. What had happened to shake the man to such a degree?

But he was waiting for her to answer. Clearing her throat and straightening her spine, she said, her voice only shaking slightly, "May I come in, Mr. Gadfeld? I would like to speak with you."

After a long silence where the vicar stared at her as if he did not quite understand what she was saying, he finally gave a quick, shallow nod and stepped aside for her to pass. She went straight to the small sitting room off the front hall, Mouse following quietly at her side, as if he understood the need to be on his very best behavior now more than any other time. She sat quickly before her shaking legs gave her anxiety away, then waited as Mr. Gadfeld settled across from her.

He looked her over, seemingly exhausted if the dark circles under his eyes were any indication, before motioning to the bag at her feet.

"Were you going somewhere, Miss Denby?"

"I was," she replied steadily. "But I decided I shall not be run off from this place I love so much. I am going to stay and fight."

His lips quirked at one corner, though there was no humor in the action. "I suppose that means confronting me."

"It does."

He nodded, as if that made perfect sense. "You shall not be the first to call me out on my actions of the past month. And no doubt you shall not be the last."

It was a much milder response than she had expected. And as she stared in incomprehension at this man who had just hours ago railed at not only herself but also Lady Tesh, and the utter silence of the house settled around her, she realized something was very, very wrong.

The vicarage had never been so quiet. With four lively

girls housed within its stone walls, it could not be. Yet the silence of the house was jarring.

"Mr. Gadfeld," she said, "where is everyone?"

A quick tightening of his mouth was his only reaction to her question. "Out," he said curtly, harshly, before meeting her gaze. His eyes were like chips of ice. "Say what you came to say. I'm quite busy."

Katrina was tempted to shrink into her seat and babble out apologies. *Be small, be quiet, don't cause problems.* It had been her mantra for her entire life, said to her over and over again during her childhood. And she had always failed abysmally, causing it to be repeated until it was all she heard in her head.

Now, however, she was tired of being small. And she was done with being quiet. And if she caused problems while doing both, so be it.

She sat forward, a new fire burning under her skin. "Firstly, I am not going to bother explaining myself to you. No matter the truth behind the scandals that have taken place in my life, no matter that I was not at fault and that nothing untoward occurred, I know you are only going to believe what you wish to believe. And that is not my problem. It is your problem, and yours alone."

His eyes narrowing was his only reaction to her words. Emboldened, she continued.

"Secondly, I am going to remain on Synne. It has become my home, and I love it and the people on it, though you would do your best to turn them against me. And if Lady Tesh and my friends want me here, there is nothing on this earth or beyond that will tear me from it.

"Thirdly," she continued, "you shall no longer punish Honoria for her friendship with me. She is a good friend, and a loving daughter. Despite what has occurred between you and I this past month, I know you have been an incredible father to her and have raised her and her sister and her cousins right. They all have good morals, are kind and giving, and you should be proud of each and every one of them."

His lips parted, a harsh breath escaping them. But Katrina hardly noticed for how desperately the words in her chest wished to be released.

"But your opposition to her wishes have caused her a grief that she does not deserve. And you shall lose her, and mayhap all of them, for all her sister and cousins love her, if you continue as you are. That is not a threat, but a fact. I know what it is to lose your family. And I would not wish that on anyone."

She rose, and stood staring down at the vicar, who suddenly looked very small. But there was one more thing she needed to say.

"I don't want an apology from you. Indeed, I don't expect you to give one to me even if I wished for it. But I will not see Lady Tesh or my friends hurt further by your agenda to vilify me. You shall cease your attacks and allow me to live my life here in peace." Then, having said all she had come to say, she made to leave. Let the vicar do with that what he would; it was not up to her, it was up to the man himself.

But as she turned to go, the vicar spoke, his voice harsh in the quiet of the room.

"One would think you are a demon sent from hell to punish me for my sins, for all your words have cut me to the quick."

Startled, Katrina turned back to look at the vicar. His face was wan, though his eyes burned with grief.

"I am not a demon, Mr. Gadfeld," she said quietly, resuming her seat. "I am merely a woman who is struggling, and who loves your daughter dearly and does not wish for her or you to suffer from loss of family as I have."

His next words, as strangled as they were, stunned her to silence. "I have already lost them," he managed. "They have gone, each and every one of them."

She gaped at him. "I—I don't understand."

He closed his eyes as if in abject pain. "Honoria was the first to go. Of course she was. She learned what had occurred at Lady Tesh's and packed her things immediately to stay with Miss Peacham at the Beakhead. And once she was gone, and the younger girls learned what had happened, they left as well, along with the housekeeper, to stay at the Master-at-Arms. They said, and I quote, *we shall not return until you make things right.*"

"Oh." She blinked, at an utter loss. "I . . . did not know."

"No," he said, sounding defeated, "I suppose you didn't. I was certain you had come here to taunt me. I can see now you did not."

"Of course I would not taunt you about such a thing," she replied softly.

"No," he murmured, looking at her as if seeing her for the first time, "I suppose you wouldn't. And though you did not wish for it, please allow me to say how sorry I am for causing such trouble. I was only trying to do the right thing. Yet I fear I was blinded by my own arrogance." He gave her a pained smile.

Katrina, blinking back tears, replied softly, "Thank you, Mr. Gadfeld."

He nodded before, heaving a sigh, he rose to his feet. Katrina and Mouse did the same.

"I suppose I should return you to Lady Tesh's house," he said, moving for the door. "I can ready the pony and cart in short order and have you home safe. And it will give me a chance to extend my apologies to the dowager. Though I am not looking forward to Lady Tesh's reaction to my groveling—for she will take great pleasure in it, I'm certain." He laughed lightly.

Katrina hardly heard anything past one very important word, however: *home*. *What a lovely word*, she thought with a small smile as she followed the vicar. She had thought that home could only be where her family was, and that to have a home again she had to return to her brother's house. Now, however, she saw that she'd had a home all this time. Lady Tesh had given her a home. And the Oddments had made her feel welcome and were like family to her. Blood did not matter, but hearts that loved one another truly did, no matter who they were or where they came from.

If only Sebastian could be part of that.

She sucked in a sharp breath. No, he never could be. And the sooner she got that through her mind the better off she would be.

Though that thought was decimated as Mr. Gadfeld opened the front door and Sebastian nearly fell through into the narrow hall.

Chapter 22

Sebastian's first instinct upon seeing Katrina standing next to the vicar was to grab her hand and pull her away from that man who had made her life hell and plant a fist in the holy man's face.

But he would never know if he would have followed through on those urges. Mouse boomed out a massive bark and bounded toward him, his massive nose headed straight for that place that had already taken a punishing blow from the beast.

Blessedly he was much quicker this time around. A swift step to the side, and the dog's snout missed his privates by mere inches, landing with a solid thud against his hip and nearly sending him sprawling backward across the flagstones.

"Mouse!" Katrina cried, lunging for the animal and pulling him back. "You naughty thing. Sebastian, are you all right?"

Never better. The words whispered through his mind as he took in her lovely face. God, he loved her, so much. He wanted to make a life with her, to have children with her, to grow old with her. And to work together, through good and bad, through every hardship and heartbreak.

But for the first time since he'd left Seacliff to come after her, anxiety took hold. And not a small bit, but a healthy dose. Not that he doubted her love for him. He knew she loved him, as deeply and completely as he loved her. But would he be able to convince her to take a chance on a life with him? She had been willing to give up her own happiness, her very future, to protect those she loved. He had never met anyone so selfless and strong. Could she overlook all the reasons they shouldn't be together and instead focus on the one reason why they should?

But he had been silently staring at her for far too long. "Your Grace," the vicar said, his voice solemn. "I am glad you are here, for I have something I wish to say to you."

At once Sebastian remembered where he was—and with whom. "I have something I wish to say to you as well, Mr. Gadfeld," he said, facing the vicar as he did before. Though this time things were so much clearer and more frightening and hopeful. And he had something very concrete he was fighting for: namely, a possible future with Katrina.

"Miss Denby is a kind, loving, generous person, who does not deserve the heartache you have caused her this past month or more."

"That is absolutely true."

"You shall cease your campaign against her, and against Lady Tesh as well."

"I agree."

"And you will repair the damage you have done on Synne."

"I will."

"Furthermore—"

But whatever he had been about to say was lost as the vicar's words penetrated the furious haze his brain was in. Frowning, he peered at the man—and truly saw him for the first time. He appeared a changed man, all the bluster gone out of him. "What was that?"

"I agree with everything you've said, Your Grace."

Sebastian blinked. "Oh. That's . . . good."

He looked to Katrina then. And for the first time since arriving at the vicarage saw how clear her eyes were. Was there still pain there? Yes. But the anxiety and fear were gone.

She seemed to have seen the confusion in his gaze, for she smiled slightly. "Mr. Gadfeld and I had a lovely talk, and things shall be different from here on out."

"Oh," he said again. All the while his heart expanded, somehow fitting more love into it than ever before. She had come here, had faced this man who had caused her so much pain and heartache, had somehow stood up for herself and changed things around.

She was incredible.

"Mr. Gadfeld was just about to bring me back to Seacliff," she said before, her gaze drifting over his shoulder, she spied the carriage in the road. She frowned. "Is that Mr. Bridling's carriage? But . . . he left for London."

"You inspired him to return and face his father. He's back at Seacliff as we speak. As is," he continued, looking at the vicar, "your daughter."

"Honoria," the man said, lines of pain bracketing his mouth and eyes.

Katrina, kind soul that she was, laid a hand on the man's sleeve. "You don't have to accompany me as you planned," she said quietly. "I'm certain everyone will understand if you postpone."

"No," the vicar said, straightening his narrow shoulders under his stark black coat. "That is kind of you to say, but this is something I cannot put off a moment longer. If I delay, the apologies will only become harder to give. Your Grace," he continued, looking to Sebastian, "if you have room in your carriage, I would be most obliged to accompany you and Miss Denby back to Seacliff."

"Of course," Sebastian said. Then, giving a curious look to Katrina, he led them all to the carriage.

* * *

Katrina could not recall a time she had ever been more tired. And yet, she could not sleep. She lay wide awake in her bed, staring up at the ceiling, the events of the past hours playing over and over in her head.

Most of it had been straightforward enough. Mr. Gadfeld had apologized to Honoria and Lady Tesh, and later to his younger daughter and nieces when they had been called to Seacliff. There had been tears—on the Gadfeld girls' parts, at least; Lady Tesh had been predictably dry-eyed, though there had been a sniffle or two upon seeing the Gadfeld family reunite. And then there had been further discussion when Honoria had shocked everyone and declared that, though she loved her family dearly, she would remain with Adelaide at the Beakhead for the foreseeable future. It would take time for the family to return to their typical closeness. But by the end of the evening—or, rather, the early hours of the morning, for they had remained talking well after midnight before they had returned to their homes—Katrina had been certain that a full reconciliation would not take long at all.

But that had not been the thing weighing so heavily on Katrina's mind in the hours since their departure. No, that honor had gone to Sebastian. Or, rather, he and Miss Bridling. To say it had been a shock seeing that woman at Seacliff would have been an understatement of the first order. This was the woman who Sebastian was destined to marry, and here she was in the flesh. And much kinder than Katrina had thought she might be.

No, that wasn't right. She had *hoped* the woman would be unkind, a veritable virago. Instead she had greeted Katrina with warm smiles—and Mouse with exclamations of delight and many, many scratches to his posterior, sending the dog into raptures—and had the audacity to actually make Katrina *like* her. Which, of course, lit a spark to the dry kindling of Katrina's guilt. She had declared her love for the woman's future husband and had taken him to her bed. Or, rather, his bed, but that was neither here nor there.

And now that woman was sleeping under the same roof as she and Sebastian while she waited to depart for London in the morning with her brother—who was thankfully still planning on returning to propose to his Miss Hutton. Lord Cartmel had retreated to the Master-at-Arms Inn before Katrina's return to Seacliff, and so she did not know if the family would reconcile as easily as the Gadfelds had. But Katrina had witnessed firsthand the affection between the two siblings, and so she was consoled that they would at least have each other.

That did not mean it was any easier to know that Sebastian's future wife was just down the hall. Or to know that, eventually, he would make a life with that woman. Expelling a harsh breath, Katrina flopped over onto her side and punched her pillow before hugging it to her and resolutely closing her eyes. But no matter how she tried to empty her mind, sleep would not come. And then Mouse, who had been snoring beside her in the bed, having refused to leave her side all night long, suddenly roused, a low whine escaping him as his attention snagged on the bedroom door. Katrina knew it was hopeless to attempt sleep any longer; she may as well rise and start her day. The sky was beginning to lighten just the barest hint, the blackest ink bleeding into indigo, a sure sign that dawn was approaching. And mayhap, if she kept herself busy enough, she would be able to get through it with a portion of her sanity—and her heart—intact.

But as Mouse leapt from the bed to pad over to the door, and she threw back the coverlet to rise, she finally saw what had captured her pet's attention: a letter, on the floor.

Frowning, she went to Mouse, who was busy snuffling at the piece of paper. "What have you got there, darling?" she murmured, bending down and picking up the missive. Someone must have slipped it under her door. But who?

It did not take long to receive an answer to that all-important question.

Katrina,

Meet me where we shared our first kiss. And leave Mouse.

S.

Heart pounding like a drum in her chest, growing louder
and louder the more she read over the short missive, she
tried and failed to stem the rising tide of hope in her. No
doubt there was a perfectly logical explanation for this. He
must want a private place to officially say goodbye. After
all, with Mr. and Miss Bridling returning to London in a
matter of hours, Sebastian had no further reason to remain
on Synne.

Yet that bit of reasoning did nothing to stop her heart
from running away with increasingly wonderful reasons for his wanting to meet her at such a place. Mayhap
he was finally going to declare himself. *But then what,
ninny?* her mind scolded. Perhaps he wished to remain on
Synne with her. *And would you be his mistress?* Possibly
he wished to marry her. *And lose his chance at saving
the dukedom?* Round and round her heart and mind went
as she hurriedly dressed and gave Mouse a hug and a bid
to behave himself before she snuck from the room and
through the dark, sleepy house, a small lamp held aloft in
her hands.

But when she finally carefully descended the steep
path to the beach in the gray light of pre-dawn, and saw
what awaited her, all those tumultuous voices quieted in an
instant.

An array of soft blankets had been laid over the sand,
pillows strewn in cushioned piles, lanterns forming a glowing halo of golden light around it.

And in the middle of it all, feet bare and wearing trousers and an open-collared shirt with sleeves rolled to his
elbows, was Sebastian.

A quiet gasp escaped her lips. But, though she ached to
rush forward and into his arms, she could not seem to move

her feet. This was no goodbye, that she knew. But what it could be she could not—would not—try to guess. If she guessed wrong, it would destroy her.

He gave her a tentative smile, then stepped from the gilded circle of light and walked across the sand toward her. "I feared you would not come," he murmured, reaching out to take her hand gently in his.

"I could not stay away even if I had wanted to," she whispered before, nervously motioning to the blankets, she asked, "What is all this?"

"This," he said as he tugged her toward the light, "is my attempt to convince you of something very important, in the hopes you shall be so dazzled by the display that you could not possibly say no."

Despite her nerves, she found herself smiling. "Is that so?"

"It is." He guided her onto the blankets, then turned to face her fully. Behind him, the faintest hint of pink was coloring the horizon as the ocean lapped lazily at the shore. But all she could see was the love in his eyes, brighter than the lanterns that illuminated them.

"First, you must know that Miss Bridling and I have broken things off."

The joy that pronouncement brought was hampered by her worry for him. "Oh, Sebastian, what of the dukedom?" She took a step closer, grasping his hand tight. "What of the people who rely on it and you? Surely you can mend things. You must return to Seacliff at once and make things right before Miss Bridling departs for London."

His gaze pierced into hers. "Is that what you want, Katrina, for me to marry Miss Bridling?"

Immediately her cheeks heated. "It does not matter what

I want. What matters is what needs to be done, which is you marrying Miss Bridling and making certain all those counting on that union are provided for."

"That does not answer the question," he said softly.

"There is no reason for me to answer the question," she insisted.

"There is a very important reason to answer it."

"What?" she demanded a bit desperately, feeling as if she had been backed into a corner, though there was not a corner to be seen here on the wide expanse of beach.

His hand came up to cradle her cheek. "I need to hear it," he replied, his voice hoarse with emotion. "I need to hear the truth, from your own lips."

Tears burned her eyes. "You wish to torment me? Very well. No, I don't want you to marry Miss Bridling. I don't want you to marry anyone else except—"

She cut herself off, unable to say what was in her heart, that she did not want him to marry anyone else except her. She wanted to be the one to carve out a lifetime of love with him, to fall asleep beside him at night and wake beside him in the morning, to raise a family with him and make him smile each and every day. It was what she had wanted four years ago. And now that she had spent these weeks with him and fallen even more deeply in love with him than ever, it had transformed into something she needed if she was to ever feel whole again.

But it could not be. It was an impossibility.

"Please," she choked out, unable to meet his eyes, "forget I said anything. Return to the house and make things right. I'm certain if you just talk to Miss Bridling she will understand and accept your hand. I won't get in the way any longer, I swear it—"

His other hand came up and he cradled her face like the most precious treasure, cutting off her words. Tears burned her eyes, and though she fought them back with everything in her, they slipped free, tracking down her face. With utmost tenderness he wiped them away.

"You could never be in the way," he whispered, his voice made all the more precious for the gentle breeze that carried it to her, wrapping it around her like a caress. "In fact, you're the whole reason I can find my way through life, through this confusing, cruel world. You're like the morning star, guiding me, lighting my way. I would be lost without you, Katrina."

And then he did the most amazing, baffling, wonderful thing: he sank to one knee before her. A sob escaped her lips.

"Don't say no just yet," he warned thickly even as he gazed up at her. "You are the other half of my heart, and I know you would gladly give up any chance at happiness to make sure those you love are protected. I also know—as you have mentioned it several times already just now"—here he gave her a crooked little smile—"that you think Miss Bridling's fortune is the only thing that will save me."

He squeezed her fingers, still held tight in his grip, as if to punctuate the point he was about to make. "The only thing that will truly save me from a lifetime of misery is your heart, Katrina. I need you by my side, the other half of myself."

She shook her head. "But what of the dukedom? What of your sisters, and tenants, and everyone who counts on you? Love is all well and good, Sebastian, but it does not put bread on the table. You—" Her voice broke, but she soldiered on. "You will grow to despise me for it."

"I could never despise you," he vowed, his eyes burning. "But if money is all that is stopping you from marrying me, what if I told you I have found a solution to my need for funds, without the need to marry for money? Would you, perhaps, consider making a life with me?"

Her breath caught in her throat, hope sparking in her chest. "Have you found a solution, Sebastian?" she breathed.

His smile, more beautiful than the breaking dawn, had the small spark of hope flaring bright. "I have. It will take some doing, mind you," he continued. "And a bit of time. But I've a mind to lease out Ramsleigh Castle."

Her heart dropped into her toes, taking her burgeoning hope with it. "Oh, Sebastian," she said. "No, not your home."

But his smile did not falter. "But that's just the thing, Katrina. The only home to me is wherever you are."

"But you'll be sacrificing so much."

"I'll be sacrificing nothing," he declared, his voice thick with emotion. "In fact, as long as I have you by my side, I'll be gaining everything I could ever want."

His gaze turned teasing then, though there was a hint of uncertainty behind it. "If, that is, you wouldn't mind forgoing the impressive castle and living someplace small and simple with me."

She exhaled a disbelieving burst of breath. "As if that ever mattered to me," she choked out.

His face lit up. "Well then." He reached into his trouser pocket and pulled out a simple gold ring with the clearest aquamarine stone she had ever seen. And Katrina thought her heart would burst from the happiness pouring into it.

"It is not much I know," he said ruefully as he held it up. "Lady Tesh was more than happy to give me one of her many—very many—rings to propose properly. But have you ever looked at that woman's jewelry? Good God, she has some gaudy taste."

A watery giggle bubbled up to Katrina's lips, and he grinned that wonderfully crooked smile of his, his eyes soft on her face.

"But when I saw this one, that reminded me of your beautiful eyes, I knew it was right. And so I offer it to you, my Katrina. I love you, with every version of myself, from the selfish boy I was, to the cynical man I am, and everything in between. And I shall love you with every rendition of myself that I become. I know life will be difficult. We will have trials and tribulations and heartaches. But I also know, with a certainty that makes my heart beat, that if we can get through them together, nothing else will ever matter."

He smiled, and his eyes glinted in the lamplight, glistening with unshed tears. Tears, she knew, that would mirror the ones in her own eyes.

"Marry me, my darling Katrina."

She swallowed hard. "I come to you with nothing, Sebastian."

"You come to me with everything," he rasped, lifting her hand to his lips, kissing it fervently. "Your sweetness, your goodness, your loving heart; those are the things that will save me. I love you."

And then, again, "Marry me."

As she gazed down into his eyes, so full of love, so certain in their future, Katrina felt all her doubts and fears melt away. He was right: if they were together, nothing else mattered.

"Yes," she whispered, a tremulous smile spreading across her face. "Yes, Sebastian, I will marry you."

"Thank God," he breathed before, slipping the delicate ring on her finger, he rose to his feet and dragged her into his arms, his lips claiming her as surely as he had claimed her heart.

* * *

Sebastian had not intended to seduce Katrina when he had brought her out here to this isolated stretch of beach. No, he had merely wished to make a beautiful spot for them where he could proclaim his love and convince her that they belonged together, no matter what might oppose them.

In that moment, however, he could not help thinking that his decision to use blankets and pillows had been positively genius. Now that he had her in his arms, and he knew they belonged to one another and no one else, he could not possibly stop at one kiss. No, one kiss became many, their lips tangling, parting only briefly to whisper words of love before returning for more. And then their hands came into play, roaming over curves and planes, loosening clothing, fanning the flame of their desire. They dropped to the blankets, one mind, one need, Katrina pulling on his shoulders until he settled between the welcoming cradle of her thighs.

He ached to sink into her heat, to lose himself in her. Instead, however, he paused, pulling back to gaze down at her, this incredible woman who had given her heart so unreservedly to him after a lifetime of believing she was not good enough for anyone.

He would spend the rest of his life making certain she never believed that about herself again.

"I love you, Katrina," he whispered, cradling her face in his hands.

"I love you, Sebastian," she replied, her voice cracking with emotion.

He lowered his head to hers again. Though now there was no rush, no haste. They had their entire lives ahead of them, together. And when, finally, their bodies joined as the sun began to crest the horizon, a new dawn bathing them in gilded light as they became one in body and heart and soul, they knew it was just the beginning of their forever.

Chapter 23

*H*ow," Honoria said later that day as she bent down to scratch an ecstatic Mouse behind the ears, "am I going to survive without seeing this great lummox during our weekly meetings?"

"Not to mention Katrina," Seraphina said dryly as she closed the lid to the trunk she had been packing.

Katrina, carefully folding a shawl, laughed as the other Oddments joined in on the lighthearted banter. Lady Tesh had invited them all to Seacliff to assist Katrina in packing for the upcoming trip with Sebastian to Gretna Green, a last gathering of the group. Katrina would forever be thankful to the dowager for such a gift. Though she could not wait to start her life with Sebastian, she would miss her friends dreadfully. They had been there for her when she had been lost and friendless, welcoming her into their group with open arms and open hearts. She would love them forever, no matter how many miles separated them.

Just as she would love Lady Tesh. That woman had been waiting for them by the open front door when Katrina and Sebastian had arrived back from the beach, her cane tapping impatiently against the tiles of the front hall. There had been a time when Katrina would have panicked to see her employer in a moment such as that, knowing the woman would guess what they had been up to on that beach just by looking at their faces.

Not now, though, knowing she had grown strong, and had the love of a good man behind her. And so instead of dropping Sebastian's hand, she had held on tight, proudly even, and strode forward without hesitation. Lady Tesh had spied their clasped fingers, and a wide grin had spread itself over her heavily lined face. And it seemed the woman had not stopped smiling since.

The dowager hobbled into the small room just then, followed not only by a prancing Freya, but also her lady's maid. That woman's arms were full of linen, a pile so high that it teetered precariously as she made her way to the bed and carefully lowered it to the mattress.

"What is all this, Lady Tesh?" Katrina asked, approaching and running her fingers over the bright white cottons and creamy laces and bits of delicately embroidered linen.

"You cannot go off to marry a duke without a proper trousseau," the woman said. "And goodness knows I have too much for any one person to use. Consider this my wedding gift to you."

Katrina gaped at her. "But you have given us so much already."

"Poppycock," the dowager said in her typical sharp tone before, smiling, she patted Katrina's arm. "You deserve so much more, my dear. You have been like a granddaughter to me, and I could not love you more if you were."

Tears blurred Katrina's vision as she looked at the dowager. "I love you, too, my lady."

For a moment Lady Tesh's lower lip trembled, and her eyes shone brightly, and Katrina thought for certain the woman was about to cry. In the next instant, however, she cleared her throat loudly and glanced around at the other women, who were all looking on the scene with varying degrees of emotion.

"But what are you all standing about for?" she snapped, even as she surreptitiously sniffled. "These things are not going to pack themselves, and Miss Denby and His Grace need to get on the road if they are to make good headway in their trip north."

"Of course, my lady," Adelaide murmured with a small smile for Katrina as she turned back to the open trunk before her.

Seraphina surveyed the new pile of linens with a frown. "They cannot cart all of this to Gretna Green, my lady. It is illogical."

"I daresay," Brownyn said, taking her own turn with distracting Mouse as he sniffed curiously at all the new items filling the room, "Lady Tesh has a plan for that. Don't you, my lady?"

"As ever, Your Grace," the dowager murmured, inclining her head to Bronwyn, "you show your incredible good sense. Of course, I will not have them cart this all with them. I may be old, but I am not senile. I shall send it on ahead to Ramsleigh Castle, ready to bring with them wherever they may wind up. Does that suffice for logic, Miss Athwart?"

But Seraphina was too like Lady Tesh to be cowed. "It does, my lady."

"Hmph," the dowager grumbled. "You are too confident for your own good, young lady."

"Oh, I think it is very much to my good," Seraphina stated blithely.

"We're a' Jock Taimson's bairns," Phineas squawked from the bedpost, cocking his head and eyeing Lady Tesh.

"Precisely, dearest," Seraphina said to him.

Lady Tesh scowled. "Why do I think that bird has insulted me?" she grumbled.

Before Seraphina could answer her, Sebastian was suddenly there in the doorway, and Katrina forgot everything else.

He grinned at her. "Hello, my future wife."

She sighed happily and smiled back at him. "Hello, my future husband."

"Hello to us as well," Honoria piped up cheekily.

"Have you finished your packing, Your Grace?" Lady Tesh asked as she sank down onto the small desk chair that Adelaide had guided her to.

"Indeed I have. And I come here offering my services if you have need of them. Though," he continued ruefully as he scanned the full-to-bursting space, "it seems you have a full house—or, rather, room—where that is concerned."

Just then Mouse, who had been quite happy with Bronwyn's attentions, perked his ears up and spied Sebastian. Tongue rolling out of his mouth like a moist pink carpet, drool flying, he bounded across the room toward his favorite person. Sebastian, instead of dodging the oncoming snout, bent down and met the dog's greeting with enthusiasm. As Mouse whined in delight and Sebastian scratched at his back, lavishing praise on him, Katrina's heart, which she thought was unable to hold a drop more happiness, overflowed.

Only one thing could put a damper on her joy: how deeply would his life have to alter for the worse in order to marry her? And they would be affecting the lives of his sisters as well; would they despise her for it?

Her anxiety must have shown on her face, for suddenly Sebastian was there before her, taking the shawl from her—which had become twisted in her grip—and clasping her hand. "Katrina, are you well? Mayhap this is all too fast for you. Would you rather we wait and have a proper wedding, as Lady Tesh suggested?"

"What? No! Of course not." She tried for a smile, but from the persistent divot between his brows, Sebastian did not believe her one bit.

But he was thankfully prevented from quizzing her further when the butler arrived in the doorway. Unfortunately, the reason for the butler's sudden presence was even more devastating than any question from her intended could be.

"Miss Denby, a Sir Francis Denby is here to see you."

The silence following that pronouncement was so absolute, the one part of Katrina's brain still capable of thought wondered vaguely if someone had sucked all the air out of the room. But the silence did not last long.

"Your brother?"

"He is here?"

"How dare he after all this time?"

"I would like a minute alone with him myself, after what he's put you through."

It was Sebastian's face so close to her own, however, his concern and love for her plain in his eyes, that snapped her out of the fog she'd been lost in.

"Katrina, do you want me to send him away? You don't have to see him if you don't wish to."

His voice shook with his fury, but was gentle nonetheless. And it gave her strength as nothing else could. No matter what, Sebastian would support her decision with her brother. She could refuse to see him, and no one would condemn her for it. In actuality, she thought as she took a quick look about the small room, from the anger saturating every face surrounding her, including Lady Tesh's, she rather thought they would be more than happy to see her set Mouse after Francis.

But she'd had the strength to confront the vicar, hadn't she? Why should this be any different?

She looked to the butler, who was staring wide-eyed at the collection of fury before him. "Please show Sir Francis to the drawing room and tell him I will be with him momentarily."

* * *

When Katrina had last seen her brother, he had been thin and wan, his skin waxen from loss of blood as he sat propped up in his bed. He had raged at her, his fury and fear plain, and had sent her from their London town house in shame. In the years since, she'd had trouble remembering the athletic, magnetic brother she'd looked up to, the image of him with hate in his eyes and close to death's door having been seared into her brain until it was all she could recall.

Now, however, except for his empty sleeve pinned to his

shoulder he could not look more different. He was no longer sickly, yet he did not resemble the devil-may-care rake of his youth, either. His features were stark and hard where they'd once been soft, his form stocky and strong where it had once been lanky and lean.

But it was his eyes that held the most difference. They'd once been filled to the brim with ennui, and Katrina had never felt as if he'd seen the person she was beyond his responsibility to her. Now, however, they were sharp as flint, and they took her in from the top of her head to the tips of her toes, as if peeling away the past four years to see everything that had happened to her since.

"Hello, Katrina," he said, his voice rough.

"Hello, Francis." She swallowed hard, focusing on Sebastian's comforting presence behind her, desperately happy that she had asked that he accompany her. She motioned back to where he stood, not taking her eyes from Francis's face for all it seemed a stranger's to her. "You recall the Duke of Ramsleigh? Though you would have known him as Lord Marsten."

Francis glanced over her shoulder, his slight start proof that he had not noticed Sebastian before now. He frowned, clearly confused by his presence before he dipped his head solemnly.

"Ramsleigh. I did not expect to see you here."

"Denby," Sebastian said in a voice devoid of inflection. "I could say the same about you."

Francis acknowledged that with another head tilt, this one in wry acceptance, before returning his attention to Katrina. "I came here to discuss something important with you. Might we have a moment alone?"

"Whatever you have to say, you can say in front of Sebastian," she said, instinctively reaching behind her. At once Sebastian was at her side, his hand sliding into hers, holding on tight.

Francis did not miss the show of solidarity. His gaze narrowed on their joined fingers before he looked to Sebastian. And to Katrina's shock, there was fury in his eyes.

"How did you learn about it?" he demanded, striding forward until he was nose to nose with Sebastian.

As for Sebastian, he tensed beside her, his fingers tightening on hers as he maneuvered her behind him. "What the hell are you talking about, Denby?"

"The inheritance. Why else would you be here sniffing at her skirts?"

"What inheritance? Denby, you'd best explain things, immediately."

"As if you don't know," her brother spat, his lip curling. "I tried to keep it quiet, to keep the news from leaking out. Yet here you are, the one man in London in need of funds more than any other. Bit of a coincidence, wouldn't you say?"

But something in Sebastian's eyes must have finally burned through Francis's anger. He stilled, his eyes narrowing.

"You must have known. Else why are you here?"

Katrina, her shock finally dissipated enough for her to react, stepped around Sebastian. He appeared agitated, his confusion plain on his face as he stared at Francis. The very same confusion that settled like a pit in her stomach and made her feel both hot and cold all at once. Looking to her brother, she said, "We don't know what you're talking about. What inheritance?"

Francis considered Katrina for a charged moment. "Perhaps you'd best sit down," he said, his tone strangely devoid of inflection. Then, before either one of them could react, he made his way to the nearest settee and dropped like a stone.

Katrina followed beside Sebastian, her legs shaky. What was he talking about? Inheritance? She had not received an inheritance. And if she had, who would have left her money?

Clearing his throat, Francis began. "It seems, Katrina, that our aunt left you quite a tidy sum upon her death."

Katrina blinked. "Our aunt?" He could not mean Aunt Willa. That woman had barely tolerated her while she had taken on the position of chaperone during Katrina's one and only—and calamitous—London season. And then later, when Francis had exiled them to that small cottage after the scandal, Aunt Willa had treated her with such disdain. Surely he could not mean her.

"Yes," Francis said, "Aunt Willa." His lips twisted. "It seemed, unbeknownst to me, she was quite wealthy. Disgustingly so, in fact."

"I...see," she said. But in fact, she did not see. Not even remotely. The woman had lived on Francis's beneficence while she had stayed with them, acting more like a surly servant than family. Even after they both escaped from that cottage, when Katrina had come to live as Lady Tesh's companion, Aunt Willa had not lived a life of wealth. Indeed, she had been frighteningly frugal, more than happy to live off the largesse of others, staying with any friend who would take her in. Katrina had even gone so far as to send her whatever funds she had managed to make, a kind of apology for the terrible position she felt she had put the woman in.

And she had been *wealthy*?

Francis must have seen her confusion—truly, how could he miss it?—for he spoke again.

"It seemed there was some contention with her estate," he mumbled evasively. "Thus the delay. But I could not quite countenance that she had left you such a sum."

Which might have stung if Katrina had been in full possession of her faculties. As it was, she could not countenance it either.

"I, of course, wished to verify that it was all above board," Francis continued. "At the same time I worked at keeping the news of your sudden windfall quiet, to protect you from any would-be fortune hunters." He narrowed his eyes, looking to Sebastian.

"For the last time, Francis," she snapped, her emotions pulled taut beyond bearing, "Sebastian knew nothing of any money from Aunt Willa."

"So you say," her brother replied, not looking the least convinced.

"I do say," she replied coldly, much colder than she had ever spoken to him before.

He pulled back, looking at her with first wariness, and then disapproval. But for the first time in her life, Katrina did not hurry to smooth things over at the first sign of displeasure. Raising her head, she said, "Why did you come to Seacliff, Francis? Why not simply send a letter informing me of the inheritance?"

He had the decency to look slightly abashed. But only slightly. "I admit I was too harsh in my last letter to you. I was...not thinking clearly. Hearing of Landon returning to England, after what he did to me..." He motioned to his empty sleeve.

Bitterness filled Katrina's mouth. Of course he would focus on how he had been affected, and not on how her life had been ruined because of Lord Landon's actions.

Ignorant of her less-than-complimentary thoughts of him, Francis continued. "I did not think a mere letter would suffice after my dismissal of you. Especially as I had hoped we could repair our relationship. We have never been close, you and me. I thought to change that."

Just days ago, Francis declaring that he wished to be a brother to her would have been the realization of the deepest desire of her heart. How many years had she wished to have the love and acceptance of her family, to be welcomed back with open arms?

But she was not that desperate, hurting woman any longer, happy with the smallest crumb of perceived affection. No, she was strong now, had learned to respect herself. Sebastian had taught her that.

She looked to him now. His eyes burned as he stared at Francis. But his expression altered when he turned to look her way, the love and patience and trust there filling her up until she thought she would burst with it.

Taking a deep breath, she returned her attention to Francis.

"If that is true, and you truly wish to have a relationship with me, I will be more than happy to. However," she continued as a smug satisfaction spread over Francis's features, "it will take time. You have damaged our relationship nearly beyond repair; my trust will not be easy to reclaim. Are you willing to work toward that?"

She did not expect him to fall at her feet with apologies; that was not who her brother had been, and she doubted the past four years would have changed him into that man.

Even so, she was not wholly prepared for the anger that saturated his features. Nor for his hurtful words. "I see," he snapped, rising. "You think now you are wealthy you can discard me like refuse? You owe me, Katrina, for all you have put me through, for all I have lost because of you."

Katrina flinched from his barely banked fury but was not about to be cowed. "See it as you like," she said, refusing to look away.

He glared at her for a long moment, no doubt expecting her to retreat. When she merely lifted her chin, he turned and stalked out the door. Soon the only proof he had been there was the faint echo of the front door slamming.

Katrina didn't move. Sebastian remained still as well, his warmth at her side a silent support. And she knew in her heart he would give her all the time she needed to process this new turn of events.

Which only made her love him more.

"Do you know," she mused, shifting in her seat to face him, "that was quite possibly the most freeing thing I have ever done."

The worry scoring his beloved face melted away at her lighthearted comment. "Is it now?" he murmured as he gently tucked a stray strand of hair behind her ear.

"It is," she said with a decisive nod. And it was true. She saw now, having finally claimed the power in her relationship with her brother, that she'd been held prisoner to her desire to please her family all these years. Now it felt as if she'd finally broken herself free.

"No doubt I will have a good cry about it later. He was

still my brother, for all he has done to pretend otherwise. As well as a good cry for Aunt Willa. She was a harridan, and absolutely rubbish at being a chaperone, but she showed she cared in the end."

She smiled wide then and held out her hand, palm up. "And because of her I no longer come to you empty-handed, Sebastian. You won't need to leave Ramsleigh Castle."

He took her hand in his and laid it over his heart. "But don't you see, love?" he said, his voice tender. "You never came empty-handed, for you hold my entire heart in your hands."

* * *

Some hours later, the carriage packed and ready to go, farewells said, Katrina stepped outside of Seacliff and to the gravel drive, sandwiched between Sebastian and Mouse. This place had been a haven for her, a place where she had found love and acceptance, and a found family though she had not realized it at the time.

Now that found family stood on Seacliff's steps, smiling broadly as, having been helped up into the carriage by Sebastian, Katrina turned to glance back. More than one face was red from crying, more than one set of eyes swollen. Yet their love and happiness for her shone through the sadness. Not for the first time—or even hundredth time—that day, Katrina felt tears well up. But she resolutely wiped them away as Mouse and then Sebastian climbed into the carriage. She did not want anything marring the view of her friends and Lady Tesh and even Freya saying their goodbyes to her.

"Be sure to write often," Bronwyn called.

Adelaide blew her a kiss. "I shall send you your favorite biscuits every month."

"Give Mouse a kiss from me every night," Honoria said. "We love you."

That last came from Seraphina. As one the other Oddments stopped waving and gaped at Seraphina; out of everyone, she was the last they expected to say such an emotional thing.

Seraphina caught them staring, and her face, red with emotion though she had not shed a tear, deepened to burgundy as she scowled at them.

"I can say such things, too, you know," she snapped.

Katrina laughed along with the others. Just then the carriage jolted into motion.

Suddenly Lady Tesh's voice sounded above the rumble of the wheels on the gravel. "Take care of my girl, Your Grace!" she cried. And then, "Be sure to visit often."

"I will, and we shall," Sebastian called back, just before the carriage turned down the drive.

The moment Katrina lost sight of those women she loved so well, the tears started in earnest. Sebastian pulled her into his arms, his hands on her back and his voice in her ear soothing her.

But her tears did not last long. Especially when Mouse decided he must join in. He pushed his nose under her hand, giving her a wet kiss and a low woof before, hefting himself up onto the bench across from them, he stuck his head out the open window, ears and jowls flying in joyful abandon in the wind.

Katrina and Sebastian, laughing, settled back against the plush squabs, their arms wrapped about each other.

"I think he will do well at Ramsleigh Castle," he said.

"Very well indeed." Suddenly his tone turned thoughtful. "But will he miss the Isle, do you think?"

She rather thought he was asking about more than Mouse, if the sudden concerned divot in between his brows was any indication. Smiling, she cupped his cheek. "The Isle will always hold a special place in his heart. But I rather think," she murmured, "that Mouse—and me—will be happy to be wherever you are."

He smiled, the future shining from his eyes as his gaze caressed her face. "Happy, my love?" he murmured.

"More than words could ever say," she said before dragging his head down for a kiss.

Epilogue

"Katrina, some mail has come for you!"

Katrina, in the process of helping Ramsleigh Castle's cook pack the last of the care baskets for the villagers, looked up as Sebastian's youngest sister, Gracie, bounded into the kitchen, Mouse at her side and a handful of letters and packages held above her head. Smiling broadly, she quickly wiped her hand on her apron before turning to the cook.

"Mrs. Aldred, do you mind finishing up here?"

"Not at all, Your Grace," the cook said, helping Katrina off with her apron before turning to bark orders to the kitchen maids to help pack up the baskets into the waiting cart.

Katrina gave Mouse's ears a quick scratch before taking the mail from Gracie with a smile of thanks. The girl, not above seventeen, bright-eyed and smart as a whip, peered over Katrina's shoulder as they made their way from the kitchen and up to the main floor.

"There is a package from Miss Peacham," she piped up, bouncing along at Katrina's side—a perfect match to Mouse, who gamboled along her other side. "What biscuits do you suppose she has sent this time?"

"Whatever they are, I'm certain they will be delicious." She gave a happy sigh. "I have missed her baking something terrible. And so has Mouse," she continued, giving the dog a fond look. His tongue lolled out of his mouth as he gazed in adoration up at her.

They made it to the green sitting room, a large space that had quickly become a gathering place for their little family. *Family*, she thought happily as Sebastian's nineteen-year-old sister, Rachel, seated in the window seat reading a book, spied them and jumped up to greet them. It seemed an age ago that Katrina had mourned the fact that she no longer had any family, when she had been desperate for a word from her brother.

Now not only did she have her found family on Synne, but she had Sebastian and his sisters and all the people at Ramsleigh Castle she had come to love in the two years since her marriage.

The two girls and Katrina and Mouse gathered about a low table. The package was quickly opened, their exclamations of delight ringing through the room as they spied the collection of ratafia biscuits within. Then, with the girls'—and Mouse's—mouths full of the delightful almond-flavored concoctions, Katrina went about shuffling through the small pile of letters. There was one from Bronwyn, and one from Lady Tesh. And there, on the bottom, was one from Miss Bridling.

"Oh!" Gracie exclaimed in delight. "Is she still with Lady Tesh? Will we see her when we visit next month do you think?"

Katrina laughed. "I have not opened the letter yet! But I promise to tell you the moment I know."

"Know what, precisely?"

Sebastian's voice, so deliciously deep as he strolled into the sitting room, sent a thrill of anticipation up her spine. No matter that they had been wed two years, no matter that they spent every night in one another's arms, her reaction to him just walking into a room had never dimmed. In fact, it had only grown stronger.

Something he knew, if the self-satisfied grin on his face was any indication. He approached, claiming the seat beside her and snaking an arm about her waist before planting a kiss on her waiting lips. Gracie and Rachel, watching the whole thing, gave happy little sighs.

"Katrina has received a letter from Miss Bridling," Rachel piped up, reaching for another biscuit.

"Wonderful," he said, his smile widening. "Her brother is rubbish at correspondence, and so now perhaps we might learn if the next generation of Bridlings has been born."

Mr. Bridling's marriage to his actress had taken place shortly after his return to London, though he had insisted on a lavish affair with all of society present to welcome his new wife. To everyone's shock—and to Katrina's relief—Lord Carumel had been in attendance, and had even insisted on throwing a wedding breakfast for the happy couple. By all accounts it had not taken the baron long to grow fond of his new daughter-in-law, and once she had found herself increasing, he had become positively inseparable from the newly married couple.

Miss Bridling, on the other hand, had done a bit of traveling before finally taking Lady Tesh up on her invitation to stay with her. She had been there some months, and the two, by all accounts, had become inseparable.

She opened her letter now, quickly scanning it as the others talked quietly. When she finally looked up, it was to find the threesome watching her intently, waiting for whatever news she had to impart.

She grinned. "Mr. Bridling's wife has been safely delivered of a healthy baby boy," she said. "And yes, Miss Bridling shall still be visiting with Lady Tesh when we arrive next month."

"Wonderful!" Gracie exclaimed before, jumping to her feet, she tugged on her sister's hand. "Come along, Rachel. I need your help deciding which gowns to bring for our journey."

"It is a month away," her sister complained, though there was no malice in the words. "Though perhaps you're right in that it would be best to start now. I do need to figure which of my books to bring, for I certainly cannot take them all. Come along, Mouse," she called as, arm in arm, the sisters hurried from the room. Mouse, with a happy woof, followed them.

Leaving Katrina and Sebastian alone.

After closing the door behind his sisters, he settled back beside Katrina and pulled her into the circle of his arms. "Well," he murmured, "this is a lovely treat. Remind me to thank my sisters later."

Later—much later—Sebastian lifted his head, his smile slightly lopsided as he gazed down at her. "You know, I don't think I could be happier than I am right now."

Katrina grinned mischievously. "Oh, I don't know. I may have something that will increase your happiness."

She brought her lips close to his ear and whispered that bit of news she still could not believe herself.

He pulled back, eyes as round as saucers, with the beginnings of tears making them shimmer. "You are certain?" he asked almost reverently as his large hand came to rest gently on her still flat abdomen.

She nodded, fighting back her own tears. "Yes, Sebastian."

Shaking his head in wonder, his gaze caressed her upturned face. "Well, look at that. I could become happier," he murmured before taking her lips in a kiss.

Don't miss the next breathtaking novel from Christina Britton, coming Winter 2024

About the Author

Christina Britton developed a passion for writing romance novels shortly after buying her first at the impressionable age of thirteen. Though for several years she put brush instead of pen to paper, she has returned to her first love and is now writing full-time. She spends her days dreaming of corsets and cravats and noblemen with tortured souls.

She lives with her husband and two children in the San Francisco Bay Area.

You can learn more at:
    Website: ChristinaBritton.com
    Twitter @CBrittonAuthor
    Facebook.com/ChristinaBrittonAuthor
    Instagram @ChristinaBrittonAuthor

*Get swept off your feet by charming dukes,
sharp-witted ladies, and scandalous balls in
Forever's historical romances!*

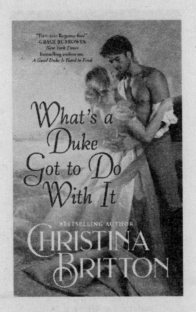

WHAT'S A DUKE GOT TO DO WITH IT
by Christina Britton

The last thing Miss Katrina Denby needs is another scandal. So when one lands in her garden and the rumors start affecting her friends, she will do anything to regain respectability and protect those for whom she cares. But her plans to marry one of the few men who will still have her are thrown into turmoil with the arrival of the Duke of Ramsleigh: the only man Katrina ever loved...and a man who is about to become engaged to another.

Connect with us at Facebook.com/ReadForeverPub

Discover bonus content and more on
read-forever.com

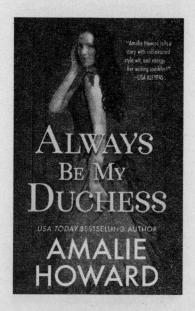

"Amalie Howard tells a
story with self-assured
style, wit, and energy.
Her writing sparkles!"
—LISA KLEYPAS

ALWAYS
BE MY
DUCHESS

USA TODAY BESTSELLING AUTHOR

AMALIE
HOWARD

ALWAYS BE MY DUCHESS
by Amalie Howard

Because ballerina Geneviève Valery refused a patron's advances, she is
hopelessly out of work. But then Lord Lysander Blackstone, the heartless
Duke of Montcroix, makes Nève an offer she would be a fool to refuse.
Montcroix's ruthlessness has jeopardized a new business deal, so if Nève
acts as his fake fiancée and salvages his reputation, he'll give her fortune
enough to start over. Only neither is prepared when very *real* feelings
begin to grow between them...

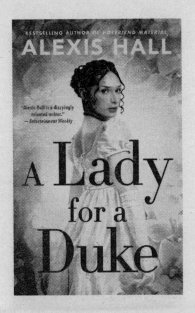

A LADY FOR A DUKE
by Alexis Hall

After Viola Carroll was presumed dead at Waterloo, she took the opportunity to live as herself. But Viola paid for her freedom with the loss of her wealth, title, and closest companion, Justin de Vere, the Duke of Gracewood. Only when their families reconnect years later does Viola learn how lost in grief Gracewood has become. But as Viola strives to bring Gracewood back to himself, fresh desires give new bloom to old feelings. They are feelings Viola cannot deny...even if they cost her everything, again.

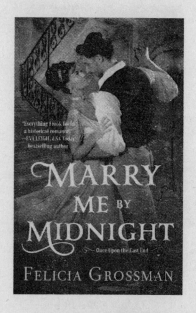

MARRY ME BY MIDNIGHT
by Felicia Grossman

Isabelle Lira may be in distress, but she's no damsel. To save her late father's business from a hostile takeover, she must marry a powerful stranger—and *soon*. So she'll host a series of festivals, inviting every eligible Jewish man. Except that Aaron Ellenberg, the synagogue custodian, provides unexpected temptation when Isabelle hires him to spy on her favored suitors. But a future for them both is impossible…unless Isabelle can find the courage to trust her heart.